THE WOLF

BY J. R. WARD

THE BLACK DAGGER BROTHERHOOD SERIES

Dark Lover
Lover Eternal
Lover Awakened
Lover Revealed
Lover Unbound
Lover Enshrined
The Black Dagger Brotherhood: An Insider's Guide
Lover Avenged
Lover Mine
Lover Unleashed
Lover Reborn
Lover at Last
The King
The Shadows
The Beast
The Chosen
The Thief
The Savior
The Sinner
Lover Unveiled

THE BLACK DAGGER LEGACY SERIES

Blood Kiss
Blood Vow
Blood Fury
Blood Truth

THE BLACK DAGGER BROTHERHOOD WORLD

Dearest Ivie
Prisoner of Night
Where Winter Finds You
A Warm Heart in Winter

THE BLACK DAGGER BROTHERHOOD: PRISON CAMP

The Jackal
The Wolf

FIREFIGHTERS SERIES

Consumed

NOVELS OF THE FALLEN ANGELS

Covet
Crave
Envy
Rapture
Possession
Immortal

THE BOURBON KINGS SERIES

The Bourbon Kings
The Angels' Share
Devil's Cut

J.R. WARD

THE WOLF

THE BLACK DAGGER BROTHERHOOD
PRISON CAMP

G
GALLERY BOOKS
New York London Toronto Sydney New Delhi

Gallery Books
An Imprint of Simon & Schuster, Inc.
1230 Avenue of the Americas
New York, NY 10020

This book is a work of fiction. Any references to historical events, real people, or real places are used fictitiously. Other names, characters, places, and events are products of the author's imagination, and any resemblance to actual events or places or persons, living or dead, is entirely coincidental.

First Gallery Books hardcover edition November 2021

GALLERY BOOKS and colophon are registered trademarks of Simon & Schuster, Inc.

For information about special discounts for bulk purchases,
please contact Simon & Schuster Special Sales at 1-866-506-1949
or business@simonandschuster.com.

The Simon & Schuster Speakers Bureau can bring authors to your live event.
For more information or to book an event, contact the Simon & Schuster Speakers Bureau at 1-866-248-3049 or visit our website at www.simonspeakers.com.

Interior design by Davina Mock-Maniscalco

Manufactured in the United States of America

10 9 8 7 6 5 4 3 2 1

Library of Congress Cataloging-in-Publication Data is available.

ISBN 978-1-9821-7987-8
ISBN 978-1-9821-7989-2 (ebook)

Dedicated to:
A wonderful pair, who deserve a future,
survivors, through and through

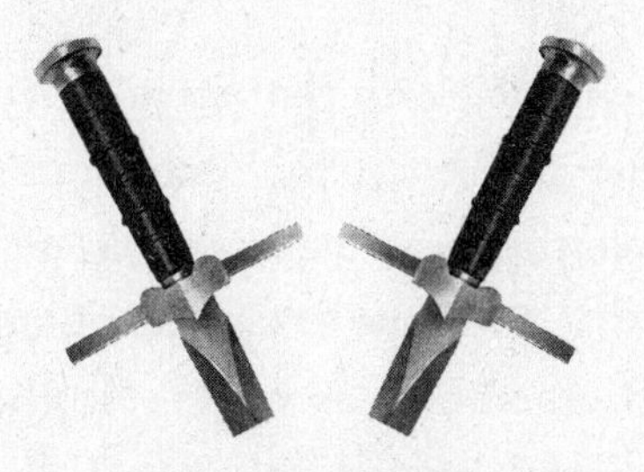

GLOSSARY OF TERMS AND PROPER NOUNS

ahstrux nohtrum (n.) Private guard with license to kill who is granted his or her position by the King.

ahvenge (v.) Act of mortal retribution, carried out typically by a male loved one.

Black Dagger Brotherhood (pr. n.) Highly trained vampire warriors who protect their species against the Lessening Society. As a result of selective breeding within the race, Brothers possess immense physical and mental strength, as well as rapid healing capabilities. They are not siblings for the most part, and are inducted into the Brotherhood upon nomination by the Brothers. Aggressive, self-reliant, and secretive by nature, they are the subjects of legend and objects of reverence within the vampire world. They may be killed only by the most serious of wounds, e.g., a gunshot or stab to the heart, etc.

blood slave (n.) Male or female vampire who has been subjugated to serve the blood needs of another. The practice of keeping blood slaves has been outlawed.

the Chosen (pr. n.) Female vampires who had been bred to serve the Scribe Virgin. In the past, they were spiritually rather than temporally focused, but that changed with the ascendance of the final Primale, who freed them from the Sanctuary. With the Scribe Virgin removing herself from her role, they are completely autonomous and learning to live on earth. They do continue to meet the blood needs of unmated members of the Brotherhood, as well as Brothers who cannot feed from their *shellans* or injured fighters.

chrih (n.) Symbol of honorable death in the Old Language.

cohntehst (n.) Conflict between two males competing for the right to be a female's mate.

Dhunhd (pr. n.) Hell.

doggen (n.) Member of the servant class within the vampire world. *Doggen* have old, conservative traditions about service to their superiors, following a formal code of dress and behavior. They are able to go out during the day, but they age relatively quickly. Life expectancy is approximately five hundred years.

ehros (n.) A Chosen trained in the matter of sexual arts.

exhile dhoble (n.) The evil or cursed twin, the one born second.

the Fade (pr. n.) Non-temporal realm where the dead reunite with their loved ones and pass eternity.

First Family (pr. n.) The King and Queen of the vampires, and any children they may have.

ghardian (n.) Custodian of an individual. There are varying degrees of *ghardians*, with the most powerful being that of a *sehcluded* female.

glymera (n.) The social core of the aristocracy, roughly equivalent to Regency England's *ton*.

hellren (n.) Male vampire who has been mated to a female. Males may take more than one female as mate.

hyslop (n. or v.) Term referring to a lapse in judgment, typically resulting in the compromise of the mechanical operations of a vehicle or otherwise motorized conveyance of some kind. For example, leaving one's keys in one's car as it is parked outside the family home overnight, whereupon said vehicle is stolen.

leahdyre (n.) A person of power and influence.

leelan (adj. or n.) A term of endearment loosely translated as "dearest one."

Lessening Society (pr. n.) Order of slayers convened by the Omega for the purpose of eradicating the vampire species.

lesser (n.) De-souled human who targets vampires for extermination as a member of the Lessening Society. *Lessers* must be stabbed through the chest in order to be killed; otherwise they are ageless. They do not eat or drink and are impotent. Over time, their hair, skin, and irises lose pigmentation until they are blond, blushless, and pale eyed. They smell like baby powder. Inducted into the society by the Omega, they retain a ceramic jar thereafter into which their heart was placed after it was removed.

lewlhen (n.) Gift.

lheage (n.) A term of respect used by a sexual submissive to refer to their dominant.

Lhenihan (pr. n.) A mythic beast renowned for its sexual prowess. In modern slang, refers to a male of preternatural size and sexual stamina.

lys (n.) Torture tool used to remove the eyes.

mahmen (n.) Mother. Used both as an identifier and a term of affection.

mhis (n.) The masking of a given physical environment; the creation of a field of illusion.

nalla (n., f.) or ***nallum*** (n., m.) Beloved.

needing period (n.) Female vampire's time of fertility, generally lasting for two days and accompanied by intense sexual cravings. Occurs approximately five years after a female's transition and then once a decade thereafter. All males respond to some degree if they are around a female in her need. It can be a dangerous time, with conflicts and fights breaking out between competing males, particularly if the female is not mated.

newling (n.) A virgin.

the Omega (pr. n.) Malevolent, mystical figure who has targeted the vampires for extinction out of resentment directed toward the Scribe

Virgin. Exists in a non-temporal realm and has extensive powers, though not the power of creation.

phearsom (adj.) Term referring to the potency of a male's sexual organs. Literal translation something close to "worthy of entering a female."

Princeps (pr. n.) Highest level of the vampire aristocracy, second only to members of the First Family or the Scribe Virgin's Chosen. Must be born to the title; it may not be conferred.

pyrocant (n.) Refers to a critical weakness in an individual. The weakness can be internal, such as an addiction, or external, such as a lover.

rahlman (n.) Savior.

rythe (n.) Ritual manner of asserting honor granted by one who has offended another. If accepted, the offended chooses a weapon and strikes the offender, who presents him- or herself without defenses.

the Scribe Virgin (pr. n.) Mystical force who previously was counselor to the King as well as the keeper of vampire archives and the dispenser of privileges. Existed in a non-temporal realm and had extensive powers, but has recently stepped down and given her station to another. Capable of a single act of creation, which she expended to bring the vampires into existence.

sehclusion (n.) Status conferred by the King upon a female of the aristocracy as a result of a petition by the female's family. Places the female under the sole direction of her *ghardian*, typically the eldest male in her household. Her *ghardian* then has the legal right to determine all manner of her life, restricting at will any and all interactions she has with the world.

shellan (n.) Female vampire who has been mated to a male. Females generally do not take more than one mate due to the highly territorial nature of bonded males.

symphath (n.) Subspecies within the vampire race characterized by the ability and desire to manipulate emotions in others (for the purposes of an energy exchange), among other traits. Historically, they have been discriminated against and, during certain eras, hunted by vampires. They are near extinction.

talhman (n.) The evil side of an individual. A dark stain on the soul that requires expression if it is not properly expunged.

the Tomb (pr. n.) Sacred vault of the Black Dagger Brotherhood. Used as a ceremonial site as well as a storage facility for the jars of *lessers*. Ceremonies performed there include inductions, funerals, and disciplinary actions against Brothers. No one may enter except for members of the Brotherhood, the Scribe Virgin, or candidates for induction.

trahyner (n.) Word used between males of mutual respect and affection. Translated loosely as "beloved friend."

transition (n.) Critical moment in a vampire's life when he or she transforms into an adult. Thereafter, he or she must drink the blood of the opposite sex to survive and is unable to withstand sunlight. Occurs generally in the mid-twenties. Some vampires do not survive their transitions, males in particular. Prior to their transitions, vampires are physically weak, sexually unaware and unresponsive, and unable to dematerialize.

vampire (n.) Member of a species separate from that of *Homo sapiens*. Vampires must drink the blood of the opposite sex to survive. Human blood will keep them alive, though the strength does not last long. Following their transitions, which occur in their mid-twenties, they are unable to go out into sunlight and must feed from the vein regularly. Vampires cannot "convert" humans through a bite or transfer of blood, though they are in rare cases able to breed with the other species. Vampires can dematerialize at will, though they must be able to calm themselves and concentrate to do so and may not carry anything heavy with them. They are able to strip the memories of humans, provided such memories are short-term. Some vampires are able to read minds. Life expectancy is upward of a thousand years, or in some cases, even longer.

wahlker (n.) An individual who has died and returned to the living from the Fade. They are accorded great respect and are revered for their travails.

whard (n.) Equivalent of a godfather or godmother to an individual.

CHAPTER ONE

Willow Hills Sanatorium
Connelly, New York

It was a stormy Halloween night when two boys, aged thirteen and thirteen and three-quarters, squeezed through the torn section of a chain-link fence hung with all kinds of "No Trespassing" signs. The one who was older by eight months got his jacket caught on a rusty grab, and the tearing sound was one week without his iPad. Minimum.

"Dammit," Tiller said as he pulled at the snag.

"C'mon. Let's get this over with."

He shouldn't have brought Gordo, but Isaac was sick, and Mark was grounded for what they'd all done the weekend before. Stupid fire. They hadn't meant it to get that big, and besides, the leaf pile was gone now and that burned lawn in the Thompsons' side yard would grow back.

As rain started to fall a little harder, Gordo came over and yanked at the jacket. "Take it off."

"I am."

Tiller shoved his ghost-hunting equipment into his buddy's chest, unzipped the front, and got out of the sleeve. Then he gripped with both hands and pulled as hard as he could—

The release was immediate, and as he landed on his ass, he got rain in his eyes and mud all over him. "Fuck!"

Gordo bent down. "I gotta be back before midnight."

Like the guy thought Tiller was going to hang around until things air dried. Sometime next week.

"Relax." He got to his feet and flapped the jacket around. Palm-cleaned his jeans. "What, are you scared?"

"No, dumbass. And we're s'posed to be online in an hour."

"Whatever."

The guy was lying about not being afraid. Which was why he'd been third choice when Tiller had decided he couldn't handle going alone. Not that he himself was nervous or anything.

Tying the jacket around his waist, he felt like he was wearing his mother's kitchen sponge, but as he looked around, he forgot about the cold and wet. The trees had no leaves on their clawing branches, and the bushes, with their twisted, finger-like extensions, seemed ready to follow the fence's example with poisoned thorns—

Overhead, lightning flashed.

Good thing Gordo also jumped.

"Where is the place?"

"Up here," Tiller said, even though he didn't know where they were going.

As they continued on, he let Gordo keep hold of the night vision cam and the EVP recorder because he was trying not to run back for the fence, and not sure whether he was going to win the argument with his feet. The deeper into the acreage he went, the more he just wanted to get the video and send it to the seventh grade group chat and have this shit be done with.

"How far is it?"

"Not far."

Except the trek felt endless, and the trees seemed to move all around them, and Tiller started to lose faith, too. So he fired up the EMF reader on his phone and swung the sensor around, the beeping noise making him think of that submarine movie his father liked to watch, the one with that guy, Stewart Seagal or whatever. The ghost-hunting app, which he'd installed for free, made him feel like he had a flashlight—

The howl came from over to the right. And it was loud and long. And it didn't sound like just a dog, even a big one like a German shepherd or a Rottie. Whatever was making that noise was much larger.

Tiller grabbed for Gordo, but the kid did the same thing at the same time, so he wasn't a wuss. As his phone shook in his hand, he almost dropped it. Which would have been a month without his iPad. Or longer.

"I want to go home."

Gordo sounded like a damned baby. Except, yeah, Tiller wanted his mommy, too, not that he was going to say anything about that.

"It's just piped in," he blurted.

"What?"

Tiller shoved the kid off. "Like how they do in haunts to scare people going through the mazes. That wasn't real. Come on, like there's a wolf inside this fence?"

"You think there're speakers in the trees?"

"Just keep going. Jesus."

Tiller put the phone back up because he needed to look like he was in control. Otherwise, he was going to lose Gordo and have to do this alone. And he was not *not* sending the video—

"I'm out," Gordo announced.

Turning around, Tiller marched back to the kid. "You want to look like an idiot after we didn't jump into the quarry this summer?" He and Gordo really should have just frickin' done the dare. Then they wouldn't be here. "We promised the footage, we're going to get the footage. Besides, nothing is going to happen."

He grabbed Gordo's arm and dragged them both forward. When more lightning flashed, they both squeaked and ducked down. Tiller recovered first, and he kept ahold of the other kid. No fucking way he was going to let his cover get away. If something went wrong, he was faster than Gordo and it was like in *Zombieland*. Rule #1: Cardio—

"See?" Tiller said. "It's just right there."

His feet stopped, even though he'd intended to keep going. And Gordo didn't argue with the no-more-walking.

As thunder rolled through the dark sky, another flash lit up the looming structure before them—and the Willow Hills Sanatorium got way too real. The rotten old building was twice the size of the school they went to, with five floors and two big wing-thingies. Broken windows, busted shutters, and nasty stains running from the roof all the way down to the weeds made the place look like it was possessed.

And maybe that was true, Tiller thought as he took in the empty eye sockets in the towering wall of the centerpiece.

"What's that?" Gordo mumbled.

"What's what." God, he should have brought . . . well, he shouldn't have come here at all. "What's your problem."

Gordo shook his head. Standing there in his Minecraft sweatshirt, with his shaggy brown hair in his scared eyes, he reminded Tiller of a fence post jammed into the ground.

The kid wasn't looking at the building.

"There's something over there." Gordo raised his arm and pointed off to the side. "There are eyes between those trees . . ."

Tiller swung himself around—and there it was. A set of yellow eyes glowing in the shadows.

"Fuck this," Gordo yelped as he dropped all the equipment and tore off.

For a second, Tiller stayed right where he was, his body incapable of motion. But then the snarl was low and carried the promise of sharp fangs and bloody stumps and—

Tiller tripped over his feet as he started to bolt away, and when he landed hard, he lost his phone. But he couldn't worry about that. Lunging back up, he ran like his life depended on it—because it fucking did—and he didn't care how long he was going to be grounded or how many weekends he was going to have to work for his dad in the yard to pay for a new iPhone.

He just wanted to get home without being dead.

And so he ran, ran as hard as he could, back for the fence, to the tear in the metal twists. To his friend. To his house, where wolves didn't howl and didn't snarl and kids didn't accept dumbass dares that took them into haunted places on Halloween with the least courageous of the neighborhood's group of seven boys . . .

In the aftermath of the rushed departures, the snarling in the barren tree line stopped. And then there was a pause, followed by moist cracking sounds, a groan or two, and a ground cover shuffle that was easily drowned out by more of the thunder's lazy, snoring travel through the ionized air molecules of the storm.

A moment later, a pair of muddy bare feet walked over to the 8S, and a human-like hand reached down and picked up the cell phone. The ghost-hunting app made a frantic beeping sound, and as the wolven turned the sensor to himself, the damn thing lit up like a Christmas tree, screaming with warning.

The male chuckled.

Until a menacing, female voice said behind him, "Don't you have somewhere to be down in Caldwell?"

The wolven glanced over his naked shoulder and flashed fangs white as morgue shrouds, sharp as surgical instruments. "I'm going."

"Just keeping you on time. You know what you have at risk."

"Yeah," was his muttered response. "You're good like that."

CHAPTER TWO

Trade & 29th Streets
Caldwell, New York

Ainhoa Fiorela Maite Hernandez-Guerrero knew she was being watched in the alley. As Rio stood in the shadows thrown by a fire escape, she could feel the eyes on her, and she slipped her hand into the pocket of her leather jacket. The nine millimeter autoloader was small enough to hide, deadly enough to defend.

What more did you need in a gun, really.

Looking around, she was aware that she was alone in a way that made things dangerous. It wasn't that nobody was around. She just couldn't trust anyone who—

Spaz came shambling around the corner into the alley, his stained peacoat and paper-thin jeans the kind of wardrobe he'd have to go to a landfill to update. The man was only in his mid-twenties, but the drug lifestyle was a nonbiological cancer, eating his body and mind away, only a husk remaining.

Until such time as even addiction couldn't animate the shell anymore.

"Hey, Rio, you got anything?" he asked.

She glanced behind her and prayed that the supplier contact she'd come here to meet was late. "Not on me, no."

"So, yeah, listen, Rio, you gotta give me some business. I mean, I'm good. I can handle myself. I mean. Come on. I can sell for you regular."

Spaz's watery, bloodshot eyes circled the alley in the manner of bats, flapping around in a disorganized way. She was willing to bet that the last time he truly focused on something was the first time he'd put a meth pipe to his lips.

As a wave of exhaustion came over her, she said, "You think Mozart doesn't know what you did with that last piece we gave you to move?"

"I told you two days ago, the guy jumped me. He took the shit after he got me."

Dirty fingers lifted up an old Soundgarden t-shirt that had more holes than cotton fibers to it. "Look."

She didn't need to lean forward to see the line in his skin. It was about an inch long, off to the side above his hip, and the thing had the red puffy profile of infection.

"Spaz, you gotta get that looked at."

"I don't have medical insurance." He smiled, showing cracked teeth. "But I could get some. If you give me—"

"It's not up to me. You know that."

"So talk to Mozart."

"He does what he wants."

Spaz's Ping-Pong-ball pupils got in the vicinity of her face and hovered around. "Can you give me some money, then."

"Listen, I'm not—"

"I gotta pay someone back. You know how it goes. And if I can't get the product or the cash, they're going to . . ."

The words drifted, and not because he was trying to do with innuendo what was obvious even without the syllables. There was such hopelessness in his gaunt face, his capitulation to his countless bad decisions now impossible to reverse or probably even comprehend, his life nothing but a speeding car swerving toward him while all he had on his feet were a pair of broken roller skates.

"Who do you owe?" she asked.

"Mickie."

Oh, shit. "Spaz. You know better than that."

"I didn't mean to."

Rio looked left. Looked right. Checked her watch. "I gotta go, I'm almost late."

Except she was in the right place and on time. Spaz was the one who had to leave—

"Mickie's gonna kill me. After he uses me for a while."

There was no need to do the math on that. No way she could live with herself if she didn't help.

Cursing, Rio linked her arm through his and started walking. And not even half a block into the parade, Spaz struggled to keep up, even though she was going only slightly faster than a Sunday-stroll speed.

"Where we heading, Rio?"

"You're coming with me."

"Ahh, Rio. You're not gonna make me go to the shelter again."

"I sure am."

As a flash of lightning licked across the sky, she looked up—and half expected a meteor to be gunning for her head, the fireball targeting her and her alone, poor, desperate, dying Spaz collateral damage from her predestined destruction.

Except no, it was only a freak thunderstorm on Halloween night about to smack Caldwell around with wind and rain and volts of sky-born electricity.

"You always take care of me." Spaz rested his head on her shoulder. "Thank you, friend."

Closing her eyes for a second, she took them around a corner and looked twice before she piloted them across the street.

"You're welcome, Spaz. And you gotta take better care of yourself."

"I know, Rio. I know."

✦ ✦ ✦

Vishous, son of the Bloodletter, watched the human woman redirect the drug addict away from where she'd been standing at the back of the nightclub. As it was Monday and the den of iniquity was closed, he could easily hear their conversation, no bass thumping in the background, no stumbling drunks or loose-jointed Molly users kibitzing and crowding the air with their inane dissertations on nothing at all.

The junkie who'd approached her was not part of Caldie's club crowd. Maybe he had been at one point in time, but he'd fallen through the net of high-functioning to the homeless level below. Next one down for him? Grave site.

Stepping out of his lean, V lit up a hand-rolled and casually smoked as he trailed her and her social services project. You didn't see a lot of dealers trying to get their customers into recovery. That was like a fry cook urging diners to watch their cholesterol. But humans, you know. They were multifaceted in so many boring ways, and this woman had herself a secret—

As his phone started vibrating, he took the Samsung out of the ass pocket of his leathers. When he saw who it was, he answered immediately. "Tell me."

"My lead is dead."

V rolled his eyes. "Quick point of clarification, Hollywood. Was he breathing when you got there, or did your beast bust out the A.1. steak sauce again."

Of all of the Black Dagger Brotherhood, Rhage was the one with the biggest appetites. Well, *appetite* in the singular now that he was happily mated to his Mary. The guy had given up all excesses except for food—which would have been fine and dandy if all he ever pounded were half gallons of Breyers ice cream and the occasional six-pack of roasted turkeys with all the trimmings. But Rhage had long ago onboarded one hell of a chaser when it came to takeout consumption, and sometimes you couldn't be sure if his beast was going to recognize who was friend and who was lunch.

"That is *so* judgy," the brother said.

"I'm just asking. That flying purple people eater you carry around under your skin like luggage has been known to turn whole stadiums of people into a charcuterie board. So it's not an unfair question."

As V brought up tall, *T. rex*, and noshy, he stayed in the wake of the human woman and her twitchy BFF, following them to what he was going to bet would be that new shelter set up by Our Lady of Perpetually Doing Good Shit on 27th Street.

"No, I didn't eat him. And I meant to only cap him in the knee."

"With your fist or your gun."

"I sneezed when I pulled the trigger."

"Oops." Overhead, more lightning skipped along the undersides of the restless clouds. "Entry wound is where?"

"In my defense," Rhage interjected, "this place is filthy. If rat poop were nickels, this motherfucker would be Jeff Bezos."

When V's goiter reflex raised its little hand in proverbial class, he swallowed that quick. He was a real male, dammit, not someone who *ew*'d at things. But God, rat shit?

"So where'd you shoot him?"

"Well . . ." The word trailed off, like the brother was tilting in for a closer look to make sure the anatomy description was right. "Let's just say he's going to have some blood in his urine."

"Not if he's dead he ain't."

"Do you *have* to be so literal. Fine, if he were still alive and capable of beer'ing himself into a stupor, he'd be pissing blood out of what's left of his sausage and two eggs. But whatever. You try and pull a gun on me, it's not going to go well for you."

"I'm glad you're okay, Hollywood," V muttered. "I'd miss our stimulating conversations. Plus, I invested in the Tootsie Roll company years ago, and I enjoy beating the S&P 500."

"Actually, you *would* miss the shit out of me."

The brother was right, of course. But like the rodent-related excremental bleurgh back there, V saw no reason to airtime any kind of awww-ain't-that-sweet emotion.

Instead, he crossed the street, and played paranormal gumshoe as the woman went—yup, he called it—right up to the shelter's double doors. As she hit the call button, and then spoke into the intercom, the guy next to her was looking around as if he were assessing opportunities to bolt. She knew better than to let go of that tattered sleeve, however.

"Anyway, can you come over here? I've got a cell phone and a laptop." Rhage sneezed again. "And my sinuses just have to share this wealth with one of my nearest and dearest."

"Aren't I lucky."

Up ahead, the shelter door opened, a man in a SUNY Caldwell sweatshirt opening things up and beckoning the pair inside.

"Okay, yeah, my target is going to be tied up for a while." Vishous glanced down the street. "So I got time."

"This shouldn't take long."

"I don't have a tracer on her yet, but she'll be easy to find. She covers a given territory."

"I can help after you come here."

"Roger that. ETA two secs."

As V hung up the phone, he looked behind himself. Caldwell was damp and dreary tonight, the twinkling spires of the financial district's skyscrapers doing nothing to relieve the oppressive doom and gloom of the freak weather front.

Then again, maybe that was just his frustration talking.

He wished like hell the Brotherhood had a better strategy for finding where that prison camp had gone. After the species as a whole had lost track of the place, and the now-defunct *glymera* had used the underground labyrinth as a dumping ground for vampires it disapproved of, there had been a recent rediscovery—which had occurred just after the location had been abandoned. The near-miss had done little but confirm its existence, and now Wrath, the great Blind King, was determined to find the lawless holding tank and render some much-needed justice to the falsely accused.

The only clue came from the drug trade that was apparently used to sustain the camp's infrastructure and population. Drug-product packaging that had been found in the underground site was now starting to turn up on Caldwell's streets again. The second Trez had found the iron cross trademark back in circulation, they'd alerted the Brotherhood.

Was it possible someone else was using the branding? Sure. Likely? Nah.

And as if they had anything else to go on.

Whatever. One way or another, the prison camp was going to be located—and Wrath was going to establish a proper penal system for the vampire race, one that would be far fairer than the aristocracy's secret racket. But when you were as impatient as V was? Everything took too long.

On that note, he moved two steps back into the shadows, double-checked that there were no eyes on him, and up-up-and-away'd himself, ghosting off to Rhage's coordinates.

Just another night in Caldwell, vampires moving through a city choked with humans, with the latter being none the wiser.

Which was one thing that could never change.

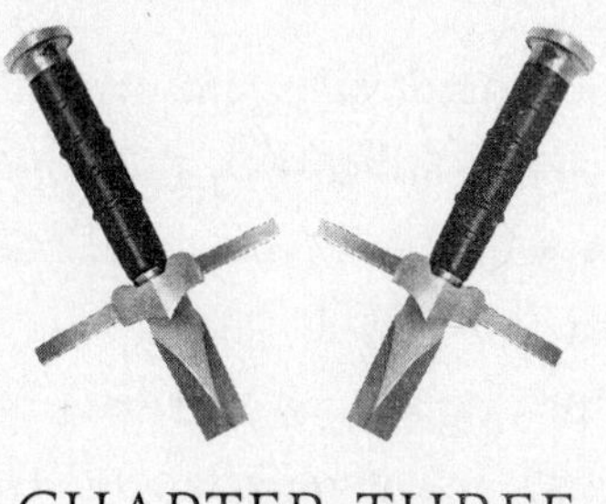

CHAPTER THREE

Rio stepped back out into the thunderstorms twenty minutes after she delivered Spaz through the doors of the Our Lady of Lourdes Shelter for the Homeless. Hopefully the guy would stay longer than the night, but she really didn't expect him to.

She was going to take care of one of his problems personally, however.

Mickie was going to back off the guy. And she'd confront the fucker now, except she was really frickin' late.

Even though the drug world didn't necessarily run to schedule, she went into a hustle, jogging back for where she'd been standing under that fire escape—

Her phone went off, the subtle ringing rising above the rustle and creak of her leather jacket. Stabbing her hand into an inner pocket, she pulled the cell out. When she saw that it was a blocked number, she pulled up short and answered in a whisper.

"Hello?"

The male voice was immediately recognizable. "Rio, you're in danger—"

"Are you out of your mind calling me on this number?" She looked around. "You want to get me killed—"

"Listen, I'm not anywhere near you, and I can't go into it right now, but your cover is blown. I'm—"

"I can't talk about this right now. And don't call me on—"

"—sending something to you outside of normal channels—"

"I gotta go," she hissed.

"Rio! You have to pull out. You've been compromised—"

"No, I haven't—"

A lightning strike burst through the night, attracted by the rod on the top of the One State Street Plaza building, which was just a couple blocks to the east of her. The flash was blinding, and the crack and sizzle of impact had her cringing back and lifting her arm over her face like a vampire. As her direct report continued to talk into her ear, she cut the call, shoved the cell in her pocket—

Up ahead, the supplier stepped out from under the fire escape.

And he was the size not so much of a football player, but an entire defensive line.

Zipping up her jacket, she pushed one hand through her short hair as the other burrowed in and locked on the grip of her hidden gun. Good thing she was wearing Kevlar under her fleece.

Rio strode forward, knowing she had to get her shit together. Everybody involved in the trade was rat smart and always reading any room they walked into or up to. She needed to get her affect strapped tight and her energy projection right. There was no way her undercover status had been compromised. There were only two people in the Caldwell Police Department who knew what she was doing, and her fake background was ironclad because she'd come over from the FBI—which had erased everything about her.

She was a ghost, floating through the streets at night, stringing together a case so that Mozart's stranglehold on the Caldie drug scene could be severed with a lifetime set of iron bars.

"You Luke?" she said crisply.

The man's golden eyes seemed to glow like candle flames, and as another bolt of lightning skipped above them, his face was briefly highlighted. Well . . . hello, sailor. He had the high cheekbones of a model, the mouth of an Italian lover, the jaw of a fighter, and the streaked hair of a nineties-era John Frieda ad.

Also, a strange scar that ran around his throat.

That last one was probably the only thing about him that made sense. There were all kinds of reasons people in the big-money sectors of the drug business ended up with things that lingered in their skin, a road map of brutal, bloody sin.

She thought of Spaz and his stab wound. And knew that was true for the underlings, too.

"Rio," came the man's low response.

Okay, that voice was smooth as bourbon in the gut, warming, relaxing—in spite of the fact that she was in the middle of a drug zone, with no backup. As usual.

And . . . was that cologne? He smelled really good.

"Yeah, that's me." She lifted her chin. "You want to talk terms."

"Not here."

"I'm not alone." Rio nodded up to the darkened windows of the building across the alley and lied through her teeth. "And I'm not leaving my friends in there."

"Don't trust me?"

"Not as far as I can throw you. So do you want to talk terms or not?"

The man stayed where he was—for a split second.

The next thing she knew he'd grabbed hold of her, spun her around, and slammed her up against the damp cold bricks of the nightclub. As his huge body pressed into her back, she was very aware of that smell of him—which, considering things were going bad, bad, bad, she should not have noticed, much less approved of.

"Get off me," she snarled.

With a yank against the hold on her arms, she tried to get her gun out. Or at the knife at her waist. Or to the pepper spray in her back pocket. Worse came to worst, she was going to bite the back of his hand and then take a course of PEP in case he was HIV-positive.

Baring her teeth, she went for—

The bullet sizzled past the top of her head, somehow charting a course that avoided both her skull and his jawline. And then there was a pinging sound as the slug hit something metal—and immediately, there was another *pop! Pop! Poppoppoppoppop—*

"I swear to God," the deep voice in her ear muttered, "if you bite me, I'm going to toss you back out there and you can get plugged full of holes."

Rio twisted her head and looked down the narrow chute between the walk-ups across the way and the club they were up against.

One of the shooters was using the blacked-out Charger he was parked in as cover. Not the worst idea given the size of its big block engine—and the fact that liquid gasoline didn't actually explode. But he'd better keep his noggin down.

That safety glass was no better than a paper napkin—

The shattering of the windshield was spectacular, the spidering cracks virus'ing out from a pinpoint hole in the glass.

The immediate blaring horn suggested that someone was taking a little nap in the driver's seat. But she didn't have time to figure out who had done the job.

Her body moved without her giving any commands to her arms and legs.

Then again, luggage didn't animate itself.

It was carried.

✦ ✦ ✦

She was a human female, Lucan thought as he picked up the woman he'd been told to meet and carted her farther away from the shooting.

When the appointment had been made, he'd assumed that Rio was a male, and the fact that the "he" was actually a "she" was a goddamned inconvenience. In an exchange of bullets, he'd have let a male die, but it seemed, well, rude, or at the least ungentlemanly, not to save the fairer sex—

"Ow!" he barked.

As that Charger was put into gear, and its set of four rubber grabbers tried to claw into the damp asphalt, his damsel in distress squirmed around, grabbed his nuts, and cranked down on his hey-that's-personals like she wanted him to sing something from *Saturday Night Fever* for her.

Instantly incapacitated, he let go of the woman and went bull rider, sinking into his knees around an invisible saddle—and thankfully, the grip was released. While Lucan blinked his eyes clear and tried to stand up straight, the woman shoved herself off of him, backing away—

Right into the path of the screeching muscle car with its pixelated safety glass, probably dead driver, and copilot who was apparently remaining under the dash while he or she steered an escape.

"No!" Lucan yelled.

The image of the woman wheeling around to face the car and getting spotlit by yellow running lights was going to stay with him forever: Her eyes popping open, her short dark hair a helmet that would do nothing to protect her skull, her reflexes not enough to save her.

She was hit fair and square, right in the legs, her body tumbling up onto the hood, her somersaults taking her in a roundabout over the busted windshield and across the roof and down the trunk: Hands, boots, hands, boots, her dark head the fulcrum around which the momentum carried her torso and spun her limbs.

The geometry was pretty damn clear. She was going to end up hitting the pavement on a headfirst landing—

Lucan sprang forward, putting all his strength into the surge, and just as he got in range, gravity won out over her forward motion, and her tender flesh started to fall with her skull leading the way—

He went airborne, throwing his body parallel to the pavement because it was his only chance to get there in time. With the wind in his ears, the stink of car exhaust and burnt rubber in his nose, and a pounding in his chest, he flew . . . flew . . . *flew* . . .

Like he was a bird instead of a wolven.

He grabbed whatever he could of the woman, locking his arms

around her and rolling in midair so that his back and not her brains took the impact of their combined weights. As they began their joined descent, he tightened his left arm, and leveled the gun in his right to the shadows just beyond the fire escape.

The shooter there was still focused on the Charger, pumping bullets into the car, *pings!* and bursts of Roman candle sparks turning the thing into a deadly disco party.

Lucan got as many bullets off as he could before he landed so hard, the breath knocked out of him and his vision went on the fritz. He told himself that the distant shout of pain was the shooter going down, but he had no proof of it. He might have made the sound.

Now . . . no more shots. Just a soft moaning.

His? The human female's? Not the shooter, too far away.

Meanwhile, the Charger was no more. The engine roar was dimming . . . and now disappearing.

Breathing. His. Hers.

Then he felt the pressure on his chest ease up and that on his hips increase. He opened eyes he hadn't known were closed.

The woman was sitting up with her back to him. Right on his pelvis.

Talk about bull riders.

As his thoughts went to places where they were naked, she was yee-hawing all over him, and things were on the hot and sweaty side of hi-how're-ya—she cursed and put her hand up to her head. Then she looked around. Twisted around. Met his eyes with ones of her own that went wide as paper plates for a second time.

"Oh, Jesus—" she barked.

The woman pushed herself off the cradle of every bright idea he'd ever had—and it was pretty clear she meant to leap to her feet. That was a no-go. She slumped to the side and grabbed for one of her legs.

"Are you okay?" he said. Or at least, that was what he meant to say. He wasn't sure what kind of fruit salad's worth of syllables came out of his mouth.

"It's not broken." She hissed as she rubbed her calf. "It's *not* broken, dammit."

Sitting himself up onto his elbows, he thought about pointing out that if a cast was required, that pep talk wasn't going to do shit for the situation. But really, why waste breath on the obvious—

Boom!

They both jumped at the explosion. Putting his arm out to shield her even though he didn't know what or where the threat was coming from, he looked down at the far end of the alley. Flames. A bonfire's worth of them. About six blocks away under one of the city's twin bridges by the river.

The orange strobe-lighting was impressive, and courtesy of the flickering show, he could see that the black muscle car was at the center of the bomb burst. And as street people ran away, he knew that soon there would be flashing blue and red lights, and all kinds of humans with badges, and spectators with camera phones.

"We gotta get out of here," he said as he stood up—and put a palm to the small of his back with a curse.

When she just looked at him, he extended the hand that didn't have a gun in it toward her.

"Do you need a doctor?" he asked.

"No."

As she left his palm out there in the breeze, he'd really had it with the way things had been going tonight.

"I'm not going to hurt you," he muttered. "I saved your life, twice. And if we keep hanging out in the middle of this fucking street, you and I might have to go for a threesome."

There was an awkward pause and then Lucan shook his head.

"Wait, that came out wrong."

Or did it, he wondered to himself.

CHAPTER FOUR

Vishous re-formed on the roof of a walk-up apartment building that had trap house written all over it. As his full weight of nearly three hundred pounds solidified in his boots—hey, he'd been working out hard, and all that iron humping was paying off—there was a creaking that suggested he needed to step carefully. Easing forward, he checked out the raw tar paper, the pockets of leaf debris that were ossifying into topsoil, and some twists that looked like clothes caught up in a crime scene.

'Cuz human flesh would be unlikely. Not a lot of Buffalo Bills in Caldie at the moment. That anybody knew about, that was.

The rooftop was long and thin because the five stories' worth of crappy flats was a shotgun, the building sandwiched between two others of equal merit and distinction. On a lowbrow domicile such as this, it went without saying there was no HVAC venting of any size, not that he felt like rolling his mortal dice on a ghosting trip down an unknown system of ductwork. But there also wasn't a set of stairs or even a hatch, and this left him with having to find a way into the top-floor apartment.

Not a big deal, though. Plenty of broken windows he could dematerialize through—

Whoop!

There it is.

Without even a snap, crackle, or pop of warning, V went into a free fall, his shitkickers breaking through the mushy roof, his body sucking through the hole they'd created, the drop so lightning fast that he barely had time to put his hands up so that his arms didn't snap off at the pits.

The weightlessness lasted one blink and a single inhale of powdered urban rot long—and just as he was wondering if he was going to keep busting through until he hit the basement, his soles hit something solid, his knees went into a bend—

And his butt bounced. Twice.

As a cloud of dust blurred the air, his forearms flopped onto padded rolls.

"Fuck me!" Rhage hollered from the far side of the debris bloom.

V glanced down at himself. Well, what do you know. An armchair.

"You want to give me a heart attack?" Hollywood demanded. "Scaring me like that?"

Across a fetid war field of stained mattresses, empty liquor bottles, and drug paraphernalia, the brother was clutching his chest like a little old lady in church who'd just learned premarital sex was a thing.

V crossed his legs at the knees and moved his gloved palm around as if he was on a throne. "You can act like a man. What's the matter with you."

"Don't you Vito Corleone at me."

"At least you caught the ref."

Rhage jabbed a finger forward—and kind of blew the tough-guy confrontation by sneezing. Three times in a row. But big, blond, and always-hungry recovered like the fighter he was.

"I liked you better before you got a sense of humor. And I know *The*

Godfather by heart. Also, before you ask, no, I'm not kissing your ring. You don't wear them, anyway."

"Oh, but I do. And wouldn't you like to know where they are."

Rhage shook his head. "That's an anatomy chart I do not need to see."

"Fair enough." V stood up. Looked to the hole in the ceiling. *Well-fuck'd* to himself. "What're the chances."

Through the ragged wound in the roof, the rain that had started to fall sprinkled his face as flaps of tar paper caught the storm's gusts and sounded like bird wings.

Rhage came over. "So you didn't plan it?"

"How the fuck am I going to plan falling through a—"

The groan brought both their heads around. Slumped in the low corner of an off-kilter sofa, a man who was twenty-five-going-on-early-grave was twitching like he was hooked up to a faulty electrical socket, his hands inching toward the red river running out of his lower abdomen.

"Oh, you're awake," Hollywood said in a cheerful way. "Great. I thought you were dead."

"Who's your friend," V asked as they went over and loomed above the guy.

Clicking now, from the slack mouth. Followed by a cough. Closer up, the human was meatier than V had first thought, and not from being fat. He was also greasier, which V supposed made him a quarter pounder, instead of a single. He had on a t-shirt that had been white probably three hundred and sixty-five days ago, and a pair of jeans that could probably stand on their own without his help.

He was armed, too—well, almost armed. There was a gun about four inches outside of his immediate reach, on a couch cushion that was a sponge for bodily fluids V would just as soon not have to culture. To be sure there weren't any more bullets flying into soft tissue that wasn't going to grow back, V confiscated the weapon, took out the clip, and pocketed the components.

Rhage leaned down and tapped the man's shoulder. "Hello?"

"I don't think he's being shy." V took out a hand-rolled and made sure the wrapper was still tight. "And that's an observation unrelated to my medical training, given that he's leaking like a busted fuel pan."

"We only want to ask you a couple of questions." Rhage raised his voice as he held a little plastic baggie marked with a cross symbol in front of that going-gray face. "You're selling this on the streets—hey, don't worry. We're not pissed and we're not your law enforcement. We just want to know where you got it."

As V patted around for his lighter, dust floated up from his leather jacket. And yeah, there was a hint of rat-vacuation to it.

Right on cue, Rhage sneezed and startled the dying man, but the revival didn't last long.

"We're out of time for talk therapy," V muttered. "I'm going in."

After he lit his cigarette, he exhaled in a stream and burrowed into the man's mind—

V cursed. "Damn, son. You gotta chill with the pipe."

Even on the lip edge of death, the guy's neurons were so overstimulated, it was impossible to isolate the memory areas, either short- or long-term. And then it didn't matter. The man gritted his teeth, reared back, and stiffened into a seizure.

V jumped out of that brain quick. "I got nothing. And he's too far gone for CPR."

"Dammit." Rhage looked over at a ragged table strewn with baggies marked with that iron cross malarkey—as well as a lappy and a phone. "I guess we take everything over there and ghost out."

In the center of the stained wooden square, there was a blue plastic-wrapped block, the corner of which was torn open, like a mouse had eaten into cheese. White powder, fine as the shit you'd brush onto a model's face, had spilled onto the table.

No wonder the guy's brain was a sparkler.

"Quite a supply," V murmured.

"He's a big dealer."

"Not anymore."

Hollywood picked a Target bag up off the floor. Shaking the thing out, he forearm'd what had to be two hundred little packets of white powder into it.

"How's this asshole hanging here by himself with all this coke?" V headed back to the couch and went face-to-face with the gaping, twitching human. "I'd think he'd have backup. Unless you shot anybody else?"

"Nope, just him," Rhage said agreeably. "He must have a reputation and a half."

The dealer's watery, bloodshot eyes rolled back as he exhaled his last breath. After which he became just like the piece of furniture, another used-up object in the squalor.

"Well, that's that." V straightened. "And maybe you and I should do some target practice in the training center during the day, true? You know, perishable skills and all that."

"I need Zyrtec." Rhage sneezed. "The problem is my nose, not my aim."

"We can get that down in the clinic, too. Come on, Hollywood, let's blow. With the blow."

As V browed-up a couple of times, the brother shook his head. "Like I said, I liked you better before you got a sense of humor."

"Why, you jealous I'm good at something else now?"

◆ ◆ ◆

Down on the ground in the alley where she'd been hit by a car, Rio was trying to rub the pain out of her left leg—and thinking of *My Big Fat Greek Wedding*. Windex. If only she had some Windex.

So maybe she had a concussion, too.

As the Charger had come at her, she'd managed to jump-and-roll just before impact, and her timing had saved her legs from being totally shattered at the shins. But that didn't mean she didn't break something or that she wasn't going to be a quilt of bruises in the morning—because the human body was not supposed to act as a squash ball.

"—have to go for a threesome. Wait, that came out wrong."

As the male voice registered, she looked to the source.

It was the supplier she was supposed to meet. The one who had saved her life. He was talking to her, but for some reason, she couldn't hear what he was saying—

All at once, the words that had registered were properly deciphered by her brain. "I'm *not* sleeping with you," she blurted.

As he stood up, he waved his palms, all just-forget-it. "Like I said, came out wrong. Do you need a doctor or not?"

"Not. Most definitely not."

It was a surprise that someone in the drug trade wanted to pull the rip cord on a call to 911 for anything, but then he knew she was one of Mozart's top lieutenants. So maybe he was just preserving the potential revenue stream. If she kicked it, or was taken out of circulation, he'd have to find another contact.

Like Mickie.

As Rio went to stand up, she braced for a lot of pain. Fortunately, it wasn't as bad as she'd thought it would be, just a matched set of bass drums in her legs. Meanwhile, the supplier—Luke was the name he was using—looked at her like he was expecting her to list to the side and knock herself out cold on the pavement. When she held her balance, he whistled under his breath.

"You're impressive as hell, lady."

Whatever, she thought. A couple thousand pounds of metal and glass coming at you gave you wings.

Talk about a Red Bull ad.

She kept all that to herself. "So let's talk pricing."

"Um, yeah, do you see that fireball down there?" He nodded to the river, where the Charger had exploded on some kind of impact, and a bright orange fire was showing no signs of burning out. Then he cupped his ear. "You hear those sirens? Shit's about to get complicated around here, especially because I shot the shooter, even if I didn't shoot the deputy. You want to talk, we're going somewhere else."

Rio hell-no'd that. But not because she was injured. She needed to find out whether the phone call she'd gotten before the shit hit the fan was connected to what had just happened. Had she been a bystander . . . or a target?

"I gotta go. We'll meet tomorrow."

Luke, likely not his real name, just stared at her. "You fuck me off, I'll go to Mozart myself."

"Yeah, good luck with that. He doesn't meet directly with anybody."

"I got special skills."

"So do a lot of people." Her bored tone was a cover-up for the stress prickling under her skin. "I'll be in touch and we'll try this again tomorrow night."

And like the Caldwell Police Department patrol units had read her mind, those sirens the guy had pointed out doubled in volume, either because twenty more squad cars were coming in their direction or because the twelve dozen that were on their way had just turned the final corner.

"Suit yourself," the supplier said. "But I was willing to make the deal tonight—and I'm moving on to someone else if you don't take more of what I gave your organization last night. Also, you owe me."

"Excuse me?"

"I saved your life, twice." His golden eyes narrowed. "You owe me, Rio. And I collect my debts."

"I didn't ask you for a damned thing."

"So you'd rather be dead."

"Than indebted to anybody? You better believe it. And you need me. You can't do the kind of business you want to with anybody but me. Mozart's is the only organization that's going to buy at the levels you're talking about moving."

"So let's get the deal done."

Rio glanced around, and heard the warning she'd hung up on haunting her. "I'll contact you at the number I have—"

The man snapped a hold on her arm. "Don't fuck with me. I have options you don't even know about."

Before she could react, he released his grip and walked off, his dark clothes helping him blend into the shadows.

"Dammit," Rio whispered as she ducked and disappeared herself.

Sticking to the club's flank, she took out her gun and measured the windows across the alley, the lane behind her, the lane ahead of her. The patrol cars screamed by one block over, and she caught sight of the lineup with their flashing lights as they crossed an intersection she could see through.

Her legs were killing her, her left one below the knee in particular.

A streak of lightning gave her eyes more than the ambient light of the city to go on—and also revealed her. As she sank into an inset doorway, she frowned and leaned back out. A moment later . . . there was another of the storm's strobes.

"Where did you go?" she said under her breath.

The supplier had somehow . . . disappeared. Unless he'd snuck into one of the buildings? Maybe. That was the only explanation. In the direction he'd gone in, away from the river, there were no corners, no cut-throughs, no going any way but forward for two blocks straight.

Maybe he'd broken out into a sprint—

She couldn't worry about it. Not right now.

Checking the clip in her gun, she relowered the weapon to her thigh and continued on. She found the body about forty feet ahead, crumpled facedown on the pavement behind a dumpster. It was a man, going by the build and the hair, as well as the size of the boots. As she knelt beside him, her brain connected the dots.

The jacket. She recognized the black leather jacket because of the red stitching that crisscrossed the shoulders and ran down to the bottom hem.

"Erie."

One of Mozart's lieutenants.

Had he been shooting at her? Or the Charger?

As she looked at the spreading red pool under the man, she thought about a killing down in Manhattan the weekend before. Johnny Two

Shoes, an associate of Mozart's biggest competition in the state, had been executed and rolled into the Hudson. The word on the street had been that revenge was imminent.

Maybe Erie had been protecting her, protecting the deal being made. Had the driver of the Charger been trying to kill her in retaliation?

Rio stretched an arm out and put her fingertips to the inside of Erie's still-warm wrist. Feeling around . . . no, there was no pulse. Making the sign of the cross, she straightened—and left the area so that she could call in the shooting details to HQ from greater safety.

That she was walking with just a limp was better than she could have hoped for.

Good thing, too, as she wasn't done with her to-do list yet tonight.

CHAPTER FIVE

Lucan re-formed at right about the place he'd scared off those two boys with their ghost-hunting equipment. Lifting his face to the rain, he let the light drops fingertip his forehead and cheeks. On the backs of his eyelids, he saw that human female getting hit fair-and-square by the car. Then pictured her rising to her feet afterward, brushing herself off, and giving him the what-for.

She'd had a strong face, her features bold, her lips full, her dark eyes big under declarative brows. Her skin had lost all its color as she forced her weight onto what had taken the impact, but she had refused to give in to the pain.

He couldn't decide whether the grit was sexy or stupid.

Well . . . he supposed it was stupid, but he found it sexy.

Wiping the rain through his hair, he leveled his head and stared straight ahead. If she didn't call him sometime during the rest of tonight or tomorrow during the day, he was going to go out to the streets and find her.

And then what? the malest part of him demanded.

"None of your business," he muttered.

You want her.

"Yeah, to get the Executioner off my back."

Aware that he was arguing with himself, he started for his new home—and by "home," he meant involuntary servitude with a roof over his head. "Prison camp" had been the old term, when they'd been underground at the old site they'd abandoned. This was the new world order, no more cells, though still underground, those tracking collars ever present.

Funny, how you could control people when, with one press of a remote, their brains were vaporized. There also weren't a lot of options for most of the vampires being held.

He was one of the few without a collar. But he needed to be able to dematerialize back and forth to Caldwell to make this deal, and there was no ghosting around when you had a band of steel around your throat.

And the Executioner wasn't worried about him bolting. The fucker had leverage over him, the kind of thing that was just as good as an explosive necklace. But it wasn't going to last much longer so he was biding his time. With one death, he was free—and he was of half a mind to take care of the Grim Reaper's work himself. It would be a mercy killing at this point, anyway, two liberations for the price of a single slit throat.

Cheap, all things considering.

Up ahead, the old human hospital building loomed like something out of a John Carpenter movie where everyone but the virtuous girl who didn't have sex with her boyfriend died in creative, bloody ways.

God, he missed the eighties. Then again, the last time he'd been able to watch a TV or listen to a radio had been right before he'd been thrown into the prison camp. So, yeah, he was current as of the spring of 1983. And maybe he didn't miss the era; he missed . . . life and the simple freedoms he had taken for granted.

Lucan stopped at the worn stone steps of the sanatorium's entrance. The central core of the building was a tower of closed windows, the floors rising up like a blocky spear, the tip of which was a tower topped with a lightning rod. On either side of this torso, there were two five-story wings of open porches, each extending at a wide angle to catch the prevailing breeze for failing lungs.

The place had been built to treat the human tuberculosis patients who suffered such cruel, suffocating deaths through the 1800s and into the twentieth century. Back then, the treatment for the bacterial infestation was fresh air, and as much of it as you could stand, no matter the season. Well, that and hacking pieces of your lungs out, or cod-liver oil, or inhaling hemlock.

Until streptomycin and other drugs came to the rescue in the late forties.

Why did he know all that about those rats without tails and their coughs? He liked his trivia, even if it was about shit that didn't affect vampires. Or vampire-wolven half-breeds.

The *New York Times* crossword puzzle had been his favorite.

Looking down the south wing, he measured the open porches that ran all the way to the far end. The patient rooms were behind the loggias, the rusted frames of the old hospital beds cluttering the tight spaces, all kinds of debris down the hallways and graffiti marking the stained and rotting walls. The north wing was the same, as was the administrative core that anchored the structure.

Everything abandoned and decaying, only the ghosts of dead patients remaining now.

Above ground, that was.

In a way, prisoners like him and the others belonged here. They'd been discarded, too. Forgotten. And most were rotting as they shuffled around beneath the earth, their only use cutting and portioning drugs to make money for yet another despot.

"One death," he said grimly as he reached for the tarnished brass pull. "One death, and I'm out of here."

There were advantages to having been excised from your family.

No more leverage when it came to your bloodline 'cuz you didn't care if the fuckers were smothered in their own beds.

The old place still had some electricity running through it, and a dusty light bulb hanging from a wire cast sad light over what had been the reception, waiting, and check-in area. From what he'd read on a plaque on the wall, the hospital had stopped treating tubercular patients in the early fifties and switched to housing the mentally ill. That had lasted until the seventies, at which point, everything had been deserted.

He didn't think anyone was going to add a bronze plate honoring the coda that included vampires.

Diverting from the open area with its moldy, toppled chairs and chipped, cheap-wood tables, he headed to the right. The north wing's hall was marked "North Wing"—surprise!—and there were administrative offices on both sides, missing doors allowing views into rooms with ceiling collapses and broken windows that had let in the weather as well as years' worth of fallen leaves. In a few spots, weeds had set up shop and started to inch ascents over the stained walls.

As he went along, he didn't bother to hide the sounds of his boots. The sentries who were watching expected him—well, maybe not back this early, but he was a known commodity, allowed to go in and out.

The farther away he went from that single bulb, the darker it got, but his eyes were even sharper than normal vampires', his wolf side giving him a night-vision-goggle effect, everything going shades of red.

Which was how he'd known exactly where to shoot back in that alley. What a clusterfuck—

"You're home early."

Lucan stopped. Well, shit. Another twenty yards, he'd be down into the basement complex. So close.

He kept his eyes on his prize, refusing to turn away from the steel reinforced door that had been an installation of the new owners.

"What's the matter, wolven. Someone take your kibble away down in Caldwell?"

"That's right," he said smoothly. "At the same time they removed your soul."

The chuckle in the darkness was like a switchblade traveling across a jugular vein. Well, it would have been, if Lucan gave a crap about being alive.

"You know I'd trade places with you if you can't handle it."

Now Lucan glanced over his shoulder, in case this verbal poking was going to elevate to prodding—and hey, he'd be good with that. He wanted to hit something.

"Too bad the Executioner won't allow that," Lucan murmured. "You can't be trusted, can you, Apex."

The vampire stepped out into the corridor, and he was a nasty piece of work, the kind of thing that even the actual killers and sociopaths in the camp gave a wide berth to. With black eyes that glittered with a predator's instinct for fresh blood, and a body that was heavily muscled as well as lightning fast, he was just as he appeared: A soulless murderer who, unlike some of the people trapped in this hell, actually deserved his sentence.

And goddamn, the fact that the male had started shaving his head hardly made him look any warmer and fuzzier.

"You don't have to come back here," Apex said. "You could just disappear down in the city."

"You know exactly why I come back. And I'm not justifying my rock and a hard place to the likes of you."

The other male's mouth lifted in what would have been a smile on another person's puss. Considering who and what he was, the movement was merely a way of flashing fangs.

"Don't get defensive over the death you choose for yourself, wolf. Or do you think this is going to end in another way for you?"

Lucan stepped right up to the full-bred vampire, getting so close that their pecs touched. Then he returned the smile, exactly as it was given to him.

"Since when do you worry about anybody but yourself." He kept his voice level. "And if you're making a threat here, how about you try something right now. I've had a shitty night and could use the fucking exercise."

Apex's gleaming onyx eyes narrowed. "You're such an animal."

"So. Are. You—"

"Hey, hey, now, boys. Can't we just take a deep breath here?"

Mayhem joined the fun and games, but more as a bandleader than a brawling participant. Throwing his muscled arms around the proverbial bomb that was about to explode, he looked back and forth.

"Come on, I want you two to kiss and make up. Then follow me. I hijacked a pizza-delivery guy heading to a football party—don't worry, I let him go, and I'll bring back his car with the cost and tips. I got the receipt as well as his insurance card with his address on it. What was I saying—oh, right. I got hot Domino's right out back. Come on!"

Apex punched Lucan's shoulders, and the double hit felt good. Then there was a pause, as if he were being given the chance to fight back. When he decided not to, Apex stepped off.

"I'm watching you."

Lucan's upper lip twitched. "Anytime, motherfucker."

The other male up and dematerialized, and Lucan broke away and paced around in a circle.

"He likes you," Mayhem said. "Under all that, he really likes—"

"Are you *crazy*?"

"Well, no. At least I don't think so. Anyway, pizza?"

Lucan rubbed his face. "Yeah, I'm starved."

"Come on, I'll take you to it."

At that, Lucan finally focused properly on the perennial third wheel. With his black-and-white hair, and colorless eyes, Mayhem was built powerful enough, and he could back himself up if he had to, but he was too goddamn easygoing to be a primary threat.

"I need to go see the Executioner," Lucan heard himself say.

"Food first. You're too hangry not to get yourself in a bad situation."

It was good advice, from a source that was better known for being annoying. But beggars/choosers and all that.

As they started to walk to the emergency exit together, Mayhem tacked on, "And the good news is that only one of the pizzas is that Hawaiian bullshit. Why anybody puts pineapple and ham together on a bed of perfectly fine mozzarella is beyond me."

"Humans are weird."

And a helluva lot less dangerous than the people I'm living with, Lucan thought to himself.

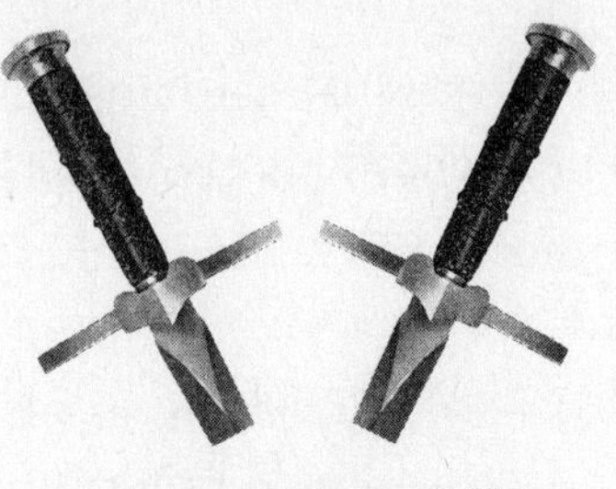

CHAPTER SIX

By the time Rio arrived in the vicinity of her last stop of the night, her left leg was humming a tune to the beat of her heart, *boom, boom, boom . . .*

Wasn't there a song like that? Charlie X or something. She'd heard it on Sirius every fifteen minutes a couple of years ago.

As she continued along, favoring the opposite side gave her a pronounced limp, and did little to relieve the spikes of pain flooding her nervous system. The good news was she had only one more block to go, and this was what Motrin was for, right? There was a half-used economy bottle of the stuff in the glove compartment of her car—and, bonus, her beater was even closer now that she'd made this rerouting from that alley.

Swinging her eyes around, she double-checked there was no one following her. The walk-ups on both sides of the street were tall-and-thins, squeezed in with mere inches between mismatched sets of aluminum siding. Occupancy was fifty-fifty at best, and you could tell which buildings were legally lived in by whether the windows were covered up. If there were drapes pulled or sheets strung between nails, there were people paying rent inside. The rest of the flats were fair game for squatting, broken glass panes and dim candlelight sad testament to the lost souls seeking refuge from their demons in the very pockets of urban Hell.

This neighborhood was incredibly dangerous after dark, a battleground for street gangs and drug suppliers, the unfortunate civilians who existed in the airspace between territory conflict and illegal commerce collateral damage in more ways than one. Thanks to the storm and all the police gathering down under the bridge, the corners were clear. But they weren't going to stay that way for long.

And she would have come anyway, even if it had been business as usual.

As she came to the walk-up she was looking for, she glanced around again. Then she went up the chipped and stained concrete steps. No reason to knock. Mickie had guards all over the place. He already knew she was here.

Pulling open the pitted door, a waft of dank-and-dreadful hit her square in the face. There were two apartments on each floor, with a central staircase lacing up the center of the building, and as she hit the carpeted steps, the ascent put so much pressure on whatever was going on in her left leg that she ended up having to use the sticky banister. At every new level, she paused to make sure she had the bead on her surroundings right: No one behind her. No one in front. Nobody coming out at her from the abandoned flats, the doors of which were all open.

That last one was the big danger. The light of the stairwell bled into the main living spaces of the dirty apartments, but there were rooms she couldn't see into, spaces that could hide all kinds of threats. The only thing she could count on was that if she weren't allowed here, she wouldn't have gotten this far.

Besides, Mickie knew that she was on his level. Which meant if anyone aggressed on her, and she were hurt? Mickie would have to deal with their boss, and nobody wanted to do that.

When she got to the topmost floor, the door on the left was closed.

So Mickie was in.

"It's me, Rio," she called out.

She did not go over and stand directly in front of the wooden panels. She put her back to the wall, reached past the jamb, and knocked hard with her left hand. Her right stayed deep inside her pocket, on the butt of her weapon.

"Mickie. It's Rio."

As she waited, she looked into the apartment across the way. Its living room had a sofa and three mismatched armchairs, the furniture arranged around an oil drum that burned wood in the winter when security had to camp out.

"Come on, Mick." She knocked again. "Don't fuck with me."

There was no chance that he'd evac'd because of the police presence down by the river. Too far away. And there hadn't been a raid scheduled. She would have known about that whether it was by ATF, FBI, or CPD, and would have put a stop to it through regular channels.

"Mickie!" She knocked again. "C'mon."

No answer. Fine. Three . . . two . . . one—

Rio gunned up and threw open the door. The second she got a look inside, she muttered, "Sonofabitch."

Across the messy living area, in the glow of the ceiling fixtures, Mickie was sitting on his couch, his head back, his body on a sprawl, his feet flopped to the sides. But he wasn't chilling. He had a massive abdominal wound, his blood seeping out to stain his dirty t-shirt a bright, Fourth of July red.

And that wasn't the only new-and-interesting in the place.

There was a hole in the roof of the building, the dwindling rain falling through the ragged aperture to turn an Archie Bunker armchair into a sponge.

Keeping her gun in her hand, she went over and pulled another two-finger on a wrist. And just like the shooter by the dumpster in the alley, Mickie had flatlined—but was still warm.

The murder was recent, maybe thirty or forty minutes ago. Not that she was a coroner.

"Great. Just fucking great."

Rio muttered all kinds of things to herself as she took out her phone, and with her left hand, texted the shooting in. Then she snapped a picture of the body as well as another of the worktable where a couple of scales, some powder residue, and a boatload of empty two-inch-square baggies were a loud-and-clear on what had been happening in the apartment.

Not that anybody would assume Mickie hosted cooking classes here.

After she scraped some of the had-to-be-cocaine off the table with her Swiss Army knife—

"I'm just going to use one of these baggies, Mick," she said. "You don't need 'em anymore, do you."

She took a picture of the sample and then put it in her pocket.

Then she went back over to the body. As she stared into the frozen face, the waxy, pale skin transfixed her, taking her back to another time she had seen a human being dead . . . back to the first time she had seen remains. Her memories of the moment she had walked into her younger brother's bedroom were so vivid that she became inanimate herself, suspended between the past and the present. And once that recollection was unleashed, there was no stopping the deluge of what she so capably kept under wraps during normal circumstances.

"Stop it," she whispered.

But the nightmare wouldn't recede. Then again, tonight she had almost died. Twice. No wonder the longest and worst evening of her life, as well as everything that had happened afterward, was dogging her.

It was a while before she could think properly again.

"You deserve worse, you sick bastard," she said.

For everything Mickie had done to Spaz—and so many others. And that was why she had come here, to warn the dealer that he was going to lay off her street friend or the consequences were going to land on his head: Even though Mickie was—er, *had been*—a sadistic piece of work, there were levers she could pull, ones that were within the bounds of the law, but that would cause him problems with Mozart.

Of course, all that strong-arm stuff was a moot point now.

And the sad reality was that Spaz was likely to find another source for what he needed. Still, no one had been as bad as Mickie.

"Rest in Hell, you piece of shit," she said. "I hope you roast—"

The soft squeak behind her brought her around—and her gun.

CHAPTER SEVEN

The Black Dagger Brotherhood mansion had been built at the turn of the twentieth century by Darius, a brother who had had a big heart, a strong dagger hand, and a treacherous hope that one day, the fighters for the race would live under a single roof with their families and loved ones.

As Vishous shoved his goatee'd mug into the vestibule's security camera and waited for the copper lock to be released, he had a thought that that male would have approved of where they had all ended up.

Damn shame the brother hadn't lived long enough to see it himself—

Clunk!

Vishous opened the seven-thousand-pound door, and the ancient *doggen* butler on the other side was a beaming smile upright and walking in a penguin suit. Fritz Perlmutter loved his job and the household he served to a degree that had been grating at first. Like, how could anyone be that excited silver-traying drinks, organizing the rest of the staff, and spot-cleaning blood off rugs?

"You're home!" Fritz exclaimed, as if V and Rhage had returned from a dangerous mission to the Arctic Circle and managed to only get frostbitten on a pinkie toe and one earlobe. "And early as well!"

Rhage plowed in, as was his way. "Fritz, my guy, I'm starved. Can you—"

"I have three footlongs pre-prepared for you. Ham and cheese, salami and cheese, and turkey and cheese. Allow me to mayonnaise them, and I shall bring them to you immediately." Fritz looked at V. "A Grey Goose and tonic for you, sire?"

All V could do was shake his head in wonder. The guy had a way of growing on you, you know? "Yeah, thanks. We're up with Wrath."

"Right away!"

In spite of the jowls and the wrinkles, Fritz headed off fresh as a sprinter out of the blocks, his polished shoes clipping over the foyer's mosaic floor, his white-gloved hands pumping to the beat of his love of service.

"It's like he's a mind reader," Rhage said as they started for the grand staircase, with its gold-leafed balustrade and its blood-red runner. "I mean, how did he know—"

"You are never not hungry, and when have I ever turned down a V 'n' T?" V held up his forefinger. "I'm not saying he ain't a genius, but guessing you're ready for a footlong is not prognostication."

"You got a point, my brother."

As they came to the second floor, the doors to the study were open, and across the pale blue room with its fine French furniture, Wrath, son of Wrath, sire of Wrath, was all heavy-is-the-head-that-wears-the-crown. Plugged into the old carved desk his father had used, sitting on the old carved throne his father had sat in, the great Blind King's wraparounds were angled down as he ran his fingertips over lines of braille. No doubt it was another report from Saxton, the Brotherhood's solicitor and expert in the Old Laws.

"Well, well, well," Wrath murmured as he looked up like his eyes worked, "back so soon. What went wrong."

With his hip-length black hair falling from that widow's peak, and his aristocratic features that had a cruel edge, he looked like exactly the force of nature he was, and had to be, if the goal was keeping the species alive and together, under the noses of humans and in spite of the persecution of enemies.

It went without saying that the brother wasn't a party to deal with sometimes. Then again, anybody in his situation, with his kind of stress, would get a little cranky from time to time—although, to be fair, even before he started really doing the king shit, he'd had the interpersonal skills of a shotgun.

"I got a door prize," Rhage said as he barged right in and planted it on one of the silk sofas by the fireplace. "Well, lots of little prizes."

As Hollywood held up the Target bag full of coke, even though Wrath couldn't see it, V shut the double doors. "All he had to do was empty the lower intestines of a dealer into the guy's own couch."

"Your beast come out?" the King said.

"Nah, I sneezed."

Black brows lifted over the wraparounds. "Really? I didn't know your nose had that kind of firepower."

"It doesn't," V answered as he took out a hand-rolled. "He had an oopsie."

"Do you need gun practice—"

"You would have sneezed, too," Rhage interrupted the King. "And no, I don't need to go to the range. Well, unless Lassiter has a target on his ass—"

"I'll volunteer the angel right here, right now." V parked it on the far side of the desk. "And can I be the one with the stapler, pinning the tail on his donkey? 'Cuz I'll tell you right now, I'ma hit that Stanley until the thing jams."

Wrath sat back, his hand reaching down to stroke the boxy head of his Seeing Eye dog. As George lifted his head in adoration, the King actually laughed a little at the joke. A rare event. Like Zsadist smiling.

"I would pay money to see that." Annnnnnnnd then shit got serious again. "So tell me what went tits up."

V flicked his Bic, sucked the flame into the tip, and exhaled. "We got some samples of the product. Nothing much else. As we said, Rhage popped one contact, and the other—well, she got busy saving the world so she missed her appointment with the middleman."

"Why don't you get into her mind," Wrath demanded. "Look under the rocks, find the worms. If that shit's hitting the streets, and she's one of the dealer's enforcers, she'll know where it's coming from."

"She doesn't. Not yet. She's working on a deal, though. Something was supposed to come of it tonight, but then—yeah, she had to go to rehab."

Wrath shook his head. "Good dealers never use their own product."

"Oh, it wasn't for her. She was taking care of a junkie." V stroked his goatee. "See, our girl down there, she's got herself a little secret. She's a cop playing among thieves."

Black eyebrows once again rose above the wraparounds. "Dangerous game."

"She's a do-gooder, trying to make up for a bad thing that wasn't her fault. She's definitely going to get herself killed in the process, but hopefully, I'll find out what we need from her before she toes up."

"You are such a humanitarian, V." Wrath leaned to the side and gathered up the dog, transferring the sleepy blond bulk from the floor into his lap. "But stay on it. We need to find that camp."

V ran through his visit to the previous location. The place had been underground, out north and west from Caldwell, a subterranean labyrinth of old cells and cavernous common places hidden from everyone and everything. Set up by the *glymera* for criminals in the 1800s, it had devolved into a debased holding tank for all kinds of minor infractions, social insults, and inconvenient people who needed to be disappeared by the aristocracy. Over time, the location had been forgotten, and in the vacuum of stewardship, a new power structure and sustaining effort had evolved, the costs of food and supplies covered by drug dealing in Caldie's downtown.

The big break on its existence had come when a female had gone into the prison camp to rescue her sister, and shit had gotten critical. The Jackal, a true male of worth who had been falsely imprisoned, had made it out alive with her, but by the time the Brotherhood had arrived on scene, the place had been partially destroyed and totally emptied out.

From a tactical point of view, V had to respect the coordination required to move that many people. It wasn't like they'd dematerialized to another location. That would have been like blowing the head of a dandelion, scattering your indentured workforce to the wind, never to be seen again. No, the illicit leadership had had trucks—and big ones. There had been evidence of a flotilla's worth of vehicles exiting the abandoned site through a roadway that ran in and out of the facility.

There had also been the leftovers of a drug-processing station the size of a small college, the details of which the Jackal had shared as best he could.

"We'll find the prison." V inhaled deep and let the smoke roll out of his mouth. "And we're gonna take control."

A subtle knocking on the door had Rhage leaping to his feet. "Fritz with the food, finally! I'm starved."

As Hollywood raced to let the butler in like he was in a deadly blood sugar drop, Wrath shook his head. "Does he *ever* stop eating?"

"Not that I've noticed," V said dryly.

✦ ✦ ✦

The St. Francis Medical Center was a state-of-the-art sprawl that just happened to be on Rio's way home. As she came up to a red light at the entrance to its complex, she looked over the glowing, mostly empty parking lots, and the glowing, always full buildings of surgical suites, testing facilities, patient rooms, and administrative offices. Even with all the well-lit signage, the idea of figuring out how to get around to the emergency room was exhausting—

Her phone vibrated in the interior pocket of her jacket, and she fished around to find it. She didn't bother to check and see who was calling. She knew who it was.

"I can't talk, I'm going to get checked out." Hitting her directional signal, she ran the red light and turned into the main thoroughfare through the acreage. "And no, I'm not bleeding. I got into a little car accident, but I'm fine."

Captain Stanley Carmichael got his boss voice on. "I'll meet you there."

"No, you won't. I'm undercover and will be using my—"

"I don't want to do this over the phone."

Rio's eyes tracked the red-and-white signs that read "EMERGENCY," and the fact that her hands and feet operated her beater all by themselves seemed a commentary on how used to dealing with emergencies she was.

"Do what," she said remotely. "Over the phone."

The emergency room was lit up like a ballpark, the bays for the ambulances and the glass-fronted entrance for walk-ins glowing like a promised land for the afflicted.

God, she hoped she didn't end up with a cast.

"Hello?" she demanded. "Will you just tell me, Captain. I'm going to have to hang up in a second as I go inside."

"What kind of car accident were you in?"

A quick memory of rolling up and over that Charger played like a ticker tape across her mind's eye. She really should have kept that detail out when she reported Erie's death.

"Just a fender bender," she said.

"Then why are you getting checked out."

"You know me, always following the rules."

There was a multi-tiered parking lot on the far side of the ER, and out of habit, she avoided it and parked instead in the open air and directly under a streetlamp. Her ring of keys made a clapping sound as she turned off the engine, and when she got out, she made sure she hadn't been followed.

"Hello?" she said into the phone. Like the roles were reversed and she wasn't speaking to a very-much-higher-up.

Captain Carmichael was actually Chief Carmichael, but he was the kind of humble man who didn't stand on ceremony. According to him, "captain" was enough when it came to titles, although he wasn't going to turn down the office and especially not the private bathroom.

"Rio."

"What."

When the captain didn't respond, she closed her eyes and leaned against the side of her car. "I'm not stopping. You're not taking me off—"

"You called in two homicides tonight. Both gunshot victims."

"I did what I'm supposed to—"

"So you know the rules. In addition to reporting in, if any officer is involved in a shooting, it's mandatory admin leave until they've been assessed by a counselor and cleared by the county prosecutor and the AG—"

"I didn't shoot either of them. And if you don't believe me, check the ballistics. My gun wasn't used."

"The rules are what the rules are. You're off the streets—"

"I'm so close to getting what we need on Mozart. Captain, come on, I just want another couple of weeks—and I can get you the supplier as well. I met him tonight, and I'm going to get the deal done—"

"Rules are there for a reason—"

"I'm being punished because I was in the wrong place at the wrong time!"

"This is not punishment. This is health and safety, Rio. I'm taking you off the case. Mozart is not as important as your life."

So he knew about the cover being blown, she thought. That's what this was really about.

And he was a good guy, so he wasn't going to spell it out to her—because nothing was less professional than an undercover cop who'd had her identity compromised. Especially one like her with federal training.

Rio looked over to the ER's entrance. An older woman and man were coming out, the man offering his arm, the woman taking it and leaning on him. She wasn't limping, but she was tilted in as if she needed help carrying her own weight. But her problem wasn't like what Rio had, it wasn't an injury. She was sick. In the bright, icy illumination, her face was too red and she was breathing through her mouth and coughing.

"—assessment later this week," her superior was saying. "And then a debriefing. After that, you're taking a couple of weeks off—"

"How're you going to replace me. Out on the street." She leaned forward, like the man was in front of her in his suit and tie. "Who'll take my place with Mozart? I'm the one who's gone the furthest, and I've worked on this for eighteen months straight. I told you, I met the supplier contact tonight—and I was about to make the deal when we were rudely interrupted by a goddamn gunfight that had nothing to do with me." *Well, at least in theory,* she tacked on to herself. "It's not my fault that the Ballous decided to ride up on Caldwell and avenge Johnny Two Shoes—and before you criticize me for holding a meeting in an alley, where else am I supposed to face-to-face my contacts? The public library? Yeah, because that'll go over *so* much better—"

"Your life is more important than this case."

"I accepted the risks when I took the job."

"There's no getting around this, so let's both be professional here. Your appointment's been made with mental health, and I'll expect to see you in my office tomorrow, shall we say eleven? Great. See you then—oh, and if you need to make a workers' comp claim for that injury, bring your paperwork from St. Francis. Goodnight, Detective."

The connection was cut, that deep, serious voice turned off like a lamp at midnight.

"Sonofabitch."

As she shoved her phone into her pocket, she thought of Spaz and wondered how the shelter was going for him. He would have been assessed by now, and had that stab wound checked out. He'd also have a hot meal in his belly and a clean bed for his body to rest on. She wished there was a way to make him stay in long enough to transition into a long-term care facility that would detox him and get him into a sustainable recovery.

But that wasn't the way things worked.

Rio watched the couple get into a station wagon. The man helped the woman into the passenger seat; then he went around and got behind the wheel. The headlights flared to life, but the couple didn't immediately leave. They were talking.

She imagined the husband was worried that the wife was sick to her stomach. Then Rio dubbed in the wife telling him she was fine, no, honestly, she was fine. He would ask if she had enough stuffing left in her to pick up the antibiotics/painkillers/antivirals/whatever at the twenty-four-hour pharmacy at that Hannaford's on the way home. If she didn't, he'd take her back first—

I'm fine, honey. Drive on.

Eventually, the station wagon eased forward, crossing the parking lot and hanging a left to hook up with the main road to the complex's exit.

Rio stayed where she was, next to her car, until she couldn't see their headlights anymore.

Then she closed her eyes—and, for no good reason, thought of the supplier from back in that alley. He was right. He had saved her life. Twice.

But they weren't going for a third time.

For so many reasons.

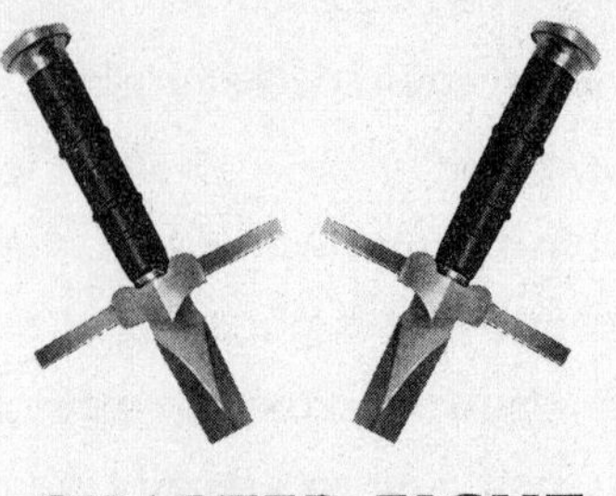

CHAPTER EIGHT

Out far to the west of Caldwell, a farmhouse with a wraparound porch, a big maple in the side yard, and a family under its gabled roof was glowing with light and warmth and laughter. Inside, there was a son who had been found, and a sister who was sunshine at midnight . . . and a male and a female who were united in love. Though the tract of land was isolated, it was hardly lonely on the acreage. And inside, the pantries were full, and family pictures sat upon the mantel, and there was so much to look forward to and celebrate: Birthdays, festival nights, even regular things like a shared First Meal or a homemade dessert for Last Meal or a book well read, a game of gin rummy well played, a practical joke well dealt.

It was a good life. A great life, by all accounts.

And as the male of the family stepped out of the front door and took a deep breath of the rain-saturated air, he lied to the one he held closest in his heart as he propped the heavy weight open with his running shoe.

"Nah, not long," the Jackal said. "Just maybe ten miles out and back. It'll take me about two hours?"

Down by the kitchen, his *shellan*, Nyx, leaned around the doorjamb. "Sounds great. Just watch that ankle of yours."

For a split second, his mate was all he could see, from her long, black hair to her familiar face, her flashing hazel eyes to her beautiful smile. In the space of no time at all, Nyx had become his world . . . Nyx and his son, Peter, and her sister and her grandfather.

They were his tethers. To the present, to the good parts of himself . . . to the decency he'd once had, and only recently rediscovered.

"I'll do that," he whispered, even though he couldn't remember exactly what she'd told him to watch out for. "I love you."

Nyx's head tilted. And then she came down to him, all loose blue jeans and baggy shirt and devastatingly sexy. She had a damp dish towel in her hand because the farmhouse didn't have a dishwasher. And actually, one of his favorite things to do was stand with her over the sink, working the sponge, and handing off to her everything he had cleaned. Or sometimes, she washed and he dried.

It was just simple stuff. But it was also the kind of thing that when he'd been in the prison camp, he'd given up on ever having.

As his female halted in front of him, something about the way she stared up into his eyes made him feel like she could read his mind. And he didn't want her to see inside of him. Not tonight. Not right now.

"I'm glad you like to run," she said. "And you can run as much as you want. I'm never going to stop you."

With a subtle lift, she rose up onto her tiptoes. As their lips met, he shook his head.

"I'm just running," he told her. "Really."

Because he wished it were true. He wanted it to be true. And yet he knew he was lying to her.

But was he? If she knew anyway?

"I'm sorry," he said softly.

"You have nothing to apologize for. Now go. Do what you have to. I'll be here."

The Jackal kissed his *shellan* again, and then he turned away and closed the door. The floorboards of the porch creaked as he went to the steps, and as soon as he was down on the ground, he fell into a jog. Then a quick running pace.

He didn't track traveling across the dying grass or the moment when lawn got traded for pavement. But he knew how far away he was from his home as the first mile was passed.

Without consciously deciding to stop, he went statue in the middle of the county road. On either side, there was a whole lot of nothing-much up close, just brush that was now brown. Farther away, though, there were mountains rising from the valley floor like they were the lip edge of the bowl that kept the earth from spilling out into space.

He pictured the way the landscape looked during the warmer months.

From time to time, just because he could, he would come out of the farmhouse when it was safe to, after the sun had not just set but pulled its golden swath away with it, and he would enjoy the smell of the fresh air.

He supposed it would take until next year to find out whether that was the normal course of things. He hoped it was.

Taking a deep breath, he closed his eyes.

A good minute and a half later, he was finally able to dematerialize.

When he re-formed, it was a couple of miles farther down the road, and into the landscape a good distance. As he focused on the scruffy ground, he couldn't immediately find what he was looking for. He had to walk around in ever-widening circles until—

Yes, there it was.

If you hadn't been searching for it, the hatch would have remained as camouflaged as it was, nothing but a sunken square in the earth marked by a bald spot in the otherwise unremarkable, spotty weeds.

But he was looking for it, and so here he was.

As the Jackal knelt down, both his knees cracked—evidence that he was sometimes truly running when he left the farmhouse. Most times.

Not all the time, though.

Whisking some of the sandy dirt away with his hand, he notched his fingers through an eye ring—and pulled the weighted panel open.

The dense stench that bloomed in his face took him back into *Dhunhd*: Dirt, mold, stale air . . . and the remnants of body odors that lingered even after the males and females were long gone. There was a ladder descending into darkness—and he turned around and lowered himself down a couple of steps, the toes of his running shoes penetrating out the back of the steps. Steadying himself, he reached up out of the hole and pulled the hatch back into place. As the darkness swallowed him whole, he had to open his mouth to breathe. There was just too much in his nose, down the back of his throat, deep in his mind—and a vicious anger blew him apart even as he stayed whole.

At least he thought he stayed whole.

Grabbing at the small of his back, he took his cell phone out of his waist pack and threw the flashlight on. The beam of icy light was nearly consumed by the void, a reminder that there was nothing so dark as the subterranean.

As soon as the Jackal hit the floor, he started walking through a tunnel that had been carved out of the dirt and reinforced by old, hand-cut beams. He had a thought that he should have brought a weapon—not that he thought there was anyone down there. The scents that weaved together were all old, nothing new.

It was not hard to find his way, even with the collapses that had occurred. A large part of the labyrinth was impassable, or too unstable to be safe, but not every part had been wasted—and he was careful.

He'd nearly died down here once before.

So he had no intention of actually fucking dying down here tonight.

A century underground. All for the deflowering of a young female of the *glymera*—that someone else had committed.

If Nyx hadn't come along when she had . . .

He would still be down here.

Going deeper, the Jackal moved the beam around. Dirt walls. Dirt floors. Dirt ceilings reinforced with more of the wooden planks. But not all of it had been like this. There had been sections of the prison camp that had been finished, with heating and air-conditioning. And privacy. And guards.

Peter, his son, had been kept in a cell in that part. With books and a bed and a desk.

Peter, his son, had also been miraculously released by his *mahmen*. Who had controlled everything before she had been killed in a fitting way, a monster getting eaten by a monster.

"Why am I here?" the Jackal said out loud.

He didn't answer himself. He wasn't sure what he was seeking, and why did it matter anyway—

Stopping short, he wheeled around. And then a deep voice said through the darkness: "Don't shoot."

✦ ✦ ✦

Rio opened the door to her dim apartment and hit the remote to shut off the security system at the same time. Stepping through, she let things close on their own and went down a short hallway, leaving the main light off. It wasn't like the place was big or had a confusing layout: One bedroom, one bathroom, one closet-sized kitchen. With gray wall-to-wall carpeting and platinum-painted walls, she felt like she was living inside an old-fashioned aluminum tin, the kind your grandmother would have kept sugar or flour in on her Formica countertop.

It did the roof-over-her-head job well enough.

As she put her keys and her purse down on the two-top dining table, she realized she'd forgotten to remove her shoes. She always took them off on the mat just inside the door. It was how she changed identities.

Staring down at her black boots, she thought of where they'd gone since they'd been put on at about—what, eight? Eight-thirty? Naturally, as she considered the night's events, an image of the supplier barged into her mind and refused to obey an eviction notice: It was from just after she'd

accine facts

e, effective, and reliable way to
from COVID-19.

side effects are pain in the area
hot, feeling tired, headache, body
ess common, fever.

ine is provided at no cost to you.

are provider if you have concerns
ine is right for you.

tly asked questions at
com/COVID19 or call the Providence
7-216-3644 (TTY: 711).

and Providence Health Assurance
federal civil rights laws and do not
s of race, color, national origin, age,

PROVIDENCE Health Plan
PROVIDENCE Health Assurance
PROVIDENCE Medicare Advantage Plans
A division of Providence Health Assurance

P.O. Box 4327
Portland, OR 97208-4327

*********************AUTO**5-DIGIT 97006
DARRYL HONG
650 SW MEADOW DR APT 115
BEAVERTON OR 97006-7125

Protect your health: get vaccinated

been hit by the car, after the world had gone spin-cycle on her and she'd braced herself for a bad impact on the asphalt.

That drug dealer's body had been her landing pad.

She could still picture the low-lidded speculation on his face as she'd looked over her shoulder to discover she was sitting on his hips . . . in a way that would have been sexual under any other circumstances, even though they were strangers.

Funny how bullets, fireballs, and dead bodies had a way of killing the mood.

Shaking her head, she measured the distance to her **Welcome** mat—and decided to keep going to her bedroom. The whole shedding her shoes routine wasn't working anymore, anyway. Lately, she was on the streets even when she was here, no matter what the hell she had on her feet.

In the glow from the security lights in the parking lot, the messy sheets on her queen-sized bed were like frosting on a cake that had been slapped on by a baker who didn't give a crap about their job. Likewise, the comforter was half on the floor from when she'd bolted out of bed at dinnertime. Of course she'd overslept. That was what happened when you didn't crash until one in the afternoon after having gotten home from work at just before noon.

You'd think being undercover would get you out of paperwork, given how shhhhhh everything was. It didn't. She had to file reports after every shift, listing with detail who she met, what the tenor and content of the conversations were like, and cross-referencing the intel with other ongoing investigations. But whatever. Part of the job.

Sitting down on the mattress, she let the backpack she'd double-strapped fall to the floor, and as it landed, she heard a chorus of little clapping sounds from inside the folds, as if there were a miniature audience in there and they were approving of her finally being safe behind a locked door.

It was the Motrin. Which she had yet to take. For a leg that she still didn't know was broken or not.

Rio hadn't made it into the ER. In the end, she'd stopped just in front of the facility's revolving glass doors. Staring through them, into the bright light of the registration and waiting area, she'd just kept thinking about her conversation with Captain Carmichael.

She refused to give up. There had to be a way to stay on the case. A loophole. Some sort of persuasion she could throw out.

And so no, she wasn't going to give her boss a medical reason to ground her. Besides, her leg was feeling better.

Okay, fine, it was numb. So she wasn't exactly sure what it felt like.

Dropping her head into her hands, she cursed as she rubbed her eyes. When she re-straightened, she was staring at herself in the mirrored doors of the closet.

If the panels were slid back, they'd reveal her closet—and talk about coming up with a whole lot of nothing-much. All she had hanging in there was her funeral dress, her job-interview suit, and a bunch of parkas, fleeces, and other winter wear too bulky to hang on the hooks just inside the main door to the apartment.

Not really much of a wardrobe. Then again, she was one of those people who were just grateful to get the naughty bits covered, to hell with fashion.

"Time for a shower," she told her reflection as she took off her leather jacket, her fleece, and her Kevlar vest.

When she didn't move, it was hard to say who wasn't listening to the bright idea. Herself . . . or herself.

As she stayed put and measured her reflection, she felt a chill and drew her Patagonia zip-up back on. Something about the warmth it brought made her wonder what that supplier had thought of her. Her dark hair was cut short, her face had no makeup on it, her dark eyes were . . . well, exhausted was one way to describe them. Bloodshot was another.

If she had to pick a third? She couldn't come up with one that was even remotely complimentary.

Yup, she was a looker, all right. And she would've liked to say she didn't recognize the hollow shell that just happened to be wearing clothes she knew she owned. Except she did. Maybe the captain was right and she needed a break, but that could come after she'd finally tied Mozart to the supplier and then—

The figure in black jumped up from behind the far side of the bed and came at her so fast, it was clear whoever it was was a professional. Right before she was hit on the back of the head, she had a brief impression of a balaclava covering the face—and then a blow to the base of her skull rendered her senseless and she slumped to the carpet.

Gasping, straining against an abrupt paralysis, Rio's self-protective instinct roared—but there was too much traffic along her neuropathways, the signals for her hand to go into her jacket for her gun, for her legs to kick, for her to fight back in some way, do—anything, really . . . getting mired in a jam of adrenaline and pain.

The man came around and stared down at her. She expected him to say something, like a movie villain would, but he didn't. He was like an anesthesiologist trying to assess whether a surgical patient needed another shot of the propofol.

He took one of her ankles. And then the other.

Now he was pulling her, her hands staying put as the rest of her body started moving—until the slack in her bent arms was used up and then everything was along for the ride and being dragged across the carpet, away from the bed. When he got out to the living area, he dropped his hold and patted her down under the arms and along the legs. One by one, he removed her gun, her knife, her cell phone, and her Mace. Then he stood over her again.

A series of electronic taps suggested the man was texting something. And then there was the *swoop!* of an iMessage going through.

Oddly, the nice-and-normal sounds calmed her. For absolutely no good reason.

There was a brief lull. Then a *bing!* as a response came through.

More pulling now. Toward the sliding doors.

It was then that she noticed there was no light shining through the plate glass panes. He'd obviously killed the security fixtures by the building's side entrance, the ones that gave a perennial glow to this part of the apartment.

She hadn't noticed exactly how dark it had been when she'd come in.

The man let her ankles go again, and used gloved hands to pull back one half of the door. The air that rushed in was wet and cold from the storms, and revived her a little.

As did the reality that he was about to remove her to his domain, wherever that was. He no doubt had an associate standing right below the balcony of her tiny terrace, the two-story drop not far at all.

Scream, Rio told herself. *Just open up your mouth and bring the house down.*

But she didn't. Instead of making noise, she waited until the man had to get close to her torso to pick her up. Dead weight was a problem, no matter how strong you were, and as the man grunted and hauled her up off the carpet—

She used the last of her strength to shove her hand around to the small of her back, and the small holster that was on the rear of her belt.

Three. Two. One—

With a fast jerk that made every bone in her body hurt, she whipped out her Taser and caught the bastard right in the side of the neck. As he let out a bark and then strained too hard to make much noise, he let go of her—and she took the weapon with her.

While he stumbled, she rolled onto her side, yanked up his pant leg, and nailed him again, this time in the calf.

Her attacker fell like a tree in the forest, the impact of his body on the floor the kind of thing her neighbors down below would have heard right away—if she'd had any. Her apartment was located over the building's rental office, and there was no one there this late at night.

Rio shoved herself up and stumbled for the door, her forward motion good, her balance for crap. She banged off the corner of the couch hard enough to rattle her teeth, but she kept going, the Taser still in her palm, a distant, persistent crackle suggesting that her hand had tightened on its own to trigger the sparking—

She ran right into the second man just as he came in through her door. He had a hood up to mask his features—and he was armed with a gun that had a suppressor.

"Jesus," he muttered, clearly annoyed. "You're a pain in the ass."

Boom!

Before she could respond, there was another burst of pain in her head. Rio's last conscious thought was that he'd struck her with the butt of his gun on her temple.

After that, there was nothing.

CHAPTER NINE

Here was the thing with people who were—as Butch O'Neal, native of South Boston, always put it—wicked frickin' jumpy. Unless you wanted a fight, it was in everybody's best interests to give 'em a heads-up, especially if you were coming at them from behind.

Down in a tunnel that had all the air freshening of a rock pit, Rhage lifted his hands as the Jackal wheeled around in front of him.

"Just me," he told the guy, "your half-brother. Don't get crazy."

The other vampire was looking rough in his running shorts and his too-thin-for-the-time-of-year t-shirt, kind of like a zombie who had decided to go on a health kick. And for an instant, Rhage went back a hundred years and change, and saw the male when their paths had first crossed—at that annoying aristocrat's place.

Back then, the Jackal had been hired by Darius to create plans for a place for the Black Dagger Brotherhood to live together, and the Jackal, as an architect, had been willing and able to do the deal with a pencil and a ruler. He'd dressed the part, too, looking distinguished and smart in a tailored suit in the style of the times, his waistcoat anchored by a gold pocket watch and chain, the collar of his buttoned-down shirt rounded, the lapels of his fine jacket notched at the top.

And now here he was in Nike Lycra. The hair and the face were the same, of course—no, that wasn't right. In the glow from his phone's little pin light, he was much, much older, his eyes ancient even though he wasn't even close to middle age.

"What are you doing here?" the male asked hoarsely.

"We got the place rigged." Rhage motioned around, even though that camera light didn't carry far—so, yeah, not a lot to see. "You tripped the security system when you lifted the hatch."

The Jackal frowned. "But I've been here before."

"We know."

"You do?"

"Yup, you want the dates? I got 'em on my phone." Rhage debated flashing his Samsung, but the guy seemed to have enough going on at the moment. "Or you can just take my word for it."

"So why did you come here tonight? Are you here to tell me I need to leave? Like I'm trespassing?"

"Nah." Rhage *pshaw*'d with his dagger hand. "I'm not playing mall cop here."

"Mall cop?"

"Kevin James as Paul Blart? Never mind." Rhage reached into his leather jacket and took out a Tootsie Roll. "Oh—crap."

"What?" The Jackal looked around. "What's—"

"Orange. I hate orange." He unwrapped the lollipop and grimaced. "You want to hop on this train? I'll give you a good one?"

The Jackal blinked, as if a discussion about candy was nothing he could assimilate given what was crowding his brain.

"Why are you here?" he demanded.

Rhage shrugged. "The intervals between you coming underground are getting shorter and shorter. I'm not an expert in anything—well, other than killing and ice cream, and who'da thought those two would ever go together. But it's clear you're going through it, and I guess I figured a little check-in wasn't a bad idea."

"I don't know why I am so drawn to this place."

"I believe that. So where're you headed? Back to your cell?"

"Ah . . . yes. No. I don't know. I didn't really have a plan."

"Lead on." Rhage debated crunching with his molars and decided against the tongue flood of citrus. Sometimes it was better to just draw the shit out. "And yeah, I'm coming, too. Sorry."

The other male stared at him, and then glanced at the black daggers that were holstered, handles down, on Rhage's chest.

"I should go home instead."

"Yeah, that's probably true," Rhage agreed. "But some times the past isn't going to let your head have the wheel. And fighting that kind of stuff is pretty pointless."

The Jackal looked off down the tunnel, and as his eyes moved around even though there was, again, nothing much to see, it was like he was walking in his mind, going left, going right, sticking to a straightaway.

After a moment, the male said, "They were . . . my family, in a way. Not by choice, but we were together with the suffering. Lucan, Mayhem—even Apex, sick fuck that he was. I feel like I've got unfinished business. I'm out—and they need to be out, too."

"We're going to find them. I was working on it tonight, matter of fact—"

"Kane died for us. For me and Nyx. We were tied up in the Hive, about to be tortured to death . . . and he pulled that collar off his neck, knowing it was going to explode. Without him doing that . . ." The Jackal rubbed his eyes. "He told me that true love was worth sacrificing for, and then he took that fucking collar off. The blast blew him to smithereens, but it collapsed the ceiling, and those poles we were tied to fell. The only reason we were able to get out was because of him."

Rhage thought of his Mary. And how he'd kept his curse to keep her alive. "True love is a sword worth falling on. He made a heroic choice."

"And he died because of it."

"That's the way it goes. Some choices are irrevocable—and are you saying you wish he hadn't done what he did?"

"I don't know."

"Yeah, you do. You just feel bad that you survived."

"I don't have a fucking clue how I feel." The Jackal turned to face the tunnel's black void. "Why the hell did he do that. And what happened to the other three. I know he died, but what about . . . fuck. Maybe you're right. Maybe that's what's eating me alive. I'm on the outside, I got a mate, I got a family. What have they got? Nothing. Hell, I don't even know if they're alive—but if they are? I won the lottery, and nothing changed for them. They're still imprisoned."

"Survivor's guilt is a bitch." Rhage thought of Phury, and everything the guy had done for his ruined twin, Z. "I know people who were almost destroyed by it."

The Jackal's eyes shifted over. "You told me I could help find the prison camp."

"I did, and I meant it." Well, up to the point where the guy might get himself killed. The pen was actually not as mighty as the sword when you were in the field. "The choice to help is yours, but it's not going to be a cake walk. There are serious risks to the mission, and we'll only be able to protect you to a point."

"I have a lot to lose," came the soft murmur. "Nyx is . . . everything to me, and I have my son to think of—and that's why I don't get it. I mean, Kane's dead. Apex is a sociopath. Mayhem actually *likes* being in prison—don't get me started on that. And Lucan has always handled himself. He doesn't need me. So what the *fuck* is my problem. I have true love, I have everything I could want . . . and I'm stuck here. Still in this prison, even as I walk around a free male up above."

Rhage locked his molars on the Tootsie Roll and bit down hard, breaking through to the chocolate center. As he started chewing, the familiar pull on his teeth as the center grabbed back distracted him from how much he didn't like orange added to anything.

Before he could respond, the Jackal threw up his hands. "I mean, goddamn . . . my female is right now in our mated home, doing the dishes that we ate our First Meal on—and I lied to her about where I was going and what I was doing. Just like I have the other dozen times I've come here. What the *fuck* is wrong with me?"

Rhage extracted the empty white stick from his mouth. "Well, at least part of it is simple."

"Oh, yeah? Which part."

"They're your brothers," Rhage said in a grim voice. "And you need to save them because when you do, you save yourself. That's why you keep coming back here, even though you have a female of worth at home. You need to save your brothers . . . to save yourself."

The Jackal rubbed his head like it hurt. "But they aren't my blood."

"Blood is not required for that job description. Trust me."

✦ ✦ ✦

Back at the sanatorium, Lucan was walking through the tiled corridors of the south wing's fifth floor. As he killed time, he read the graffiti spray painted on the walls. It was remarkably unoriginal and the kind of thing, like the unconfusing layout of the hospital, that had been easy to memorize. A few trips through and he had the fonts, the colors, the map of it all down cold: Names in block letters. Couples in hearted algebra equations that ended in "4EVA." The occasional satanic bullshit just for effect. Oh, and a line or two from Edgar Allan Poe—which he only knew because they were marked "—Edgar Allan Poe."

The storms of earlier in the night had washed through, and the moonlight that pierced the open porch and flowed into the patient rooms gave him more than enough to read the human missives by. As he went along, the fallen plaster crunching under his boots, the hoots of owls a distant radio station of fauna-tunes, he decided that the illumination was like sunlight at the end of the day, the beams long and slanted as they crossed the corridor in a regular pattern.

Four a.m., he decided. It was probably close to four given the lunar position in the sky full of stars.

Soon enough, he'd have to go down underground with the others, and that was why he always came up here before the dawn locked him away. The wolf in him needed to breathe, had to be free—and this was the best he could do to honor that side of his bloodline.

So that it didn't consume him.

But maybe it had already.

Trying not to think about the madness, he refocused on his promenade. There was one particular patient room that he felt drawn to, even though he couldn't say that it was any different from any of the others. It had become a talisman of sorts, though, and as he approached it, he tracked the numbers on the doors: 511. 513. 515—

517.

It was a bad-luck number, violating all his rules. He liked even numbers, with his favorites being 2 and 4.

But 517 it was.

As he paused in the doorway, it was as if there were someone inside and he was waiting to be invited in. Which was fucking nuts. And yet as he threw a leg over the threshold, he felt like apologizing for intruding.

Just like all the spaces on the floor, the room was about ten feet square, and the set of rusty bedsprings strung between their rusty head- and footboards took up most of what open area there was. The only other furniture a small table and a stool. Both had been upside down, and about two weeks ago, he'd righted them and arranged the pair so that if there had been somebody in the room, they could have written a letter home. Or maybe read a letter from their loved ones.

And then he'd moved the empty, decaying bed support so that if someone had been lying on a mattress on the setup, they could have looked out of the flap doors and through the porch's open-air arches, to the sky.

Fucking sap that he was. But there had been suffering here. Great, unimaginable suffering and sorrow, humans dying long, protracted deaths, surrounded by others doing the same. He'd never been a big fan of the other species, but something about this place, about the sheer magnitude of the numbers of those who had died here, gave him a shot of sympathy.

He knew what it was like to be doomed by something outside of your control.

Stepping past the table and stool, he pushed his way out onto the porch. The loggia was fairly shallow, but long as the entire wing, and as he went to the rail and looked out over the sanatorium's hill of skeletal trees and dead grass, he imagined the humans who had lain here, knowing they had something incurable in their bodies, aware that people just like them were disappearing from the rooms beside their own—and not because they were being cured and leaving healthy.

They had been prisoners here, isolated from the general population, through no fault of their own.

As he leaned over the drop, he glanced down the building's elevation. From this vantage point, the enormity of the structure really struck him. Although not that tall off the ground, with its enormous, embracing wings, it seemed to stretch as far as the eye could see, like an ocean.

And yet for all the floors, and all the porches, there was nobody else staring out like he was.

No one but him, and maybe Mayhem and Apex, ever came up here. The prison camp's operation was underground, in the vast subterranean rabbit warren of spaces in the basement levels.

The sanatorium was literally the perfect location for a bunch of solar-avoiding vampires running a drug-processing business. Much better than that happy-hands-at-home system of tunnels they'd been in before. Not that the move had gone well. About two hundred prisoners had died soon after arrival, something about the new environment being the last domino to fall in their miserable existence, their strained hearts and bad lungs giving out.

Good thing they had the chute for the bodies here.

Just like when the place had treated humans with a terminal disease, the dead had been sent down a thousand-foot-long shaft that bottomed out at the base of the rise the building sat on. But unlike when those humans had been removed, the vampire bodies didn't need to be carted away on the railroad tracks down there. All that was required was a little sunlight, and then the ash was so fine, it blew away like snow in a sub-zero wind.

"It's a beautiful night," he said to all the nobody around him.

And that was when he thought of the woman. Rio.

The wolf in him was called to her, sure as if she knew his soul's name and spoke it in a pitch only he could hear . . . sure as if she saw deeply into him and forgave him for his sins, his bad breeding, his worse choices since he'd been imprisoned here.

But humans did not read minds. They did not even know that vampires actually existed—and some of those with fangs and a hankering for blood had mated, willingly or not, with wolven. To create sons who were accepted nowhere.

And who ultimately were double-crossed and sent to prison camps run by evil aristocrats, and then, worse, criminal homegrown madmen.

"Fuck," he muttered.

That female was just a tool to be used in this game he was getting increasingly disinterested in playing. Nothing more.

What the hell was wrong with him.

Turning away from the vista of bare tree limbs and dead leaves on the ground, he pictured what the porch would have been like some ninety years ago, the beds plugged into docking stations as if they were rowboats in danger of drifting off on the current of the wind.

He'd seen the pictures, down in the records room in the basement. He'd read the logs of the dead—or at least flipped through them.

He felt as helpless as those haunted patients had in those old black-and-white photographs, nothing to look forward to, no choices to be had, no future to speak of.

Sick of himself, sick of the place, sick of . . . everything, Lucan took himself back inside. As always, before he could leave the floor, he had to look at the patient room directly across the way. 518.

Unlike the treatment spaces in the front of the building, these back rooms had no access to any porch, just a single window. Same beds, though. No tables or stools, however.

During his perusals of the records room, he'd learned that the back side was where the people who were going to die were moved to. No reason to try the therapy of the air, anymore. Had they known what the shift across the hall meant?

They had to have known.

Just like he'd known when his cousins had come to him with that look in their eyes . . . he'd known they were going to kill him and he had been ready for the fight.

Except instead, they'd framed him for the murder of a vampire so they could get him permanently out of the way without having any blood on their hands.

Cowards. They'd always been cowards.

Lucan walked off to the stairs that ran down the terminal of the wing. After he pulled open the creaky fire door, he jogged the descent, dodging the debris in the stairwell, the empty, faded beer cans, melted candles, and dingy red balls that the humans thought the ghosts of the children would move cluttering the way.

With every step, he thought of that human woman in the alley.

How could she be involved in such a horrible business?

And no, he wasn't being sexist.

Even an asshole like him wouldn't have a damn thing to do with drugging if he'd had a choice.

But maybe she didn't, either. Maybe she was just like him. Trapped.

She was playing a dangerous game, though. It was one thing to be on the supply side, like he was. Distribution on the streets was how people got killed, and she was in the thick of it.

Then again, she'd walked away from being hit by a car like she was Wonder Woman.

Clearly, she was immortal.

CHAPTER TEN

Rio came awake with a gasp and a jerk that brought her head up. Before she could focus on where she was, a quick physical inventory commanded her full attention: She had a screaming pain in the back of her skull, a gag was in her mouth, and she couldn't move her arms or her legs—

She was in a chair. She was tied to a straight-backed chair with her hands behind her and her ankles locked in place.

And there was water falling in front of her.

Water? Wait . . . was that a *fountain?*

As she blinked to get her eyes to work properly, the inconceivable became improbable . . . which then transitioned into the yes-that's-actual: It appeared that there was, in fact, a white marble fountain about five feet in front of all her going-nowhere, and the details were getting clearer by the moment. From its wide basin to the stylized, carved carp in the center that was standing on its tail and arcing water out of its mouth, the fixture seemed like the kind of thing that belonged in a castle or museum.

What do you know, the rest of the room was just as fancy, great lengths of lemon-yellow silk pulled shut over what she guessed were tall, thin windows, the floor a black-and-white chessboard of marble squares, the walls covered with painted murals of pastoral scenes.

But what did the decor matter. Whether she was in a Versailles-wannabe or a trap house, she needed to get out of here.

Pulling at her hands, straining to kick her legs free, she got a catalogue of all kinds of pain. She had a sharpshooter in her neck, like her head had been slumped mostly to the left, and her shoulders were screaming, as were the tops of her thighs. Everything below the knee was numb on both sides, and it was a toss-up whether that was good or bad. Probably bad, because she was going to have to make a run for it and she knew if she couldn't feel her feet, that wasn't going to go well.

Twisting her wrists, she got nowhere, and her ankles were so immobile, it was like they were going to have to be surgically removed from the spindles of the—

"You're awake."

Rio's eyes flared. *Mozart?*

The voice was coming from directly behind her; except when she went to look over her shoulder, she saw nothing but more of the decorations. Glancing in the other direction, the same was true—and she had the sense he was stepping out of her view, keeping himself hidden.

Like he always did.

A hand snaked around in front of her face and removed the gag. "I'm sorry if your Uber lift was a little rough."

Rio took a huge breath. And then another.

"It wasn't the ride," she said hoarsely. "And if you'd wanted to meet me, I could have just come over."

"But then you'd know where I live."

They were going to kill her. Even seeing this one room of Mozart's house was too much for his hyper-privacy routine.

"Ever hear of a blindfold?" Her words were slurring, and she deliberately let them run together. "Or if you don't want to out your address, we could have met somewhere neutral."

"I prefer to have people come to me."

"No you don't. You refuse to meet with anyone in person."

"Well, let's just say your unique charms seduced me."

Staying out of her sight, he moved around, hard-soled shoes sounding sharp over the hard stone floor. As the man paced, she searched for anything with a reflective surface. The fountain wasn't any help, but there was an ornate fireplace set with unburned birch logs—and on its mantel, there was a fancy golden clock that was operational. By tilting her head, she could almost catch a reflection in the circular glass that covered the face.

She didn't get very far with an ID, though.

"So you've created a problem for me," Mozart murmured.

"And you've given me two concussions. Are we even?"

"No, I'm afraid we're not. Mickie wasn't worth much as a human being, but he was very useful to me."

"I didn't kill him."

"I never thought you were a liar."

"That's because I'm not lying."

It was a relief not to have to pretend about anything concerning Mickie. She wasn't sure she was up to keeping newly created falsehoods straight. The old ones, about who she really was and what she was doing on the streets, were like the route home to her apartment. So well-trod, they were rote even when she wasn't thinking too clearly.

"I went to see him at his place, got there and he was dead."

"I don't believe you."

As she tried to find some plausible deniability even though she was speaking the truth, she pictured Mickie on that soiled sofa of his, looking like Al Bundy had tripped and fallen into a Jordan Peele movie.

More with Mozart's pacing. "You're an ambitious woman."

"Can you let me go now?"

"I looked into your background. I didn't find anything."

Just her constructed identity that was nothing special. "Some people don't lead interesting lives."

"You've done good work for me."

"I know. And unless you kill me for something I didn't do, I'm going to continue working for you."

"If you'd wanted his job, you could have asked."

"I've been doing his job anyway. Killing him would have just been more work."

While she kept the conversation going, she listened for sounds beyond the room. Smells. Anything that was happening outside. The clock over on the mantel said it was seven so it had to be morning. It seemed impossible that she had been out cold long enough for it to be after dark.

"How did they get me out of my apartment?" she asked, even though she could guess that her abductors had followed through on the sliding glass door/terrace drop evac plan.

"You Tasered the hell out of a friend of mine."

"Did you expect me to shake his hand after he came at me from behind? Dragged me across my carpet by the ankles?"

There was a chuckle. "Rio, Rio, what am I going to do with you."

"You're going to put a bag over my head, let me loose from this chair, and take me back to my apartment. I will formally take over everything Mickie was doing, although I'm not going to work out of his headquarters, they're disgusting."

"You think I'm going to let you go."

"Yes, I do. Because otherwise you're down two people high up on your food chain. And who are you going to replace us with?"

"That's my problem, not yours."

"I am your solution."

There was a long pause, and Rio straightened as much as she could in the chair. "Hello?"

A hand landed on her shoulder and she jumped. As Mozart tightened his hold on her, pain shot down her arm.

"What am I going to do with you," he said grimly.

Rio closed her eyes and remembered the frantic phone call that had come in just before she'd met that supplier.

"Fine," she muttered. "I don't give a shit. I killed Mickie and I'm not sorry about it."

"Why did you lie."

Rio pulled at the ties around her wrists. "I'm not exactly a guest here, am I. And from everything I know about your financial situation, you can afford to replace this nice marble floor if it gets all bloody. So an arduous cleanup is not going to stop you from putting a bullet in my head."

There was a long pause. "I hate liars, Rio. I really fucking do."

A black-and-white image was lowered in front of her face, and she recognized the candid photograph immediately. It had been taken from a distance at her graduation from the FBI academy, at the secret ceremony that was supposed to have had no record and certainly no photographers.

Her face was younger and a little fuller, and that smile? It hadn't made a reappearance since, as far as she could tell.

"Lucky for me," Mozart murmured, "I have friends in all kinds of places."

So this was how she died, Rio thought.

Ever since she'd found her brother's dead body on the floor in his bedroom, she had wondered what her own last breath would be like. Whether she went from an accident or if it was an illness that got her. Whether she was in roaring pain or a fog from being medicated. Whether she lingered or if it was quick.

Some of those questions were going to be answered today. Soon.

Oddly, she thought of the couple who had walked out of the emergency department the night before, the old man and the old woman, helping each other not to just the exit of a building, but to the big departure.

"Officer Hernandez-Guerrero, what am I going to do with you."

Rio closed her eyes and mouthed a silent prayer. All things considered, that was a rhetorical question, wasn't it—

The pinprick in her upper arm was sharp, and she whipped her eyes down and to the right.

A hypodermic needle was sticking out of her upper biceps, and as she gasped, she tried to rotate her limb to get it out. But like that was any . . . kind . . . of a plan . . .

Everything slowed down, not just inside her body with her breathing, heart rate, and thinking, but outside of herself, too, the whole world turning to molasses.

Her last image, as she lost consciousness, was of that antique golden clock, the curlicues and lovely, painted face full of roman numerals the kind of thing a princess might have had in her bedroom.

And then she knew nothing, sensed nothing, felt nothing.

CHAPTER ELEVEN

That night, as soon as it was dark enough to leave the suffocating lockdown of the sanatorium, Lucan dematerialized to downtown Caldwell. When he re-formed, it was on the roof of the club he'd met the woman beside. As he returned to his corporeal form, the rhythmic beat of the music's bass line came up through the soles of his boots, and on the breeze that wafted around the building, he caught the scents of the humans in the waitline.

He took out the portable phone he'd been given. Still no response from Rio.

He had called the number four times since they'd parted.

Even though she'd said they'd meet again, he had no time or place to go on. He came back here because . . . what really were his options.

Had she died during the day from internal injuries? Been killed?

Gotten fired the old-fashioned way, right into a coffin?

Heading over to the roofline, he looked down over the lip edge. The alley was empty, nothing but scattered litter, a car that was parked on the far side, and a lineup of trash bins that had been recently emptied by someone lazy or careless, their lids flopped back, their filthy maws still open. As the wind changed direction, the temperature was downright cold, the unseasonable warmth of the evening before gone, the winter flexing its muscles already.

Swinging up and over the roof's molding, he hit the fire escape's top level with a clang—and he didn't hide how much noise he made as he descended the back and forth of flights and landings. When he got to the lowest set, he didn't put the ladder down; he just pulled a dangler, hanging on by his hands and dropping to the ground.

Breathing in the air, he sifted through the scents coming to him: Motor oil and gas from that car. Rotten food from the dumpster around the corner, the one where that shooter had been. Fire from somewhere, probably down under the bridge by the river, where the homeless crowded around barrels and used lit trash to keep warm.

He was guessing that both the Charger mess and the body of the shooter had been long removed. No doubt the human police had had a field day with the pair of crime scenes.

"Where are you, Rio," he murmured. "I'm waiting for you."

Like his voice had magical powers over that woman, like he could summon her to him?

Yeah, whatever, he thought. It was more like the other way around—

Down at the head of the alley, a handful of humans turned the corner and came striding toward him. Stepping back, Lucan stayed in the shadows thrown by the weak security lights. It was a pack of four men dressed for the club, all in black, their hair spiked up, their pushing and shoving not from drink or drugs but anticipation for the night ahead.

He was guessing they looked as good as they were going to. By four a.m.? All that put-together was going to be rough as fuck—

Abruptly, they stopped in front of a sunken doorway and one of them got out a phone. A moment later, a guy in a "STAFF" shirt opened the way inside and motioned all quick-quick-quick, like he was letting them in without them paying.

The door clapped shut.

Lucan crossed his arms over his chest. Glanced to the left. Glanced to the right. As his fangs tingled with aggression, he had to walk down to the corner because he couldn't stand still. Every three or four strides, he rechecked the cell phone the Executioner allowed him to have . . . which was a waste of time.

If she'd called, it would have vibrated.

If she'd texted, it would have vibrated.

As if there were a third option? Fucking hell—

His senses came alive in warning before his nose informed him of exactly what was about to enter the alley—and his body moved on its own volition to relative safety: One moment, he was walking along against the building across from the club; the next, he was ducking down behind the parked car.

The two figures came out of the shadows at the head of the alley and stopped by the fire escape.

Vampires. He could tell by the scent—and not aristocrats or civilians. Fighters. The one on the left was blond and as wide-shouldered as a span bridge. The other one had black hair, a goatee, and an expression on his face like the world bored him to death. They were both dressed in black leather, and he knew that the bulges under their biker jackets were not only muscles.

They had plenty of gunmetal on them.

They stayed just out of the reach of the security lights, hulking shadows that, if he hadn't scented them because he was downwind, even he might not have noticed.

Goddamn they blended into the night well.

"—nah, this is where she was last evening," the one with the goatee muttered.

Lucan's upper lip curled back. But what were the chances—

"She was here waiting for the contact." The male took out what appeared to be a thin cigarette and put it between his teeth like he wanted to bite something that bled instead of lit up. "She took that human to rehab. That's all I got, Hollywood—because of your little sneezing fit."

As a Bic was taken out and thumbed, the brief, flaring flame highlighted both their faces. Lucan did not recognize them.

"It wasn't a fit, V. It was one, single achoo."

"Sneeze, cheese, whatever. If you hadn't had your ges-gun-dheit moment, I would have gotten to her—"

The vampires went silent as another round of humans came down the alley, three this time. At the back door to the club, they stopped and texted. A moment later, the same security guard opened things and shuffled them in.

Lucan disappeared the cell phone into the pocket of his jacket. Then he welcomed some of his wolven to the forefront of his consciousness—not enough to change himself into his other form . . . but enough to sharpen his senses even further.

As he closed his eyes, he knew he had to be careful.

Back last night, when he'd toyed with those human boys who'd snuck through the chain-link fence, he'd known that the kids were so far beneath his wolf that he hadn't been worried about his other side going after them. They hadn't been a threat at all, and he hadn't been hungry. And like all predators, there were only two occasions when his wolf was going to go on offense. One was out of hunger; the other was to defend territory. Otherwise, the calories expended didn't compute.

These big-ass vampires? He was going to have a problem, especially if the wind changed directions and they scented him. For one, they were a match for his aggression, far more deadly than any human walking around Caldwell. But worse? They were talking about that female of his—not that she was his—and that was a recipe for two servings of fresh meat, even if he had fooded up before he'd left the prison camp.

And if he killed them? He wasn't going to find out what else they knew about his female, was he.

Not that she was his.

✦ ✦ ✦

Vishous knew that something was wrong in the alley. He could feel it in his marrow: Something was . . . not right.

Narrowing his eyes, he looked back over at the rear door of the club. Three humans had just gone in there for free, while up around the front of the building, there was a bottleneck of a waitline, all kinds of people trying to get in to get drunk, get it on, and at least attempt to get home in one piece.

He glanced over his shoulder. Given the way the wind was blowing, he could scent whatever was behind them—so it was up in front where the problem had to be.

"Look," Rhage was saying, "I think we go back and pay the guy I sneezed on a visit."

V exhaled, the smoke moving away from his face. "He's dead, remember."

"I didn't kill his apartment. That was your attempted murder when you fell through the roof."

As nearly irresistible as it was to correct the brother that he hadn't planned to do that break-and-enter descent, V let it go and focused on a car that was parked about forty yards down. It had a little red blinking light on the rise of the dash, the on-and-off beam projecting up the inside of the windshield.

So the Hyundai was locked and there was no one in the front seats. But the back? Who knew. The trunk? Maybe there was a body in there.

He had a rat-smart sixth sense for death. And like who his *mahmen* had been, and living with Lassiter, he would have given up the premonition bullcrap if he could have.

At least then, if he didn't have this kind of radar, he would have been sure the twitch he had going on was his actual instincts instead of some kind of witchy stuff.

"Someone's going to come looking for all that iron-cross-marked product we took. " Rhage stomped his shitkickers like he was itchy to get a move on. "Maybe we can use them to get us to the big buyer—who will ultimately get us to the supplier."

"Assuming the body's been found, the cops have been there all day—so nobody's going anywhere near that trap house—"

"Is something wrong?" Rhage blurted. "You look weird."

V shook his head back and forth slowly. Then answered in the affirmative: "I think we need to go up to the roof. Right now."

One of the things that Hollywood had going for him—in addition to his movie-star looks and the kind of hollow-leg eating habits that would have made him a Nathan's Famous champerino—was that he could go from casual to combat-ready in a split second.

And you never had to tell him anything twice.

The brother unholstered a gun, nodded—and the pair of them dematerialized up to the roof of the building across from the club. As they re-formed, V marveled that he hadn't even had to tell the brother which side of the alley to go on. Rhage just knew.

Remaining in sync, they scoped out the flattop with its hip-height HVAC equipment and its battened-down hatch roof access. As the wind whistled in V's ears, he outed his own gun. On his nod, they walked in the direction of where the Hyundai was parked as, off in the distance, a car horn beat out a series of staccato yelps, its alarm triggered by God only knew what.

When they were in range, V put up his gloved hand and lifted his forefinger on a one count. Then his fore- and middle fingers for two. And finally his fore-, middle, and ring—

All at once, he and Rhage stiff-armed their guns and trained them over the edge, onto the car.

But there was no one taking cover between the sedan and the building's flank.

"You want to fill it full of holes?" Rhage asked grimly. "I got a suppressor and I can turn it into a fucking sieve."

"No." V kept his muzzle on the Hyundai and looked across to the roof of the club. "Not yet."

"I'm going down there. If something's under that—"

V slapped a hold on the brother's sleeve. "Call Butch. I want backup before we get any closer."

"You got it."

Rhage outed his phone and hit send. As the soft ringing burbled by the fighter's ear, V shook his head at himself. Then lowered his weapon and cursed.

Maybe he was just losing it.

"Hey, cop," Hollywood said beside him. "It's time to get the troika back together, my brother. Your roomie and I want you to come play with us. We're four blocks away from you, by the club at—"

"No," V cut in. "Tell him to meet us at that apartment. Give him the addy. He can be there in eight minutes by car."

Rhage frowned and lowered the bottom part of the phone from his mouth. "You sure?"

V took one more look over the roof, at the car. "Yeah, I just got a hair across my ass tonight, true? Tell my cop where to meet us."

Rhage reholstered his gun. "Roger that. Hey, Butch, scratch that. You need to meet us over at Thirty-Second and Market Street—"

"Hold up," V said. "What the fuck is *that*?"

✦ ✦ ✦

Underneath the car he'd originally snuck behind, Lucan stayed spread-eagled and back-flat'd on the pavement, his head turned away from the undercarriage and toward the building. The vampires were up on the roof. He'd guessed correctly that that was where they were going the instant they'd ghosted from the shadows, and he'd never hit the asphalt so fast in his life. Tangling with that pair was the last thing on his to-do list.

Fuck, he hoped they stayed up there.

And as he heard their voices above him, because it was just a two-story building and his wolf side had ears better than a radar detector, he pictured the fight that was going to roll out as his wolven took over, and they got out their guns, and humans all around went for their goddamn cell phones to take video—

Naturally, things promptly got more complicated. Because it was just the kind of night he was having.

Across the alley, the back door to the club swung wide and a set of staccato heels came racing for the driver's side of the car. The woman stopped right next to him—and then fumbled and dropped her keys. As she leaned down to pick them up, the ends of her long blond hair trailed into his field of vision—

Beep-beep.

Running lights flashed as she unlocked the sedan with her remote, and Lucan tried to calm himself so he could dematerialize out—but he didn't get far with that. His wolven side was too close to the surface, still triggered by those male vampires, still too excited that it had been given even a little freedom to come forward.

Great. The damn thing was liable to eat this woman who was wrenching open the door—

"Hey! Where the fuck do you think you're going?" A human male came bursting out of the club after her, talking at a volume that suggested he'd swallowed a bullhorn at some point in his life. "What the fuck! Leaving me like that! Fuck you, Maria!"

The woman threw herself into the car, slammed the door, and punched the locks. Then she cranked the engine as the man came up and started pounding on the windows and yanking at the handle.

"You bitch!" *Pound, pound, pound.* "You fucking—"

Lucan had a brief stare-off at a pair of black loafers. Then the woman put things in gear and stomped on the gas.

Under the car, he had to think fast. No dematerializing because there was no chance to calm himself—and she had cranked the tires so hard to the left that he was directly in the path of the rear set of radials. Oh, and then there were the two vampires still up above him, who were looking for the same woman he was.

And surprise, he was the supplier who apparently they ultimately wanted to get to.

Fuck, he mouthed as he reached up into the fruit salad of the Hyundai's underbelly and grabbed on to whatever he could.

As the wheels spun, and the smell of burning rubber got into his nose, and that man at the window kept yelling, Lucan planked the fuck out of himself, pulling his shoulders off the asphalt and extending his legs out straight. With abs burning, and his ass clenched tighter than a pair of gaffer grips, he held on for dear fucking life as the car's tires found purchase and there was a thump.

Like the man had jumped in front of her and she'd hit him.

Christ, what was wrong with this alley? Was there some kind of mow-down quota that had to be reached every night?

That was Lucan's last thought as the Hyundai got rolling and he had to use every ounce of strength and each brain cell he had to make sure his cheeks didn't get the polishing of a lifetime.

He couldn't say he'd spent much time considering the relative attributes—or lack thereof—of his posterior region, but the one thing he was suddenly really fucking clear on?

He wanted to keep all of what his mama gave him.

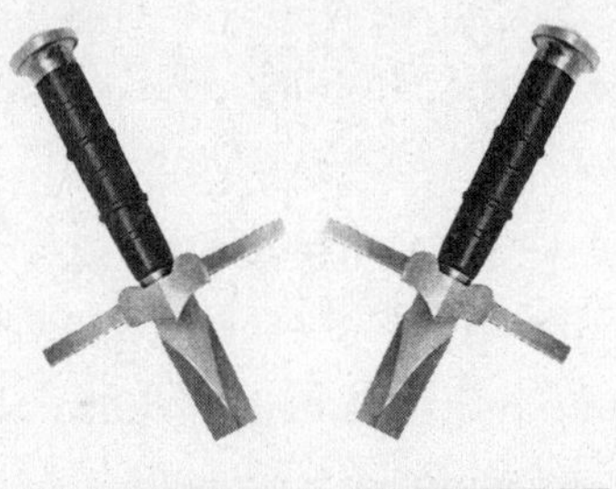

CHAPTER TWELVE

Homicide Detective José de la Cruz knew it was time to head home for the night, but he looked around the murder scene one more time. But like anything had changed since two seconds ago? It was still a dump that had been co-opted by drug dealers, with a hole in its roof, a bloodied-up sofa, and enough coke residue on that busted-ass table over there to give a grown man marching orders. The body that had turned the couch into the biggest Band-Aid in the world had been removed about an hour ago, and the techs had finished up with their photography and sampling about thirty minutes before that. Now, it was just him and—

"It true you're retiring, Detective?"

José looked across at the kid he'd been partnered with for the last six months—who was actually thirty and had a wife and two children at home. Treyvon Abscott was tenacious, a little bit arrogant, and smart as hell. With his perfectly tended fade and his navy blue departmental perma-fleece, he looked more like a Marine who was off duty than any kind of donut-munching homicide detective—

"Yup, I'm calling it a wrap on this job." José snuck a hand under his blazer to pull his pants up over his dad-bod belly. "Sixty-four days left. Not that I'm counting."

Trey walked over to the sofa and stared down at the blood-stained cushions. "Hate to see you go, sir. We're going to miss you."

In spite of the guy's casual khakis-and-fleece action, which was worn no matter the season, no matter the weather, there was a formality to Treyvon that José approved of. Then again, when you felt tired in your bones and weary in your soul, you appreciated when someone two decades younger than you paid you a little respect.

One newbie last year had tried to call him Joey, for fuck's sake. He'd nearly slapped that nickname right out the guy's mouth.

"Nice of you to say that." José closed his notebook and ran his forefinger over the cover. To think he wasn't going to have to buy another of these spiral-bound steno numbers. "So I think we're done here, Trey."

"Yeah, not much to go on."

"Nope."

And yet both of them hesitated to leave. Which was the sign of a good detective, wasn't it. Until you got your answers, you couldn't let anything go.

Maybe that was why he was so tired after all this time. Too many questions with blank spaces after them, the catalogue of what he considered failures weighing him down. He was praying that retirement would get him not only a gold-plated watch from the department, but a cord-cutting from all that shit, a freedom, from everything that haunted him.

Dead children. Brutalized women. Innocent men who had been in the wrong place at the wrong time.

Missing partners, who disappeared without a trace.

"Maybe the bullet will turn up something," Trey said.

"Maybe." But José didn't think so. This was all very professional—and not as in the shooter's gun skills, but the drug trade context of the murder. "Well, I'm gonna head back and type up the report."

Trey frowned. "You sure? I can do it."

"It's my night to cover the desk. Besides, Quiana will appreciate the extra set of hands with that new baby of yours. How late were you out on scene last night?"

"I don't remember."

"And here comes the next generation," José muttered. Then, a little more loudly, he felt compelled to add, "Be careful. This job can not only eat you alive, but your whole family."

"You're still happily married."

"I'm lucky. I hope the same for you."

"My wife understands me."

"Just make sure you take time to understand her. That's the tricky part."

"Yes, sir." Trey looked over at the worktable. "Listen, if you hear anything about that missing undercover officer, will you let me know?"

José frowned. "We have someone missing?"

"That's the rumor."

"Who?"

There was a pause and the younger man put his hands in his pants pockets, a physical parallel for whatever he was keeping to himself. "It's a female. I don't know. I just heard something. Maybe it's a rumor."

No, José thought. There were no rumors about that kind of stuff—and there was a protocol for all undercover assets. They had to check in every twelve hours to their administrative contact with a code when they were actively working a case.

"That fucking Mozart," he muttered, thinking of the dealer who had taken over the city. "What else do you know? Did she miss her check-in—"

"I got nothing else."

So that was why the detective didn't want to go home. Trey was waiting for the other shoe to drop about the absent officer, and José wasn't about to badger the guy into revealing his sources. He could guess how the intel drop had happened. The identities of undercover personnel were need-to-know only, but clearly the administrative contact was reaching out to homicide—and undoubtedly had some kind of personal relationship with Trey that made that easier.

José had had his own share of those phone calls over the years, and the fact that he didn't get this one was yet another sign things were moving on without him already.

"If anything comes in," he said, "I'll let you know immediately."

"Thanks."

As their eyes met, they both knew what the "anything" was: A body. They also both knew that sometimes you didn't even get that. There were plenty of missing people who stayed gone, and plenty of cases that were still cold. Take this scene. Yeah, they had a corpse, but you could bet your Dunkin' that the ballistics on the bullet inside the guy wasn't going to link to anything. And there was so much contamination here at the scene, they weren't going to find many prints that were useful or fibers that meant anything.

Just one more murder in the brutal drug world.

"Go home," José told the guy. "Tell that nice wife of yours I want more of her gumbo."

"I will."

Trey went to the exit and glanced back, a tall, strong man with smart eyes and a serious expression. "I'm gonna call you after you're off the force. And not just for coffee."

"Anytime you need me to look something over, I'm there for you."

"Thanks, Detective."

As the last partner he would have in his professional life walked out and hit the creaky stairs, José turned back to the sofa. The bloodstain was still red now, but by the time this ruined piece of furniture ended up in the dump, the mark would be brown. He pictured the couch when it had first been bought from some kind of showroom or depot, the pattern fresh, the cushions perky and pointed at the corners, the feet square on the floor. If inanimate objects could die, then this one had suffered greatly on the way to its final occupant's occupancy, battered, stained even before the pool of blood, worn out.

José tried to imagine not doing this anymore, not standing in the middle of a murder mess, trying to put the puzzle pieces together—and he succeeded beautifully at the task. He was going to spend more time with his girls, help his wife out around the house, cheer at graduations, cut birthday cakes, light off fireworks, take care of the dogs. No more Christmases being missed or Thanksgivings lost.

Hell, if he wanted to celebrate Groundhog's Day, he was going to do it.

Fishing in the summer. Homemaking beer in the fall. Cozy winters and cheerful springs.

No more dead bodies.

No more . . . missing bodies.

No more questions with no answers, no trails, no nothing.

Even though he didn't want to think about his old partner, Butch O'Neal, he couldn't help it. Coming to the end of his career had brought up all kinds of loose ends, and Butch was the loosest of them . . . maybe because it felt like that cop from South Boston, with his *Good Will Hunting* accent, and his hair trigger, and his incredible nose for the truth, was still with him.

José could still remember walking into his old partner's apartment that last morning. As usual, he'd been braced for a body, not because someone had murdered the guy, but because Butch had drank himself into a stupor, fallen down in the bathroom, and cracked his skull open.

Or maybe overdosed because he'd added a prescription chaser to all the booze he pounded at the end of every night.

That particular bright-and-early, José had been aware that he'd gotten addicted to the cycle of peaking anxiety as he knocked on Butch's door and let himself in, and then the sweet relief when he'd find his partner in that sloppy bed, passed out, but breathing. The ritual of aspirin, water, and throwing the guy into the shower had been part of his day.

Except that last morning . . . there had been no one there. Nobody asleep facedown in the sheets. Or slumped on the couch. Or one-arming the toilet.

And in the days and weeks that had followed, there had been . . . nothing. No clues, no evidence, no body. Disappeared. But given the way Butch had handled himself and the hard life that he'd led? José couldn't say he'd been surprised.

Nah, he'd just been heartbroken.

He glanced back at that couch. "Nothing worse than trying to save someone."

As the good Catholic he was, José had spent a lot of time praying for his former partner. He'd also missed the guy, and not just on a personal level. Like Trey, he wished Butch could have been here on this scene, be back at HQ going through files, be knocking on doors and asking questions.

O'Neal had been sucky at real life, but a helluva detective.

What a haunted man.

From time to time, José dwelled on him, and when the memories got too painful—which was almost immediately—he'd switch to imagining that Butch was living in a parallel universe on the flipside of Caldwell, with a beautiful wife and a bunch of strong protectors around him—

As a sharpshooter pierced through José's frontal lobe, he groaned and stopped going down that rabbit hole. It was just fiction anyway, something his mind coughed up when he couldn't handle the fact that there hadn't been a body to bury.

Rubbing his face, he knew he was never going to get over all he didn't know about what had happened to the guy. And it had always made him feel for those families who never got their justice.

"Where did you go, Butch," he said out loud.

He was used to talking to his favorite partner, as crazy as he knew that was—but had long ago decided, hey, people used their dogs as sounding boards, right?

Heading for the door, he flipped off the overhead light, and closed things behind himself. Picking up a roll of yellow police tape that had been left on the floor outside, he ran it across the portal, stringing the official-business banner between a set of nails that had been driven into the jamb. Then he affixed a fresh seal to the juncture and signed it with his pen.

As he went to the stairs, he jacked up his slacks again and patted his belly. Maybe he'd take up running. Touch football. How about the basketball games at church on Tuesday and Thursday nights?

The stairs were stained and dusty—but what wasn't in this building—and they squeaked and creaked under his street shoes. Then again, as he considered the roof damage to the crime scene, the fact that the structure was standing at all seemed like a miracle. On that note, he stuck to the wall side of the steps. When he came to the floor below, he—

A shuffling sound, like rats hightailing it across a bare floor, brought his head to the right. The apartment directly below the victim's had a closed door. Unlike the rest of the units.

Surely someone had checked to see if anybody was in?

He walked over, curled up a knuckle, and went a-rapping. "Hello? Detective de la Cruz, CPD." He reached into his jacket and got his badge ready to flash. "Hello, do you have a minute to talk to me about your upstairs neighbor?"

It was hard to believe anyone was inside, though. The dealer clearly did so much business here that he'd want to secure the entire premises—which, according to records José had searched on his phone, had been abandoned by its commercial real estate property owners, foreclosed on by its bank, and then been left unpurchased for the last eight years.

José looked across the hall. That door was lolling open. Turning back, he knocked again.

"Hello?" he said more loudly.

A muffled shuffle was all he got in return, which suggested inhabitation by something larger than a medium-sized dog—but if the person didn't answer, there was no way he had probable cause to enter. It could be a cat, somebody taking cover, a man or a woman just living their life.

Which had to be entwined with that dealer's.

"I'm going to leave my card." He took one out of his wallet and pushed the stiff square into the doorjamb. "I'd like to ask you a couple of questions."

José waited a little longer; then he kept going down the stairs. It was frustrating, but he would try again—and set up a surveillance outside of the address. The person or people in there had to leave for food at some point. He'd cross their paths sooner or later.

Just as he stepped out of the building, a black Escalade pulled up across the street. Between its darkened windows and matte black rims, it was clear that it belonged to somebody in the same chosen profession as the victim's.

Not a lot of Door Dash deliveries in a vehicle like that. Or Lyft rides.

Maybe a diplomat. But like they'd get rerouted to a neighborhood like this?

Well, shit was about to get more interesting, wasn't it.

He looked left. Looked right. No other cars around, either parked or traveling over the chipped pavement. No other lights on in any of the buildings on the block. Nobody walking the sidewalks or in any window, anywhere.

Considering he was all alone, maybe meeting whoever drove that thing in the open air was better. Not that he couldn't be gunned down out here in the street, it just made it a little less likely than in that stairwell, for example.

Where was Butch O'Neal when he needed the guy. That Southie madman had been the best backup—

The SUV's driver's side door opened, and a long leg extended out. Black slacks—no, leathers. And then—

José froze. And couldn't believe what he was looking at.

Who he was looking at.

◆ ◆ ◆

"—leave my card. I'd like to ask you a couple of questions."

As the male voice permeated the closed door across the way, Rio strained against the gag in her mouth, trying to make a sound that the man could hear. When that failed, again, she arched against the ropes that bound her neck and her feet. She was lying on her side, her hands tied behind her back, her body strung tightly between two fixed points that she couldn't see.

For all her efforts, the best she could do was make a swishing sound against the floor—but there was no way the soft noise was going to travel far.

With a strangled groan, she twisted her neck as much as she could—until, in her peripheral vision, she could see the glowing square of the stairwell's light bleeding around the doorframe. Down at the bottom, the man's feet cut a pair of reassuring shadows into the illumination.

On the far side of the barrier, Detective de la Cruz, who she knew, who was widely respected throughout all divisions, knocked one last time . . .

That set of shoes stepped away, the line of light at the floor now unbroken, once again.

As his footfalls receded and then went down the rickety steps, Rio's long shot turned into an impossibility.

Gritting against the twist of cotton in her mouth, she screamed in frustration—or tried to. She was weak, and as the pressure flushed her face, she felt like the back of her skull was going to blow out. Or maybe that was the hangover from the drugs.

When she had come around from whatever Mozart had injected into her, she had been totally disorientated and nauseous—and the first thing she had worried about was vomiting. With the gag, she was liable to choke to death. Then, as her stomach had stopped churning so much, and she'd found no new injuries, she'd tried to see what she could about the decrepit room she was in. The windows were covered with blackout drapes, but the lengths were loose so the daylight had seeped through and created somewhat of a glow.

Enough for her to see. Enough for the video camera that was mounted on a tripod in front of her to record her.

There had been nothing else of note, no one with her, and nobody and nothing she could visualize off in the other shadowy spaces.

She knew the layout, however. Knew the smells, too.

Mickie's building. She was in Mickie's trap house. And there were people upstairs, directly above her. All day long.

At least, she assumed it was all day. Time had been a fluid thing, and only the progression of light had been a concrete measure that hours were passing. Well, that and the sounds of voices, male and female, and so many footfalls up and down the stairwell. There had been a lot of people in the building, and she knew who they were and what they were doing.

They were the homicide team.

Mozart had staked her out right underneath the crime scene.

Sick fucking bastard.

And now that they had pulled out, she knew that someone would be coming for her. Mozart wasn't going to leave her alive here forever. The day and the beginning of the night had just been the mental-torture foreplay before the real fun and games for her began.

He'd done this before to people. She'd heard the rumors, knew that he liked to watch.

Desperate, she arched her back and strained her shoulders, pulling against the rope around her neck. When her airway started to close, she shifted the effort to her legs, dragging them up until her throat once again refused to let any oxygen through.

She got nowhere. And under other circumstances, she would really have respected the attention to detail that had to go into a setup like this. If she'd had just a little more leeway, she could have gotten someone's attention by banging her feet, her head, her arms.

They'd definitely done this before, maybe in this very room.

And very soon, all of those professionals above, who had worked so hard on Mickie . . . were going to have another scene to work when Mozart and whoever he'd hired were done with her. Not that he was going to do the messy work with his own hands.

Adrenaline surged at the thought of what was coming for her, but there was nothing to fight and nowhere to go, and—

Off in the front of the apartment, the sound of a door opening was soft. Her eyes shifted down her body.

What was that smell? Like . . . sweet and death at the same time.

The chuckle in the darkness was quiet. "I think we're alone now."

Footsteps came up to her and the figure stopped at her knees. "Isn't that an old pop song? Tiffany, I believe the singer was. I'm old enough to have heard her on the radio."

Rio's eyes strained against the darkness and her body jerked as she tried to get a bead on the man. Other than his slight accent, she had nothing to go on.

"Would you like to see me?"

A light flared, the lantern the man held in his right hand coming alive with an LED illumination that was icy bright. Her murderer was dressed in black and had a tight black hood pulled down over his face, looking like some kind of wraith out of a nightmare.

Recoiling and blinking, Rio tried to think. Then worried about her breathing as her nose was stuffing up and there was nothing going in and out of her mouth because of the gag. As panic choked her, the man put the lantern down and stepped forward.

When he knelt down next to her, he was careful to stay out of the camera's way, and she could feel his eyes on her as he looked her up and down.

With a steady hand, he pulled the mask off himself. "I'm pleased to make your acquaintance, Ainhoa."

He had pale skin tone, pale, nearly white eyes, and white hair. His age was . . . unknowable. He was not young, but he wasn't old, either, his lean face unlined and hawkish.

There was a sharp sound of metal on metal, a switchblade triggered.

The blade entered her visual field, shiny and clean, and the hand that held it was wearing a dark gray glove. In the back of her mind, she thought that the reflected light on the honed steel was the color of the man.

Icy cold.

"We're going to have some fun now."

The knife left her eye line—

As she felt the tip in between her breasts, she groaned and the man laughed again. "We're going to have so much fun, Ainhoa. And I shall call you by your given name as we work through this process together. Although I've heard people call you by Rio, I prefer to be formal about things. No reason to be common in this."

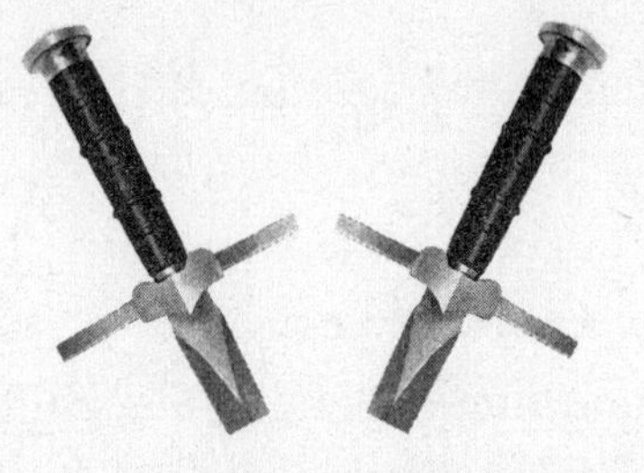

CHAPTER THIRTEEN

As the Hyundai sped away from the alley, Lucan knew he wasn't going to last long under the damn thing's belly. His hands were sweaty from the effort of holding his two-hundred-and-sixty-pound weight up off the blur of pavement—and the engine was transferring more heat down every piece of metal he was gripping or next to. And the woman was continuing to accelerate.

She was swerving, too. So if he timed the drop wrong, he was going to get mowed flatter than grass.

Meanwhile, his abs were screaming in pain from this death plank, his pecs and biceps were worse—and the going was rough, every manhole and sewer-access panel in Caldwell passing under the car like the woman was steering for the things.

"Fuuuuuuuuuuuuuuuuuuuuck," he growled through gritted teeth.

The car lurched around a corner—

The brakes were hit so hard that he didn't get a chance to form an opinion about releasing his hands. His body just shot forward as the car stopped short, momentum taking control of his destiny as he was propelled out from under like a missile.

Lucan had a brief image of the front wheels passing on either side of him and then the front bumper—

Blaring. Honking. Flashing lights.

Sudden death.

As he exploded into the intersection, the vehicles traveling through on a green light swerved and stomped on their own brakes. Twisting onto his side, he bounced along the asphalt and the car chaos, Ping-Pong'ing off the box grille of an old Toyota, before rolling up the sloped hood of a low-slung Pontiac from the eighties. As the firebird stencil made an impression in spite of the danger he was in, he thought of his female from the night before.

Not that she was his.

And then it was time to stop with the freestyle acrobatics. Kicking out on the windshield of the Firebird, he jumped himself into a change of direction, and got the fuck out of the way on a tight tuck—

Just as a series of impacts crunched and crackled in the center of the intersection, vehicles crashing into each other.

Lucan's boots landed flat on the ground and the second he felt his feet under him, he burst into a run. Zeroing in on the shadows in front of him, he plunged himself into darkness to get cover. When he was sure he was out of sight—not that those humans were focused on anything other than their airbags—he slammed his back against a dumpster that was empty, given the hollow *clang!*

Panting, he caught his breath and focused on the pileup. Out under the dangling traffic lights, a collection of body-repair jobs had replaced the previous going concerns of five vehicles—but his blond unknowing Uber driver was not having it. Even though she still had the red light and there was a junkyard of automobiles in front of her, she shot up onto the sidewalk, bypassed the accidents she'd played a solid role in creating, and hit the gas.

Given the asshole who'd come after her, Lucan couldn't say he blamed the woman.

Closing his eyes, he listened to the humans as they got out of their cars and had one of two reactions: Half got onto 911, and the other half started yelling.

He'd never thought of a pileup as a personality inventory test before, but there you go.

When his breathing had calmed and his heart slowed, he had one good thing going for him: His wolven side had fully retreated, and it was a relief not to have to rein it in.

As sirens sounded from far away, that was his cue to split. But when he tried to dematerialize, there was no shift of his molecules, no ghosting.

He tried again.

Nothing.

And that was when he realized that one of his feet was soggy in its boot, like he'd stepped in a puddle. Looking down, he shook his head because he was not seeing what his eyes seemed to be reporting: He was absolutely not staring at a dark, spreading stain on the outside of his jeans' pant leg. He just wasn't.

When his eyes refused to follow orders, he thought, okay . . . fine. There might have been a stain running down the outside of his calf, but it was motor oil. Yeah, that was it.

It was *not* blood. In spite of all the copper in the air.

✦ ✦ ✦

Out in front of the trap house, José tripped over his feet as he bumped right into his unmarked. When his body hit the front bumper, he had to put his hand on the hood to steady himself—especially as he got a clear shot at the man getting out of the Escalade.

His dizziness did not improve as he got a proper look at the driver.

Across the street, standing straighter, taller, and broader than José remembered . . . was his old dead partner. Sure as if José had conjured Butch O'Neal out of thin air by wishing the guy was still around for backup.

And what do you know, Butch seemed equally poleaxed.

The two of them walked forward like a pair of zombies, meeting in the middle of the road.

As José blinked, he decided that he knew what this was. This was a dream, conjured up after he went home from the scene he'd been at all day long. With his wife in school, and the kids busy, he'd obviously had too much of that leftover *carne asada* from Tuesday and had fallen asleep on the sofa. Preoccupied with his own retirement, his subconscious had burped this little not-actually-happening over the ol' brain transom and—

"Hi," Butch said roughly.

"You're taller." As José spoke the words, he had the weird conviction that they'd done this before. Not in the middle of this particular street, but in other alleys, roads . . . and at church. "Than I remember."

"It's the shoes."

They both looked down, and José whistled. "Nice boots. What brand are they?"

"We just call them shitkickers."

"Badass." José smiled a little. "Are you okay?"

The moment he asked the question, he winced, that headache coming back.

"I'm thinking I need to ask you that." Butch cleared his throat. "It's good to see you again, old friend."

José forced his eyes to focus, yet they weren't unclear—and then he heeded an internal conviction that he had to talk fast because Butch wasn't going to last. Or rather, this dream wasn't going to last.

Yes, this was totally a dream.

"I'm retiring," he blurted.

"You are?" Butch seemed shocked, his eyes bugging. "Wait, for real?"

"Yeah. I'm tired of getting calls in the middle of the night, and I've gotten too stuck in my head. Plus I'm old, now."

"You're not old." There was a desperate edge to that familiar voice. "Don't talk like that."

"I got my pension, you know. I'm staying one month after it kicks in—hey, you look great, by the way. I mean, so healthy. You've turned your life around."

This was a good dream, he decided. Considering the raw material, he was lucky it wasn't a heartbreaking nightmare involving a lot of blood.

"I met someone," Butch whispered. "I fell in love and I married her. She's too good for me."

José smiled even as his head really started pounding. "I swear we've had this conversation before—but then I'm asleep and imagining this, aren't I. I always hoped you'd find a nice woman and settle down."

"You're a good friend, José."

"Why do you look so sad if you're happy?"

"I miss you."

Such simple words. That went through José's chest like a scalpel.

"We were a good team." José shut his eyes and then rubbed them. "God, my head hurts."

"I think you better go."

"Why do I feel like we've done this before?" he mumbled. For the hundredth time. But that was what happened in dreams, wasn't it. Things were always a little skewed, a little wonky . . . real, but unreal.

He'd wanted to see Butch one last time before he retired, before José wasn't out in the downtown at night anymore. Like maybe his retiring would stop these dreams from happening, like they were the same as his badge and his service weapons, something he had to turn in at his exit interview.

"We have done this before."

Opening his eyes, José nodded. "I think we have."

Butch's hazel stare shifted to the left, and he focused on something over José's shoulder. "I gotta go, too."

Pivoting, José did a recoil, even though . . . he somehow wasn't surprised. Two men had arrived at the trap house's front door and they seemed to be waiting for Butch. One was huge and blond and looked like a movie star. The other had black hair, tattoos at one temple, and a goatee. Both were dressed in leather.

José turned back to his old partner, a strange feeling coming over him. "We have done this before, haven't we."

"Yeah, we have."

"And this isn't a dream, is it."

"Life is a dream, José. The whole thing is one long fuzzy fiction, and I'm glad you're getting out of homicide. It's dangerous on the streets—"

"You need to come find me," José cut in. "I've been running into you out here, haven't I. But no more paths crossing after I step down. So you need to come find me."

Okay, this was nuts. Because even as he repeated himself and struggled against confusion, which was very dream-like, he felt the need to communicate with his old partner like the guy was actually in front of him, and he was still at the trap house, and they were together for not the first time, not by a long shot.

"Promise me," he gritted out through his teeth.

"Sure, I'll find you. Now you better go. Your head hurts wicked bad."

"God, yeah, it does." José stepped back. "I'm really glad you're okay."

"Me, too," came the sad reply.

As he took another step away, and another, Butch just stood there.

"You better pick one side or the other," José said. "Or you're going to get hit in this street."

"I've already picked my side," the guy whispered. "I had to—"

An argument back at the curb brought both of their heads around. Over on the sidewalk by the building's entrance, the blond- and black-haired men were going back and forth.

"Are those two your friends?"

"Yes," Butch said. "And I know they look like they're about to kill each other. Don't worry, it's unlikely there'll be any permanent damage. Well . . . pretty unlikely."

José stared at his old partner. "Where did you go, Butch. I need to know. Please, just tell me something that I can live with every day. You were the big cold case I never solved."

"You won't remember this, José—"

"You're wrong." Shaking his throbbing head, José grabbed Butch's arm and mumbled through the pain—a panic he couldn't lose dogging him. "You have to tell me. Because . . . I do remember these meetings. And it's killing me."

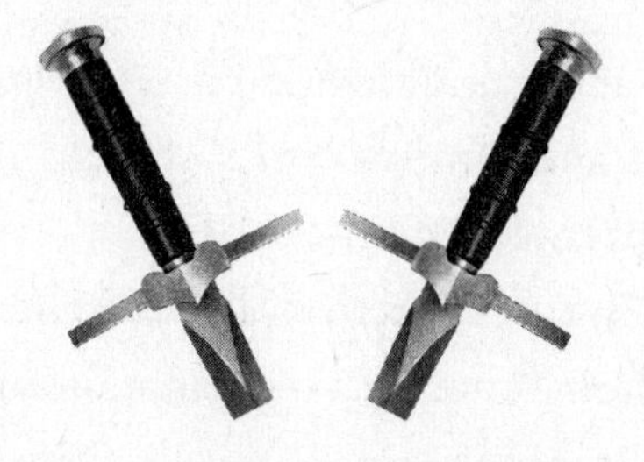

CHAPTER FOURTEEN

As Vishous watched his roommate and that cop meet in the middle of the street, he literally wanted the homicide detective to get sideswiped by a school bus. Then run over by a garbage truck. And maybe after that . . . something that involved an Army tank. A troop transport vehicle lineup that was fifty units long.

Oh, wait. How about a whole span bridge's components on their Wide Load motor-mattresses.

It was such a satisfying fantasy, the end result being that human homicide detective bag of carbon-based molecules laid out so flat that he'd be a stain.

Too bad four-wheeled hardware on that scale was not often seen in neighborhoods like this one. Or anywhere, all at once, ever. It'd be like winning the automotive Powerball and getting to point to where the parade drove through.

The thing was, something about that José de la Cruz guy bugged him to all get-out and he could feel the rank-and-nasty rise in the center of his chest. Again. Caldwell was a big city, but a small place, when you were talking about the underworld parts—where the Brotherhood hunted their enemies and humans woke up dead from lead injections, stabbings, and drug overdoses all the time.

Which meant homicide detectives, like Butch's old partner, crossed the paths of the brothers, if not on a regular, monthly basis, at least once or twice a year.

And every time Butch and José de la Cruz orbited each other it was the same, the two of them meeting face-to-face and staring into each other's eyes as if they hadn't just done that six fucking months ago.

Once was more than enough for the display, and—after *how* many years of this?—V was sick and fucking tired of the "Kate Winslet/Leonardo/bow of the *Titanic*" show.

Of course, on the human's side, it was a case of Lewis and Clark, each OMG-it's-you a fresh news flash because his memories were always scrubbed. But did Butch *have* to look like he missed the guy so fucking much? Jesus Christ. Make out with him, why didn't he.

Not that V cared on any deep level.

It was just annoying.

Hell, V was fine with it . . . just waiting here on the sidelines, for the hundred and fiftieth time, watching his best friend go all Bambi-finds-his-fucking-mother with a fucking human—

Whatever.

From out of nowhere, an image barged into his mind, and the damn thing was both specifically vivid and a composite of a lot of separate, but identical, events: He saw himself running into a dark alley and finding his roommate down on the ground dying, the stench of *lesser* thick in the air, an evil halo not so much surrounding Butch, but emanating from his very pores.

Back when the war with the Lessening Society had been ongoing, vampires had been hunted by the Omega's army of undead slayers, and the Brotherhood had been the only defense against those predators. Stabbing them with a steel blade in the chest could get them off the planet, but they didn't go to Hell.

Well, not in the Judeo-Christian sense.

They went back to their maker, in an endless cycle of regeneration, the Omega turning more humans into slayers, and keeping the population of vampire stalkers relatively constant for centuries. But then Butch, former homicide detective, had entered the picture. Captured by the evil itself, he had been tampered with before he'd been rescued. Finally, he'd been turned because he was a half-breed—and he had somehow survived the jump-started transition.

The guy was the best kind of cockroach. Unkillable.

His journey had been the *Dhestroyer* prophecy made manifest, V's roommate capable of stopping the slayers from returning to their maker by inhaling their god-awful essence into himself.

V looked down at his gloved hand. The lead-lined-leather Michael Jackson action protected everyone and everything around him from the fierce, destructive energy that glowed within his palm, a little gifty from his PITA mommy, the Scribe Virgin. The damn thing had been a handy—natch—weapon in some circumstances, but it was trouble, too.

When it came to Butch, it had been a lifesaver.

The former cop from Southie had been the prophesized one, but V had been a necessary component, the second, critical cleanup step. Whenever his roommate had been down on the ground, stewing in the Omega's vile swill, all V had to do was take the male into his arms, hold him tight, and let the light fly.

Like an existential HEPA filter.

Together, they'd brought the enemy of the species down.

As partners.

Now, though? With the Omega all bye-bye? That special closeness was gone—

"Whatever," he muttered as he got out his phone.

"What's wrong?" Rhage asked.

"Nothing."

Rhage glanced back at the apartment building. "You want to go in and leave those two at it?"

"No." V scrolled through God only knew what and saw nothing. "I'm not leaving him out here alone."

"He's not alone. He's with his old human buddy."

Why wasn't social media more interesting, V wondered as he thumbed past what turned out to be Instagram. Oh, right. It was boring because he didn't give a shit about people in general, humans in particular, and anything that had to do with pets, food, children, hashtags, influencers, inspirational quotes—

"Are you jealous?"

Vishous glared over at the brother. "Of what?"

The way Rhage's eyebrows went tent pole and he took a step away was probably a clue that V needed to chill.

"I'm not fucking jealous of *that*." Vishous nodded toward the happy couple in the street, but didn't look over there again. "That's not his life anymore. He's with me—us, I mean."

"Do you want some chocolate? I got M&M's—"

"What? Why would I want chocolate?"

"It cheers people up." Hollywood took out a plastic baggie full of bright and cheerful little UFOs. "Here—"

V batted the calories away. "Yeah, you can fuck off with that."

"Why? It has that chemical that simulates the feeling of falling in love." Rhage opened the bag's top. "Fritz puts them in a Ziploc for me because sometimes the regular packaging breaks open when I'm in the field. I hate chocolate in pockets, all melty. It's like putting your hand in poop—"

"Oh, my fucking God, please stop talking—"

"—except you can eat it, of course."

"*What*."

Rhage popped a handful into his piehole and chewed. "I'm just trying to distract you from Butch's family reunion."

"They are *not* related."

"Just like we're not related, right?"

"Shut up."

"It's okay to be jealous—"

"I'm not jealous!" As V's voice rose, Butch and that homicide detective looked over—so he lowered his volume. "Shit ain't like that."

"There's a reason they call it *bro*-mance. I'm just saying." More with the palmfuls and the chewing. "And what are you embarrassed about? I get jealous, too, sometimes."

"Of what. Anybody eating something anywhere on the fucking planet."

"No, of people."

"Stop projecting onto me."

"I'm just saying it's totally normal to feel left out when you see two people who have a special bond. Butch and that guy worked together for how long—"

"I do *not* need a history lesson."

"—and went through a lot of shit together—"

"Oh, like he and I battling the Omega was a trip through Chuck E. Cheese?"

"—and given how close you and Butch are, it could feel weird to see him with somebody he's equally close to."

"He lives with *me*," V snapped.

"And you're right, Chuck E. Cheese is awesome."

"What?" V blinked at the brother. "You know, a conversation with you is a real experience."

Rhage put his hand over his heart. "That is the *nicest* thing you've ever said."

Shaking his head, V dug into that Ziploc and shoved some M&M's in his mouth. As he chewed, he tried to pretend he wasn't watching his roommate stand in the middle of the street with V's archnemesis, Detective Luthor.

"FYI, I'm never jealous of Marissa," he said around all the chocolate.

"Why would you be? She's not a threat. She's his mate—"

"Which is my point." V went in for more candy because he was absolutely *not* perking up in the slightest already on just one swallow of the stuff. "I don't want to be his fucking *shellan*."

"Exactly. You want to be his best friend." Rhage nodded out to the street. "And don't worry, you are."

Okay, V wasn't relieved by that statement. Just like the M&M's didn't help.

"No offense," he muttered, "but I think you need to leave the psych business to your Mary. You couldn't be more off base if you were talking about someone else entirely—"

At that moment, there was a vibration in V's free hand. Lifting his phone, he was so fucking relieved it was a text to the whole Brotherhood. As he called the message up, and Butch and Rhage also got their Samsungs out, V hoped it was something serious enough to demand immediate attention, but nothing that involved death or dismemberment.

Well, not among the Brotherhood, at least.

"Shit, shadows," Rhage muttered as he put away the candy. "And not the good kind."

"We gotta go." V did the same with his cell and raised his voice. "Butch, we're out."

As his roommate looked over and nodded, Vishous studiously ignored a little surge of triumph—like he'd won a race and the trophy was a former-alkie, Southie ex-cop with a great sense of style, more loyalty than the moon to the earth, and the best laugh in the whole world short of Jane Whitcomb's.

But there was no real competition here, especially because as if a human could ever be a threat? Whatever. Rhage had his head wedged on the jealousy thing—

Out in the middle of the street, Butch finally got moving—but it was to close the distance between him and his former partner. There was a pause, and then the two embraced.

Fortunately, that crap didn't last long—and as Butch came over to V and started coordinating where they were all going to meet up, that homicide detective de la Cruz got in his unmarked and drove the fuck away.

"I'll ride with you," V said. "As backup. Let's go."

"Good deal," his roommate agreed.

And justlikethat, everything was back as it should be.

Almost.

As V got into the Escalade's passenger side, even though the SUV was technically his ride, he glanced across the console and couldn't help himself.

"You gotta quit it with the interactions. Going in and out of his memories like that, scrubbing him so many times, it's no good."

Butch stared through the front windshield for a moment. Then he started the engine. "Yeah, I know. But he's retiring. So no more running into him around town anymore."

Wow, this was not another sort of relief, V told himself.

But damn, his roommate looked so fucking sad.

"You had to pick," V said. "One side or the other—and you did."

"I don't want to go back to my old life." Butch shook his head. "I had nothing then. I have everything now. When I see José? It reminds me of the way I was and I hate how I left him, just disappearing. That poor bastard saw me at my worst, and stuck by me, and what did I do? Not even a goodbye, an explanation . . . a reassurance. Makes me feel like a shitty friend."

"You're not that."

Butch shrugged and put them in gear. "I was to José. I was the worst friend to him, and all he ever did was take care of my sorry ass and treat me with respect. Makes a male feel pretty goddamn small."

V frowned and stared out the window as they proceeded down the street. "You could never be small. You have the biggest heart I know, and you're a male of worth. Always have been."

"You're biased."

"I cannot be biased. I am too logical for that."

Just like he was waaaaaaaay too logical to be jealous of a human. Who wasn't even in his roommate's life anymore.

"I wish I could make it up to José somehow. I hate to leave him hanging, and yet he can't have any memory of me in the present."

"You gotta leave it, cop. There are some things that just have to be left, true?"

Next to him, Butch nodded.

And then neither of them said anything else.

✦ ✦ ✦

When Lucan left the accident(s) in the intersection, he didn't immediately know where to go. But while he was in a state of molecular scatter, his mind connected two dots, and he rerouted to a block of mostly abandoned walk-ups. As he re-formed across the street from the one he intended to go into, it was a case of *surprise!*

Like a couple of bad pennies stuck to his shoe, he found the blond- and the black-haired vampires in their matching leather zoot suits, hanging out in front of the battered entry of the five-story fall-down Lucan intended to enter.

Looked like it was a goddamn vampire convention—and he had a thought that if the goateed one was trying to find Rio, too, then this was a good place to be. Lucan had been here one time before, when he'd dropped off the samples of product for Mozart's people to try as well as the baggies to send out into the streets. It seemed a good bet that Rio could be here, also—or, if he could find a human with knowledge of her, he could break into their brain and get some clues.

Except there was trouble in his not-really-paradise. Those fellow members of Caldwell's paranormal underbelly didn't seem in a big hurry to get a move on. There was even a third member of the species in the center of the road, talking to a human.

Great.

While Lucan impatiently waited for whatever business was going on to conclude, he checked out the abandoned apartments. All of the levels were dark—no, that wasn't right. In addition to what appeared to be a light in the lobby, there was a subtle glow in the windows on the fourth floor on the left, like a heavy sheet or maybe even a proper drape had been pulled into place over all the dirty glass.

"Jesus, will you get on with it," he muttered as he crossed his arms over his chest and leaned up against a spray-painted set of stairs.

After about twelve hundred years, the vampire and human combo in the street hugged each other; then an unremarkable car took off, a hulking black SUV drove away, and the blond vampire walked into the shadows and dematerialized.

Lucan gave things another minute or so, in case anybody forgot their wallet or their proverbial house keys, and then he limped forward and crossed the road. As he went along, his boot was even soggier, but he was operating under the truism that that which was not acknowledged did not exist. So no, he was not bleeding down his pant leg and into his fucking footwear. He'd stepped in a puddle, on this dry night, with his waterproof boot.

Nothing to see here, we're walking, we're walking . . .

Literally.

Going up the stone steps to the apartment building's door, the bite of pain every time he put weight on his left leg was added to the list of shit he was ignoring. And he had to admit he was relieved that he didn't have to fight with a lock or anything as he yanked things open. Given the crime in the neighborhood, there was nothing preventing a walk-in from anybody; then again, it wasn't a surprise there wasn't anything worth stealing in the place.

Other than the drugs on the fifth floor. And those would be guarded.

In fact, he could expect a twelve-gauge welcome wagon at any second.

As he waited for a bunch of heavily armed humans to rush out at him, he looked around the front hall. There was an apartment on each side of the building, and both doors were open, revealing interiors that were covered with dust and grime and furniture that was broken or upside down. The smell in the air was a dense compaction of old rot, and human urine, and ridiculously, he hated the idea of that woman walking by a place like this, much less coming inside.

But it wasn't like she was a civilian or even a user. She was knee-deep in it.

Just like he was.

And what do you know, he didn't want that for her, either.

What was it about sexual attraction that the shit made you find virtue in the object of your banging desire? He guessed it was some kind of guilt-free filter, so that you didn't feel bad about wanting to be with someone who was on the fringes of morality.

As it dawned on him that no one was coming at him, he went to the base of the stairs and put his left, sloshy boot on the first step. Measuring how many landings were ahead of him, and dividing them by the sum of everything he didn't care about—other vampires, humans, the drug trade itself—he was struck by a wave of fuck-this.

He'd been telling himself all day and all night that finding that woman was about getting the deal done, but maybe it was his sudden exhaustion—or a bog-standard, long overdue, reality check—that made him see the truth behind his mad scramble.

He was actually looking for her because he wanted to know that she was alive. That she didn't need a doctor. That she was going to be okay after the fun and games of the evening before.

It had nothing to do with buying and selling the prison camp's powdery wares.

If she was dead, or even if she wasn't, that knowledge was not going to get him further with his own plans. If anything, it was going to tangle him in bullshit that had nothing to do with what he had to accomplish for himself.

This was worse than a wild-goose chase. This was going to rain shit on his own head.

The job he had to do was connected with that woman only if she was the one with the money. Other than that, she was not his business, and he needed to connect with that other guy, the one who'd taken the product originally.

Lucan looked around. If there were no guards here, there was no product here. No dealers here. No business here.

Unlike in that stretch of ten blocks between all those clubs, down by the bridge. Where he'd found the man he'd initially dealt with, before the woman had stepped in to do the negotiating.

Besides . . . if someone didn't answer the phone when there were millions on the line?

He knew what had happened to her, even if he didn't have the details.

On that note, he turned away from the stairs, and twisted his back to release some of the tension in his spasming abdominals—

What was that noise?

As he froze and held his breath, he listened. Out on the street, a car with loud music trolled by. Someone hollered at somebody else. In the distance, there were sirens—then again, when weren't there sirens in downtown Caldwell.

Sniffing at the air, he just got more of the same. And the smell of his own blood.

Lots of the latter.

"This is bullshit," he muttered as he went to the exit.

His eye on the prize needed to stay where it had been before that woman and he had crossed paths . . . and he'd ended up in a ditch.

CHAPTER FIFTEEN

Rio felt the switchblade's tip move from between her breasts to down onto her abdomen. The point was doing a helluva job on both her fleece as well as the thin cotton t-shirt underneath, the layers giving way, her skin registering the contact with a shiver of warning. She didn't know whether or not he was cutting her yet because she both was numb and hyperaware at the same time.

But whether it was happening now or not, things were going to head in that surgical direction. Fast.

"I really like to film these kinds of things," the man said softly with his accent. "Mozart needs proof, but I like videos as well for my personal souvenir. Smile for the camera."

The blade disappeared, and he gripped her chin and forced her face over to the tripod. As she breathed hard through her stuffy nose, the nostrils flaring and sucking in, flaring and sucking in, she felt the switchblade snake down to her breast, the tip making a circle around her nipple.

"You're going to be so pretty when I'm done with you." The tone was soothing, as someone might placate a patient who was about to get a medical procedure done. "And don't worry, I'm going to make sure you feel everything I do to you. If we have to take breaks for you to catch your breath, we will. And when the end comes, and I enter you properly, you're going straight to heaven."

Rio squeezed her eyes shut and thrashed against the ropes, her body fighting for its freedom on its own, her brain taking a back seat to the high-octane fear coursing through her veins.

The man took a break from the teasing and sat on his heels, watching her as a child who had picked the wings off a fly might regard the insect's futile suffering.

She ran out of energy pretty quickly, and then she was limp and sweating, in spite of the cold.

"So pretty," he murmured as he tilted his head and then brushed her bangs back with the switchblade. "I wish I could take out the gag. I want to hear everything you have to say to me, and I want to kiss you—"

The door to the apartment blew off its hinges, not opening but falling in, the panel hitting the floor with a clap and a cloud of dust, its screws bouncing free as they ran off across the bare floorboards.

After that . . . Rio wasn't sure what happened.

The man with the switchblade was attacked, but not by another person. It was an animal, a huge . . . dog? The massive gray-and-white canine bounded into the space and launched itself at Rio's torturer, punching the guy on the back with its forepaws so that her attacker fell face forward—then latching on to the nape of the neck with tremendous fangs.

The man tried to fight back, the switchblade swiping in wide, useless circles as the animal managed to keep him pinned on his stomach by planting itself on his back. And then there was a banging, the man's torso lifted and slammed down, lifted and slammed down, the dog heaving its great head up and down, the bludgeoning turning the pale features of its victim to a crimson red as the nose was broken.

When the man went loose-armed and utterly limp, the dog shifted its bite to an arm and rolled the deadweight over, like it was thinking this all through, as if there were a specific strategy to what was happening.

Then it cocked its head, as if confused.

The pause didn't last, and things got even bloodier now. The beast tore the front of the throat open and then went to work . . . on the face.

Squeezing her eyes shut, Rio trembled, and her nausea came back—especially as that strange smell she'd caught as soon as the man had revealed himself grew loud in her nose. And without her eyes tracking the carnage, the sounds of it all got unbearably loud: The wet slopping, the ripping, the crunching that had to be bones.

Rio was next.

That was her final thought as her blood pressure gave out entirely and she—

✦ ✦ ✦

Rio resurfaced into consciousness slowly. Her head was pounding and she was sick to her stomach . . . and every time she breathed in through her nose, she choked on the stench in the air. Like roadkill and old-lady powder—

"It's okay, you're okay."

Her lids flipped open. Someone was kneeling in front of her, someone her memory told her she knew, yet she couldn't place . . . a man who was beautiful in a harsh way, his handsome face both stark and concerned, his dark hair on the long side—

His hair was wet. Was it raining?

Given the way his mouth was moving, she had a thought that he was talking to her, and that was when she saw the camera on the tripod behind him. All at once, the whole sordid mess came back to her, from being knocked out at her apartment, to drugged at Mozart's, to what had happened here—

She needed to warn him. She needed to tell him about the—

"Dog," she croaked.

As the word came out, she realized she no longer had the gag in her mouth. With a punching expansion of her lungs, one that caused pain everywhere in her body, she breathed in so deep and so hard it was as if she sobbed. Or maybe she was sobbing? And then the tether around her neck tightened and she moaned in fear.

That deep male voice cut through her protest. "It's all right. I'm just going to untie you. I have to pull on the ropes a little to do it. Shhh . . . it's okay. I'm going to take care of you."

All at once, the tension around her throat was gone—and then she heard a shuffle and felt tugging at her ankles. Able to lift her head, she looked down herself and saw . . .

Luke.

It was the supplier, Luke. That's who he was, and his eyes were full of worry and warmth as he looked at her—

"How . . . find me?" she groaned as he went back to work and cut what appeared to be nylon climbing rope with a knife—

Between one blink and the next, she saw the switchblade he was using right next to her face . . . felt it between her breasts . . . heard the pale man's accent tell her they were going to stop when she had to catch her breath.

Rio let out a choked sob. "Oh, God. He was going to kill me—"

"Don't think about that right now." Luke collapsed the switch, and came back up to her head. "I'm going to get you out of here."

Strong arms gathered her as if she were cut glass and pulled her into his heavy chest. Even though she didn't know him, and had every reason not to trust him, she wanted to put her arms around him in gratitude. But she didn't have the strength.

"I can't walk," she mumbled as she turned her face into his neck. "My legs . . . I can't feel them."

God, he smelled good. More of that cologne he'd had on before—and it was strong enough to cut through that horrible smell.

He glanced over his shoulder to the door that had been broken down by that animal. "I've got to get us a car—"

"Mine is . . ." Back at Mozart's—no, at her apartment. Which was miles and miles, and a lifetime, away. "Gone."

"I'll figure it out." He set her back a little. "I'm going to lay you down, okay?"

After he'd lowered her onto the floor once more, he got to his feet and went over to a pack of some sort. "Maybe there are keys in here."

"What . . . happened . . . dog?" What if the thing came back—

"He's gone." Luke spoke absently as he continued to rifle through whatever was in the bag. "He's how I found you, actually."

It was then that she turned her head—and retched. Across the room, looking like he'd been holding a bomb to his chest when it exploded . . . was the white-haired man: His naked body was sprawled in the far corner, a bloody smear pattern tracking across the dirty floor like he'd been dragged over there.

"Dear God," she mumbled.

Whether it was the desecration of that body, or dehydration, or that cloth gag, her mouth was like steel wool, the inside of her cheeks chewed raw, her tongue nothing but a dry slab between her rows of teeth.

"Okay, I found a car key, but it's not safe. I'll bet they'll have a tracker on it . . ." He tossed a key fob at the mangled remains. "Fuckers."

Luke rose to his full height and stared at the wall, and that was when he properly registered to her for the first time. He was wearing black pants that didn't reach his ankles and were tight around his thighs, and a black leather jacket that was zipped from hem to collar. The jacket also seemed too small, a gap of taut flesh around his hips and lower belly showing. And he was barefoot, too.

But like she was going to argue with the sartorial choices of her savior?

Or the wet hair, she noted numbly as he pushed the waves back again.

When he returned to her, he looked away sharply and she worried he'd been wrong, that the dog had returned. But then his gentle hands realigned her cut-open fleece and shirt, making sure her breasts were covered.

"You need to take this."

Her eyes refused to follow her command to focus. But eventually, she recognized what he was holding out to her. A gun.

"I have to go find us a car," he said. "And I know there's no one in the building. You're safer here than you are down on the street, especially if armed."

It took everything in her not to beg him to take her along. But he was right.

"Help me . . . up. Prop me on the wall."

Luke closed his eyes briefly. "Yes."

Bending down, his hands, his big, careful hands, slipped under her arms. As he lifted her, she hissed in pain, and his face paled.

"I'm so sorry—"

"Move me," she ordered, "just move me."

Biting down on her molars, she endured the agony of a change in position, her arms and legs screaming as the joints, which had become locked, were forced to bend. And then, when she was leaned on the flat wall, her torso just slid to the side, her energy spent, her body refusing to work.

Luke ended up having to relocate her so she was in a corner.

"Gun," she grunted.

She tried to lift her hands to hold it. She couldn't.

Luke got the pack thing and put it carefully in her lap. Then he situated her forearms on the bundle and set the gun between her palms, training the barrel at the door at what would be chest height on an average man.

"I've got it," she said. "You go . . . I'll take care of myself."

There was a pause. And then Luke surged forward and pressed a kiss to her forehead.

He was gone after that, rushing out the wide-open doorway.

As Rio took a deep breath, her ribs were like a steel cage around her lungs and nausea rose again. Then her vision receded to a fine point—although it came back quick enough.

Shifting her eyes over to the dead body, she swallowed compulsively. In the light that shined in from the stairwell's fixture, the gleam of blood seemed evil—and then something moved.

Or . . . at least she thought it did. Probably just an autonomic jerk of muscle fibers.

Well, no doubt, it was that—considering most of the muscles of the chest were gone, and she wasn't even sure which part of the glistening remains was the face.

She refocused on that open door and trained all her strength on her trigger finger.

In case she needed it to pull hard.

CHAPTER SIXTEEN

Lucan hit the walk-up's staircase on a leap, jumping down landing to landing, swinging himself around by the banister. At the ground floor, he ignored the front entrance and shot to the back hall. Breaking out through the battered door at the end, he found a series of parking spots in the alley, but they were empty—of cars, that was. Discarded mattresses, a broken TV, and a couch that had its inner stuffing exposed to the elements took up the shallow asphalt square.

As he cursed out loud, he tasted anew the blood of the man he'd eaten.

Even though his wolf had done the chewing, as usual, he was left with the aftereffects, his full stomach not the kind of third wheel he needed right now.

Taking off at a jog, his bare feet were silent over the damp, cold pavement of the alley. When he got to the first intersection of a proper avenue, he looked left and right.

And jumped out in front of a car.

As the headlights splashed across him, he put both his palms forward like he was Superman and could pick the thing up by the front bumper—and then, because he was no hero at all, much less one that was super, he had to jump out of the way when the tires locked and the skidding started.

Momentum being what it was, he sprinted forward to keep up with the driver's side window, and the second the sedan came to a halt, he locked eyes with a—shit, it was a kid behind the wheel, a human young who couldn't have been much older than fourteen or fifteen, not that Lucan knew a ton about the aging cycle of the other species.

Actually, it was two kids, and they were arguing with each other, like over who'd chosen to come this way. Then both doors punched open and they bolted from the scene, taking off so fast, Lucan didn't have time to get into their brains and demand that they give him control of the vehicle.

Might be the only thing that went his way tonight, Lucan thought.

The deserters had left the engine in gear, so without any brake pedal pressure, the sedan was rolling forward at an idle. Hopping in, he yanked the wheel around and hit the gas. The passenger's side door flopped wide on the turn, but as he righted the course to straight, it clapped shut.

For no good reason, he noticed that he smelled fast food and glanced across the console. The passenger side's wheel well was filled with Burger King bags, and that pair had obviously just stopped for some more grub. There was also something else in the air—fake strawberry and tobacco smoke.

The car was clearly stolen. Not exactly the complication he was looking for. He'd have preferred to tamper with the memories of a human so that he didn't have to worry about the Caldwell police having an all-points bulletin out on Rio's escape route away from that walk-up. But he had no time to spare to look for a better four-wheel option.

Back at the walk-up, he pulled in next to the deconstructed sofa, slammed the gearshift into park, and jerked the keys out from the steering column. It was a good thing that the beater was so old. In the last couple of months, he'd learned that modern cars had remotes that could live in a pocket or a bag and didn't have to be plugged into the ignition.

Those boys might well have taken the ability to secure and restart the thing with them.

Stretching across the seats, he pushed down the lock on the passenger door. Then he was out and locking the driver's panel with the key.

He'd never moved so fast in his life: In the rear entrance. Back down the dark hall. Around the base of the stairs and then up the steps three at a time, his hand grabbing at the balustrade and hauling his weight up.

Fourth landing now—and he remembered how he'd left her with the gun.

"It's me," he said before he jumped into the open doorway. "Rio? Don't shoot, it's me—"

"I'm here," was the weak response.

Lucan all but flew into the shitty apartment, expecting to see the woman slumped on the floor. She was not. Her head was listing to the side, but other than that, she was precisely where he'd arranged her, like a rag doll abandoned by its maker.

God, she looked bad.

Yet her eyes were shining fiercely, and that nine millimeter was angled right where it needed to be.

Her body might have been failing her; her will was not.

As he rushed over to her, time fell into a crawl. It seemed like a hundred years until he was kneeling by her side again, and the sight of her so battered and bruised was etched into his mind, indelible. From her matted short hair, to the blood that stained her sliced-open fleece and shirt, to the ligature marks around her pale throat, she was nothing like the woman he had met the night before.

And to think he'd almost ignored that sound he'd heard, that prickle of awareness that he'd had out in front of the building as he'd been about to leave.

If he'd been even ten minutes later or had taken off . . . she'd have been hurt in ways that were intolerable to consider.

That bloody, naked corpse over in the corner hadn't paid enough.

"Let's go," he choked out.

When he went to take the gun from her, she shook her head. "I'll cover us. You just carry me out of here, and I'll shoot anything in our way."

Her voice was stronger than it had been, and he took a moment to respect the warrior that was just under her skin. Then he slung the pack her attacker had brought with him onto his shoulder, scooped her up—and grimaced as she gasped and grunted in pain. As he marched them into the light of the stairwell, he glared across at the mangled body.

Out in the common landing, he had to give her credit. Despite her condition, she kept that weapon pointed right in front of them. The job required both her hands, but he knew that she wasn't going to drop the weight.

She was going to protect them . . . as he did his very best to save her life.

✦ ✦ ✦

It went without saying that if Luke hadn't shown up when he did, Rio would have been dead by now.

That was the thought that she used to distract herself from the waves of burning agony that lightning'd through her muscles and bones. The trip down the stairs was incredibly painful, each rushing step a jarring reminder of everything she had been through.

So Luke had saved her three times, as it turned out.

Maybe she was a cat, though. And still had six left.

When he bottomed out by the front door, Luke paused and turned left, turned right. Courtesy of her iron grip on the gun, the muzzle swung around to both of the open apartments. No one came out of the darkness on either side.

"We're going out the back door," he said.

And then the pain started up again as his long strides carried them both down a narrow hallway that had sheets of vinyl wallpaper peeling off from the ceiling and trash scattered to the sides of the corridor, a Litter Sea parted by those who had created the problem.

The back door had a small window set about five feet up from the floor, the opaque glass crisscrossed with chicken wire. Luke kicked the thing open—and right outside was an old two-door Cutlass sedan. Navy blue. With a pinstripe.

He went around and unlocked the passenger side with a key, the old-fashioned way. Then he had to tilt her down so he could pull the handle, and there was a metal-on-metal squeak as he opened things.

"I'll be as careful as I can—"

"Just drop me in there so we can go."

Rio tried not to pass out as he set her in the seat, but her body was as limber as a brick wall—and felt just as liable to break apart under sufficient pressure. As her lips peeled off her front teeth, she closed her eyes and leaned out, in case she threw up.

Maybe that drug was still in her system.

She felt the gun get taken from her hands, and she was more than fine with letting it go. Breathing in and out of her open mouth, she tried to focus on something to keep herself conscious . . . keep herself alive—

That cologne of his. She trained all her attention on the way that Luke smelled—and whether it was the placebo effect or there actually was some kind of magic in whatever he'd aftershave'd himself with . . . eventually, she was able to bring herself back from the brink.

Like he knew she was ready to get buckled in, Luke carefully pushed her shoulders into position so she was properly in the seat.

"I'll get the belt." Luke's voice, so deep, so level, was right in her ear. "Just keep breathing."

Good advice, she thought to herself.

After he pulled the strap over her torso and clicked it into place, he closed her in and she watched him with blurry eyes as he bolted around the front of the car. When he had to pause and flipped the set of keys around in his hand, she made a move like she was going to reach over and pop the lock for him. But there was no lifting her arm.

At the rate her body was refreezing in its current position, she was going to have to be surgically removed from this car.

Fortunately, Luke did not have her problems with mobility. He all but pile-drove himself in behind the wheel, and the easy way he tossed the pack into the back seat without any effort was not the kind of thing she'd ever thought she'd envy. As soon as the engine turned over, he threw them in reverse and stomped on the gas.

"Don't hurry," she mumbled as they jerked back. "No accident."

"Right." He K-turned at a more reasonable clip. "Try and sleep. We've got a ways to go."

"Where." Finishing the sentence was too much like work. "Kidnapping me?"

His head whipped around. "What the hell?"

"Guess I'd be in trunk, then." She tried to smile at him, but all she could manage was to turn her head in his direction. "Right?"

"That's not funny."

"Little funny."

"No, not at all."

And then they were off, traveling toward the river at only slightly faster than the thirty-mile-an-hour limit. She watched him instead of the street. He was bearing down on the steering wheel like he might rip it off its column, sitting forward as if he could get them to wherever they were going quicker if his face was closer to the windshield.

As the pain ramped up, and she felt that horrible retching sensation threaten the back of her throat, she moaned. "I think . . . need a doctor . . ."

"I know. I'm going to take care of it."

She was going to tell him to just take her home, but that wasn't safe. Mozart was going to find out sooner or later that his hitman hadn't just failed. He'd been eaten. And with only one bloody body at the scene? Her old "boss" was going to guess she was still out in the world, somewhere.

With all kinds of information on him.

"Where dog come from," she heard herself say.

When Luke didn't respond, she figured he had no better idea than she did. Or maybe she hadn't said that out loud? She just couldn't seem to connect to the world, the agony in her body the kind of thing that so completely overwhelmed her senses, it was hard to break through its haze and connect to anything outside of herself.

The Northway's Trade Street on-ramp came up way too quickly—and she suspected she had lost consciousness for a minute or two, the angle of the car rousing her as they hit the incline and accelerated. When they flattened out and headed north, she took a shuddering inhale.

"Where . . . going."

Luke glanced over, his face grim in the glow of the dashboard. "It's safe, I promise. Try and rest, okay?"

"Three times," she said.

"Huh?"

"Saved me . . . three times."

He went back to staring out at the road ahead. "And I'll do it a hundred times more, if you need me to."

His words were spoken so softly, she wasn't sure if she'd heard them right. If she had? Well . . . then he was a criminal with at least some kind of a moral compass, wasn't he.

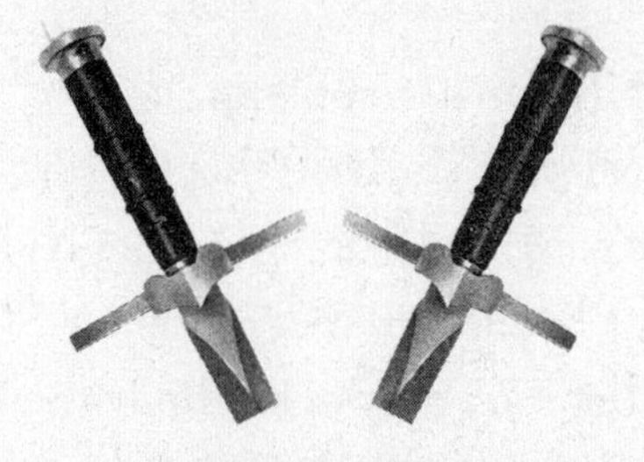

CHAPTER SEVENTEEN

About forty minutes after Lucan finally got off the Northway, he pulled the stolen Cutlass onto an overgrown drive and proceeded a hundred and fifty yards off a county road that had had less traffic than a goat path.

As he went along, he kept checking on Rio. She was looking . . . dead. Her skin was gray, her mouth lax, her body motionless except for the kind of rapid, shallow breathing that was not a good thing. Over the course of the trip, which had been longer than it should have been because he'd had to make sure they weren't being followed, she'd settled against the doorjamb, her torso tilted away from him—though her face had stayed angled so that if she opened her eyes, she could see him.

And now he was worried he wasn't going to be able to get her out of that seat. Get her the help she desperately needed.

The lane ended at an aluminum-sided farmhouse that had seen better days. Pulling into a single-vehicle, open-air carport, he hit the brakes and killed the engine.

She didn't move.

"Rio?"

At the sound of his voice, her eyelids twitched and she groaned, but then she seemed to sink back into sleep. Or maybe it was a coma.

"I'll be right back," he said. "Just hold on."

Getting out, he shut things back up so that she'd stay warm, and walked over to the rear door of what he intended on being their temporary refuge. Unfortunately, the very modest two-story house was just as rough as that apartment building—and he had a thought that someday, he'd take her someplace nicer.

Which, considering where he was starting from, might include locales with such exotic luxuries as running water, reliable electricity, and central heating.

The back entry into the kitchen had an overhang that was barely hanging on, and he tested the door's lock. When it held firm, he turned his shoulder to the panels—

And broke the fucker open.

The air that wafted out was as cold as the night, and not moldy at all—which meant there were so many windows broken, there was always plenty of breeze going through the rooms. He'd been inside once before, back when the prison camp had taken up its new residence. He'd roamed the landscape constantly back then, his wolven side desperate to get out and move under the moonlight after so many decades of forced, subterranean confinement. He'd always come back to that sanatorium, however.

The Executioner had started right off with the leverage shit.

Then again, when you had levers to pull and stuff you had to get done, you didn't sit on your ass if you wanted to create an empire.

Lucan stepped into the kitchen. The house had been abandoned sometime in the seventies, he was guessing—because the rusty, avocado appliances and mustard-yellow linoleum floor were in the style that was popular right before he'd been thrown into the prison camp. The windows and walls were a matchy-patchy of faded sunflowers, and without any furniture to speak of, it was like a museum exhibit on rural, aspirational living that had been robbed.

A quick check through the other four rooms on the first floor yielded nothing. Quick walk around of the five-room second story was the same. He wasn't surprised; his nose had told him up front what it took his eyes six minutes to confirm. But he wasn't really interested in what was aboveground.

The cellar door was under the stairs and it was shut solid, yet opened just fine. As he looked down into the darkness, his hand went to get inside his jacket—but then he realized he wasn't wearing his own clothes. And it wasn't smart to use a phone for a flashlight, anyway. Tracers happened, which was why he'd turned his burner off.

Going over to the cabinets and drawers, he didn't expect to find anything, but there was a surprising collection of crap left. By a stroke of luck, he found a candle, and lit it with a match from a box marked "Joe's Steak Shack."

Okay, fine, the candle was actually the number "5" and it had dried frosting on its foot, the forgotten marker of someone who was that age. Or 15. 25. 35 . . .

Pinching the bottom of the number between his fingers, he was careful going down the rough staircase.

Well . . . what do you know. There was a candelabra on a stand right at the base, as if the owners had had their electricity go off a lot and wanted to be prepared. Using the 5, he lit the cobwebbed four-arm and felt like Vincent Price as he moved the anchored flames around.

Fabric, everywhere. And tubs, which he assumed were for dyeing. Also long tables that looked like they'd been built in the cellar from assembled wood.

"Pretty fucking perfect."

Putting the candles down, he gathered up bolts and bolts of fabric, and shook them out to make a soft bed. He chose behind the stairs as a location—so that if anyone descended the steps during the day, Rio'd have time to hear it and be ready to shoot whoever it was.

She would be safe here—at least that was what he told himself.

And he wasn't going to be gone long.

At least not while it was still dark out.

✦ ✦ ✦

The next time Rio woke up, she was stretched out on a bed in a candlelit room. As she went to sit up, the world spun around so she laid back on the mattress.

Except it wasn't a mattress. It was . . . heavy sheets. Layers and layers of—no, fabric, like you'd find at a Jo-Ann's, all kinds of different patterns, weights, and colors.

Totally disorientated, she tried to see beyond the halo of golden light thrown by the grouping of candles. Where the hell was she—

It all came back in a waterfall: The white-haired man with the switchblade coming at her as she was bound and gagged on the floor. The dog attack. Luke freeing her and carrying her out to a car. This abandoned house, which she had a hazy recollection of being moved into.

Now she was here, in the cellar, on this bed of multi-colored fabric—

Voices up above. Now footsteps that made dust fall from the boards over her head.

A door opening and a beam of light piercing down the steps ahead of her. "Rio, it's me."

At the sound of Luke's voice, she shuddered in relief—and became aware that she'd lifted up a gun and pointed it at the open-board staircase in front of her.

The reality that he hadn't left her undefended meant that he, and anybody with him, did not intend to hurt her. But considering how much rescuing he'd been doing over the last little bit, did she really still doubt his savior act?

Then again, old habits of self-protection died hard.

"I'm here," she said in a rough voice.

"I have help."

There was a pause, and then she saw his legs at the top of the rough wooden stairs. She knew they were his because he was wearing those strange, tight, too-short black pants—and through the open frame of the stairs, she watched him take things one step at a time. Was he injured?

No. He was helping someone in a tan-colored robe, someone who seemed to have bad balance.

It was slow going.

And when he was finally on the concrete floor, he put out his arm for whoever was with him and brought them around, into the light . . . oh, so it was a limp, the person had a limp, a bad one—and their whole head and body were covered, nothing showing of the face, a mesh drape hiding the features.

"She's here to help you," Luke explained.

Rio glanced at him, needing to refresh everything she knew about his face, his body, his energy. In the flickering light, he looked ferocious and his body seemed huge. Next to him, the robed figure was slight and came up to his pecs.

It was a woman under there, Rio thought.

"Will you allow me to examine you?"

The voice was, in fact, female, and also smooth as silk, and for some reason, Rio pictured whoever was under there as having long, dark hair.

"I got hit on the head," Rio said on a mumble.

"So I may examine you?"

The accent was odd, a mixture of French and something Romanian. Not that she was a linguist.

"Sure."

She didn't even bother to ask whether the woman was a doctor or a nurse. Or a vet. Anything was better than nothing, and it was not safe for her to be seen at so much as a doc-in-the-box. Mozart had resources everywhere in and around Caldwell—

"You're a nun," Rio blurted as she put the gun aside. "That's what you are."

As the woman lowered herself down onto the edge of the fabric pile, she relied heavily on Luke's arm—and then addressed him. "You will leave us now, and allow me your flashlight. Thank you."

Luke hesitated.

"You will leave us," the woman said more sharply. "You are not her mate. It is improper for you to attend to her. Go."

After a moment, Luke looked at Rio. "I'll just be upstairs."

"It's okay," Rio said. Even though she feared she was lying to him.

"And you must needs get her some food and drink," the nun ordered. "Now. She is dehydrated and requires nourishment."

Luke did not seem like the kind of guy who took orders. But he skulked off for the stairs like he'd been yelled at by an elementary school teacher.

After his heavy weight clomped up the steps, the robed figure's mesh-covered face turned to Rio. But the woman didn't say another word until Luke had closed the door.

"Tell me, female," she said gently, "what happened to you."

Rio's eyes watered. And she intended to speak . . . but she suddenly didn't have any air in her lungs.

"Oh, female. I am so sorry." A soft hand took her own. "Just catch your breath, we are not in a hurry here."

"I'm okay." As Rio breathed in deep, she winced. "I really am."

Was she? She didn't know for sure. Or maybe at all.

"Where do you hurt?"

Everywhere. "My head is the worst. They hit me with a gun, I think. At least twice."

Determined to be a good patient, even though there was nobody around with a clipboard to judge her performance on convalescent compulsories, she went to sit up. The pink-and-white fabric draping her to her chin fell down—

Revealing her cut-open t-shirt and the red line where the tip of the switchblade had cut into her.

Rio stared down at herself. And then with shaking hands, she drew the two halves together so that she was covered.

"You are going to be all right," the woman said sadly. "At least physically. I shall make sure of that."

Between one blink and the next, Rio found herself back on the floor of that apartment, tethered tight between the stakes, that shiny silver blade going—

The trembling took her over fast, her whole body caught in a flood of flashback adrenaline.

"Come, let us attend to your head," the woman said after a moment. "We shall start there."

Or at least Rio thought the words were something like that.

She suddenly couldn't hear very well over the screaming inside her skull.

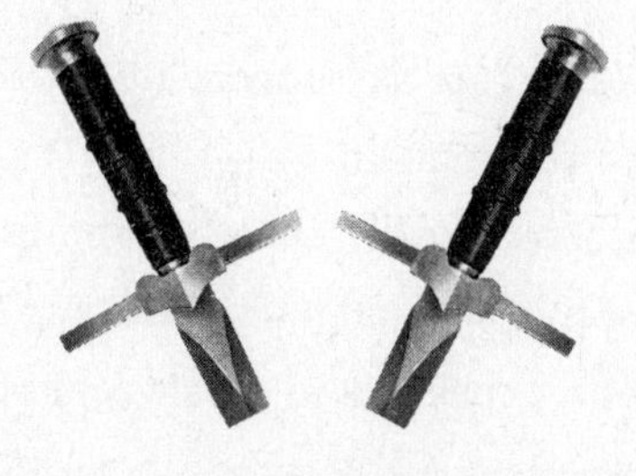

CHAPTER EIGHTEEN

Lucan stood in the empty, antiquated kitchen, staring out a dirty window, trying not to think about what was happening down below. As time stretched to an unbearable limit, and he felt like he was either going to punch something, explode into a shower of cartilage, or put his head through the wall, a set of headlights pulled into the long drive and came down to the farmhouse.

He palmed up both guns and looked down at the weapons. One was from the prison camp, signed out to him for use only against humans in the drug trade. The other was from the pack he'd lifted from the apartment. He knew how many bullets were in the former—didn't have a clue about the count in the latter.

Going over to the door, he back-flatted against the wall and looked out. As the headlights were killed, his wolven eyes adjusted.

A hatchback was right up to the rear bumper of the stolen Cutlass, and when Mayhem got out with three pizza boxes, Lucan whispered a prayer to the Elder Wolf, even though he didn't believe in it. Her. Whatever the fuck it was.

"I owe you," he said to Her as he stepped out from the house. Then he spoke more loudly, "You made it."

Mayhem was characteristically cheerful, the male raising the boxes up like they were a trophy given in an obstacle course competition. "I got you cheese, pepperoni and cheese, and sausage, pepperoni, and cheese."

"Did you also—"

The prisoner nodded over his shoulder. "I snagged a gallon of bottled water. It was the best I could do. It's in the back—here, take these."

Lucan accepted the stack of boxes, sandwiching them between his palmfuls of nine millimeter, feeling the warmth, smelling the melted cheese and the sauce.

"I'll come back for the water—"

"I'll bring in the—"

"No."

Mayhem stopped in the process of opening the back. "Why not. You said you needed help."

"Stay here," Lucan snapped. "You're not coming inside."

He went into the house, put the food load down on the chipped countertop, and bolted back out.

"Forget it," he said the second he stepped out. "Don't even start."

Mayhem was leaning against the hatchback, arms crossed over his chest, the gallon of water dangling from two fingers. And he wasn't smiling.

"I'm not talking about it." Lucan strode forward. "Gimme the water. I owe you. And that's as far as we're going."

"You've got a problem, prisoner."

"Maybe, maybe not. But whatever it is, it isn't your business."

"Sure as hell is. You told me to come out with food. You get caught with—whatever the hell is going on here, and I'm in on it."

"No one knows you're here."

"No guarantee on that. You know the way shit is in the camp. There are few secrets, and those rare things that stay hidden will be used against you."

"Then the less you know, the better, right?"

"No, in this case, the less backup you have—and the more danger I'm in."

"I don't need backup."

"You needed pizzas. And what are you going to do for food tomorrow—"

"I'm going to get it myself. Time for you to go, Mayhem—"

"I know you brought that nurse here." As Lucan narrowed his eyes, the other prisoner shook his head. "So one of two things is going on. You're either fucking that female in the robes, or she's treating someone for you. Since your request didn't include a dozen red roses, I'm thinking it's not about dating."

Lucan leaned in and snatched the water. "Do yourself a favor and stop thinking about me and this house and all the shit that is not going on."

"*You* asked me to come here."

The "asshole" was implied in the tone.

"And now, I'm telling you to get the fuck out."

For the first time, Mayhem's eyes flashed with an aggression at odds with his generally yeah-cool-whatever personality.

"You don't want to go this alone, wolven," the male said in a low voice as he yanked the water back. "And I'm not talking about whatever the fuck is happening in this sieve of a house. I'm talking about the prison camp. We're down to three hundred males and females, and the Executioner needs every one of us. You're allowed to go to Caldwell and make the deals because he's got you fucked hard if you don't. That leeway doesn't go on forever. You're going to be missed unless someone covers for you, or were you planning on leaving here in less than an hour for check-in?"

"Fuck." Lucan paced around. "I can't go yet."

"Then what are you doing about check-in." When Lucan didn't respond, Mayhem held out the plastic jug. "My price is I want to know what the hell is going on. The food and water are free."

Lucan let his head fall back so he looked up at the shining stars. Then he leveled his stare once again. "Why the hell do you care?"

With a shrug, Mayhem replied, "I don't have anything better to do. And I haven't been allowed to watch TV for how long? Your drama is going to be my new favorite show."

"This is not a fucking game."

"Didn't say it was. But I did say you need me and I quoted my price. What do the words cost you."

Rio's life, Lucan thought.

"Jesus Christ," he muttered.

"Excuse me? I'm more like Lucifer."

"No, you're more like a toddler." After a tense glare, Lucan grabbed the jug. "You're not going down in the cellar. You stay on the first floor."

As he turned away, Mayhem stuck right on his heel. "Where are your shoes?"

"Not on my feet."

"I can see that."

Opening the back door, the two of them stepped into the kitchen—

Mayhem stopped as his nostrils flared. And then he shook his head. "A human. This is about a fucking *human?*"

At that moment, the cellar door opened and Nadya, the nurse, pulled herself up the last step by the jamb.

Both Mayhem and Lucan jumped forward to help, but she batted them off. And after she caught her breath, she said the one thing Lucan didn't want to hear.

"We must bring her in. She has had two blows to the head and she needs monitoring. I cannot stay here much longer and you are not going to know what to do for her if she has a seizure."

Mayhem threw his hands up, went over to the pizza boxes, and flopped the top one open. As he bit into a slice, Lucan cursed.

And cursed some more.

✦ ✦ ✦

José had just been leaving headquarters, having finished the write-up on the scene at that trap house, when his phone rang. And now he was not on the way home, but heading across town to the urban-most edge of the suburbs.

Home had been the plan, but not the vow. He knew better than to promise his wife anything off-duty related after all these years. It was a good rule of thumb, and one that he was not going to miss when it was no longer an operational imperative.

"Yeah, yeah, I see it." He switched his cell to his other ear, the one that had always been better at its job. "It's brick, right? Three stories—yeah, I'm just pulling in now. Yup, there you are."

Parallel parking his unmarked in between a truck and a minivan, he got out and locked up. His headache, which had been a constant background noise for a good hour or two now, had mysteriously disappeared as soon as he'd answered the call from the captain. Who refused to be known as chief.

All things considered, it should have been the opposite way, he thought as he waited for a couple of cars to pass by. But focusing through discomfort was either a habit or a skill for him.

Either way, he'd refined it over time.

With the coast clear, he jogged across the two lanes. Or shuffled, was more like it.

"Captain," he said as he lifted a hand.

Standing next to the entrance of an unremarkable brick apartment building, Captain Stanley Carmichael was dressed in plain clothes—which was to say that he was wearing a dark suit. His tie was unknotted, however, the blue strip of silk hanging loose. The man was also smoking, the cigarette between his teeth halfway done, two crushed stubs by his scuffed loafers.

"Thanks for coming, José," was the exhausted greeting.

"Stan, what's going on."

As José came up the short concrete steps, he shoved his hands in his pockets, and thought about the many times they'd stood together and all the different contexts of the proximities: The two of them had gone through the academy at the same time, back a hundred and fifty million years ago. José hadn't had a lot of patience for the political side of things, however; he'd been too interested in solving crimes. His buddy, on the other hand, had excelled at the palm pressing, but not in a fake way. Even as Stan had risen through the ranks, he'd still stayed plugged in at every level of the hierarchy, from the newbies to the rank-and-file cops to the mayor herself.

"I got a problem," the captain said.

When the guy just looked off into the distance and continued to smoke, José leaned against the railing on the other side of the brick stoop.

There were times when questions were invasive, even if you'd been invited into the conversation, times when silence and collected breath were preparation for the hard stuff about to come.

"Okay," Stan said, "let's go in."

The captain dropped the cigarette with a lot of tobacco still remaining before the filter. Crushing it with the tip of his loafer, he opened the outer door into an anteroom with mailboxes. Past that lineup of little squares, there was a second entry that was all glass, and Stan unlocked it with a code that he punched into a keypad.

The lobby on the far side had institutional carpeting, dreary wallpaper, and an elevator with a cockeyed "Out of Order" sign taped to its panels. The smell was a cross between Crock-Pot, fresh coffee, and fabric softener; not exactly nasty, but just a lot in the nose. And meanwhile, underfoot, the floor creaked like maybe it could have used a couple more support joists rising up from the basement.

It could have been any one of a thousand such buildings throughout the city. The state. The country.

As they went forward, the captain who refused to be called chief didn't say a thing, and José was content to follow—because he wasn't in a hurry to hear the story. He already knew the subject, even though he didn't have the name yet, and he could guess the circumstances, even though he didn't have the fact pattern.

The staircase had short-stop steps that were deeper than usual, and José bet a lot of people tripped on them because they weren't the standard height and depth. At the top of the landing, the captain went left. Two apartments down, he stopped in front of a door that was no different from any of the others in the hallway. Out of habit, José looked left and right, noting all the doors with numbers that began with 2 because they were on the second floor, and whether there was anyone peeking out of a doorway at them, and if there were any unusual stains on the runner.

The captain took a nitrile glove out of his pocket, snapped it on, and slid a single-soldier key into the dead bolt face. With his forefinger and thumb, he turned the brass knob and then pushed.

The apartment on the far side was dark and stuffy, lit by an overhead fixture in the center of the main living area. As Stan went to take a step forward, José grabbed his arm—

"Stop."

The other man froze like a statue. "What?"

José pointed to disruptions in the carpet. "Scuffs and blood. This is a potential crime scene, captain."

There was a moment where Stan closed his eyes, and then he seemed to deflate. "You're right."

"We can't go in without booties. Is there a body?"

"I don't know. That's why I called you."

"Stan, come here." José pulled the man back out into the hall, the apartment door shutting itself with the key still in the lock. "Talk to me. Who the hell lives here?"

"Rio Hernandez-Guerrero, she's one of our undercovers. She was involved in two incidents last night. I put her on administrative duty pending assessment as per protocol, and she was supposed to come into HQ this morning. She never showed up, never checked in. We reached out to our sources downtown, no one's seen her. Her car's out front. Her cell phone's been inactive. And she hasn't been here—"

"Someone went through this apartment already?"

"Officer Tan from Internal Affairs did a welfare check at one. There was no response to his knocking, so he entered, turned the light on, and did a walk-through. We gained access because Rio's old patrol partner still had a key and gave it to us." The captain nodded over to the door. "Tan came back and checked at four again. Nothing. No one."

"Okay." José checked his watch even though he had an idea of the time. "And just to confirm, no one's heard from her since you spoke to her last night?"

"No one. She said she was going to go get treated at the St. Francis ER. I have a buddy inside the hospital and he said no patient was registered under her undercover name or her real one. And none of our informants or undercover officers on the street have seen her or heard anything about her."

"Family?"

"None in Caldwell. She's got some distant cousins out of town, and they haven't heard from her either."

"Husband, boyfriend, roommate?"

"None that we're aware of."

"And she was reporting to who?"

"Me, basically. So I feel really fucking responsible for her."

José gave the man's shoulder a squeeze. "Stay here in the hall, Stan."

The captain nodded. "I got a glove if you want it?"

"Yeah, sure." José had nitrile gloves of his own in his inside pocket, along with booties, but he took what the captain offered because sometimes people needed to feel like they were helping. "Thanks."

Gloved up, and with his street shoes covered, José entered the apartment. There was a short hall that led to an open area with a couch and TV, and a galley kitchen. The closed doors in the space were closets and maybe a half bath. Across the way, a sliding glass door let in the ambient light from the security fixtures outside of the building.

A body had been dragged across the carpet, the heel marks a twin track that was dotted with red spots.

He followed the trail to the open door of a bedroom. Inside, the windows were covered with blinds that were partially open, and in the twilight from the external source of illumination, he could see signs of a struggle on the mattress, the sheets and blankets on the floor, a pillow off-kilter by the headboard. Streaks on the fitted sheet also suggested blood.

This was bad.

José front and centered his phone and called up a familiar number out of his contacts. After two rings, a female voice answered.

"Kim, it's me," he said. "Yeah. Good. You? Great. Listen, I know you're off tonight, but I need a little help at a scene—" He closed his eyes. "You're the best. Let me give you the address."

When he hung up, he just stared at the bed. He had heard of an officer by the name of Hernandez-Guerrero on the force, but he hadn't known she was undercover. Which was the point, wasn't it.

This had to be the woman Trey had talked about.

Shit.

CHAPTER NINETEEN

The best memory Rio had of her younger brother, Luis, was from the afternoon they'd taken their grandfather's fishing boat out onto Saranac Lake. They'd been twelve and ten, and she'd been in charge of the fifteen-horsepower, hand-crank Evinrude outboard motor that had been mounted on the stern. As they'd putted along, there had been a hypnotic quality to the way they'd rocked a course along the shore. She hadn't been much for the worms and hooks and poles, but she'd liked being in charge, and Luis and the boat had been her own little kingdom for the time they had been alone.

When she'd finally cut the motor, she could remember clear as day the two of them out there in a calm bay, the subtle sway of the hollow tin hull and the sunshine on her head and shoulders and the bright blue sky over the dark evergreens like a dream.

She was back there now, in the boat, looking past the honey-colored wooden seat in the middle. Luis was at the bow with a line in the lake, his brown eyes fiercely trained on the bobber as if he were willing a smallmouth bass to bite. He had been a scrawny kid with a big mouth, the former a fact of the scale, the latter bluster to cover a tender heart and a worried nature.

If she had known what was coming, she would have been nicer to him that day. She would have been more careful with him, too.

He'd been less hearty than everyone had thought, and that had been at the root of everything that had followed.

Then again, she'd had to find a way to rationalize it all without blaming him. Right after the overdose, she'd tried on what it felt like to hate him, and she hadn't been able to live with that.

As the boat continued to rock, her thoughts drifted into fragmentation, nothing sticking, not even the supercharged past—

"—scent? We need to mask it."

"I shall take care of that."

A man and a woman were talking, very close to her, and that was confusing because how the hell did that happen in the middle of a bay? Giving up on making sense of anything, she was relieved that she recognized the voices, especially the male one. And talk about smells. There was something earthy in her nose.

It wasn't until she forced her lids to open that she realized they had closed, and as her eyes strained against a dense darkness, there wasn't much to see—and not because her vision wasn't working. It was so dim, only a weak glow of light up ahead orientating her.

Oh, and forget the boat stuff. She wasn't on a lake; she was being carried, her legs bent over, and her torso braced on, someone's strong arms, a long stride creating the back-and-forth motion.

"Luke?" Or at least, that's what she tried to say. The name came out like a croak.

"It's okay, we're almost there," he replied tersely.

In the back of her mind, she was aware that she was in deep trouble, and not just because she was an undercover cop going deeper into a drug supplier's wherever: She had a feeling she was much more seriously injured than she could comprehend—which was what happened when your brain was the thing wounded most on your body.

As her lids weighed seven hundred pounds apiece, she let them slam back down again—and it was right about then that she became aware of an echoing to the footsteps around her, as if she'd been brought into an open area. The smell was different, too: Astringent with a hint of lemon bloomed in her nose. Which was better than the oppressive earth-stink before.

"Over there," the female voice said. "The last one in the row, please."

More rocking. Then she was gently put down, and something was pulled over her. After that, there was the sound of a match striking and then a sweet, woodsy scent.

Incense, she thought.

"This will mask the scent." The woman was brisk, as if she were in charge. "But no one comes here. The Executioner believes it's bad luck."

"Okay," Luke said quietly. "Hey, thanks for this."

"I am doing this for her."

"Is she going to live?"

I don't know, Rio answered for herself.

As fear spiked into her chest, she threw out a hand. A leather sleeve was just where she needed it to be, and she grabbed on as if it were a lifeline.

Because it was.

"Don't leave me," she moaned.

There was a pause. Then that drug supplier, Luke, made a vow they both knew he could not keep: "Never."

✦ ✦ ✦

Lucan didn't know what the fuck he was saying. Hell, he barely knew where he was. This had *not* been part of the plan.

But as he knelt on the floor next to the hospital bed, he had to wonder what the hell he'd thought was going to happen? Rio was much too injured to be in that cold farmhouse by herself all day long.

Of course, now he had big problems—and so did she, over and above her bruises and wounds. In the prison camp, survival odds increased greatly the fewer people on your list of dependents. Like, if you only had one person, yourself, to worry about, then you automatically knew where everybody who mattered was.

Courtesy of his savior-reflex, he had her . . . and his other little issue.

At this rate, he was going to end up with a tally to rival the census bureau.

The nurse, Nadya, came back over with a shallow pan and some soft towels. "I need to cleanse the wound on the back of her head. Please roll her toward the wall."

Lucan glanced around. The large storage room they were in had all kinds of old medical supplies on shelves, and discarded packs of whatever-the-fuck on the floor, and bins full of stuff that had to be way too degraded to use. Somehow, the nurse had also managed to find and roll in seven usable hospital beds. Two were occupied now.

Over at the far end of the lineup, the other patient was hidden by sheets that had been nailed up in panels around the mattress. For privacy.

Fuck, Lucan thought. He wished this was a proper clinic.

"Hold on, Rio," he murmured. "I'm just going to move you a little."

She groaned and stiffened as he shifted her weight onto her side. And when he had a good look at the wound on the base of her skull, he cursed.

"You shall have to step aside for me to get to her."

Lucan repositioned himself farther down the mattress. As the nurse knelt where he'd been, her robes pooled around her, and she bowed her head for a moment in prayer. He felt like he should join in, but he didn't believe in anything.

Although maybe the fact that this female seemed willing to help was proof the Elder Wolf existed. Who the hell knew.

The water Nadya had brought over was clean, drawn from the well. The gauze was likewise fresh, having been taken from some of the left-over supplies. He wished there were X-rays. Surgeons. IVs. Whatever Rio might need—

As the nurse patted at the gash, Rio moaned in pain.

"I'm here," Lucan said and put his hand on her leg.

"Good," the nurse murmured. "No stitches needed."

"How long do you think it'll take her to recover?"

"We'll see." The hood of the robing with its mesh facial shield turned to him. "I don't know a lot about human healing, other than it is much slower than ours. Where did you find her?"

"Downtown. In Caldwell."

"Did you hit her with your car?"

As if Rio were a stray dog. "No, I didn't. I just . . . had to help her."

"You did the right thing. It is never wrong to show compassion, no matter who or what the creature is."

Lucan totally didn't agree with that, so he kept his mouth shut—

Down at the far end of the bed lineup, the sheets hanging from the ceiling moved as if caught in a gentle breeze, the undulation reminding him of a candle flame anchored by a wick, swaying from a draft.

What came out from behind the thin, makeshift curtain made no fucking sense at all.

Apex stepped through an opening in the panels, and as he emerged, the male didn't bother to look over, look around. Which was as uncharacteristic as the guy setting up a kissing booth: As a paranoid sonofabitch with a kill instinct more finely tuned than an assault rifle's trigger, he never didn't check his surrounds.

Instead, he didn't even seem to notice Lucan. Or the new patient who scented like the human she was because that incense hadn't taken over the air yet.

The prisoner just drifted out of the storage room, passing his hand down his face like he was either trying to erase what he'd seen.

Or wiping away tears.

"I don't get it."

"I beg your pardon?" the nurse murmured.

"Nothing."

"Let us prop her on her side like this with something. She will rest more easily without weight on this injury."

Lucan bolted to his feet because he was desperate for a fucking job—and yet, for a split second, the supply room was a chaos that his brain couldn't assimilate into assessable sections. But then he went over to a folding table and grabbed a cloth-wrapped bundle of what had to be sheets. Somehow, they were clean, another miracle.

"How about this?"

"Yes," Nadya said. "Put that against her posterior. She is too weak to hold herself thus. I would run an IV, but I do not trust what is in those glass bulbs I found. I will sterilize more water and ensure she partakes even if I have to rouse her properly."

After he made sure Rio had the support she needed, he stepped back. "I have to go to check-in."

The hood turned to him sharply. "Yes, go if you wish to protect her. I do not want to gain notice, and if you are searched for, they might come here."

"What about you? What if you need—"

"If I can take care of him," she nodded down the bed lineup, "I can take care of her. And no one looks for me at check-in anymore. I shall have to thank the Virgin Scribe for the Executioner's strange superstitions."

"I'll leave right now."

But it was a long moment before he could make himself start walking. And he couldn't say goodbye to Rio.

Talk about your premonitions. He felt as though if he spoke that word, he might condemn her to death. Or something.

What the fuck did he know.

After weeding his way around the stacks and shelves, he pushed open the door into the basement corridor and dragged a tired hand through his hair.

There was a lot he didn't get about his situation, himself, right now. And part of the conundrum was that he and Apex apparently had something in common.

Both of them were deeply worried about somebody.

And that was bad news in the prison camp.

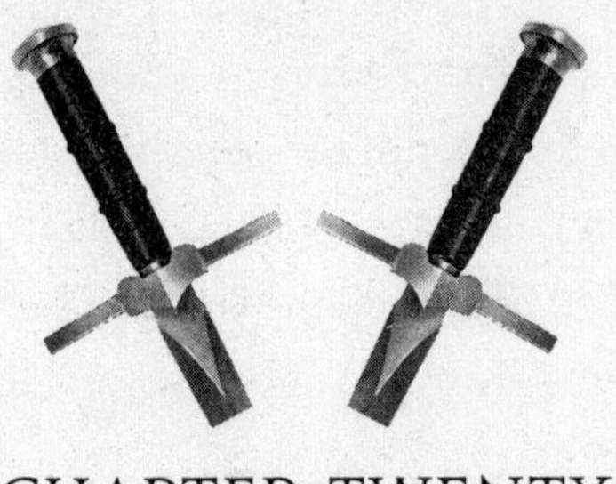

CHAPTER TWENTY

The Black Dagger Brotherhood mansion was quiet, all the lovebirds snug in their beds, not a creature a-stirrin'—

Except for the one whose skin was crawling. Whose bones were aching. Whose body was demanding a type of sustenance that had nothing to do with air or water or food. Or blood.

In the billiards room, Vishous stood alone at the bar, a rocks glass filled with Grey Goose swirling, swirling . . . swirling . . . in his gloved hand. His mouth was open slightly, and he breathed through his parted lips.

Exhale. Exhale. Exhale.

Sweat had bloomed across his forehead, and he wiped at it in a series of swipes, as if his whole arm had a tic. Underneath his muscle shirt, his pecs were spasming, his abdominals twitching. From time to time, he jerked his head to the left, to the right, the upper vertebrae cracking.

He closed his eyes and listened to the roar inside his skull. Too many thoughts. Too much gasoline from emotions he refused to think about. Talk about. Acknowledge at all. Opening his lids, he checked the time on his phone. Then he stamped a shitkicker—and regretted making the noise. The last thing he needed was interaction with anybody.

He would have waited at the Pit, but he was too itchy.

And he prayed to his *mahmen* who didn't exist anymore that Lassiter would not come into the room. Into the foyer. Into the fucking house.

Please, oh Great Virgin Scribe in all your drapey-drapey, if you've ever loved me, and I know you didn't, but still, just don't let that fallen angel—

Turning his cell phone screen up, he checked the time again. Then he lifted the glass, put it to his lips, opened his throat—and tilted his head back. He took the three inches of vodka on a oner, the burn lighting a fire down his esophagus and into his gut.

It didn't help with the sweating. He cleared his brow again—

Bing!

V nearly dropped the glass as he jerked the phone up. Opening the single text that had come through, he saw what he hoped to see, what he needed to see.

Just a single period.

.

He took another drink from the glass, catching only the drops that were left. Then he put it aside, wrapped both hands around the granite edge of the bar, and bowed his arms. Bracing his weight, he tightened the muscles of his shoulders, and then went all the way down his spine with the flexing. Heat now, blooming throughout his body.

Behind the fly of his leathers, his sex thickened. Hardened.

Pushing off, he wheeled around and stalked through the room. On the way out, his hip banged into one of the pool tables and the pain made his cock pound with its own heartbeat.

In the grand foyer, he crossed over the mosaic depiction of an apple tree in full bloom in total silence, glancing up the red-carpeted stairs to the open doors of Wrath's study. Off in the distance, he could hear *doggen* talking in the kitchen and someone was running a DustBuster out there, the high-pitched whine as loud as a concert to him. It was well after Last Meal had been cleaned up, and too early to start prep for First Meal, the downtime typically meant for sleeping for the staff. Nonetheless, Fritz had set up a rotation of skeleton crews so someone was available to the household at all times.

Skirting around the base of the staircase, he went to the hidden door tucked under the great carved-wood and gold-leafed rise. Entering in a code, he was aware that his palm was sweaty as he opened the way under the earth.

He took the steps two at a time, and when he broke out into the underground tunnel to the training center, he nearly ran.

But there were two people coming at him.

Tohr and Xcor were walking side by side, towels looped around the backs of their necks, their huge bodies glistening with sweat. As V approached the half-brothers, he was dimly aware that they were talking to him, telling him Jane was still in the clinic—

Yeah. He knew that.

—asking him how he was, saying they'd had a good workout in the gym.

He put his cell phone in front of his enormous hard-on. "Yeahgoodthanksrightgoodyupokaybye."

Or something to that effect. He had no clue what was coming out of his mouth and he didn't care. He just wanted the syllables to make enough sense so that neither of those two fighters delayed him to make sure he wasn't having a stroke.

When they kept going, and so did he, he took a deep breath.

Maybe his last one of the day.

When he got to the door into the training center, he paused. It was getting harder and harder to keep from orgasming. Every step forward, each shift of his weight, stroked the tight leather over his cock and squeezed his hypersensitive nut sac.

And with the anticipation and the images going through his head, his arousal was on the knife-edge of release.

His hand trembled as he punched in the passcode, and the muffled *thunch* as the dead bolt retracted made him swallow through a dry mouth.

As he passed through the office's supply closet, his shoulder caught a box of envelopes and pulled it off the shelf. He left the thing where it fell in a scatter.

On the far side, the little glass-fronted room with its computer and desk was empty and dim, the illumination from the corridor beyond offering a false moonlight.

V kept going, pushing open the glass panel and stepping into the concrete corridor that ran all the way down to the parking area to the right and all the way down to the pool and target range to the left. Drawing a long inhale through his nostrils, he scented Tohr and Xcor . . . and no one else, thank fuck. If Fritz decided to come down here and clean? V was going to send that butler back to the kitchen to service an order of fifty-two footlongs for Hollywood. No doubt Rhage would be overcome with gratitude.

The problem with living in a huge household with lots of help was that sometimes discretion among staff and the natural circadian rhythm of vampire sleeping patterns didn't go far enough. You wanted real privacy, the kind that meant you weren't just alone with someone, you were isolated from everybody else.

Lowering his head, he got to moving again, his eyes locking on the worn, steel-toed tips of his shitkickers. The training center's medical clinic was something he had built his Jane as a kind of engagement/mating present. And actually, they'd done a lot of the work together. She had helped with the drywall of the build-out, and she had planned all of the treatment spaces from the examination and recovery rooms to the OR itself.

As he came up to her section of the facility, all of the doors were closed. Except for one.

The last one was cracked ever so slightly, the kick-stopper deployed against the tiled floor, a two-inch seam of glow revealed in the gap to the jambs.

V put his gloved hand down to his erection. He couldn't help it—

The hiss he let out seemed loud as a car horn.

He knocked. When there was no answer, he pushed his way in.

The patient room was lit with black candles on tall stands, the pin-point flames agitating as he walked in.

The hospital bed had been stripped and moved away from the wall; it was now in the center of the room, the foot of the mattress facing the door. All of the other furniture, the chair, the rolling table, even the framed painting and wall-mounted TV, had been removed.

Swallowing again, he toed up the door stopper, and as the panel eased shut, he turned off his phone. There was a little closet, and he put the cell in there, on a shallow shelf. After that, he pulled his black muscle shirt out of the waistband of his leathers and took the thing off. Stretching his arms over his head, he arched back, trying to loosen the tension locked along his spine.

When he undid the buttons of his fly, his arousal jumped out—

Oh. So he'd come sometime during the trip down here.

The orgasm hadn't even registered, his erotic anticipation was so great.

Bending low, he peeled the leather down his thighs, and when he got to his calves, he realized, Mensa member though he was, that he'd forgotten to unlace his shitkickers. He took care of the problem quick . . . and then he was kicking the heavy weights off his feet and shucking his pants. The last thing he had to remove was his socks.

Even though he was a neat freak, except for the living room of the Pit, he crammed his clothes into the bottom of the closet—

As he turned around, he stopped.

V did not move. Except for his cock.

It kicked at the front of his hips.

Across the warm glow of the clinical room, Jane, his *shellan,* was in her ghostly form, nothing but a shimmering shadow that distorted the flat wall she stood in front of.

Without a word, she pointed to the hospital bed.

V opened his mouth and began to pant. On legs that felt seriously unreliable, he did as he was commanded, going over to the mattress.

The institutional-grade five-point restraints were laid out across the latex bottom sheet—

With a groaning curse, he orgasmed again, jets of come shooting out of him, speckling the floor. Just the sight of the black nylon straps with their buckles and hooks was enough for him—and this time, he felt the release.

But it did nothing to drain him. He was a well that was going to take hours to empty.

And he needed this.

Instead of going around to the side to lie down, he all-foured it, mounting the foot of the bed and prowling up to get in position, his erection bobbing, the tip of his long sex brushing the latex sheet until he wanted to scream in frustration.

The good kind.

When he was where he needed to be, he stretched out on his back. That was when he started shaking badly enough to rattle his molars. This was the hardest part for him. Even though he knew who he was with, even though he had asked for this, even though this was what he required . . .

He was a Dom for a reason. Loss of control was the fundamental fault line in his psyche, the earthquake that tore him apart.

And that was the point.

When he was ready, when his arms would listen to his mind's command, he stretched one and then the other out at a ninety-degree angle, laying the backs of his hands on the far sides of the heavy cuffs. Down at the other end of the bed, he moved his legs apart, placing his ankles on one, and the other, of the straps there.

And then he had to hold it together. As his chest pumped up and down, and his eyes watered, and his heart thundered, he had to force himself to stay in place.

While his mate, the woman he loved, watched him.

The longer she watched, the harder he had to work to keep ahold of himself.

"Fuck," he said as his jaw locked. "I can't . . ."

Time went eternal on him, and he felt hot tears seep out the corners of his eyes. Deep inside, he hated himself for what Rhage had seen in him. He hated the petty jealousy over a relationship Butch didn't have anymore . . . with a human man who was no longer in his roommate's world, much less his life.

V was a fucking weak piece of shit, and he wanted that toxic knowledge out of him.

So he clamored and quaked on the hospital bed.

As his female gave him absolutely nothing to go on.

Vishous had never loved Jane more.

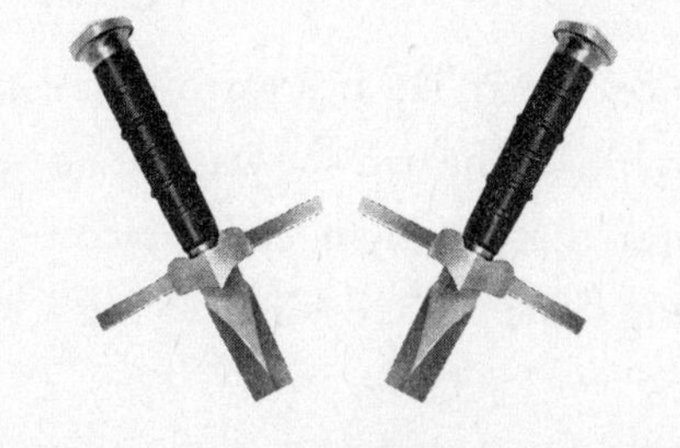

CHAPTER TWENTY-ONE

Rio's eyes flipped open, and this time, as she called on them to focus, it was different. She was back. She didn't know how else to describe it. On the disjointed trip to—where the hell was she?—she had come and gone, her senses trying to penetrate a fog of incomprehension that stemmed from the knocks on her noggin. Now, though, as her lids went wide, she was fully aware, fully functional.

Yes, in pain. Yes, lost, wherever she was.

But her mind was cranking over again.

After confirming her basic physical functions were ongoing, her brain was all about orientation: She was on her side, staring at a wall that was gray, but not painted that color. It was concrete blocks stacked and mortared together. Further, she was lying down on something that was soft. And there was something pushing against her lower back, keeping her in place—

When she went to move her head, a bomb burst of pain lit off, but she'd better get used to that.

"You want something to eat?"

At the male voice, she rolled her torso over—and groaned at the pain. Luke was right beside the bed she was on, sitting on the hard floor. He had changed out of that too-tight leather jacket—hey, check her out, she was remembering details—and was wearing a loose sweatshirt the color of a cloudy sky.

"Where am I?" she demanded.

As his brows went up, she assumed he was as surprised as she was at the strength behind the syllables. Either that or she'd just spoken gibberish.

"You're with me," he answered.

"And where are we?"

"Here."

Rio took a deep breath—or tried to. When she didn't get far with the inhale thing, she wasn't sure whether she had broken some ribs or was just stiff as hell. With that debate ongoing, she gritted her teeth and pushed herself upright.

Luke reached out as if he were prepared to catch her as she collapsed—or maybe exploded, given the bracing tension in his face. But she made it far enough on her own so that she was sitting on her hips. Turning her head, she grimaced. Half her neck was a steel band that did not appreciate any attempt to maneuver it. Her shoulders were the same.

But she was alive.

"I want to go," she said. "Now."

He pointed across a cluttered room full of boxes and shelves of God only knew what. "There's the door. You want me to help you?"

When she looked surprised, he said dryly, "I'm not keeping you here. You're free to leave whenever you want."

"So where am I."

There was a telling pause. "You're—"

"Here, right." She pointed to the mattress she was on. "Here."

Lickety-split, memories came to her: She remembered the phone call she'd answered as she had rushed to meet Luke in that alley for the first time, her direct report's warning urgent and rough. Then she recalled coming to in front of that marble fountain, Mozart putting that photograph in her face and saying her real name. And finally, she was back on the floor of that fetid apartment, bound and gagged, listening to her colleagues walk around above her, for hours.

After which came the switchblade, the dog . . . Luke and his rescue.

The culmination of it all was ironic as hell: Luke had brought her exactly where she had wanted to go all along.

She was close to the supplier's lair, if not actually inside of it.

She knew this in her gut.

Rio eased back against the wall. Then cursed as the injury on her head raised its proverbial hand in ouch class.

"Yes, I'm hungry." She tucked one arm behind her skull at an angle where it didn't hurt. "And thirsty. And I'd like to go to the bathroom."

"I can help you with everything—"

"There was a nurse," she blurted.

"There still is. She's just out grabbing something to eat. She'll be back."

"What did she say was wrong with me?"

"Head injury."

"Ah, and here I thought it was my elbow."

Rio looked past him at a row of empty hospital beds. At the end of the lineup, there was what she assumed was one behind a privacy curtain. The rest of the place did not resemble a hospital or a clinic in the slightest. In the muted gleam of two bald light bulbs hanging on wires from the ceiling, she saw there was no medical monitoring equipment. No nurses or doctors. Not even running water in the form of a bathroom or a sink. And then there was the debris, all kinds of boxes and bins and shelves full of things that had antiquated labels on them.

She had to get out of bed and go exploring—now.

"Ladies' room, please," she said. "I'm assuming you have one?"

He nodded and got up. "We have to—well, go out into the hall."

"Hopefully it's not far." Liar. She didn't care how far she had to go. "I'm a little wobbly on my feet."

"Considering you've been out cold for about seven hours, I'll take that as an improvement."

Rio hesitated at the little duration news flash—and tried to put together a timeline. When the effort of adding and estimating the different stages of her adventure made her head pound, she put out her hands and Luke firmly took them with his own. After she shifted her feet off the mattress, he pulled her upright—

She made it only halfway to goal. For some reason, her knees refused to straighten, so to keep her balance, she had to stay bent at the waist.

"Do you want me to carry you—"

"No, I'm going to walk. Thanks."

Well, shuffle was more like it.

She had to rely on him more than she wanted to—and she thought about the old couple coming out of the emergency room from the other night. Little had she known then she'd soon be playing the role of the wife, with the other half of the duo the supplier's rep.

Luke was really steady for her. Let her pick the pace. Didn't rush her, and seemed ready to stay with her even if it took a decade.

The support and kindness felt . . . weird. And also . . . lonely.

Because it was nice of him, and she didn't have anyone in her life to fill that "nice" role, head injuries or no head injuries.

Plus she was pissed off she was so weak—except then she figured it might be to her benefit. As she recovered more and more, she could keep up the act, and the more compromised he thought she was, the less he was going to keep an eye on her. And that was going to give her a chance to—

"Whoa, okay, I got you."

Without any warning, the floor rushed up to greet her and there was nothing she could do to stop the abrupt introduction. Luckily, Luke scooped her body from its free fall and hefted her into his arms.

And that was when she became acutely aware of him.

He was incredibly strong, his muscles cording up under his thin sweatshirt. Then again, she had the sense that he could have been wearing chain mail and she would have been all, *Hey . . . pecs.* Plus that cologne of his. What the hell was it?

No five o'clock shadow on him. And a great jawline—

"No."

He looked down at her. "What?"

Flushing, Rio shook her head. "Nothing. Let me get the door for us."

She reached forward for the handle, but he pulled her out of range. "I need to check first."

"For what?" When he didn't answer, she pretended to be unaware of what she'd asked. "You can put me down?"

Luke set her on the concrete floor like she was a shot glass on the head of a pin, and as she was grateful for the wall's support, she wondered where she could get some food. Calories would help wake her up. And give her the energy to investigate.

Meanwhile, the door he opened was really solid, made of steel, it looked like, but the paint was flaking on the other side, and the corridor that was exposed was dim—

Okay, wow. It smelled like 1972 out there, a combination of cigarette smoke, carpet cleaner, and not-been-vacuumed-for-a-while.

"All right." He came back over and hefted her into his arms again. "We'll be quick."

In the hall, she tried to get a bead on what kind of a building they were in—and decided it was a *building*. As she looked around, the scale of everything was too large for a residential home, and even too big for a lot of institutions, the corridor easily fifteen feet across and God only knew how long.

The light bulbs seemed to go on forever in both directions.

Yet there was no one anywhere she could see and she heard no voices, no sounds. But there had to be people of some sort here. Why else would you need seven hospital beds? As her brain worked the multipliers, she knew that this was a massive drug operation, on par with the ones in South America.

This was definitely the big supplier they'd been looking for, Mozart's equivalent on the other side of the business.

The thrill of the chase revived her even further.

If she could get out of this alive, she was going to be able to bring down the whole enterprise. This was the reason she had been doing her job for the last three years. This was everything she had—

"I can wait outside," Luke said, "but I think it'll be better if I come in with you."

"Huh?"

Oh, right. He'd opened the way into a bathroom that was lit with—yup, another light bulb on a wire. But at least the faded tile floor and the basin and toilet were clean, the place smelling of the same astringent as the clinic-type area. There was also a shower in the corner, with no curtain.

"Heck of a first date this is," she blurted.

When she realized what she'd said, she started backstroking, but he cut her off while he carried her over to the porcelain throne. "Considering how things started between us, I think we're actually making headway on the road to appropriate. Assuming you don't fall off the loo and knock yourself out."

Rio had to laugh. "Just put me on the seat and let's hope for the best."

"And then I'll make your whole day."

"How's that," she gritted as her stiff, sore body protested being lowered down to the toilet.

"I have a toothbrush and toothpaste in my pocket."

With a sharp look at his too-handsome face, she couldn't believe that some Oral-B and a little Crest made her feel like she had won Powerball. But he was right.

"Oh, my God," she murmured. "I could fall in love with you right now."

Guess that was a good thing, she decided, considering she was about to drop her pants in front of the guy.

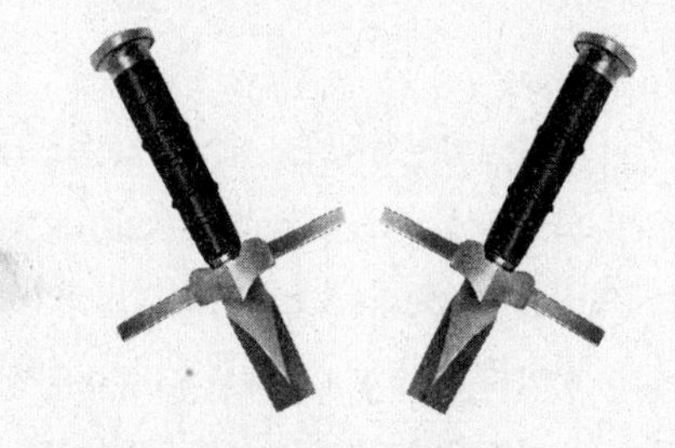

CHAPTER TWENTY-TWO

Just as Vishous couldn't stand the anticipation and dread a second longer, his *shellan* came forward, floating over to him. As she closed in, he realized her ghostly body was naked, her high, firm breasts tempting his mouth and his hands, the cleft of her sex something that made him lick his lips. He was also beyond ready for the straps, for the buckles. The initial fever pitch of fear and anticipation had leveled off, and now he needed more gasoline on his fire.

He had to have the actual trapping, the tangible tying down, to keep himself tripping on adrenaline—

Jane went by him, moving over the floor like an apparition. Because she was one.

And that was fucking hot as fuck.

The moan that came out of his throat was ragged, his need denied, his body pricking with—

Jane went to the door. Turned around. Looked into his eyes.

And then, with her right hand, the one she operated with, her dominant side . . . she slowly turned the lock into place—the copper lock, the one that he had put on the door just two months before.

For exactly this purpose.

The thing was, he had sold his penthouse at the Commodore a while ago. That place, where he had had sessions with females, with males, with humans, hadn't appealed to him after he'd mated his Jane. So he'd let his wooden worktable go. He'd given away his tools of the trade. He'd thought he'd moved on from the sadomasochism shit.

But internally, he had not changed. He still needed this outlet.

This patient room was his new playground.

Their new playground.

V started to pant as Jane returned to the foot of the bed. As she stopped, she looked up his body. Then she touched his ankles with her hands. In spite of her ghostly form, he felt the warmth and substance of his mate, and knew her for the miracle that she was, back from the dead, a gift from his *mahmen*, the Scribe Virgin. Tears speared into his eyes as he remembered holding her lifeless body in his arms, and staring at her cold, grotesquely white skin.

Yet she was here with him now and would be forever.

It almost made a disenfranchised son wish he'd reconciled with the female who had borne him.

"What do you want, Vishous," Jane asked in a low voice.

"I want . . ." Fuck, he couldn't breathe and he was pretty sure he was going to come again. "I want you to buckle my ankles."

"Why?"

"I want you . . . to control me."

"I already do." Jane lowered her chin. "You're mine."

Vishous arched his back, his pierced nipples tingling, his single ball sac tightening, his cock jumping up and slapping back down on his abdominals. Jane was the only female who had ever seen this side of him, the only person he could really go to for this sacred space of submission, this exchange of power that ran in only one direction: to her.

In the past, he had played her role, and gotten off on it, but there had always been a detachment to the experiences—and it wasn't until he'd known his *shellan* that he'd realized a truth about himself that was a shock. He had been a Dom . . . because he had wanted to be submissive.

You had to have trust for that to happen, though.

And Jane was the only one—

"I will do what I want to you. So no, you don't get the buckles."

V bit his lip. "Please—"

She rubbed his ankles . . . and went up to his calves. "You do not get them. You are going to keep yourself just as you are. Or things will not go well for you."

Jane walked up to the head of the bed. Staring down at him, she played with the tips of her breasts, as if she knew what was tingling on him, and with her forefingers drawing little circles, she bit her own lip.

A mirror of him.

"Please," he groaned.

In the back of his mind, he wondered what his brothers would think if they saw him like this, all laid out and at-the-mercy. The embarrassment nearly caused him to lift out of the trance he wanted to be in—so he stopped thinking like that.

To get himself jacked back into the erotica, he turned and looked beyond his *shellan*.

There, in a chair in the corner, he pictured his roommate, Butch, sitting in utter stillness. Watching with hazel eyes. And liking what he saw—

V's cock kicked so hard, it felt like he was coming—

"No, you can't do that right now," Jane said. "You're a patient who needs treatment first. I have to get my instruments."

The panting got more intense as she turned away from him and floated to the side door that opened into the next examination room. Opening the panel, she reached in and pulled something forward. A rolling table. That was draped with a surgical cloth.

V undulated on the latex sheet, his skin catching on what was underneath him, the adhesion pulling on his ass, separating his cheeks. He moaned again—and looked over at Not Really There Butch.

"Yes," V breathed. "I need to be examined. I need to be treated."

His eyes rolled back in his head. And when they finally refocused, Jane was putting on a nurse's uniform. She buttoned it only around the waist, the top half left open so that her breasts showed, the bottom half loose so her sex peeked out. Reaching to the rolling table, she picked up a—

"Mask," he moaned. "*Mask . . .*"

As V started to come, and couldn't stop, he watched her put a white latex mask up to her head. With deft hands, she pulled it down and arranged it properly over her features. The effect was as if she had shrink-wrapped her face, her lips pouffing out of a hole while her green eyes flashed out of two cuts, the rest of her anonymous. Alien. A stranger he knew and yet could not recognize.

Hot jets landed on his abs, even his pecs, too, and he had to fight to keep his arms and legs splayed out—because he wanted to do what she said. He wanted to follow commands.

Because otherwise she wasn't going to give him what he wanted.

Jane moved the tray into his visual field. And then she stomped on the lift for the bed. With a whirring sound, the head lifted enough so that he could see the top of the roller table—and when she was sure he was staring in the right place, she picked up the corners of the drape and pulled them back—

Stainless steel syringes. The old-fashioned kind with the glass bellies. A dozen of them.

And that wasn't all.

There were clamps. Lots of clamps, big as the sets on car batteries.

"Please . . ." V mumbled. "I can't hold myself . . ."

"So you need the ties? Because you're weak."

He looked at Not Really There Butch. His roommate lifted a brow and nodded.

"Yes," V said hoarsely. "I'm weak."

"You have to earn your ties."

"How," he asked the alien who had his *shellan*'s voice. "What do I have to do?"

Jane lowered the head of the bed back down, and then did the same to the entire mattress, the sinking feeling making him nauseous—or maybe that was just his excitement. When there was a bump and things could go no farther to the floor, Jane walked up and around the top. There was some bumping and shifting, and then the headboard partition that held the pillows on the bed disappeared.

Jane mounted the mattress right over his face, one knee by each of his shoulders, her body becoming fully corporeal, a ghost no more.

V cried out her name as he looked up at her glistening sex.

"You know what you need to do," she said.

And then she sat on his face.

Vishous let all his hunger out, devouring the folds that were at his mouth, nuzzling with his nose, sucking and eating with a desperation that made him sweat. On top of him, Jane rode him, the suffocation the sweetest kind, the lack of oxygen making his lungs burn, her taste and scent turning the rest of him into a bonfire. And then she was coming into his mouth, pressing his head down into the mattress, arching over him.

There was satisfaction at the pleasure he gave her—because his tongue was inside of her as he made her orgasm—but also a delicious dread, because he was earning the very thing he hated: His binds, his imprisonment, his at-the-mercy, which was what he feared and what he needed—

All at once, the veil of the unbuttoned skirt was gone, and so, too, was his mate's glorious sex. As the cooler air hit his hot face, he looked wildly at her. His Jane was flushed and breathing hard, her breasts spilling out of the open uniform, her nipples pink and hard.

He smiled at her, knowing he had done his job well.

She did not smile back.

But she didn't fuck with him. Down at his feet, she drew the straps over his ankles and tucked them into their buckles. After she cranked them tight, she did the same with the ones at his wrists—and also the torso restraints that crossed his chest and locked into a belt she drew across his waist.

When she was finished, he bucked against the bed, yanking, pulling, the terror multiplying until it choked him. He fought hard and got nowhere, his torso locked to the mattress, his arms and legs the same. Sweat poured out of him, running into the come on his stomach, at the same time his mouth dried out from his heavy breathing.

Jane stood by the side of the bed and played between her legs as he tested his binds, that white plane of latex over her face fucking with his mind—

Extracting her fingertips from between her legs, she brought them over to his mouth. Slipping them inside of him, he nursed desperately at her taste.

And he was still sucking as she reached over for the first clamp.

She locked it on the skin that covered his ribs, the bite of pain making him gasp. The second, she bit into the flesh over his belly button. The third clipped onto a pull of skin at his pelvis.

Removing her fingers from his lips, she came back and leaned over, letting him suckle at one of her nipples as she—

"Fuck!" he cried out as she clipped one and then the other of his own tips.

She let him lap at her as she continued to clamp him, the points of pain merging into one great grid of sensation, his body held in place as much by the compass formed by the grabs as by the straps and buckles—

She took her breast from him and looked him over. Punching the toggle on the bed with her foot, she lifted his head up so he could see what she had done. There were twenty of the clips, nipping at his skin, the pinched portions stinging, turning red.

Jane toyed with the clamps, flicking at them with her fingertips.

And now the work began. The pain was his foe. No more of him trying to beat emotions he didn't give a shit about, no more feeling an existential weakness but a physical one, no more preoccupation with things that made him jealous for no good reason—instead, he focused on the pain, on getting the best of it, on triumphing with his mind so that he could—

A syringe appeared right in front of his left eyeball.

As a fresh load of adrenaline rocketed through him—

Jane captivated him as she took the sharp tip of the needle and pressed it vertically into her nipple, the pink nub giving way, yielding around the tiny intersection.

Vishous stared to pant again.

Removing the syringe from her breast, she put it to his sternum and drew it down the center of him.

When she got to his cock, which was straining and hard and about to explode again, she took the sharp tip and drew a circle around his pierced head. Then she went lower, to his one remaining ball.

The other had been cut off long ago—but in his brain, his wires got twisted. Sharp things in that area opened up a floodgate of pain, old pain, the kind that was so toxic, you gagged.

This was where he had to go, he realized.

He'd thought it was about simple restraints and submission tonight, but . . . no, it was deeper than that. He had to go to the seat of his weakness, further down from being possessive over his roommate, further still than anything that had to do with conventional masculinity.

He had to go back to the beginning.

The origin story of his pain.

Only by glimpsing at the core of the hurt could he rebuild his strength. And maybe not get so fucking rattled over what was really nothing.

Jane in the white latex mask turned her head to him, nothing but lips and eyes and a skull. In the back of his mind, he recognized what the pause was all about. She was giving him a chance to say the word that would stop all of this . . . the three-syllable word that would get him out, no more restraints, no more mask, his beautiful female holding him, soothing him, as she removed the clips one by one.

But no. He wanted to go into the mouth of the beast. He wanted to open up the coffers that were filled with sacred, tarnished terror from the abuse he had suffered. He needed to release the pressure that had gathered there, and there was only one way to do that.

He needed blood to flow.

Glancing over, he stared at his roommate who was not really there.

Sorry, Butch, he thought at the apparition of his memory. *You have to go. This is too private, even for you.*

As much as V needed the cop in his life, as close as he was to the brother, there was one and only one person on the planet who was going to see this part of him. And of course, the vision nodded—although that acquiescence wasn't just because V was doing the visualizing. The real Butch would have understood the way things had to be.

Not Really There Cop got up and lifted his hand, as if he were saying goodbye to Jane, as if the two of them had come together and planned this. Then he nodded at V with a grave kind of love in his face. When he turned away and opened the door out—it appeared that an Almost Marissa was waiting just outside in the corridor, a worried look on her face as if she were hoping V was okay, and worried that maybe he might not be.

She also nodded at Jane and lifted her hand to Vishous. *I love you,* she seemed to mouth to him.

"I love you both, too," he said to the couple.

Then the door was closing and the outside world was closed off and it was just Jane and him . . . and the black hole in the center of his soul, that vast barren landscape that she had done so much to heal, but which nobody and nothing, not even her true love, could eradicate.

Into the mouth of the beast, he thought. *Swallowed whole and digested.*

And after that? He would feel better, like a lancing of an infection had occurred.

V looked back at Jane. Except she wasn't Jane. She was the gatekeeper of his nightmare poison, and he needed her to open that fucking vault.

Yet she waited. And waited. In the great, terrible pause, his anger grew inside his skin, her anonymity making it possible for him to set other faces to hers, other visages that belonged to enemies that had nothing to do with the Lessening Society and the war, and everything to do with wanting to break him down when he'd been a young.

Like that of his sire, the Bloodletter.

Baring his fangs, V growled, "*Fuck you—*"

He screamed so loud, his own ears hurt.

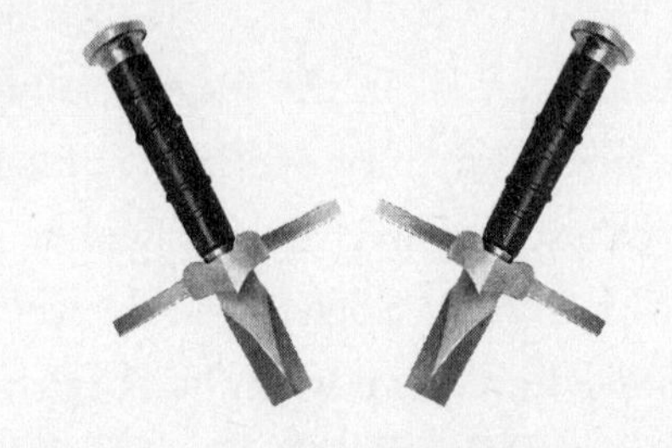

CHAPTER TWENTY-THREE

Rio had wanted a shower during her field trip to that clean, yet ancient bathroom. She didn't get one, but the toothbrushing had been transformative. And now she was alone in the hospital bed, a stalk of incense burning next to her, the patient at the other end of the lineup of beds breathing roughly behind the curtains. The nurse in the robes had been back when they'd returned, but she was gone now. And so was Luke.

It had been clear after he'd resettled her on the horizontal, and then had a tense conversation with the woman in the far corner, that he hadn't wanted to leave. They had both had to go, however.

Luke had told her he'd be back soon. Whatever that meant.

Lying on her side, because it was the only option with her head wound, she was exhausted but hyperaware, listening for clues, looking for shadows among the supply stacks. With every minute that went by, she was getting stronger—maybe it was the pep talks she was giving herself, maybe it was her commitment to her job. Maybe it was the fact that she could hear noises above her . . . movement, things passing from left to right, on wheels. Carts, she decided.

No voices, though. And she couldn't say that she heard footsteps.

She really had to get out of this bed and—

The door opened, and she knew by the size of the figure that entered that Luke had come back—oh, and he had a rolling cart with him, like something you'd deliver meals on in a nursing home. Maybe more of the same was what she was hearing overhead? He was pulling it with him, the bump-bump, *whrrrrrrrrring* of the sets of wheels loud in the dim quiet.

He didn't speak until he was in range, and he kept his voice down when he did. She wasn't sure whether it was for the other patient's benefit—or because he was hiding from someone. Then again, she did not belong here, so he might well be protecting her.

Or himself for harboring an interloper.

"I brought the shower to you," he said. "And food is on the way."

Rio had to smile. "You read my mind, huh."

Standing over her, he seemed to be scanning her internal organs as he looked her down from head to toe. "You're doing better."

"I am."

He nodded and sat beside her. "I won't look."

"At what—oh." She shrugged. "I'm not shy about my body. Who cares, you know? It's all just anatomy."

"That's a clinical way of looking at nudity."

She motioned with her hand. "And we're in a clinic. Of sorts."

Luke pulled the cart a little closer. There was a big basin on the top level, the water inside of it steaming slightly. He'd also brought a bar of soap and a hand towel that was spotted, but folded like it had just been laundered.

"Here, give the towel to me." She put out her hand. "I'll take care of it."

He nodded as if relieved, and got the terry cloth wet. Wringing out the length, he put the warm bundle in her hands.

It felt so good to cover her face and pull the moist weight down to her throat. As the heat was lost quickly, she returned it to him, and they worked out a system where they passed the damp wad back and forth. As she went on to her sternum, she realized she'd been given a loose-necked shirt at some point. Her own, the one that had been cut open, as well as her fleece, were underneath, and as she swiped the cloth—

The sting was a surprise. Even though it shouldn't have been.

Like a knife wound, even a small one, could heal in a matter of hours?

Pulling the borrowed shirt down farther, she stared at the red cut that ran between her breasts. Her bra remained in place, the wound bisected by the clasp, the little unmarked place below the fastening like a speed bump the tip of the switchblade had gone over.

Between one blink and the next, she was back on the floor of that apartment, tied down, unable to stop that man with the—

"What did he do to you?"

At first, she wasn't sure who was talking at her. Then she looked over to Luke. "How did you know where to find me?"

"What did he do."

Rio pulled the shirt's gaping neck back up. "Nothing."

"Jesus."

"He didn't hurt me like that."

As her savior merely stared into her eyes, it was obvious they were both thinking the same thing: *He could have.*

"That dog just happened to come in at the right time," Rio said lamely. "It was the craziest thing. But why were you in the building? Did you come to see Mickie? Is that why you were there?"

"Yeah." Luke rubbed his face as if it hurt. "I was looking for Mickie. You know . . . you should get out of the trade."

Rio lifted her chin. "So should you. It's hazardous for everyone's health."

When he shook his head, she said, "Oh, no, don't you dare harder-for-a-woman on me. That could *easily* have been you on that floor."

"The hell it could have."

"If there was a gun in your face—"

"I'd tell them to pull the fucking trigger. And then I'd smile as they blew my brains out against the wall."

For a split second she didn't take him seriously—but then she got a load of the dead eyes staring through her.

Maybe no talking, she thought. No talking was probably better.

She had seen that look before, and it had killed her entire family.

Shaken, but determined not to show it, Rio put her hand out to accept the rag—and realized she had lost the rhythm. He was still rinsing the thing. When he put the towel back in her palm, she set herself to work again, doing what she could to clean under her arms, and across her stomach. Then she stared at her legs.

They weighed one ton apiece. Easily. Maybe two.

"Can you help me take my pants off?" she asked.

✦ ✦ ✦

Under different circumstances, Lucan would have taken those words in a totally different way. There was nothing sexual going on for him at the moment, however. Not when he thought about that cut skin running between Rio's breasts, and how she'd been strung across that floor, and how that fucking human piece of shit had—

"Yeah," he heard himself say. "And don't worry, I won't look."

"You are a virtuous man, Luke."

Not usually. She was changing his batting average, however.

Getting to his feet, he waited for her to undo the fastenings at her waistband. Then he took the bottoms of her slacks and pulled them free of her legs carefully. As he did, his eyes went to the hanging drapes around the far hospital bed and stayed there.

Which was ridiculous. And not because he was trying to afford her some modesty.

He wanted to make sure no one else saw her. But like anybody else could see? Was looking?

He felt a protective surge, however. He couldn't help it.

With the pants off, Rio groaned as she sat up higher on the pillows—

and then she was rinsing the washcloth out herself and moving it down her thighs, her knees, her calves. Pivoting around, he gave her his back.

For what that human man had done—or almost done—he felt the need for some kind of atonement even past death. In spite of the fact that chivalry had been the last thing he had ever worried about before.

"I think I'm finished."

He glanced over his shoulder. Rio had laid herself back down on the pillows and pulled the sheet over her. With her eyes closed, he guessed she was falling asleep and didn't blame her—

"You went to Mickie's because you couldn't find me?" she said with surprising strength.

When her lids popped back open, her eyes were sharp even though there was exhaustion in her face.

"Yeah." He sat on the floor by the bed. "I thought maybe you would be there."

"You were looking for me?" she repeated.

"We had a date, remember."

For a long moment, he felt her study his face—and he wondered what she saw of him, in him. Then decided he probably wasn't going to like the answer to that.

"How did you know the address," she asked.

He shrugged. "I just did."

"Had you done business there with Mickie before?"

"Worried you're going to get cut out?"

As his words seemed to sink in on her, she frowned at him. "You don't know, do you."

"I know lots of things." He crossed his arms over his chest and felt the sweatshirt he'd pulled on stretch tight over his pecs and his biceps. "What subject are we on?"

"Mickie's dead."

Now, the way she looked at him—like she was measuring his reaction in case he'd killed the guy and was keeping it from her—made him feel as tired as she looked. But like he needed to care about some woman in the business and what she thought of him?

"You want me to be shocked?" he murmured. "Seems like that's what you're waiting for—you think I killed him?"

"Did you?"

"No, but I know what you're thinking. You're wondering why I would admit to it. Especially as you work for Mozart. Most dealers take it personally if you put their people under the ground. Gets 'em cranky."

"And you know this how?"

"I'd take it personally if I were your boss."

"Principles, huh."

"Practicality when you're trying to move product. And on the subject of principles, I got you out of a shit situation, didn't I. A couple of times. And I didn't have to."

"But maybe you needed to keep me alive so you could get your deal done. If Mickie was dead, and you have no other contacts to get to Mozart with, you're stuck. Where are you going to sell your supply. Did he make you angry or something?"

Lucan looked away from the bed. After a moment, he got back on his feet and took the towel from her hand. Putting the cold cloth in the porcelain bowl, he pushed the rolling table forward.

"I'm going to take off," he said. "I'll be back at nightfall—"

"To return me to Caldwell?"

He kept going down the row of beds, until he stopped and looked back at her. "Can I be honest right now?"

"That's your choice, not mine."

Lucan glanced away. Shook his head. Refocused on her. "I don't know you from a hole in the wall, and yeah, I'm aware I'm a fucking drug dealer. But so are you. You might want to rethink the holier-than-thou routine, at least while you're here. You need me, and I don't appreciate being slapped with the asshole label after I saved you how many times?"

"Three," she murmured. "You saved me three times. And I didn't mean to insult you."

"Is that an apology?" He put up his palm. "Wait, that's my choice how I take it, not yours again, right? Well, I wouldn't push me too hard, if I were you. I've been told I can be a terror to deal with when I'm pissed off."

"Like I said, I didn't mean to piss you off. Just asking questions."

"People in our business don't ask questions. Maybe you should remember that golden rule."

As he started walking away again, she said stridently, "I do need you. I do need your help. And thank you, for getting me out of that apartment in one piece. I'm not making sense, and I should probably just go to sleep—but, yeah. I didn't mean to get on you."

It took Lucan a moment to realize two things: One, he'd stopped moving. And two, he'd looked over his shoulder at her again.

As the human woman stared up at him, from that bed, she seemed so much smaller than he knew her to be when she was talking or on her feet. But then time wasn't the only thing that was relative. Power was, too.

And she had some kind of power over him.

Of course, he didn't like to admit this, just like she didn't like the reminder that he had saved her. They were a pair, weren't they. At least for the next twenty-four hours, take it or leave it.

"I shouldn't have brought you here," he muttered as he continued to the exit.

Funny, he wasn't sure who he was talking to on that one.

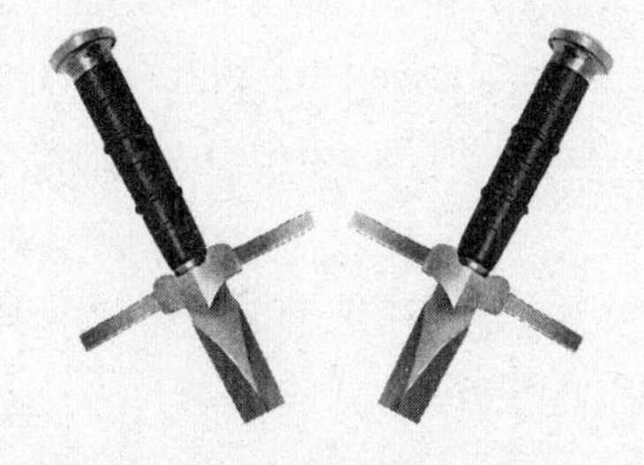

CHAPTER TWENTY-FOUR

The thing about knowing all kinds of shit about how vampire body systems worked . . . was that with the nitty-gritty details stuck in your head, the mystery was gone. You were aware of exactly what was happening when you were hungry. Tired. Had a twitch in your eyebrow, a tickle up your ass, a grumble in your stomach, an ache at your shoulder. There was a marching band of medical terminology inside your brain that had a song for every symptom and for every function both normal and abnormal.

So it was really fucking hard to just exist. Even if all the other pressing, incidental, and middle-of-the-road issues in your life receded in your mind, even if you closed your eyes, put noise-canceling headphones on, and floated in a tub of water calibrated to your precise body temperature . . . you still had the idle hum of your corpuscles to think about.

Sometimes, though, even the most rigorously logical of minds put down the gauntlet of thought, and went offline.

Now was one of these moments for Vishous.

As he lay on the latex-sheeted hospital bed, he was floating on a cloud, his body cotton candy. The inside of a good sofa cushion. Wonder Bread.

And his brain, his magnificent, complicated, PITA brain . . . was likewise, the integration complete.

He smiled.

Off in the distance, he could hear water running in a sink, but he didn't worry about it. He didn't worry about anything. He just was. With nothing teeing up his hair-trigger mind, no pain in his heart, no choking grip of the past threatening to suffocate him, he was able to be in the moment to such a degree that he became just another second clicking by, inseparable from the eternal instant.

Bliss.

Taking yet another deep breath, he opened his eyes and looked down his body. The bed was at a tilt, so he could see the bruising on his ankles and his wrists, the skin there bright red and inflamed. Likewise, all over his legs and his torso, patches of red dotted him like he was a leopard. And at his hips, his cock was in a well-used, exhausted deflation off to one side.

The cleanup was done, the blood and come washed away, the tools removed, the session over.

But it wasn't like it had never happened. The pain had receded to a glow, like a banked fire to warm his hands by, something to cozy up to and relax beside, not anything that could ever, ever hurt him.

And that was true both for the shit on the outside of him . . . as well as what was on the inside.

All he knew was peace—which was what he had been after.

Jane came through the connecting door. She was dressed in surgical scrubs, her hair a mess, her face still flushed. As their eyes met, she paused and leaned against the jamb. Crossing her arms over her chest, she smiled slowly.

And that said it all, didn't it.

When V extended his arm out to her, she came over. Bent over. Laid herself across his big-ass chest. Her lips were soft as they brushed the side of his neck, and his palm was slow over her back, and his heart was full, as was hers.

"Can you help me back to the Pit," he asked after a little while. "I want to be in our bed."

"Absolutely."

Jane straightened and stroked his hair. Then she offered him her hands, and he pulled himself up and shifted his legs off the table.

That was when he saw the chair. Over by the door.

Butch actually had been here. And so had Marissa. Hadn't they.

Unsure how he felt about that, V met Jane's eyes. "I am . . ."

"Surrounded by people who love you," she finished for him.

Yes, he thought. That was so true.

With a sense of feeling lucky, he put his bare feet on the tile and stood up. The next thing he knew, Jane was pulling a set of scrubs on him, top first, then the bottoms. He was stiff as he started for the way out, and his mate was right beside him, his arm looping across her shoulders so that she took some of his weight.

When she opened the door, he was hit with the characteristic smell of the training center: part cement, part shampoos and conditioners from the showers by the weight room, plus a whiff of far-off chlorine from the pool and a tinge of gunpowder from the shooting range.

The whole of it was beyond pleasant to breathe in.

It was . . . home.

As they started off at a slow rate, it was the best walk of his life, the pair of them bumping hips and shuffling along—well, he was the one doing the shuffling, Jane was strong as ever as she led him down to the office.

There was still nothing in his mind as they entered the underground tunnel. Continuing along, their pace stayed at a stroll, like they were in a city park, on a sunny day in the fall, just another pair of lovers perfectly in tune with each other. From time to time, he leaned over and kissed her forehead. Just 'cuz he wanted to. And halfway to the Pit, she reached over and entwined her fingers through his dangling dagger hand.

"I want to feel like this forever," he murmured.

"How's that?"

"At peace." He kissed her above her brows again. "And grateful."

Unfortunately, this rare feeling of relaxation wasn't going to last. As powerful as it was, it was also fragile, incapable of surviving the punches of the real world. He was going to get maybe twelve hours like this—no more than that, though. Sooner than later, the texts would come from the field, and the IT shit in the household would resume, and then other crap would fall on his head. Gradually, the tension would seep back in, tightening the nape of his neck, stiffening his spine, shortening his temper. And then later, much later, something big-ish would happen. Like Butch running into his old partner again, or Wrath wanting to engage something other than a civilian at the Audience House, or fuck all only knew what.

And then he would be where he had been.

But as for now . . .

Even the prospect of returning to his touchy normal was nothing but a figment floating off on the periphery, not anything he had to worry about at the moment, just something he accepted as inevitable, but wasn't going to dwell on.

When they came to the door to go up to the Pit, Jane punched in the code. The short stack of steps was rough on him, and he needed the little balustrade as well as Jane's steady hand. Not that his reliance on either bothered him. And then he was cresting the rise and stepping into the shallow hall that ran between the bedrooms.

His and Jane's. Butch and Marissa's.

"V?"

The male voice down in the living area was yet another balm to his soul.

Jane rose up on her tiptoes and kissed him on the mouth. "You go hang for a bit, I'm heading to bed."

"You worked hard tonight."

"So did you."

They smiled for a while. Then they kissed again, and said *I love you* without speaking a word: All it took was the eye contact—and yup, V was totally looking forward to coming down to their bedroom and easing between the sheets to find his *shellan*'s warm body.

But first, his roommate.

Limping down to the open area in front of the carriage house, he supposed he wanted to check to make sure everything was cool. Not because Butch didn't know what V liked—hell, the cop had dipped his toe in those waters just before Jane came into the picture. But because . . . well, because.

V found the former cop on the leather couch, a Lagavulin in one hand, the Roku remote in the other, the TV shimmering with blue light in front of him. Butch was angled forward, one foot still on the coffee table, as if he had been aimlessly flipping through channels in a recline and had just sat up.

"Hey?" the guy said as he looked over.

"Hey. So . . ."

"Yeah."

"Really?"

Butch nodded. "Mm-hm."

Just as V and Jane had shared a whole conversation in a glance, now he and Butch were talking in silence, too. All it took was that exchange of single syllables, ending in a proverbial doubleheader.

Hm'er, as was the case.

Butch had never been totally comfortable with what V needed from time to time. Jane, on the other hand, had become not only very comfortable, but also very damned good at going there with him.

Jesus, he loved that female.

But his roommate had always accepted him. Without any reservations.

And that was a kind of true love, wasn't it.

As V went over to sit in the sofa's other corner, he mostly kept the wincing to himself as his butt made contact with the cushions and accepted his weight. And then he let his head fall back against the padded rise behind his shoulders. After a nice, long siiiiiiiiigh, he put one, and then the other, of his bare feet up next to the cop's. Beside him, Butch resumed his own sprawl.

While the TV continued to drone on, V focused on the images, the sound, the—

"*Mystic Pizza?*" he said.

"Whatever. It's wicked classic."

Vishous chuckled. And then they just sat there and watched Julia Roberts dump an entire load of manure into an old school Porsche.

"Man, I bet they never got the smell out of that car," Butch murmured. "I mean, vacuuming only goes so far."

"You don't need an air freshener for a job like that. You need a lake to sink the bitch in."

From out of the corner of his eye, V saw Butch's arm flop onto the vacant cushion between them, the palm of his dagger hand laying flat.

Vishous's own arm moved.

And as he laid his leather-gloved hand on his roommate's bare one, the grip that held him was firm. Strong.

As permanent as anything mortal could be.

"You'll always be the number one asshole in my life," Butch said in a soft voice.

In any other circumstance, at any other time, V would have brushed the comment off. Instead, he squeezed hard.

Even in his post-session float, he couldn't explain how important that reassurance was to him—and how special it was to be accepted for who he was by not only his mate, but his best friend and Marissa. As extreme as he needed to get every once in a while, it was a blessing to be embraced without exception . . . loved.

"And you will always be my roommate," V murmured.

"We still ain't datin'."

Vishous laughed and rubbed his thumb back and forth over his eyebrow. "No, we ain't."

They continued to hold hands, and watch the movie, and sit side by side. It was so comfortable and simple; it was like they had done this all their lives. And the good news, V knew, was that they would be doing it . . .

. . . for the rest of their lives.

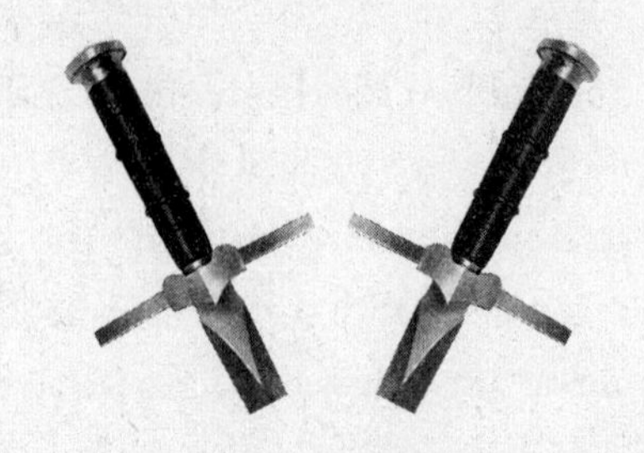

CHAPTER TWENTY-FIVE

As Rio went to get out of the bed, she was aware that she had a couple of different purposes for going vertical: She needed to go to the bathroom again—that was pretty clear—but there were other reasons to get up and move around, most of which were tied to the sense that she was running out of time. Luke had to know that she was a liability if she stuck around.

He was going to have to get her out of here.

So she had to learn what she could about the building, the operation, the people before she left.

Therefore, it was by force of will rather than actual strength that she got up on her feet and walked by the empty beds. When she arrived at the curtains that hung from the ceiling, she hesitated.

"Hello," said a hoarse voice from inside the draping.

She cleared her throat. "Hi."

When there was nothing else from the other patient, she glanced over her shoulder to the door that led into that long hall with the light bulbs. "Do you need anything?"

As if she could find something other than trouble in this place she did not know and did not belong in?

"No. Thank you."

Such a rasp. The kind that meant death was prowling around his bedsprings.

"What are you doing," the patient said. "Here."

She found herself wanting to answer him. Maybe it was the veil that separated them—and not the one that was hanging in front of her face. The man on the other side was not long for the world, whereas she had just come through her trials to survive once again.

At least she assumed she was going to get herself out of all of this alive.

"I don't know," she murmured. "What I'm doing here."

"You don't belong."

"No, I don't." Rio snapped out of the thrall she could feel herself falling into. "I'm just visiting."

"People do not visit here."

"I . . . I have to go."

When there was only silence, she turned away. Stumbled away. As she got to the door, she fumbled to open it.

Rio gasped and jumped back.

Out in the hall, sitting with his arms on his bent knees and his forehead on his arms, Luke was like a sentry who had fallen asleep at his post—

He came instantly to attention.

"Hi," she said. Then she lifted her hand. Like that would explain something . . . that didn't have her using him to get information that would put him in jail.

Although why should she care about double-crossing a criminal?

"Leaving so soon?" He stretched his arms over his head and rolled his heavy chest out. "The accommodations not working for you?"

"Actually, that bed is not bad at all."

"How's your concussion?"

"Better. Any idea what time it is?"

"I can't take you back to Caldwell yet. It's still light out." As she frowned, he shrugged. "We're discreet in these parts, what can I say. And I'd think you'd also want to keep your head down."

"All things considered, I think we can both agree I haven't been taking very good care of my noggin lately. If I were a supervisor, I'd be fired for negligence by now."

He actually smiled a little at that.

Rio went across and sat down next to him. As she put her knees to her chest, she didn't want to mirror his position so she rerouted her legs, stretching them out in front of herself.

"So how much do you know about concussions?" she asked.

"They hurt, but you can sleep 'em off. And I'd say you're following that medical advice nicely."

"Trying to, at least. But yeah . . . did you know they can cause personality changes."

"Really? Like what—wait, is this where you make an excuse for being bitchy after I saved you. Three times?"

"Oh, my God, you read minds." She pulled back a little and put her hands over her heart. "Or you're just really intuitive. P.S., is this working?"

His eyes returned to her and she could tell by his tight lips that he was trying not to smile. "Three is not my favorite number, you know."

"Why not?"

"It's not divisible by anything but itself and one."

"So you're an even man."

"I am."

Rio fiddled with the loose shirt she was wearing. In the back of her mind, she realized that she *still* had on the one that had been cut—and a claw of remembered terror came back.

But she had no time for that kind of stuff.

"You didn't answer my question," she murmured.

"Was there one?"

"Is my charm offensive working?"

Luke looked down the hall. Both ways. "I'm lying out here like a guard dog, aren't I? And that was even before you started this non-apology strategy."

"Non-apology? Come on, I have head trauma. Cut me some slack."

"Apologies generally include the word 'sorry.'"

"I knew I forgot something." She cleared her throat. "I'm sorry that I was rude."

"You're forgiven."

"Great. And does this mean, provided I lose the attitude, you might be willing to save me again?" She put her hand out. "Not that I'm looking to find myself in danger again or to be rescued by anyone but myself."

He laughed a little. "You know, that last one does not surprise me in the slightest."

"I'm an independent woman—"

"I know. For example, you didn't realize I was out here and you were ready to leave on your own."

"No, I didn't know where you were exactly, but I was very aware you were still"—she motioned around—"in the vicinity of where this is. And I wanted to go to the bathroom."

After a moment, he nodded. "Okay."

Well, crap, she thought. Neither one of them could truly trust the other.

And then she realized the silence had gotten stony. "So what can I do to pay you back for saving me?"

✦ ✦ ✦

Lucan blinked at where his mind went as Rio tossed out that inquiry. Then he glanced up and down the corridor again because he had to do something with his eyes that did not involve her lips.

"Nothing. Protection's a free service offered to females who are tough as nails."

"That's gallant of you."

"Not really. It's because I'm lazy and self-interested. If you're a hard-ass, I don't have to be a hero that often. Damsels in distress are a fuck ton of work."

Rio laughed softly. "I can respect that logic. We're in a dangerous business, aren't we. Self-protection always has to come first. So, let's start as we mean to go on, and say three time's a charm and you won't have to do the rescue stuff with me again."

"Deal."

He extended his hand, and as she clasped his palm, there was a strange look in her eyes. And he felt it, too. That sexual charge.

"So," she said as she retracted herself from the contact. "Any-who . . ."

"You want a shower while you use the bathroom? It's safe right now."

Her stare returned to his. "It is?"

"Well, -er. It's safe-*er*." He nodded to the bathroom. "I wish I could get you some fresh clothes, but all I have to offer is running water."

"That's okay." Her lids closed and her head fell back a little. "A shower would be amazing."

Lucan got up first, and when he put his hand down to her, he knew he wasn't being chivalrous. He wanted to know if—

Yup, there it was again. As she grabbed on to what he offered, the heat he'd felt on that shake went up his arm, through his chest—and right down into his cock.

Fuck.

Ordinarily, he was not the kind of wolf to turn down any opportunity to mate. With Rio, though, he held back—and told himself it was because she was a complication he didn't need, a human in the midst of vampires.

Not because he was doing a protection number on himself.

Stepping ahead, he opened the door to the bathroom. "I promise not to look."

"Like I told you, I'm not shy."

She said that as she walked by him. All casual. Like what was under her clothes was no big deal—even though he could confidently say it was all he'd been thinking about since he'd sat his ass down on the cold concrete outside of where she'd been sleeping.

Lucan glanced at his watch. It was ten in the morning. One good thing about vampires was they did hibernate in the daytime. No one was going to be around for at least another six hours. Hell, even the guards slept at their stations up above, far from this hidden corner within the rabbit warren of subterranean spaces.

Slipping into the loo, he pushed the door closed and locked it. He had the gun the Executioner didn't know he'd picked up downtown tucked into the small of his back—he had to check the one he was given in and out each night, so this other nine millimeter was a major find.

But he didn't like the fact that there was no escape in here.

He glanced up and saw a large grate in the ceiling.

Scratch that.

There was not a *great* escape. A grate one, though, definitely existed.

"I'll sit here," he murmured as he went over, put the seat down, and parked it on the toilet.

He turned and faced the wall, and tried not to picture what she was doing as he heard the water begin to fall. She would start with the shirt, he imagined, the loose one he had found in the back of the car he'd stolen and put on her. He'd had a choice between that and a Domino's polo that was stained with sauce, like the guy who either had owned the car or stolen it had worked there.

And she was taking it off.

"Am I losing my mind, or is this hot water?" she said.

Lucan smiled to himself. "It's hot."

"How?"

"Gas line into hot water heaters."

"I'm just curious, but what is this place? A school that closed down or something?"

"Something like that." And then he changed the subject. "I'm not going to do anything inappropriate, you know. Just thought I'd throw that out there."

"Do you think I'd be locked in here with you if I thought there'd be a problem?"

Her voice was easy and calm, and he wasn't sure whether she was so confident because she had a better opinion of him than she should or because she was very capable of handling herself. More likely the latter.

Had she taken the cut t-shirt off? That fleece? God . . . if he hadn't come into that apartment when he had? Well, that just didn't bear thinking of, did it.

Lucan knew she'd gotten under the water when she sighed and the pattern of rain was interrupted. And he really tried not to imagine what she looked like, naked, glistening . . . soap dripping off her—

They didn't have any soap, he realized. No, wait. They did.

Leaning to the side, he took a bar off a divot in the sink's shoulder and held it out straight without turning his head. "Couldn't tell you what kind this is, but it'll have to do."

"Thanks. I'm not picky."

As she took the bar from him, his peripheral vision picked up on all kinds of skin, gorgeous skin. And even still, as he re-angled himself so he was staring at the wall by the toilet at a point-blank range, he had an impression of what her spine looked like as it plugged into her—

"This isn't half bad," she said with a sigh.

Actually, it was. He shouldn't be thinking about things involving . . .

"Will you relax," she said through the spray. "You would have done something already, if you were going to—and besides, I'm not that special."

"Huh?" He went to look at her and stopped himself. "What did you say, I mean."

"That's why I'm not worried about being in here with you. You had your chances to be a problem—and I was out of it, too. And besides, I'm not a beauty queen. I'm just a woman."

Lucan didn't respond to that. How could he tell her that she was so much more than special—

Wait, what was he thinking here?

"How did you end up in the business?" he blurted. So he could get out of his own head.

"How did you," she countered as the smell of cedar bloomed in the humid air.

"Touché."

The sound of the water was variable, and he imagined she was running that bar over herself. He'd never particularly loved any kind of soap, but he could get used to the smell of this particular bar in his nose.

"I was drafted into the business," he muttered.

"How? By who?"

"Long story. Now it's your turn."

"What, like this is strip poker, but without the cards and the clothes?" There was a pause. Then she laughed. "Guess I already lost part of that one. The strip part, that is."

"You're avoiding the question."

After a moment, she said, "I don't know. Everyone has to be somewhere doing something."

There was resignation in her voice. And as the water was cut off, the dripping was loud.

"Here," he said as he pulled his sweatshirt off. "Use this as a towel."

"Oh, you don't have to—"

Lucan stretched his arm out again. And when she took what he offered, he realized he'd just screwed himself.

Her scent was going to be on the sweatshirt, and he couldn't afford to have that smell in anyone else's nose. To vampires, humans were easy to pick up on—and the other species was most definitely unwelcome in the prison camp.

Plus the Executioner liked fresh meat for his trophy wall.

"Let's get you back in bed," he heard himself say. "Quickly."

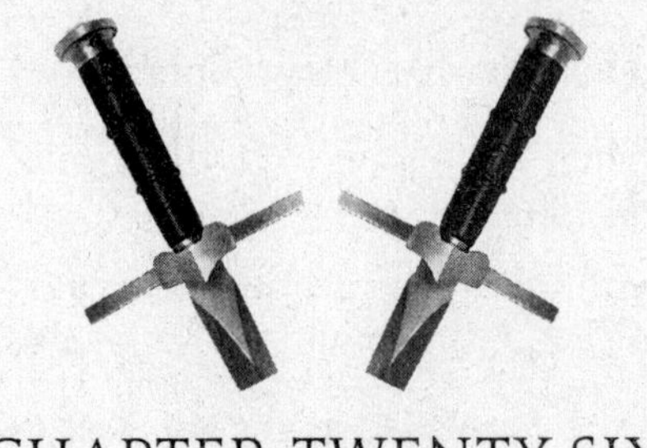

CHAPTER TWENTY-SIX

José went back to the trap house as soon as he'd logged enough sleep to be competent to drive without endangering public safety. As his unmarked rolled to a stop, he looked through the foggy car window at the facade of the walk-up. It was so cold that his breath and his hot coffee had sweated everything up, but he couldn't say that he needed a big visual refresher course on what the place looked like.

He'd been staring at it in his mind all night while he hadn't been sleeping.

Opening his door, he got out. The air was straight-up November, about thirty-five degrees, with a bite of humidity that in a month would mean snow was coming. As it was, there was a drizzle hovering just below the cloud cover. He didn't think it was going to turn into a full-on rain, but what the hell did he know.

As he walked across the road, he stopped in the middle and looked down. A compelling sense of loss made it impossible to keep going, and as that headache from the night before came back with a vengeance, he decided it was a good goddamn thing he was retiring.

He was wearing out, the chassis of focus and determination that he'd built his professional life on top of now rickety and unreliable from mental fatigue.

Cursing, he started up with the footwork again, and as he came to the walk-up's door, he slipped a Rolaids into his mouth. Maybe if he could take some time off and eat better, he'd be able to quit the chalky savior stuff.

Although to be fair, he had sucked back a lot of leftovers at two a.m. last night because he'd had so much to think about. That undercover cop had still not shown up, checked in, or been found, alive or dead. But at least his buddy in CSI had done a great job at Officer Hernandez-Guerrero's place and documented everything like it was a crime scene.

Because he knew in his gut it was one.

Nothing much to go on, yet. The bloodstains were likely the missing officer's, and the fingerprints had been hers and hers alone. Although maybe something would turn up. All downtown patrols last night had been on the lookout. They still were. And they would be until they found . . . whatever they did.

With a yank, he pulled things open—

"What the *fuck*."

As his eyes focused on the trail of blood down the stairs, his nose got filled with a crap ton of not-right. The smell was sickeningly sweet and totally overpowering, to the point where he recoiled.

Recovering fast—like he wasn't used to bad stenches?—he took some booties out of the pocket of his sports coat and slipped them over his shoes. Then he snapped on two gloves. Stepping up to the blood, he looked down the hallway to the back entrance. He guessed whoever had been leaking badly had headed out that way—because why would you come to a place like this if you needed medical help?

José got his phone and put in a call to dispatch as he walked down the corridor, making sure he didn't step in anything.

Dispatch answered as he opened the back door and leaned out. "This is de la Cruz." He gave his badge number. "I need backup."

Nothing unusual in the shallow parking lot other than a couch that had seen way better days, a broken TV, and some typical city litter. No body. No severely wounded person down on their face on the pavement.

As he gave the address, he walked out a little. The blood trail continued off to the left so he followed it to an abrupt end point off to the side of the alley. Like whoever had been leaking plasma had gotten into a car and driven away.

Ending the call with dispatch, he went back to the rear entry and retraced his path to the base of the stairs. Taking out his pocket light, he shined it on the steps and followed the trail up to the second floor. The third floor. When he came to the fourth—

Over to the left, the door that he'd knocked on the night before was open . . . and the blood went inside the apartment. Or came out of it, was more likely.

Palming up his service weapon, he closed in, and sure enough, his business card had fallen to the floor. Someone had stepped on it and left a partial bloody shoe print—

As the beam flashed inside, he saw the pool of blood immediately. It was off to one corner.

"Detective José de la Cruz, Caldwell Police."

In his gut, he knew announcing his presence was a waste of time. And when there was no response, he swept his weapon around in a coordinated movement—which was when he saw the stakes that had been driven into the floorboards. There was nylon rope tangled around each, like someone had been tied to them, and there was a major disturbance in the dust.

Evidence of thrashing.

He thought of the missing officer.

"Jesus H. Christ," he muttered.

Out to the back of the flat, he caught sight of a rotted kitchen. To the front, there were some rooms, at least one of which was a bedroom, going by the stained bare mattress on the floor.

Moving carefully and choosing his foot placement so he didn't compromise the scene, he went past the bleed-out and peered into the other spaces. Blackout drapes covered the shitty windows, as they did throughout the place. Nothing was on the bed, on the floor . . . other than some errant trash that, like everything else, had a layer of dust on it.

José went back out to the main room, to the stakes. Lowering down onto his haunches, he inspected the frayed nylon around one of the wooden stabs.

It was bloody.

As his cell phone went off, he checked the screen and answered quick. "Treyvon, I was about to call you—"

The other detective cut him off. "They found undercover officer Leon Roberts in the river. 'Bout an hour ago."

José frowned. "Leon?"

"Guess my source was wrong. It was a male officer missing."

No, José thought. *It meant there were two of them.*

"I know Leon. He was a good kid." Who was Trey's age, actually. "I mean, young man. Man. He came up through third district patrol like I did. I met him a couple of times."

"You remember everyone." There was a sad note to Trey's voice. "He was in my class at the academy. He was floating facedown . . . got caught in a residential dock. Owner called it in and the ID was made by one of the first responders who played against him in softball on Saturdays."

Closing his eyes, José swept his face with his palm. "Dammit. How'd he die?"

"Gunshot to the back of his head. Very professional. Unlikely there'll be water in his lungs." There was a pause. "Look, he's not married, but I know his parents are still alive. I was thinking maybe you as a senior representative of the department could—"

"Yup, I'm on it." José glanced at the blood on the stake. "But I can't leave my location until other officers get here."

"Where are you?"

"It's your day off."

There was a rustling, as if the guy were pulling on clothes. "Address, please."

Shaking his head, José looked to the ceiling. And then said with resignation, "Right where you left me last night, just one floor down. Watch the blood as you come up the stairs."

Things on the other end of the connection got quiet. "There was no blood on the—"

"There is now. We have another scene. I just called it in—and I think you should stay home with your wife and kids, but you won't. So do me a favor."

"Anything."

José took a deep breath—and rubbed his nose. The weird sweet smell was enough to make him rethink his pending request. But then his stomach growled anyway, a sign he was in the right profession, he supposed.

At least for the next month.

"Bring me coffee and donuts. I forgot to eat when I left. Thanks," he said before he ended the call.

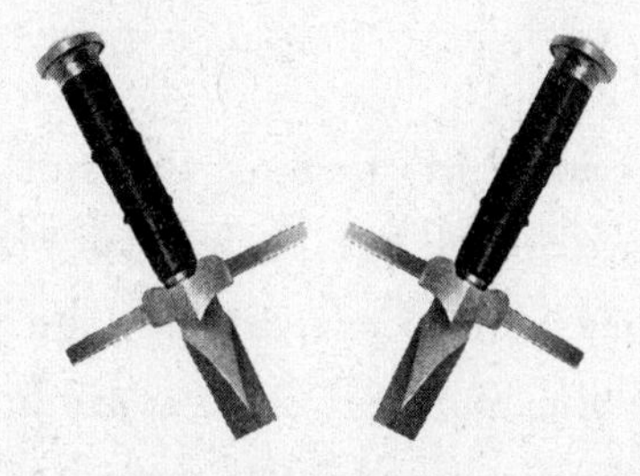

CHAPTER TWENTY-SEVEN

There was hot water, yes. But no heat.

When Rio's showering was done and she'd turned off the spray, she was surprised at how quickly the temperature dropped. Yes, there was warmth and humidity in the bathroom's tiled confines, but not enough. The only solution she had was getting dry and clothed. Too bad she didn't have a—

"Here, use this as a towel," Luke said.

Crossing her arms over her bare breasts, she looked at him . . . and caught her breath. He was turned away, facing the wall, the sweatshirt held out blindly toward her.

He was also bare chested, the muscles of his torso fanning out along his shoulders, across his back, around his ribs.

"Thank you," she said roughly.

Taking what he offered, she put his sweatshirt to work, aware that as she passed it over her skin, that cologne of his was getting all over her. And she liked it. Liked the smell of it, but liked even more the fact that it was his.

"Let's get you back in bed," he said. "Quickly."

"Okay. Thanks."

She folded the sweatshirt, turning the soft cotton over in her hands . . . and then she dried off her wet hair with it. For some reason, as her breasts swayed, they felt heavier—and hey, she wasn't thinking about the cold anymore, was she. Suddenly, she was as hot as the tropics.

Before she got way ahead of herself—too late—she set her make-shift towel on the side of the sink and put her clothes back on. As she drew her pants up her legs, she remembered when she had put them on.

A lifetime ago.

Meanwhile, Luke was still facing away from her, but had changed his position. His elbow was now plugged into his knee, his chin on his fist, that muscular back of his curved thanks to his height. His pose made her remember a picture she had seen in an art history book of that old sculpture, *The Thinker*.

And then she didn't really think of anything.

She had known he was big and strong. She had felt that when she'd been carried by him. But she hadn't expected him to be so—

"Here's your sweatshirt back," she said as she picked it up again.

Put it on, she thought. *Please.*

And not because he was ugly. Because he was so much the opposite of ugly.

"Don't worry, I'm decent," she muttered.

As he turned to her, his eyes stayed on her face. Like she was still naked.

"Thanks." He took the damp fold. "You ready to go back?"

She should have glanced away as he dressed—what was good for the goose and the gander, or . . . how did that saying go?—but she didn't. She watched as he straightened on the toilet seat and pulled on what she had just had all over her naked body.

And when he couldn't see her for that brief moment, she reeaaaaally watched him. His pecs and abs were worth the look, flexing as he went through the bog-standard movements of putting on clothes, turning the simple work into something . . . spectacular.

Smoke show, she thought stupidly. *That was the vernacular, wasn't it?*

Luke got up on his feet. "Feel better?"

Well, she was not cold in the slightest anymore. And she wasn't thinking about all her aches and pains, either.

"Yes, I am. Feeling better, that is."

"I can't get you food quite yet. I thought I could, but it's too dangerous. Everything's shut down here until just after dark, so there are restricted areas I can't get near without causing a problem." He shrugged. "But as soon as the light is gone in the sky, I'll take you back to Caldwell, and we can stop somewhere on the way."

So they *were* out of town. "We don't have to rush. Remember the situation you found me in? I need a little time to figure out where I can go that is safe. Who I can talk to. What . . . I'm going to do. How long can I stay here?"

Luke crossed his arms over his chest. "You can't stay here, but there's another place we can go. For a limited period of time."

Rio frowned. "Where I was when the nurse first came to me. In that basement with the fabric."

"Yeah, you'll be safe there. For one night. Maybe two—but it's not a permanent solution."

"It doesn't have to be. And thanks . . . I owe you."

There was a moment of silence—and in her head, for some insane reason, she saw herself hugging him; pictured the embrace so clearly, she could almost feel the warmth of his body against her own.

"Come on, back to bed," he said in a low, resonant voice.

Like maybe he had gone there in his head, too.

In response, all she could do was nod—and follow him out into the corridor. As she was behind him, she felt free to look around, but she didn't learn anything new. Still just a long, rough hallway with bulbs hanging from wires. No one around, no sounds that she could hear other than their footfalls.

When they were back inside the clinic area, she whispered, "Who is that patient?"

Her question was ignored as they passed by the hanging sheets, and then they were over to the bed she'd been in and he was offering her an arm to steady her balance as she lowered herself down. The incense had burned out, and he got some more from a drawer and lit it.

Pulling the blankets around her, she remembered back in the days when she was little and she'd had a cold. Her mother had been so good at taking care of her: Unlimited TV, bowls of ice cream to soothe a burning throat, anything she wanted to eat at any moment, cold compresses for a hot forehead. Under normal circumstances, things had been totally regimented in the household, all kinds of schedules of chores and homework, all expectations to be exceeded, or at worst merely met, failure never an option.

Her mom had been a whip-and-a-chair kind of parent, taming her two kids into virtuous human beings who went to church, did the rosary on the regular, and never talked back.

It had not been easy growing up in such an unforgiving way.

But one set of the sniffles and a slightly elevated temperature? The whole house of demanding cards went into a free fall.

Total pampering.

Sometimes, usually after grades came out and Rio got a shellacking and a half for the two Bs she always got (math and Spanish), she would deliberately go out and get a chill or head over to a friend's house if they'd missed some school in the previous week because of a flu.

She had needed the reassurance, the comfort, even if it had been unconnected to the offense of her not being perfect.

"Are you okay?" Luke asked.

So quiet. Just her breathing and the soft crackle of the incense getting started.

"I didn't see my life," she whispered. "When I knew he was going to kill me. I thought . . . I was supposed to see my life, you know?"

Luke stood over her, looming and silent. Then he said, "That's because you're a survivor. Survivors like us, we stay in the present."

"Everyone says you see your life. Right before you die."

"And how many dead people you talk to lately?"

Rio blinked. And then smiled. "Good point. And I guess I wasn't *dying*. Maybe that's when it happens."

Luke winced. Then looked away. Looked back. "Move over a little."

She stared up at him in confusion. "What?"

"You need someone right now. I'm not much, but I don't see that you have any other options."

Actually . . . he was wrong. He was more than enough—and that made her nervous. "Okay," she said.

Rio groaned as she pushed her body over, and then the mattress, such as it was, tilted to one side—and Luke had stretched out next to her.

Before she could form a coherent thought, she cleaved to his big, warm body, curling against him. With a quick shift, he settled her head on his arm.

"I can hear your heart beat," she murmured.

"So I have one. Good to know."

"Where do you get your cologne?"

"Cologne? I don't wear any."

Guess it was fabric softener, she thought as she wondered where he did his laundry.

Her eyes drifted around the room, casing the empty beds, the boxes and supplies, the draping around the other patient. From time to time, there were clunks deep in the inside of the building, the low percussive noises like the settling of cold in metal supports or air going through old pipes.

"I really am thankful you came when you did," she whispered. "I wasn't going to make it without you."

There was a period of silence, and then the rumble of Luke's voice reverberated up out of his rib cage and into her ear. Into her mind. Into her . . . soul.

"He deserved what he got," he growled.

Rio propped her head up on Luke's pec. His chin was so near and his lips were so . . . full. Above his cheeks, his eyes were closed, and his lashes were long and thick. He looked remarkably at peace considering how aggressive his voice was.

"Do you shave twelve times a day?" she murmured.

Those lips twitched in one corner. "Mind if I ask where that came from?"

Bringing her arm up, she touched his jaw with her forefinger, brushing it softly. "So smooth. I've never met a man with dark hair who didn't have a five o'clock."

"How many men have you met and gotten close enough to, to see their beard?"

"Five o'clock shadows are not state secrets."

"Sorry, did that come out bad?"

"Depends on your definition of bad. You sounded jealous."

There was another pause. And then those lashes lifted, revealing glowing golden eyes that were so brilliant and hot, they were like the sun itself.

He focused on her. "Maybe I am."

✦ ✦ ✦

Lucan had spent a lot of years not giving a shit about anything or anybody, including himself. Being in prison for your mere existence kind of turned you into a dissociative sonofabitch—assuming it didn't make you a confirmed misanthrope.

Mis-lycan-thrope, in his case.

So it was kind of . . . surprising, in a fuck-me sort of way . . . that he found himself wanting to reassure this human woman.

And do other things to her.

"Is that a problem," he asked. Even though he knew he wasn't telling her the full truth about himself. Any truth, really.

But he was sure she had secrets of her own, and that was the nature of the drug trade. You took people at face value and protected yourself. It was a rule so fundamental, it didn't have to be spoken.

Survivors, both of them. And as he'd said, that meant you stayed in the present. On every level.

"No," she whispered. "It's not a problem."

Lucan closed his eyes because he didn't want her to see into him and find out how aroused he was. Where his thoughts had gone. Where his hands wanted to go.

She moved up higher on his torso. "You want me to prove it?"

"Prove what?"

He lifted his lids again. She was so close now, he could see the flecks in her brown eyes.

"That it's okay if you're jealous?" she murmured.

"Does it involve my mouth?"

"What makes you ask that?"

"The way you're staring at my lips right now." He reached up and brushed her damp hair back. "So do you want to do something about this? Or ignore it. It's your choice."

"If I understand what you're talking about, it's a two-sided thing. You also get to choose."

His eyes locked on her mouth. "Oh, I've already made my decision."

There was a pause. Then Rio moved up a little higher on his chest. As she lowered her head to kiss him, she closed her eyes, and he liked that. It was as if she wanted to concentrate everything she had on the contact.

Lucan did the same, his lids shutting.

He expected her to be bold. She wasn't—but she wasn't timid, either. Her mouth brushed over his, and he relished the sensation, the velvet, the warmth. Except he was a greedy asshole. They might be only kissing, but in his mind, they were naked and he was mounting her, finding his way in between her thighs until—

The sound was far off, a banging noise. A door slamming? Then there were footfalls coming fast.

Rio's head lifted, and they both looked across the cluttered storage room.

"There's a gun under the bed," he told her. "Stay here by the incense. Do *not* leave this mattress."

Lucan moved quickly, rolling her free of him and then covering her up. He took two steps forward and doubled back.

Kissing her quick, he vowed, "We're going to pick up where we left off. Sometime before I take you back."

She started to say something, but he took off before she could speak, pausing only by a stack of folded clothes to pull on a fresh sweat-shirt. At the door into the corridor, he listened before opening things up, braced to attack. Then he swung the heavy panel open.

Out in the hall . . . there was a rhythmic pounding, and the shit was getting louder.

Stepping out, he closed the storage room's door behind him—

Mayhem rounded the corner at a run. "You've got problems," the prisoner said as he came to a halt.

You have no idea, Lucan thought.

"The Executioner's been looking for you since dawn. It took me this long to break away without being trailed."

"Why? I checked in. I returned my weapon."

"I don't know what the problem is, but you better show your face before the guards make a serious effort to find you."

"All right. Let's go."

The two of them jogged away, heading for the corner Mayhem had bolted around.

When they'd taken the left, Lucan grabbed the other male's arm. "You better go your separate way now."

"Fuck that. There might be a reward. Besides, if I turn you in, I don't look like I'm with you. It's self-preservation—and a good decoy for you in case things get complicated with your little secret."

"Excellent point."

They continued on, making fast work of the ins and outs of the basement. It had taken Lucan about three weeks on-site before he knew the way around the multi-layered underground. So many wide lanes and smaller offshoots, with all kinds of rooms and larger spaces. The architect who'd designed the building had clearly known that there were things that had to be hidden, truths that compassionate healers did not want their vulnerable patients to know.

Like the fact that three morgues had been required to handle the number of dead who'd apparently needed processing.

Down at the very far end of the basement, he and Mayhem got to a fire door that was brand-new, and punching through, they went up two flights of stairs. Without saying a word, they both passed in front of another fire barrier.

There were three subterranean levels, and this middle one was where the prisoners bunked. Above that? Party time.

On Lucan's nod, they ascended another two flights, and stopped again.

"You ready?" Lucan said.

"Born ready, wolven."

On the far side of another fresh-as-a-daisy fire door, Lucan smelled the cocaine in the air, dry and tingling, like it was radioactive fallout in the nose and down the back of the throat.

This was the business level, where the processing happened behind doors that were locked with copper and guarded with guns. At the moment, however, there was nothing getting cut, weighed, and parceled out into packets in the workrooms, the prisoners still in their sleep cubicles, all checked in. After nightfall, they'd be woken up, fed, and forced to come up here to work the job they were being kept alive to do.

Sadly, this building really was perfect for what they needed. The Command, now dead, had had it all planned out, but had been killed just as the move from the old location was happening.

Which was how the Executioner had declared himself ruler of the prison camp.

On that note, Lucan started walking past the product rooms, toward a wall of fresh Sheetrock about twenty feet across and ten feet tall. The expanse was both new—and stained: All along its flat plane, there were pegs set at intervals, with greasy straps that hung loose and ready for further service. Behind the beating posts, that Sheetrock had soaked in the blood that had flowed—and you could smell it, too. The whole area was air-stained with both the plasma bouquet of torture and the new-built-house perfume of chalk and sweet pine.

As they closed in on the Executioner's private quarters, the pair of guards on either side of the inset door palmed up their guns.

Unlike during the Command's era, they were members of a private guard, hired to maintain order—as opposed to culled from the prison population.

"I'll let him know you found him," the one on the left said.

The steel door set into the Sheetrock opened and closed.

"You can go," Lucan muttered to Mayhem. "I'll make sure you get your reward—"

He caught the scent first, and it was the kind of thing that made the nape of his neck prickle.

Letting his head fall back, he breathed in deep. And then a howl started to curl in his gut and rise up out of his throat.

The sound of his people was cut off as the recessed steel door opened once again.

The black-clothed figure that emerged had a bald head and narrow, calculating eyes. And the male was carrying something in his arms, something that was large and furred—and limp as a rug rolled up in itself.

The head and forepaws dangled off to one side, the back paws and tail to the other.

The Executioner threw the dead wolf at Lucan's feet.

"I believe this is one of yours," he announced.

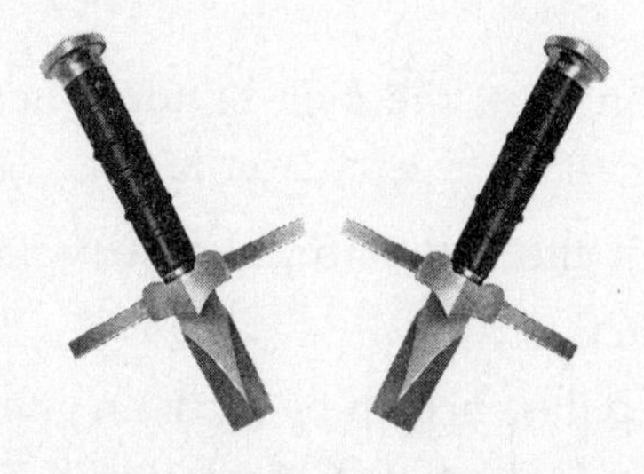

CHAPTER TWENTY-EIGHT

When the door to the makeshift clinic area opened, Rio sat up. "Luke—"

The man who stepped inside was not him. And the way that harsh face snapped in her direction . . . made her wish that she had pretended to be asleep. She didn't need to know him for it to be clear that being alone with someone like this should come with a Surgeon General's warning.

As his eyes narrowed, he took a step toward her and his upper lip peeled off his front teeth.

Which exposed tremendous teeth, teeth that surely had been cosmetically—

Rio scrambled to remember where Luke had told her that gun was. Under the bed. It was under the bed.

She lunged forward, diving under the mattress—

In some kind of *Matrix*-like time bend, the man somehow managed to cross the entire room in the blink of an eye: Just as she felt the cool barrel under her hand, a rough grip locked on the back of her head, right where she'd been hurt, the pain blinding her and rendering her limp and paralyzed.

As her vision went checkerboard, she had a split second's clear sight of the nine millimeter.

Rio cursed as he pulled her up by the hair, grabbed her around the throat, and hauled her bodily off the bed until her feet dangled. Slamming her against the wall, he put his face directly into hers and smiled like a demon.

Fangs. He had fangs.

Or rather, they looked like fangs.

"Fucking Lucan," he snapped while she began to choke and claw at his hold. "He's complicating shit he needs to leave well enough alone. So I'm going to take care of you for him—"

"Stop."

The word was spoken so softly, Rio could barely hear it above the ringing in her ears. But the man who was aggressing on her, with those canine-like teeth, whipped his head in the direction of the draped patient bed.

"Let her . . . go."

The voice was so weak, yet its effect was like that of a shotgun to the man's temple. As those hostile eyes seemed to pierce the fragile barrier strung from the ceiling, his whole body went as immobile as hers felt.

"Now."

Her manhandler cursed. And then he—

"Gently." There was a pause. "No matter her origins, she is a patient, as I am."

Rio's feet touched down toes first. Then the balls and arches made contact with the floor, and finally, her soles. After that, the man with all the teeth took her arm and settled her back down on the bed—and he didn't let go until she could hold herself up while she gasped for air.

When she was steady, he turned away and went over to the curtains, pulling a flap aside and disappearing into the interior.

Even though she was still getting her breath back, Rio snapped into action, falling to the floor and grabbing the gun under the bed. Her hands were shaking—until she saw how much the weapon was moving back and forth.

A quick shot of self-preservation stilled things. Calmed her down. Cleared the panic from her head.

With a tingling adrenaline rush, she rose to her feet, braced and ready to bolt.

Nothing but murmuring now, from that hidden bed: Two voices, deep and low . . . were having an argument, like the one who'd gone Popeye on her was getting reprimanded.

"What the hell," she muttered.

The boots she'd had on were right next to her on the floor, and she put them on one-handed, keeping the butt of the gun in her palm. As she futzed with the laces, she kept checking the curtain over and over again, bobbing her now-throbbing head up and down.

If one more *fricking* person hit her in the back of the skull, she was going to lose it.

Probably literally. When her brains leaked out of her goddamn ears.

Back on her feet, she focused on the makeshift clinic's door. It didn't matter that she had no clue where she was. A nine millimeter was a helluva map, wasn't it—and she didn't want to wait for Luke to come back. He was a complicating factor when he just couldn't be.

As always, she had to do her best to balance getting information with getting herself hurt or killed, and the instability in this environment was obvious. Even though she wanted to fully explore, she was going to have to gather what she could on the way out. Ending up in a grave was not the way to bring Mozart and these suppliers to justice.

Glancing down at the bed, she remembered the kiss she had had with Luke.

No goodbye.

And the next time she saw him, it might well be after she got him arrested.

Why the hell, after all these years of not being particularly interested in sex, did she have to be so attracted to someone like him? She'd been doing just fine living like a monk.

At least she could go right back to the celibacy. Not a problem. Especially after what had happened on the floor of that apartment.

Rio started to move toward the door, tiptoeing in her boots, trying not to put her full weight into her feet—what, like she could command gravity or something?

No squeaking, she thought at the floor beneath her feet. *No creaking*—

Oh, it was concrete. Right.

As she went by the empty beds, she counted them down. And as she came up to the drapery—

There was a choked sound of pain from inside the sheets.

Rio stopped. The two men were still talking softly—there was another groan, now, as if someone who hurt all over was attempting to find a better position. And failing.

Go, she told herself. *Get the fuck out. Right now.*

When she realized that her feet had stopped, she looked to the door, as if she could refocus their effort. Or will the exit to come to her.

After a moment, they did start moving again.

Not toward the way out, though.

✦ ✦ ✦

In front of the Executioner and his wall of Rorschach tests, Lucan dropped down onto his haunches. Around the throat of the dead wolf was a steel collar, but not the kind that came with the tracking or the explosion-upon-removal stuff. Releasing the buckle on the generic restraint, he took the thing off and eased back.

Was there enough life left in the still-warm body's cells for the change? If Lucan had still been staying in the territories of the clans, he might have recognized the patterns of gray and white and brown in the fur. But it was a long time since he'd been near his bloodline—

okay, half of his bloodline—and God knew his brain had jettisoned those memories for more useful ones tied to surviving in the prison camp—

There was a hissing sound, like air was escaping from the lungs due to rib compression. And then the transformation began, the fur that had been totally static moving in waves as each individual follicle retracted into its pore, sucking back into the wolven's shifting corporeal form. While this was happening, the fore- and hind legs began to elongate and re-form, the front paws differentiating into hands with separated fingers, the back ones pushing out into bare feet. The torso also expanded, shoulders protruding on both sides of the narrow canine chest and causing the body to roll over so that it was faceup.

So that the gunshot wound in the center of the chest was visible.

Meanwhile, down below at the waistline, the pelvic girdle broke outward and flattened to accommodate the thickening thighs as well as organs consistent with the male sex.

The face was what he was waiting for.

Up at the head, the muzzle retracted and the short nap fur disappeared, the nose, chin, and cheeks emerging as the bone structure changed, above them the flat forehead and arching brows manifesting—

The eyes flipped open and focused on Lucan, as if his scent had registered. Then the mouth started to move, the words more breath than syllable, blood speckling the lips.

The attempt at communication didn't last. A gasp cut it off, and then there was coughing, weak coughing . . . followed by the utter stillness of death.

"Jesus," Lucan muttered as he stared into that face.

"So you do know him."

Lucan looked at the Executioner, the other male a powerful figure in all that black, all those weapons. "I can't believe you went all the way up that mountain to kill this sonofabitch. If you expect me to be pissed off or more motivated, you're shit out of luck. I hate the fucker."

The Executioner smiled, his glittering eyes that of a murderer who enjoyed killing as much as a normal person might be happy with a nice dinner or a good night's sleep.

Like death was something so natural, so required to his well-being.

"Oh, you're motivated enough, aren't you," the male murmured.

"So why'd you go to the clans and risk a problem? My kin are assholes who will eat their own—literally. You don't want to get their attention, trust me."

"I didn't go to the mountain. He came here. Who is he?"

Lucan narrowed his eyes. "My cousin."

"This is a family reunion, then. How sweet."

Not even close, Lucan thought as he started to pace around in a circle, memories clawing into the center of his chest—

Before he could stop himself, or go through any of the many reasons he should keep his emotions in check, he took a running soccer kick and nailed the corpse in the gut. On impact, the dead arms and legs flopped, and the head kicked hard on the concrete floor.

He did it again. And again. And again. And—

Something warm splashed up on him. He looked down.

Blood was on his fresh sweatshirt and he brushed at it even though he wasn't bothered by the stain. He just needed something to get himself off the soccer train.

Refocusing on the Executioner, Lucan demanded, "Did you think it was me when you snuck up on him? Is that why you shot him?"

"It's daylight. I can assure you I was not the one who pulled the trigger."

The guard, Lucan thought. Some of them were humans, or so he'd heard. But who knew whether the rumor was true.

Lucan shook his head. "No, they thought it was me—that's why you went looking for me. They thought I'd gone AWOL, and when they brought this to you, you had to check on me to see if it was. What's Mayhem's reward going to be for delivering me to you?"

"He gets to live another night."

"Lucky him, this place is an amusement park just *full* of fun and games." Lucan crossed his arms over his chest. "Your guards thought they'd done you a favor, because they didn't know our arrangement—which is what happens when you hire mercenaries. They only get part of the job right. And you thought you'd lost your connection with Mozart. You were pissed, and because this wolf didn't have a collar, you weren't sure whether it was me or not. Oops."

"You make a lot of assumptions."

Whatever, he thought.

"All I know for sure is that you don't want this kind of trouble." He nodded down at the body. "When he doesn't come back, others will search for him."

"And exactly what kind of trouble do you think I'll be in?"

"If they get into this facility, it'll turn into the biggest takeout restaurant you've ever seen—and you're on the menu."

The Executioner smiled again, flashing his fangs. "No one can get in or out of here without my knowledge."

Oh, really, Lucan thought. "Aren't you a clever little bitch."

The Executioner stepped forward until they were nose to nose. "Watch yourself, wolf. You can easily be in your family member's position."

"He's not my family, at least not in his opinion. That's how I ended up here. And if you want to put a bullet in me, do it where it counts." Lucan put his arms wide. "Right in the heart."

As the Executioner's face hardened, it was clear that the male didn't like the shift.

And not in the wolven's assumption of its human-like form.

The power dynamic was not what it had started out as, with Lucan the only one who had a weakness to exploit. Now . . . the Executioner wanted something only Lucan could provide.

Tricksy, tricksy.

"I'm waiting," Lucan snapped.

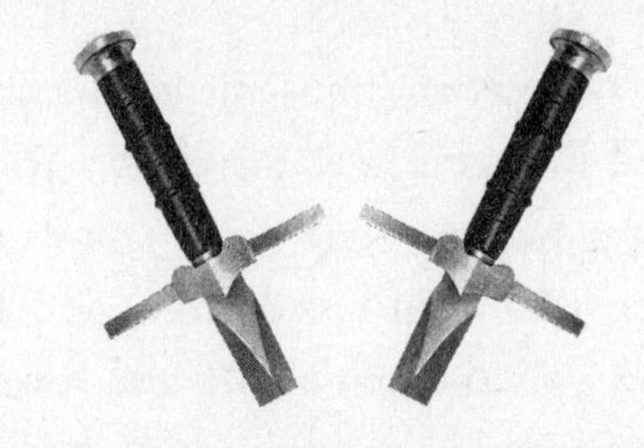

CHAPTER TWENTY-NINE

Even as Rio was telling herself that she needed to get going, explore what she could, find a way out, get back to Caldwell . . . she parted the curtains that fell from the ceiling. Over on the bed, lying on his back . . . a burn patient was in a terrible state: His face was a raw wound, the features swollen and glistening, the eyes forced shut by the injuries. The rest of his torso and arms were just as bad, nothing but raw meat that was left unbandaged, likely because any kind of gauze would just stick and become entangled—

The man who had attacked her burst up from a chair that had been pulled in close to the bedside.

Before he could come at her, she put the gun up to his face. "Sit the fuck down, this isn't about you."

The chuckle from the patient cut through a subtle whirring sound. "Yes, Apex. Do sit down."

There was a tension-filled moment. And then "Apex" lowered himself back into the chair.

Rio again turned her head toward the poor man in the bed. His only treatment, that she could see, was a small fan set on top of a cardboard box, the cooling air traveling across his ravaged skin.

"Are you okay," she said roughly.

Stupid question.

"My dear," came the response. "How kind of you to ask."

Rio glanced at the Apex guy. He was watching her like in his mind he was ripping her arms off with his bare hands and beating her to death with the stumps. But he didn't make another move toward her. It was as if he were a predator and his leash was in the patient's hold.

Rio approached the other side of the bed. She kept the gun up, just in case.

"Can't the nurse help you? Or can we get you to a doctor?"

The patient didn't turn to her. His face stayed angled straight at the ceiling above him, not that he could see anything. She was willing to guess it was just too painful for him to move anything, even in the slightest way.

No doubt mere breath was a struggle.

"I am as well as I can be." The patient's rasp was softer now, as if he were running out of strength. And yet his tone and accent struck her as highbrow. "I am simply waiting out a process that began some weeks and weeks prior. And you, how fare you? Have you been aided?"

Looking around again—but like she'd missed anything?—Rio saw no monitoring of vitals, no IV, no medications.

"You need to go to a hospital."

The other man answered. "You don't know what the fuck you're talking about."

"Excuse me?" Rio lowered the gun. "Oh, so the condition he's in is totally compatible with life. Right. Glad you pointed this out to me, because I was assuming he needed some medical help—"

"Just what we need, a human with a savior complex—"

"As opposed to you, who're just sitting here as he—"

"This is not your business—"

"*Enough,*" the patient said with exhaustion.

Rio closed her eyes, and realized she was way out of line, speaking about how dire his circumstances were.

She cleared her throat. "Were you in a car accident?"

Again, the injuries appeared consistent with severe burns, and while she gathered her thoughts, she was trying to figure out what could have caused—

Okay, she was stupid. A meth lab. Of course. Unless she thought they were making cookies here?

"We need to get you help," she heard herself say.

The patient inhaled slowly. Then he spoke through an agonizingly slow exhale. "You are kind, but you are in enough trouble yourself. Does Lucan have a plan for getting you back where you belong?"

"I'll get myself back."

The chuckle from the douchebag on the chair was no doubt a chauvinistic commentary on her abilities—except like she hadn't heard that before? Also, she might have a head injury, but at least she could stand on her own two feet—and, bonus, she had this cute little nine millimeter accessory that didn't make her ass look fat and brought out the fuck-off that was never far below the surface of her baby browns.

"I should not underestimate her, Apex."

That's right, she thought at the patient.

Then she calmed herself and stared down at the bed.

"We have to do something for you," she murmured as she noticed his hands for the first time. One was missing all its fingers.

When there wasn't a response, she glanced up at that face. The lips had parted so he could breathe, and the shallow inhales came at a panting speed. And then there was a groan—after which, a slightly calmer rhythm.

He'd passed out, she was willing to bet.

"You're in pain," she whispered to him anyway. "Dear God, are they not treating your pain?"

"No, we're deliberately letting him stew in it," the other man—what was his name? Apex?—muttered. "Because we get off on a male of worth suffering."

Rio closed her eyes. "I can't imagine how much it hurts."

"He is stronger than all of us combined."

She looked over at the chair. Apex was sitting forward, his hand on the bed right next to the patient's ruined one—but not touching it. Because that would have been unbearable, no doubt.

"Is there nothing here that can help him?"

"We're lucky we have a bed for him," the man gritted out. "Most of the medication here expired two decades ago and is degraded. There's nothing we can do."

"How much longer do you think he has?"

Eyes that were dark as the corners of Hell lashed over to her. "Will you get the fuck out of here. I'd kill you right now, but he won't let me. I promise, though, if you're still here the second his heart stops, I'm coming at you."

"Aren't you scary," she said in a bored tone.

Ignoring the guy, Rio paced up and down inside the drapery—which is to say, she took three steps up and three steps back.

Wasn't that a line in a Bruce Springsteen song? she thought.

As an image of her brother came to mind, she stopped at the foot of the bed—and tried not to get confused between the past and the present. But the stillness of the patient . . . reminded her of what she had seen when she had broken down the door to Luis's bedroom. She would never forget the way her brother had been lying there on his back, against a pillow stained with his own vomit, his blue-tinged face . . . angled directly up at the ceiling, as if he had been watching the hand of death as it had come for him.

Rubbing her eyes, she stared at the patient again. Even when unconscious, he had a frown on his face and a tension in his body.

There was no relief for him. Anywhere.

She thought of her brother. And felt sick.

"We have drugs here," she said roughly.

"What?" Apex snapped.

"This is a fucking drug factory, right? There are drugs here."

Apex opened his mouth as if he had a tic that involved telling her to go fuck herself and was giving in to it again.

She shook her head at him and spoke quickly, even as between each blink, she saw her brother's dead face. "There's heroin. Here on-site. I've seen it on the streets marked with your iron cross symbol. You don't just sell cocaine, and opiates are opiates—they make pain go away. If we can get him a small dose of heroin, he'll at least be comfortable."

Blink. Her brother. Blink. Her brother—

"That shit kills people."

No kidding, she thought.

"Only if you give him too much," she said. "And I know . . . how to titrate it. I won't let him have too much." Rio went around the foot of the bed and stood in front of the man. "Take me to where it's cut. I can test it. Then we come back here and help your friend. Partner. Husband, whoever he is to you."

Apex slowly rose to his feet. God, he was huge, a living, breathing billboard for a beatdown.

He jabbed her in the shoulder. "I don't need shit from you."

Why am I doing this? Rio asked herself.

Well . . . because she could see more of the building. He would know how to get around, where the drugs were processed. Helping the patient would help her.

"You don't need me?" she demanded. "Really? Well, for one, you're sitting how many rooms away from the solution to his suffering and you clearly haven't considered it. Two, do you know the dose? Enough to give him relief but not kill him? His respiration is already compromised, and I'm guessing his blood pressure is low. You don't know where that line is, do you."

"Are you a nurse?"

She thought back to all the conversations with ER docs immediately after, and since, her brother's death. She'd had to know exactly what had happened, down to the molecular level, from his body weight to the cut of the drug, to what else had been in his system. She'd had to . . .

"No, but I know a lot about overdoses."

The man stared down at the patient.

"He is never not in pain," she said hoarsely, picturing her brother's face whenever he'd thought no one was looking at him.

Apex passed a palm over his eyes. "Never. He suffers constantly."

"Show me where the drugs are. I'll take it from there."

There was a long silence. Then Apex shook his head. "You don't need to come with me. I'll bring it back—what do you need?"

As he stared at her, there was a blank look in his eyes.

Rio frowned. "Do you know the difference between the heroin, any cocaine or meth, and the cutting product? And what about fentanyl?"

"Of course. So what do you need?"

He was lying, she thought.

"You know this with enough certainty you're willing to risk killing him?"

"And how are you such an expert."

"I'm betting my life on my knowledge, aren't I," she said. "If he dies, you're offing me, right."

As she just leveled a stare at him, he shrugged. "So tell me what you need."

A drug dealer who didn't know his wares. Unbelievable.

"What do you do around here other than look after your partner," she murmured.

"He's not my partner."

"Brother."

"No."

"Friend, then."

The patient coughed a little. And as they both turned toward the man, a slight smile marked the distorted mouth.

"You must excuse him," the patient said. "He doesn't know what a friend is."

Rio leaned over the bed. "We're going to get you something to help with the pain."

There was a shuddering breath. "I do my best to bear up. I am weary, though . . . and growing wearier."

She reached out to pat his arm, but caught herself. "We're going to take care of it."

Looking up, she pegged Apex with dead serious eyes. "Aren't we."

As she waited for his answer, she saw her brother standing just inside the curtain, dressed in the jeans and the Nirvana t-shirt he'd been wearing when she'd found him dead.

Luis was so real, she felt like she could reach out and touch him.

And that was when she was forced to recognize the real reason she was doing this, the true driver.

She was revisiting her brother's overdose and using what she'd had to learn. Like if she could ease the suffering of the patient . . . it would somehow recalibrate the too-much her brother had shoved in his vein all those years ago.

It was some existential algebra that didn't make a lot of sense.

Nothing was going to bring her dead back. Or set right all the bad things that had happened afterward.

These were two totally unconnected events, and no matter the outcome here, it would have no bearing on what had come before.

"Aren't we," Rio repeated.

✦ ✦ ✦

As Lucan faced off at the Executioner and dared the motherfucker to shoot him in the heart, he was picturing all kinds of happy things. Like biting the vampire on the front of the throat. Then ripping the flesh free and spitting it out.

After that *amuse-bouche*, there was a peg fantasy, where he took the male by the armpits and pushed him against that wall so hard, he was punctured by the dull wooden points.

And behind door number three? Something involving a chain saw.

The latter was a pipe dream, really, considering he was completely surrounded by absolutely no Black & Decker. But the other two hypotheticals? They were goers.

"No?" he drawled when he wasn't popped in the chest. "Is that a no?"

Considering the amount of metal on the guy—as well as dripping off both of those guards—the no-trigger on all those fingers wasn't from a lack of available bullets.

"Where is my deal, wolf," the Executioner said softly. "Where is my money."

Lucan smiled in a snarl. "I'm working on it."

"Are you? I don't see any forward motion from that contact of yours downtown. I have kilos to move, kilos I made a large investment in—and nothing from you. I'm beginning to think you're not the male for this job, and I believe you know how I fire people."

The male lifted a hand toward the wall.

Lucan didn't bother looking at all the obvious. His mind was down in the basement, with Rio. If he died now? Or at any time before he got her off the property?

"You need me."

"No, you're expendable," the Executioner murmured. "Don't forget it."

I should never have brought her here, Lucan thought. But what had his options been? He'd had no idea how to help her. How badly she was hurt.

"You will bring me the deal at the end of this coming night." The Executioner stepped off. "Or I will replace you. There are others who will be helpful."

Apex, of course. He was the other one attached to Kane.

"Do we understand one another?" the Executioner demanded.

Motherfucker, Lucan thought. Then again, there was only one thing that mattered right now, and it had nothing to do with drugs.

"Yeah," he muttered. "So am I allowed to go now that you've enjoyed this little verbal masturbation session? It's meant *so* much to me—"

The Executioner moved fast, outing a flashing knife and putting it to Lucan's jugular. "Watch your tone."

Lucan smiled—and leaned into the blade. There was a bite of pain, and then the scent of fresh blood.

Taking a finger, he ran it through the wet spot and then licked the red stain off.

"Hm," he said. "It never tastes as good when it's your own, does it."

The Executioner rolled his eyes. "You're a sick fuck."

"And you need me to stay alive."

"For a little longer. And it's all up to you."

Lucan turned away. As he met Mayhem's eyes, he winked. And then said to the guy, "Collect your prize, asshole. You fucking burned me."

Mayhem's mouth twitched—and no doubt he would have winked back if he hadn't been facing the proverbial firing squad.

"Even if it's nothing," the male shot back, "there's still the satisfaction of turning you over to the proper authorities. An ass pat is good enough for me."

"Survival," Lucan said as he started walking. "That's all he's giving you."

The Executioner spoke loudly. "You better make sure you do right by me, wolf. Or your friend Kane's going to be put out of his misery—slowly."

Glancing over his shoulder, Lucan stopped and narrowed his eyes. "I'll get you what you need. And you better be prepared for war when that scout lying there dead at your feet doesn't return to his pack."

"Accidents happen in nature, you know that."

"With bullets?"

"They're never going to find the body to discover the truth."

So the Executioner hadn't lied about the wolf coming here rather than being hunted where the clans were.

"You better hope so."

"Your kind is overpowered here, wolf."

As Lucan started walking again, he wasn't going to keep arguing over an indisputable fact. If there was one thing he'd learned after all these years, it was that reality wasn't interested in anybody's opinion.

Striding down the corridor and passing by the workrooms, he thought back to the night when Kane had sacrificed himself to free the Jackal and his mate. The couple had been up on the dais at the Hive, tied to the posts that had run floor to ceiling. There had been no way of saving them from the Command.

Lucan had been there. Others, too.

Kane had taken his collar off, and the thing had done what it was designed to do upon removal. It had exploded—and brought down the house, so to speak. Or a lot of it. The collapse of the ceiling had toppled those huge posts, and in the chaos, the Jackal and his mate had gotten away.

Lucan had found Kane in the rubble. The collar blast had somehow been turned away from him, maybe from a malfunction, who the fuck knew. Instead of blowing him up, the transfer of energy had sent him flying backward—not that there hadn't been plenty of damage. He'd been burned severely in his face, down his chest, and on his hands, and then there had been the impact against one of the Hive's stone walls.

Right after the blast, there had been no intention on Lucan's part to do anything other than save himself. But as soon as he'd tripped over the body, he hadn't been able to leave the male. He'd picked up that former aristocrat and started running as hard as he could toward the evacuation route. Luck, or maybe it was divine intervention, had put a Jeep in his path. He'd thrown Kane in, jumped behind the wheel, and hit the gas.

He'd followed the caravan of semis and other trucks because he hadn't been thinking right. And it wasn't like he had any other resources, any viable plan. Freedom, in that moment, had not been the best move. Inside the prison camp? He knew how to function, and he knew there was help for Kane.

So he had driven to the sanatorium, and gone underground . . . and found the nurse, Nadya.

They had been doing what they could for Kane ever since, not that they were helping much—and when the Executioner heard about Lucan's savior routine, he had smiled and removed Lucan's collar.

And told him that either he went into Caldwell and became the face of the prison's drug operation or Kane would be killed.

Slowly.

Lucan had given in to the leverage not because of any friendship or particular loyalty to the former aristocrat. It had been more . . . about the sacrifice the male had been willing to make in that moment when it had counted most. Long before, Kane's beloved female had been killed, and he had been framed for her murder—which was how he'd ended up in prison. That he had seen fit to destroy himself so that two others could find for their lives what he had not only been cheated of but cursed with imprisonment for, had put the "noble" in "nobility" as far as Lucan had been concerned.

In the horrible confines of the prison camp and the cold, heartless fight for survival they were all locked in, it had seemed like the kind of gesture that had to be honored.

And now they were here, with Kane just hanging on in the subterranean storage room, some internal life force inside of him too stubborn to let him die. Due to their biology, vampires healed without scars unless there was salt involved, and did so faster than humans ever could, but that didn't mean they were immortal.

Lucan had no regrets except for Kane's suffering. After all, it felt good to have a principle that you didn't have to be ashamed of when you were falling asleep. But God, it was hard to feel like a hero considering the state the male was in.

Down at the end of the corridor, he took the stairs one floor lower—and entered the sleeping area. He was surprised there wasn't a guard front and center, but then he caught movement as someone stepped out of the shadows. There was a pause. Then the male figure disappeared again.

Always watching. Always waiting.

Cursing to himself, he stared down the hundred or so rows of berths, thinking about all the prisoners wedged in like they were objects, rather than living beings. As his anger stirred, he started walking again, crossing through the pools of lights thrown by the ceiling fixtures. The vertical, four-by-eight-foot cubicles were stacked three up from the floor, all of them open at the one end, endless pairs of feet, shod and unshod, facing out into the space. Ladders were mounted to the right of each opening, and the snoring was muffled, but pervasive.

As he breathed in, the density of scents was nearly overwhelming, but there was also that fresh pine smell from the fact that it had all been newly built up, just like the work rooms, the Executioner's wall and private quarters, and the other security provisions. The construction had been done before the relocation by God only knew who, and he had to admit, it had all been thought through.

Too bad it was positively inhumane.

His assigned space wasn't far from the stairwell, and he'd always been glad he'd managed to get a top, rather than a bottom or middle berth. Ascending the ladder, he slid into his slot, crossed his feet at the ankles, and folded his arms over his chest.

He wanted to go to Rio, but he couldn't risk being followed.

And putting her right in the hands of the Executioner.

As the dim snoring got on his nerves and everything felt itchy, he decided it was too bad he didn't have that old cassette player anymore. His sole possession had been destroyed during the collapse, and he missed the thing, even though he'd had only one tape.

Duran Duran had had other hit singles in addition to "Hungry Like the Wolf."

They'd had one called "Rio."

Hadn't they.

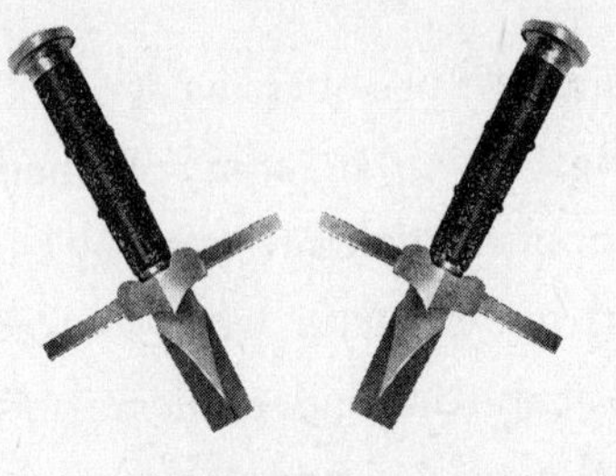

CHAPTER THIRTY

Just as Rio turned away from the bed, the patient spoke up. "Lucan will take care of you."

She glanced over her shoulder. "Actually, I . . . I am on my own—"

"He saved me not only when he didn't have to, but at great peril to himself. You can trust him." The patient's tone got more strident. "And that is why you, Apex, shall ensure no harm comes unto her. She is Lucan's."

Rio braced herself for an inner, private rager in her head about how women, especially women like her, were not anyone's pseudo possessions. But when she just felt a little warm spot in the center of her chest, she wondered when in the hell she'd regressed into 1950s traditional sex roles.

Then again, maybe she just had a low-level staph infection from having an open wound on the back of her head.

That's right, she thought. The flush was probably just bacteria in her bloodstream making her run a slight fever.

"Apex?" the patient demanded.

After a moment, the other man let out a grudging *mmrumph* sound. Which, all things considered, could have meant anything from "yes, I'll chill on the whole murder thing" to "what are you going to do to stop me from that bed you're in"—although when the patient nodded a little, it appeared that, at least between the pair of men, the translation was acceptable as an agreement.

"Do not endanger yourselves—"

Coughing cut the patient off, to the point where Rio worried there would be nothing to treat by the time they got back. But then those lungs seemed to settle.

"Come on," Apex said grimly.

When Rio went to pull back the curtain, he clapped a hand on her forearm. "I go first. Always."

His voice was soft. His eyes were like a pair of assault rifles.

"You can lead on," she drawled. "But I'm not going to yes-sir you, so I wouldn't hold your breath for that one."

Apex's brows rose. And then he I-go-first-always'd out into the open area. As Rio stepped through, too, she—

Something came down over her head, something soft, like a massive cobweb—and she immediately fought against the flapping, now-heavy weight.

"Stop it," Apex snapped. "We have to mask your scent."

"What?"

There was a tug, and then everything settled off her shoulders. Looking down at herself, she said, "The nurse's uniform?"

"That one was used for the last bed change and is on the way to the laundry."

Explains the stains, she thought.

Apex went over and opened the drawer of a desk that was right out of a secretary's office from 1980. When he came back, he started rubbing her down.

"Wait—what are you doing—"

The man's hands were quick and impersonal, passing over the folds of the buff-colored robe fast and hard. With every swipe, more of that incense smell wafted up into her nose.

"It's the best we can do," he muttered as he tossed the brown sticks back onto the desk. "Now listen to me, when we're out there, don't fuck around. Follow behind me, keep your head down, and . . ."

When he just stopped talking, she glanced down at herself again. "What?"

"You don't know, do you," he said remotely.

"Know what?"

"Where you really are."

"You want to draw me a map? That'd be great. Thanks."

"I'm not talking about location." Apex shook his head and yanked the hood piece up, the mesh swinging into place over her face. "This is fucked up. Just so you know."

"Really." Rio arranged the screen with impatience. "I hadn't noticed. I thought I was at the Ritz."

"Let's get this over with."

"I couldn't agree more."

At the door, she hung back—because of all the *grrrrr* he-man bull-crap the guy was throwing around—while he leaned out and checked the corridor. Then on his signal, she joined him—except as she fell in beside him, he elbowed her back so he was the tip of their spear.

"And do you have your gun?" he hissed.

"No," she muttered, "I left it behind because it didn't match my outfit."

The man cursed. "How does Lucan stand you."

"I'm wondering the same thing about your patient."

Apex stopped dead. "He is *not* mine."

"Right. Which is why you were crying next to his bed—"

"Don't push it, female."

Under the hood and the screen, Rio made googly eyes at him—and knew it was for the best that he couldn't see her face.

When he resumed the forward motion, she resolved to stop poking at him. As fun as it was, she needed to start memorizing where they were.

She was going to have to write it all down as soon as she could.

And hey, the good news about pairing up with the guy? Apex so completely annoyed her that she wasn't thinking about her dead brother as much anymore.

Yay.

◆ ◆ ◆

As Lucan lay in his berth with his eyes closed, he went back in time, his short-term memories like a spool of celluloid film run in reverse, people sucking out of doorways instead of walking through them, corridors flowing in the opposite direction, words he'd spoken called home to his throat, his lungs.

And then he was where he didn't want to be, but couldn't get free of.

The way you're staring at my lips right now.

So do you want to do something about this?

Now he went forward, but in slo-mo, savoring the way that woman had looked at him, the way she'd scented, how he could feel the softness of her breasts against his hard chest. And then there was the contact of her mouth against his—

The groan that came out of him was something he swallowed. And to make sure the sound stayed inside, he repositioned himself a couple of times—which didn't mean shit considering he was tight as a key in a lock. Not a lot of room . . .

As his hips rolled, the erection that had johnny-on-the-spotted because of everything he was thinking about rubbed against the backside of his fly. Baring his fangs as they lengthened, he moved his arm so that his hand was in range—and then he thought about what he was going to do.

Did he really want to jack off in here? While she was down in that clinic on her sickbed—

Well, technically she wasn't ill. She was hurt.

"Oh, that's *so* much better," he muttered.

Closing his eyes—because hey, you never knew, maybe he could sleep instead of be a dirtbag—he . . . went right back to the moment when she'd dropped her mouth to his.

His hand didn't require any order from his brain to move a little and cover his—

Lucan hissed. The weight of his palm along the top of his thick shaft juiced him up to the point of not saying no. Kicking one leg out as far as it could go, which was not far at all, he thrust his pelvis like he was penetrating that woman's hot, wet sex.

More with the hissing.

And then he didn't give a shit who in the other cubicles heard him.

He was back on that bed with Rio, and he was kissing the ever-living shit out of her—and because this was a fantasy, he curated Kane out of the clinic's picture and locked the door that had no lock.

Then Rio's clothes disappeared without her or him removing them, her breasts exposed to his eyes, his hands, his mouth.

And then they were changing positions. She was . . .

"Fuuuuck," he groaned as he yanked down his fly and sprang his cock.

In his daydream, Rio pushed him back and then got up on all fours.

Looking around her shoulder, her eyes shone with sexual heat. *I ache, Luke. Can you help me?*

Or something like that; her lips were moving, but he wasn't really hearing her. Not that he needed her to tell him what to do.

The glistening stripe between her legs was all the conversation he needed.

Lucan mounted her in a surge, and his erection pierced into her sex—

The orgasm that exploded into his hand was translated into the fantasy: As his palm went up and down, yanking, pushing, pulling, and come jetted out onto the front of his pants and the hem of his sweatshirt . . . in his mind, he was pumping her full of his scent.

Marking her.

To the point where he bit her on the shoulder to hold her in place and reached around to the top of her sex—

She was not wolven.

That one god-awful realization cold-watered the whole goddamn thing. In an instant.

As his hand stopped and his fantasy derailed from its track and went free-falling off the bridge of his delusions, he banged his head back into the hard pallet. A couple of times.

She wasn't even a vampire who could just look down on him for being a half-breed wolven—because females of worth did not fuck creatures like him.

Rio didn't even know his kind existed.

Either of his kinds.

And if she found out, it was not going to be the sort of news that made things better for them. Easier for them.

Possible for them.

"Fuck," he groaned as he looked down at himself.

In the glow from the lights out on the ceiling, he saw more than he needed to about his reality, and by extension, the two of them.

The fact that he'd ejaculated all over himself and now had a sticky, cooling mess to clean up seemed like a perfect commentary on everything.

Especially their future.

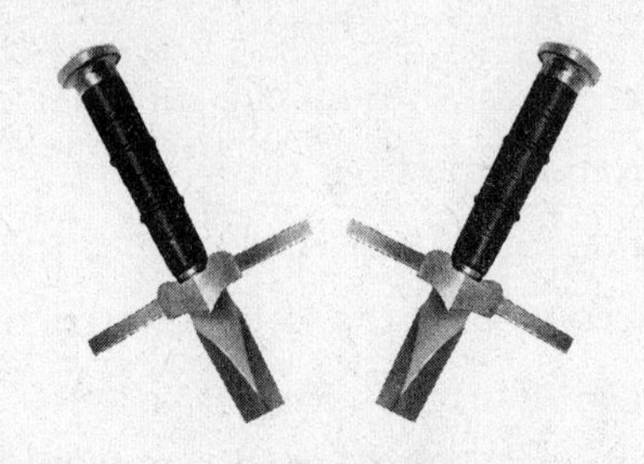

CHAPTER THIRTY-ONE

Rio had *vastly* underestimated the scale of the place—and the operation. The staircase she and Apex used wound its way around a landing, and when they got to the next floor up, he stopped and seemed to gather his thoughts as he sniffed the air like he was searching for evidence of a live fire.

While he did . . . whatever the hell he was doing . . . she looked through the chicken-wire glass in a heavy fire door. The corridor on the far side was easily sixty feet long and ten feet wide. A series of light bulbs dangling from raw wires illuminated its progression to a far-off end . . . and she wasn't sure what she was seeing.

The walls had cutouts in them, little curve-topped holes stacked three to a group and spaced far enough apart to accommodate ladders that led up to the middle and top levels. It was almost as though they were sleeping compartments of some kind—

"Come on," Apex hissed. "We don't want to be caught here."

"Then why did you stop." She glanced back at him. "What are all those spaces?"

"None of your business."

As he pulled her away, she did some math in her head. Assuming they were a kind of bunk system, there had to be—Jesus, several hundred workers in the facility.

"How many people are here?" she said, even though she'd already done the estimate, and even if she hadn't, he would certainly not help her. It was more like she couldn't believe the total.

"We're going all the way up to the main floor. It's more dangerous in some ways and less so in others."

"Well, I'll put that in my Yelp! review of this place. Thanks."

When they got to the next floor, he didn't give her a chance to stop at the fire door. She caught only a glance through its window down another long corridor. Unlike the one under it, the level seemed to be far more brightly lit, and there were no sleeping pods. The walls were also finished, although only with raw Sheetrock from what she glimpsed.

At the next landing, Apex stopped at a steel door that had no window in it. Pressing his ear against the steel panel, he seemed to not even breathe as he listened.

Then he turned to her. "The lowest two floors are totally underground. The next one up is mostly so. This one is not at all, however, so I'm going to have to move fast. As soon as I open the way, we're heading to the first door on the left that's unlocked. It's a break room. It will be empty and the windows are boarded up, so it's safer. On three. One . . . two . . . three—"

Apex ripped open the metal panel, and then recoiled as if he had been hit with toxic gas. Lifting his arm to his face, he ducked down low—and jumped forward in a defensive crouch. Even though she didn't smell anything dangerous, Rio echoed his protective stance, drafting behind his bulk, holding her breath as a vague impression of moldy carpeting, peeling walls, and a crumbling ceiling registered. Out in front of them, weak sunlight streamed across the corridor in sections, and he dodged around the stripes of faded gold.

Right ahead of her, Apex was breathing heavily, like he was struggling to stay conscious, and his speed was slowing. As they passed doors, she tried the knob of every one of them. All were locked—

"Oh, God," she muttered as the man faltered and fell down.

When he tried—and failed—to get back on his feet, she stood over him and looked around. Had he been shot? She hadn't heard anything.

Rio grabbed his flailing arm and dragged him off the carpet. "What's wrong?"

"Help . . . me . . ."

There was nothing in the air that was bad, no one else was around, and he didn't appear to be bleeding or wounded by a bullet. But now was not the time to ask questions.

Hauling him onto her, she threw his arm around her shoulders, braced his weight, and tightened a hold on his waist. Together, they limped forward, weaving a sloppy path down the corridor, her robe disguise tripping her up. She looked into every open door, noting the toppled office furniture, the graffiti, the occasional view out into a scruffy landscape of leafless trees. At each space, he told her to keep going.

"How much farther," she grunted.

"There . . ."

Okay, that narrowed their end zone down to absolutely nothing in particular.

Just as she was about to drop him, his hand shot out and grabbed on to a knob. With a powerful crank, he released the mechanism and threw the door wide—and then he shoved himself off of her, falling forward like a drunk, landing facedown with a bump of useless limbs.

"Shut the door—shut the fucking door," he groaned.

Rio shot inside, but didn't slam things—because there were people under them. Maybe above them, too. And they'd made enough noise with their footfalls.

As she carefully closed them in, instantly, everything went pitch dark, and her only orientation as she floated in space was the sound of the man's tortured breathing. Her eyes did adjust, however, shadowy outlines of a stretch of countertop, a sink, a table on its side, and one spindle chair in the corner pulling free of the void, thanks to a soft glow around the panels that had been nailed over what she assumed were window frames.

"Dumbwaiter," Apex said on a wheeze.

"Excuse me?" Rio lowered herself to her knees. "And what the hell is going on? Are you hurt?"

"There—it's a dumbwaiter. Your weight will lower it down. When you're ready, I'll pull you back up."

"No offense, but breathing seems like a challenge for you right now. How 'bout we focus on that first?"

"Go—I'll be all right. I just need a minute."

Rio looked to where he was pointing. Across the way, there was a panel in the wall that was demarcated by molding. The inset square was maybe three by three feet and it had a handle down at the bottom.

The man coughed and made her think of the patient. "Once you get down, you'll know what you see. Do what you have to and call up the shaft when you're ready for me to pull you up."

"I have my gun," she murmured, more to herself than to him.

Even though he was a disrespectful pain in the ass, she didn't want to leave him. Still, they had a job to do, so she got up and moved across the room, chunks of plaster gritting under the soles of her feet. When she got to the dumbwaiter, she lifted the panel. It was so dark, she had to feel around to get a sense of the size.

"I need to take the robes off. I won't fit otherwise."

"Do what you have to."

It was a relief to cast off the suffocating hood and take a deep, free breath. Then she put a foot into the space and grimaced as the inside of that thigh burned in protest.

"I should have gone to more yoga classes," she muttered.

"What's that?"

Rio glanced back. Apex was still lying there like a dead fly on a windowsill, his arms and legs curled up like they hurt.

"Are you sure you're going to be—"

"Go."

Rio reached in and found a lip on something that she could get a pretty good hold on. Pulling herself into the three-by-three-foot cubicle, it was alarming the way the pulley-rigged box rocked in its intra-floor track. And goddamn, as she squeezed her head to the side so her shoulders fit, the tender spot on the back of her skull hollered like a banshee.

"Please don't kill me," she announced as her eyes bounced around the tight interior—and could tell her nothing about the chances of her plummeting to her death.

"As long as you don't fuck around, I won't."

She glared out of the dumbwaiter. "I'm not talking to you. And you were wrong, my weight's not doing anything to move this thing. I suppose I should take it as a compliment, but it's a problem."

There were a couple of quick-draw inhales, and then Apex grunted and got to his feet. Dragging himself over, he braced himself against the wall.

"I'll close the door and lower you manually."

"How—"

He opened a flush panel in the wall. "Hang on."

Rio closed her eyes and pushed against the walls that crowded her, like they were people she could get to move away. "It's not me who has to do the hanging. Is this thing rated for my kind of weight?"

"We'll see, won't we."

He pulled the dumbwaiter's door shut on her.

There was a bump. And another.

Her breath was loud. So was her heart—

Squeak. Squeak. Squeak . . .

The descent was slow—and agonizing because the human body was not meant to pretzel into a space barely big enough to fit a picnic cooler. With every bump in the track and halt as Apex switched his grip, she had to fight the terror that something was going to snap and she was going to straight-shot down God only knew how many floors to egg-shatter all over—

This time, the bump was different.

"Stop," she said, projecting her voice up the shaft.

"Shh," was the response. But hello, he stopped.

Muttering about bossy men, she felt around the panel in front of her and found a handle at the bottom—which kind of begged the question whether the makers had anticipated the thing being used as an emergency elevator during the infiltration of a drug den to save a patient a little pain on his way to his eternal reward.

Rio gripped—no, it wasn't a handle, it was a bracket—and pulled. Pulled hard. Put her shoulder into—

Squeak!

Wincing, she froze. When nothing came at her, she forced the panel farther up. She was fighting against its function, some kind of resistance locked in to prevent exactly what she was doing.

Guess it was a *no* on the prognostication powers of its fabricators, at least when it came to someone like her being cargo. Either that or they'd been worried about bagels and cream cheese or maybe a fruit plate busting out and making a bid for freedom.

When she had the panel all the way up, she stuck her head into—

"Holy . . . shit."

The well-lit area was the size of a large classroom, and as if it was used as one, there were a couple dozen tables set up in three rows. Each table had a pair of chairs set on one side, and a lineup of scales, bowls, and tools on its surface, including little hammers and straight-line pastry knives. Down on the floor, boxes were set at regular intervals, and there were rolling bins dotting around. At the far end of the workspace, there were two proper desks, a couple of stepladders, and—

She recognized the cellophane-wrapped bales in the far corner instantly—and was not surprised to find that the kilos of drugs were locked into a metal cage bin that was five to six feet high.

Extricating herself from the dumbwaiter, she moved silently between the tables, her brain snapshotting everything at the same time it did some math. Twenty-four tables, two people a table, that was forty-eight workers. And yet there appeared to be several hundred of those sleeping compartments.

So there had to be more workrooms.

The implications made her head spin. An organization of this size did not just appear out of nowhere. It was part of an evolved strategy for disseminating a huge amount of product. Clearly they had been selling a lot of drugs for a long time, and yet why had no drug market intel from the streets mentioned a big whale like this?

Then again, there were always cycles of preeminence, the eras coming and going as arrests were made or deaths occurred. Maybe this operation had come here from another part of the country, ready to make the most out of Caldwell's close location to Manhattan and further accessibility to Vermont, Massachusetts, New Hampshire, and Maine.

As she passed by a table, she paused and opened one of the cardboard boxes on the floor. It was full of little baggies . . . and each had the stamp of the iron cross on it.

How far up did Luke go in the hierarchy? she wondered.

Probably pretty far. She needed to get him to talk on their way back to the city.

Continuing on, she went to the locked-up kilos and couldn't even estimate the street value. Well, she could—and it was in the millions and millions. How much product was on hand in the whole operation? And how did they get it in here? There had to be things like loading docks and other storage facilities to handle the pre- and post-processed drugs. With what she was seeing here? They could take in and put out kilos and kilos and kilos of cocaine and heroin in this place—and they clearly had the contacts with the importers to keep a steady stream of it coming.

It boggled the mind—

The sound of a door handle catching snapped her head around—and just as the way in opened, she dropped down to the floor.

All the way across the room, a man in a black uniform entered and hit a light switch that made everything even brighter.

Heart pounding, Rio looked through the legs of the tables and around the cardboard boxes as his boots started walking . . . to where the hatch of the dumbwaiter was still shoved up.

Proof that someone had gotten into the room.

And was still inside.

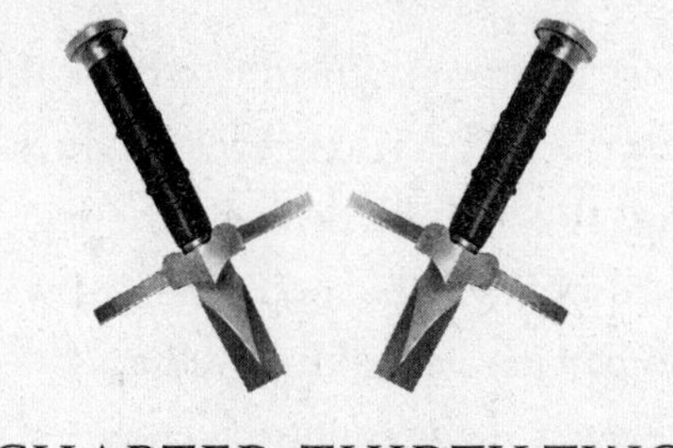

CHAPTER THIRTY-TWO

In the end, Lucan couldn't stay put. After he came all over himself, and then buzzkilled that vibe with the hello-my-name-is-Wolfie-and-not-'cuz-I'm-related-to-Beethoven, he had to go see Rio.

He told himself it was to make sure she was safe. Also told himself that if anyone was following him after the showdown with the Executioner, they'd have gotten bored by now of waiting for him to do something.

And he might have further mentioned to his inner critic that the Rio-related wanderlust was *not* tied in any way to the kiss that had started the handshake deal with his dumb handle. Not at all. In the slightest.

Whatsoever.

But yeah, there was a lot of internal monologuing going on as he shifted out of his cubicle and walked off for the stairs. He knew the guard down at the other end wouldn't question the departure—just like there had been no problems with his late arrival after check-in. They were used to him coming and going on his own, courtesy of his work with the Executioner.

Pulling open the fire door, he was quick-footed as he descended to the lowest level—

Lucan stopped. Sniffed the air.

Incense . . . and Kane?

Nadya, the nurse, must have come up here, he thought as he started again with the jogging.

Bottoming out at the base of the stairs, he glanced back at where he'd come from, peering through the latticework of the balustrade's supports. When he didn't see or hear anything, he strode off toward the clinic. The hall seemed like it went on forever, and as soon as he came up to the storage room's door, he opened it wide and looked down the row to Rio's bed—

It was empty, with the sheets, such as they were, messy . . . as if she'd gotten up in a hurry. As his heart slammed into his ribs, he leaned back and looked out into the hallway.

Of course. The bathroom.

Telling himself to get a grip, he went across to the closed door. The scent of the soap she'd used lingered in the air, but it was faded—and he was relieved he couldn't catch any sniff of her. They'd managed to camouflage her successfully.

With an excitement that was totally inappropriate, he put his ear right to the panel. It was cold against his face.

And got colder when he could hear nothing on the far side.

He knocked. "Rio?" he said softly.

There was no response.

Glancing up and down the corridor, the prison camp seemed really fucking dangerous all of a sudden.

Like the last however many decades had been a party?

"Rio?" More with knocking. "Rio. Answer me or I'm coming in."

He shoved at the door with his shoulder—and got a big ol' fat nothing as it opened wide. She wasn't in there.

Lucan raced back to the clinic and walked directly down to the bed she'd been in. Bending low, he looked under the mattress. The gun was gone.

"Sonofabitch—"

"Lucan?"

His head whipped to the drapery hanging around Kane's bed. "You okay?"

Not that there was anything he could do to help the guy if he wasn't—for so many reasons. But mostly because he had to find Rio.

"Lucan . . ."

If it had been anyone else, he would have fucked them off. Except just as the Executioner had discovered, and Lucan knew all too well, the aristocrat was someone he couldn't help but take into account. Even if it was just going to be briefly. Like it had to be at the moment.

Going over to the draping, he yanked it back—and turned his face away for a second. Every time he saw the male, it was a fresh horror.

"Hey," he said, "I'm dealing with something, but later I can—"

"She is with Apex," came the frail interruption. "Your female."

"*What.*"

◆ ◆ ◆

Lying on the floor of the workroom, Rio tracked the guard or whatever the hell he was as he progressed down to the dumbwaiter. Clearly, he knew something was out of place, but then again, she couldn't have left a bigger clue if she'd gone neon with a Las Vegas arrow flashing at the damn thing.

Glancing behind herself, she measured the drug bundles in their cage—and discovered that the load was on a platform with wheels.

That just so happened to have the same amount of clearance as a car.

With as little movement as possible, she flattened herself onto her stomach and pulled herself forward using her bare palms and her knees. As she closed in on the undercarriage, she tilted her head to the side, and prayed—*prayed*—that she didn't jostle the cage or—

"It's some kind of—I don't know what the fuck it is. It's like a box in the wall. No, it wasn't like that before. No shit, I'm not going up there—"

The words stopped short, but she couldn't tell whether it was because the man had noticed her or just been interrupted by whoever he'd called.

When boots started stomping in her direction, she feared it was the former.

Staring out from underneath the cage's platform, she tried not to breathe at all as a set of military-grade footwear come down to the bin—and stopped right in front of where she was hiding.

"Do you think I can't smell you, human?"

There were a series of grunts and her cover was moved off to the side, rolled clear away. As it revealed her, Rio wondered what kind of lead shower would fall on her head if she pulled a pivot-and-trigger. But considering that was her only chance—

Out of the corner of her eye, she caught a little red dot skating across the floor—and as it went out of her field of vision, she'd have bet both her eyeteeth that the laser sight was pegging her in the back of the skull.

"Get up."

There was no reason not to comply—and one very trigger-finger-ish reason to do so.

Rising onto her hands and knees, she looked around her arm. The man was standing right next to her, about three feet away, the toes of his boots pointed at her just like his gun was. Above his thick neck, his face was bored.

"You're never making it out of here alive," he said.

His eyes were some shade of blue, and they were moving over her body, but not in a sexual way. More like he was measuring her for a coffin—

"I fit in small spaces."

"What?"

"I'm retractable."

He shook his head. "Shut the fuck—"

Justlikethat, Rio sprang to her feet, palmed his weapon between her two hands, and diverted the muzzle. As the guard caught up with what was happening, she ripped the gun out of his lackadaisical grip and jabbed it right up into his crotch.

"You're going to want to move really carefully," she gritted. "Anything fast, I'm going to get nervous—and jeez, I get twitchy when I'm anxious. Click, click, oopsie."

She jumped back so that he couldn't grab at her.

"You don't know what you're doing," he said grimly.

He was still looking disinterested rather than alarmed, clearly in the camp that women were never much of a threat. And maybe she should feel complimented that he'd called her a human—as opposed to all the other derogatory nouns in his playbook.

Backing up, she went as far as the nearest table—

From out of nowhere, a strange confusion hit her like it was a tangible blow to the head, her thoughts scattering to the point that, as the gun she'd taken from him lowered of its own volition, she couldn't stop it: Even though she ordered her arm to stay up, it refused to obey the command—and as she started to fight to keep the weapon pointed at the guard, a piercing headache flashed across her frontal lobe.

The man walked up to her and said, "Give me the gun."

"No . . ."

And yet sure as if she had a remote and it was in his hands, Rio turned the weapon around and placed the nine millimeter grip-first into his palm.

The guard smiled now, revealing sharp canine teeth. "As I was saying, you don't know what you're doing."

Rio opened her mouth to—God, she didn't know what. She couldn't think at all. The impulse to communicate was there, but her entire vocabulary was unavailable.

And then things got worse. Her feet started walking, taking her forward . . . toward the door across the room, the one he'd come through.

As her body routed around the tables, she told herself there had to be a way out of this. She just needed to think—

"Open the door for me, would ya?"

Like he wanted to prove who was in control, she watched her hand reach out and turn the knob. Then she pulled things wide and stood aside as he passed by.

"Come on."

She followed him like a dog brought to heel, her body not hers to control, her will—off somewhere else.

Without being ordered to—verbally, at least—she walked down the hall in a trance, heading for some kind of wall with thick sticks protruding out of it and a door inset in the center—

All at once, her mind was flooded with images of horror, men and women strung up on those pegs, beaten with crowbars, with hammers, with lengths of chains—and then left there, the blood dripping off their battered bodies and pooling on the floor.

A figure in black, not the guard, but someone else, was smiling as he watched them die.

She had no idea where the gruesome slideshow came from, but it was as vivid as if she had witnessed it all personally, as if it were her own memories.

"He's going to have fun with you," the guard drawled. "You're just his type."

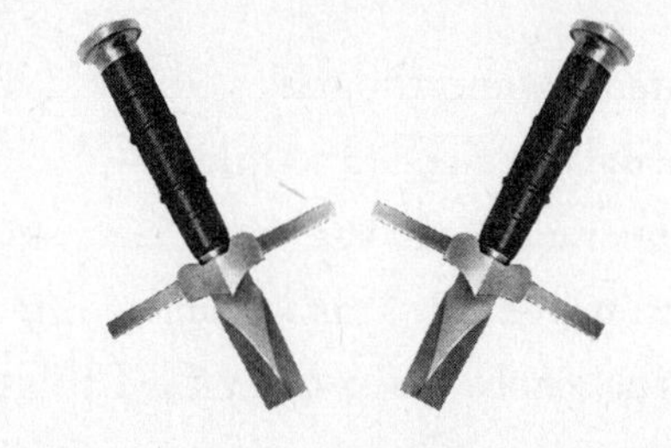

CHAPTER THIRTY-THREE

Lucan rushed back to the stairwell. Goddamn it, he'd smelled the incense coming down the steps, but also the nurse? That was why he'd been thrown off—Rio must have been put in one of Nadya's robes to mask her scent.

What the *hell* was Apex thinking, taking that human woman into the mouth of the monster. Helping Kane was fine, but *fuck*.

As he arrived at the landing of the workrooms' floor, he looked through the glass window in the fire door and tried to see if there was any disturbance. Everything seemed locked tight and business-as-usual for the daytime hours. And down at the far end, the pair of guards were in place in front of the wall—and there was nothing on any of the pegs.

Maybe she and Apex had gotten in and out already.

Either that or the Executioner had taken her into his quarters for a private party. Where that fucking madman would bite her jugular and drink her dry just for shits and giggles—

Directly overhead, a door opened and closed.

Lucan dematerialized into thin air and re-formed on the underbelly of the landing above him, hanging aloft like a bat, ready to pounce on—

Apex stumbled down the steps, weaving from side to side. "Not now, wolven. We got a problem—"

Releasing his grip, Lucan dropped down in front of the vampire, and went for the bastard, grabbing his throat and forcing him back.

"She wasn't supposed to leave the clinic!" He punched the other male into the wall. "What the fuck were you thinking—"

"It . . . was . . . her idea. Her . . . i . . . dea . . ."

The words came out as he banged, banged, banged the dumbass piece of shit into the concrete over and over again.

"Executioner . . . has . . . her."

Lucan stopped with the bread dough routine. After a split second of total shock, he shoved his face forward, baring his fangs. "You better hope she lives. Or I'm going to kill you with my bare hands—"

"I tried to stop her, asshole!" With a shove, Apex broke free—but then tripped over his own feet, fell onto the steps, and slumped like he was out of gas. "*Fuck.*"

"I don't believe you," Lucan hissed.

"You want to argue with me or save her life? We need to get her out of the Executioner's private quarters. I heard them talking from where I was—"

"Fuck you. No one can trust you—"

Apex shot up and got right back into Lucan's grill. "She was trying to help Kane. For that alone, she deserves better than dying at the Executioner's hands—or underneath him. So you can bet her fucking life you can trust me on this."

Between one blink and the next, Lucan remembered Rio strung between two stakes on the floor of that apartment, that human cutting open her shirt with that knife.

"I owe her," Apex announced.

There was a pause. And then Lucan lowered his head. Rubbed his aching temples.

"Since when did you grow a conscience?" he muttered as he went over to the doorway and checked through the glass again.

Apex cracked his knuckles. "Since I've been sitting at the bedside of that male of worth in the storage room. And then listening to that female of yours get manhandled by a goddamn guard."

Lucan couldn't even think about that last one. Or his head was going to fucking explode. "Like morals are something you catch like a cold."

"Shut up, wolven. You can't bust her out of there alone and you know it. You need me."

As Lucan assessed the guards on duty at the wall, he shook his head . . . but couldn't argue. "We have to go for a frontal assault. Take out the pair by the door, get into the private quarters—"

"The guards'll call for reinforcements if we rush them, and the backups are only one floor down. We need a reason to get close."

Lucan frowned. Then it came to him.

"I know what to do." With a quick yank, he pulled open the door. "Make like you're in on it all."

"As if I've never done that before," Apex muttered.

The two walked forward at a leisurely pace, Apex a couple of feet behind, as was his way. He never, ever made a pair with another, the I-am-an-island bullshit a cliché except for the tally of his kill count. Which was about to go up by at least one, maybe two guards—

They'd gone about halfway down the hallway of workrooms when gunshots rang out, the *pops!* muffled and distant. As the guards glanced toward the door to the Executioner's private quarters—because, hey, those kinds of noises were not that unusual—Lucan ditched his plan to talk some bullshit about the deal and lunged into a run—

Apex yanked him back, and spoke under his breath. "You have to pretend you don't care. You make like it matters, and the Executioner is going to have your balls really in a grip. You want in there to help her, you have to chill."

It took every bit of self-control for Lucan not to explode into a sprint, but in the back of his mind, he knew it was unlikely she was merely wounded. The Executioner only shot to kill. He liked his torture wet and messy—and it wasn't until he was done or bored that he'd cap someone.

Unless someone was a physical threat, of course, and Rio, as a human woman, would never be one of those.

"I'm going to kill that bastard with my bare hands," Lucan growled.

"And my job is to make sure you have plenty of time to do that."

One of the guards pointed off toward the stairwell's entry. "Go back to your quarters. Right now."

"Yeah, no." Lucan came to a halt, putting his hands in his pockets and rocking back and forth on the toes of his boots. "I'm well aware of what the Executioner has in there. Right now, as you say."

The guard leveled his gun right at Lucan's face. "I know you have special privileges, but fuck you."

Lucan leaned forward, puckered up, and kissed the muzzle of the weapon. "You're so cute. But the Executioner needs to know that that human female with him? She's his only way to Mozart. She's the source down in Caldwell that he's asked me to negotiate with. I brought her here to prove that we had the capacity to meet the supply she wants. We lose her, we lose all his business he planned for, paid for, is expecting, you know the drill."

As light dawned on the guard's Marblehead, that gun started to lower and Lucan shrugged. "If he's just plugged her full of lead? He's shit out of luck and he's going to blame you for not telling him who she is. Better hope the holes are somewhere that doesn't leak a lot—"

"Fuck," the guard said as he went for the door and entered a code. "Sir, we have a problem—"

As the way was opened, both of the guards, and then Lucan and Apex, funneled into the Executioner's private quarters. And what they saw was—

"Rio?" Lucan breathed.

In the center of the large open space, next to the army field desk that had been set up by the foot of a mattress . . . the human woman was standing over the dead body of the Executioner, the gun Lucan had given her in her hand.

She looked up—and did a double take, like seeing Lucan was the last thing she'd expected. Although as levels of shock-and-awe went, Lucan was feeling like he was totally winning in that department. Had she really just—

"He was going to kill me," she announced. "It was justifiable homicide."

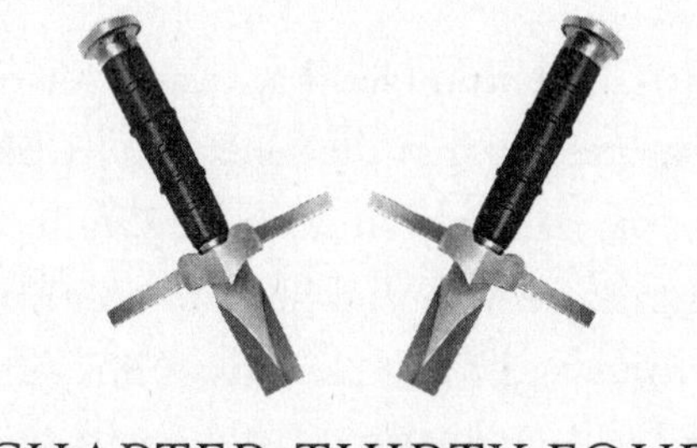

CHAPTER THIRTY-FOUR

Rio couldn't tell who was more surprised. The four men who rushed into whatever the hell space she was in . . . or the man she'd just killed with two bullets to the heart.

The shooting had happened in the blink of an eye. She'd been marched into the room and the guy in black with the shaved head had stood up from that table over there—and looked at her as if she were fresh meat.

The cold happiness on his face had been something to remember. Especially as he'd taken out a knife with a blade as long as his arm.

After he'd been informed where she'd been found, he'd excused the two guards, and the sound of the lock getting turned had been like a coffin lid secured over her body.

So self-assured he'd been, so completely in control. And in spite of her mental confusion, she'd known she had only one chance, given that tremendous, sword-like weapon in his hand.

Out with the gun. Two shots just like she was drilling targets at the range: Right into the center of his chest.

Real blink-of-an-eye stuff.

In the aftermath, he'd stumbled backward, looking at his sternum like he was baffled at the fact that the lead slugs hadn't bounced right off him or something. She hadn't been interested in his death throes other than monitoring him to be sure that he didn't get his hands on another weapon in his last three and a half seconds of life. After a couple of final twitches, he'd stayed still, and just as she'd wondered what the hell to do next—

The welcome party had burst in.

Luke jumped forward. "Are you all right?"

Rio was in his arms next.

She didn't know who went for who first. She didn't care. As she squeezed her eyes shut, she just held on to that strong, warm body, and breathed in his cologne, and felt gratitude for being alive.

Not that he wore cologne. God, he smelled like home . . .

Dimly, she was aware of a strange cracking sound. Then another. Followed by two duffle bags being dropped on the floor. Had he and Apex brought luggage?

Who cared. In this moment, Luke was what mattered.

"We've got to get you out of here," he said.

She pulled back and touched his face. Then came to her senses. "Not yet. I need to help—"

Rio didn't finish the thought as something in the background caught her attention. Looking around Luke's muscled arm, she blinked. A couple of times.

The two sounds she'd thought were bags hitting the floor had not been about any kind of Samsonite. Apex had done something dramatic to the two guards. The two men were both lying facedown—no, wait, their bodies were on their stomachs. Their heads were facing upward.

Meanwhile, the guy was walking over to the open door and calmly shutting it. Locking it. "We've got problems now."

"More," she corrected numbly. "We have *more* problems."

As she stated the obvious, a series of Caldwell Police Department rules and regulations weaved their way around the fact pattern of everything that had just happened with the man and the big knife and the handgun she still had in her palm.

She was in over her head. Big time. And her allies in the situation were a pair of drug-dealing killers.

"All right," Luke said as he started to pace around like he was thinking.

When he came up to a display of rifles mounted on the wall, he nodded like he'd sought their advice and decided to do what they'd told him to. "We need to play this like we've taken over. Apex, you and Mayhem will stand guard out in front of here until nightfall. No one will question it. Then, as soon as it's dark, I'll take her out—"

"Brace yourself for the head of the guards." Apex went over to check out the bald guy. "They've been looking for their opening all along, and they're going to see this corpse as a challenge, not a done deal. And do you really want to run this place?"

"We'll deal with that as it comes." Luke glanced to the closed door. "In the meantime, we make this death really fucking obvious. We hang the body up outside on the wall. It's a coup. We're in control now."

Apex shook his head. "It won't last. The guards are going to attack."

"It doesn't have to last. All I need is nightfall."

While they talked, Rio did some walking around herself, the contents of the large space finally registering properly. Things were set up as a military seat of command, the bed and an old forties wardrobe the only civilian furniture, the rest of it collections of rifles and guns, what she knew were explosives—and then other supplies including food, water, and camping equipment, like the man had been prepared to get gone at a moment's notice.

Coming up to a rudimentary conference table, she tried to look casual as she checked out all kinds of documents with columns on them. Everything was handwritten—which made sense as there was no computer or electronics around that she could see—and the data was organized by dates, weights, and dollars. Wait, there was also a list of names and times.

She needed to copy this all somehow, even though that was crazy.

And where's the money, she wondered.

With this sort of scale, there was going to be a crap ton of cash somewhere on the premises, and that presented both a security and a storage challenge.

Just before she turned away, she saw the cell phone. It was a newish one, without a protective case, nothing but a flat plane of glass you could access the world with. Glancing across at Luke and Apex, she put her hand out and scooped the slippery unit into her palm.

It didn't fit in her side pocket. Too big.

So she turned her back to the pair of them and put it down the front of her pants, inside her underwear.

When she pivoted around again, Apex had the dead guy up off the floor, the knife that had been in that hand falling loose and bouncing in a clatter.

"I'll take care of this," he said. "And find Mayhem."

With an utter lack of bother, like he was doing nothing more than moving a sack of potatoes around, he went over to a keypad, entered a series of numbers in a pattern, and opened the way out.

And then she and Luke were alone.

Well, as long as you didn't count the two dead guys on the floor. But really, they weren't going to interrupt much, were they.

"I need to put both of them out there, too," Luke said in an apologetic tone.

As if they were a pair of houseguests who had overstayed their welcome.

"I can help." She glanced over at him. "We'll do it together."

✦ ✦ ✦

"Are you okay?"

As Lucan asked the question, his eyes were making like they were tied to a brain that had any kind of medical training, going up and down Rio's body, searching for injury. More injury, that was. But she seemed all right. Her color was good and he could scent no blood other than the Executioner's.

Goddamn, the woman was like a cat with nine lives.

"Yeah, I'm all right." She continued her walk around, stopping over by the back door that led out into the parking area. "There's a keypad here. I'm taking that means it's got a lock on it."

"Yeah, everything's secured—" When she went to pull at the handle anyway, he put his hands forward. "Wait! Stop!"

She froze. "What?"

"Don't open that."

"Oh, you think it's alarmed?"

No, he didn't want to take any risk that it would let in a stream of daylight—because unless there was a nuclear-winter-worthy cloud cover in the sky, he'd end up a flaming ball of vampire.

"That's right," he lied. "We have to be careful. We don't want more company."

Rio dropped her hand and nodded. "You're right." She glanced back at him. "I don't know that I'm thinking right."

"Jesus, I wonder why."

He went over to her and held his arms out. The fact that she came up right against him was a relief.

"How did you do that?" he said as he looked at the bloodstains on the floor.

"Shoot the guy?" She shuddered, her strong body quaking. "I was just lucky. He underestimated me, and so did his guard. I wasn't searched. I had the gun. I used it. If they'd stripped me, I would have been in big trouble."

Stripped. As in weapons. As in . . . clothes.

In a surge of aggression, Lucan became furious enough to want to go out to the wall and kill the Executioner all over again.

"I'm going to get you back to Caldwell," he told her as he closed his eyes. "There are vehicles here, and I'll get a key, and . . ."

As she pushed herself away from him, he cleared his throat and prayed she wasn't going to argue with him. "What."

"I can't leave yet." She crossed her arms over her chest and stared at the guards Apex had taken care of. "I need to help that patient down in the clinic."

"That's not your problem."

"If not mine, whose? They don't know how to give him pain relief safely, they need me to help. I can get him—"

"Do you not remember what just happened here?" He pointed to that bloodstain by the bed. "How many near misses do you need before you stop rolling the dice with your life?"

She just shook her head. "I'm not leaving here until I help him. So you need to get me back in that room with the drugs—"

"Oh, come *on*—"

There was a series of beeps on the far side of the door, and Lucan put himself between Rio and whatever was coming in—

Apex entered with Mayhem tight on his heels. The latter clapped his hands and rubbed them together.

"Nice work, Lucan! How the hell did you get a clean shot at the Executioner?"

As Rio's eyes flared, Lucan muttered, "I didn't."

"Executioner?" she said.

Mayhem looked at her. Looked at Lucan. "*Exhibitioner* was what I meant. That motherfucker—'scuse my French—used to go around flashing people all the time. I mean, if I never see his pollywog and two lily pads again, it will be too soon. Phew. Thank God you shot him."

This was followed by a fist pump offer directed at Rio.

After which everybody just blinked at the guy.

"What?" Mayhem asked as he lowered his arm.

Like he was totally surprised that no one at the BBQ wanted to try his four-day-old, fermented homemade slaw.

"*So* glad you're here," Lucan said dryly. Then he turned back to Rio. "Listen, you're going to forget about Kane. You're leaving these quarters—"

"Don't you *dare* too-dangerous me." Rio glared at him. "I've earned the right to be taken seriously instead of coddled like a civilian—and the proof was right there at your feet until that body was taken out of here like a bag of sand."

As she jabbed a finger at where the remains had been, Lucan wanted to yell at the top of his lungs. Instead, he tried to rein himself in. "I know you want to take care of Kane, but he's fine—"

"Is that his name? Well, Kane is dying by inches, and he's in constant pain. Do you want to go through that? Or would you rather be spared some of the suffering by those around you who are able. What would you want, if it were you."

From over by the door, there was a soft curse, and Apex walked off sharply.

Rio continued to speak stridently. "That poor man's dying is not something you can stop, but his agony is. So someone is going to help me get some heroin to test and then we're going to take care of him." She glanced around at all of them, her eyes narrowed. "I'm not asking for permission, gentlemen. I'm looking for partners."

Mayhem spoke up at that. Of course he did. "As in crime? Partners in crime? Because we are sooooo good at that. I mean, we gotchu on the felony thing. Totally."

As Lucan pictured himself slapping the guy into silence, Mayhem shrugged. "What I say wrong now?"

Sweet Jesus, was all Lucan could think.

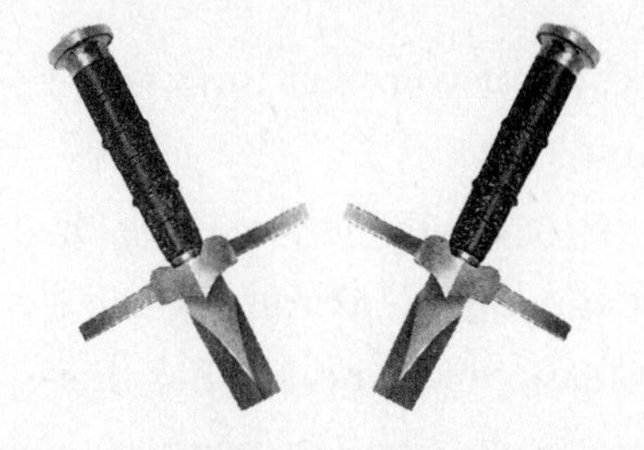

CHAPTER THIRTY-FIVE

"No," Vishous said. "The Jackal's not going to be involved in this search for the prison camp. Period, end of."

As he laid down the law, everyone in the King's study looked over at him. Including George, who you'd think would have been stone cold sleeping as he lay under his master's great carved desk, by the clawed feet of the great carved throne.

But nope. The golden retriever was alert and judging him, too, evidently.

Which just meant the dog was as nuts as the rest of them.

"The guy's not a trained fighter," V pointed out from his frilly silk chair. "And he's emotionally involved. That's a recipe for disaster if you're talking about being out in the field. Why are we bringing a liability into a situation that's already unstable?"

As Rhage and Butch stared at him like they were debating who had to answer the rhetorical, V looked around at all the French blue—and pictured the room redecorated with blood-red drapes and black walls. Maybe a rack in the corner. A display of whips and chains just to set the mood right.

You know, instead of Marie Antoinette, more like Metallica meets dungeons, no dragons.

No offense, Rhage, V thought as he took out a hand-rolled.

Across the way, the great Blind King leaned into his desktop, Wrath's heavy upper body flexing, the black muscle shirt he always wore stretching to accommodate the shift in bulk as he plugged his elbows into the blotter. The tattoos of his lineage, which ran up the insides of his forearms, flashed their design, particularly as he church-steepled his fingers.

"He knows how the prison camp runs, though." The King's wraparound sunglasses made the rounds among the troika, connecting the dots between Rhage and Butch on the sofas and V on his satellite bergère, even though the male couldn't see. "That's helpful intel. He knows the people in there, the power structure, the way it functions."

"But that was before." V recrossed his legs and sank further into the down-stuffed cushion under his ass. "At the new site? Who knows what it's like. And if we find it—"

"When," Wrath cut in.

"—I don't want to go into a raid worried about someone getting popped because they're having a moment with their long-lost buddies. We've got the full Brotherhood, the Band of Bastards, and the other fighters to coordinate. That's a lot of moving, stabbing, shooting parts—and we're all trained for this shit. I mean, Christ."

Over by the crackling fire, Rhage cocked an eyebrow. Then reached into the pocket of his SUNY Caldwell sweatshirt and pulled out a bag of M&M's.

Fuck off, V mouthed as the brother jogged the shit.

"It's the first rule of combat," V continued. "Don't bring civilians into a fight. You'll just end up saving them instead of actually getting the job done."

Butch, who was dressed in one of his slick Tom Ford suits, put his dagger hand up. "I think the Jackal's got a helluva lot of heart, and I'm not sure why locking him out is a thing. We're just looking for the place. When we find it, he can dematerialize to safety."

"You think he's going to do that?" V couldn't believe he had to argue the obvious. "You really think that guy with 'a helluva lot of heart' is not going to try to save his little friends the second he gets the coordinates?"

On that note, V started patting around for his lighter so his nicotine delivery system could get its groove on. When he couldn't find the damned thing, he cursed himself.

How was it possible that he'd left his Bic behind? Oh, right. Up until about five minutes ago, he'd been so relaxed and loose, he hadn't assumed he'd be smoking anything. Then this bright idea had been floated out at what was supposed to have been a brief, nothing-new-on-the-prison-camp-but-we're-going-back-out-on-the-streets meeting.

No wonder yoga had to be done three or four times a week to work for most people. Calm had a shelf life only as long as your next crisis.

"I think the Jackal's earned the right to choose." Butch shrugged, those hazel eyes focusing on the middle ground in front of his face, as if he were gathering his thoughts. "Like Rhage reported, the poor sonofabitch didn't want to leave the other prisoners behind and hasn't gotten over it. If that's the crucible he wants to fall on, who are we to stop him? It matters how you leave things—and who you leave behind."

So V's roommate was thinking about his partner again.

Great.

V started patting pockets on his chest that he didn't have.

On the far side of the coffee table, Hollywood jostled the M&M's bag again, a soft rustling rising up from the candy.

Fuck off, V mouthed.

Why? Rhage lip-sync'd back. *You know you'll feel better—*

"I don't feel bad now!"

"What?" Wrath demanded.

V burst to his feet, and went over to try to be casual by the marble fireplace. "Nothing. I'm fine—I'm perfect." He glared at Rhage. "Look, the Jackal has a mate now. A son, too, from what I've heard. He's got a shot at living his life. He needs to count his fucking blessings and sit on the sidelines, true? This isn't his business."

Over at the desk, Wrath shook his head. "I think maybe you're a little off today, V. Are you hungry or something?"

"Maybe too sober?" Rhage added helpfully.

"I'm fucking fantastic. You want me to drop and give you ten to prove it?"

One of Wrath's black brows lifted over his wraparounds. "You don't usually worry about other people's family lives. Especially ones you don't know."

"Fine, a hundred. We'll do a hundred. Just to prove I'm great."

V dropped down to the antique carpet, punched his palms into the delicate, swirly rug, and assumed a plank position. Then he pumped it out.

"One, two, three—"

"It's the Jackal's choice," Butch said over the counting. "That's my point. If it were me, I'd be eaten alive by the fact that I didn't get others out."

"—eleven, twelve—"

"Is he really doing push-ups," Wrath muttered. "Jesus, V, give it a rest."

"—eighteen, nineteen, twenty—"

"No one is paying attention to your pneumatic display." The King cursed. "Can one of you get him back on track? And I'm going to let the Jackal—"

V upped the ante on his volume. "*—twenty-three, twenty-four, twenty-five, twenty—*"

"—MAKE HIS OWN DECISION." Wrath spoke up loudly. "If the motherfucker wants to be involved in finding the place, and then go in with you when you do, it's up to him. But you bunch of maladjusted meatheads have to let him know the score. He gets left behind if things go tits up, and his life will not be prioritized above any of yours. If he's fine with that playing field, I'm not going to get in his way."

"That's fair," Butch hollered.

"Good," Rhage barked over the counting. "Glad we got that settled."

"—*thirty-one, thirty-two*—"

"Will you stop him," Wrath ordered, "before I throw a dagger at him."

From out of the corner of his eye, V notice Rhage bursting up—which kind of made sense. Wrath was capable of a lot of things, and could handle himself in a fight even without his eyesight—but you didn't necessarily want to be in range of him pitching a blade across a room.

"—*thirty-three, thirty-four—OW!*"

A tremendous weight landed on V's back, like someone had dropped a car on his spine from three stories up. And as his elbows gave out under Rhage's cop-a-squat, the rug rose up to slap him in the pie-hole.

"Get off me," V growled.

The bag of M&M's appeared next to his eyeballs.

With a roar, he snatched the candy and pitched Rhage off, the brother flying backwards across the room, antiques no doubt cringing everywhere.

Except Hollywood somehow managed to flop into a lie-down on the sofa he'd started out in.

"Nailed it," he said with a wink as he put his hands behind his head and relaxed like the stretch-out totally worked for him. "And I'm just taking a page from your armchair example, my brother."

V headed for the door with the M&M's, ripping open the bag and pouring some in his mouth to chew—because it was either that or he was going to be up-close-and-personal with Rhage's shit-eating grin in a way that would cause a lot of swelling in the guy's pretty features.

"I think you're all making the wrong call," V said around the melted candy in his mouth. "And if you'll excuse me, I have to go find a lighter."

"Are you eating chocolate?" Wrath asked as V yanked open the way out.

"No, I'm not."

As he poured more M&M's down his gullet, he caught sight of Rhage glancing over at Butch, and making little circles next to his head.

"Oh, and P.S., we haven't found the new location yet," V said over his shoulder as he stepped free of the study. "So the Jackal and his co-dependency issues with people in his past are a moot point."

God, where had his post-session float gone?

It was like that shit with Jane hadn't even happened, he thought as he finished the bag out in the hall.

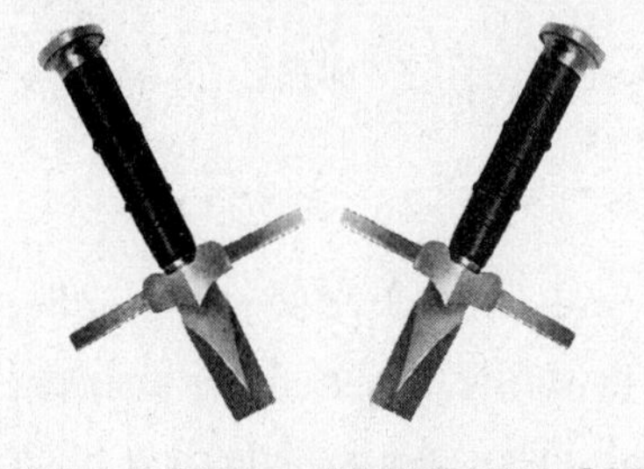

CHAPTER THIRTY-SIX

If she wants to go to the workroom, we go with her."

As Apex laid things out like that, Rio appreciated the unexpected ally. Walking up to him, she nodded at the door. "All you have to do is take me back down the hall. I've got the layout of the room. I'll be in and out in a second with a sample."

Looking over her shoulder, she cut Luke's protest off. "I know the drugs. I sell them. When was the last time you were picking between bales of white powder and knowing the difference between coke and heroin? You're a negotiator, not a processor, right?"

"It's not that hard," he said remotely. "One lick and I know the difference."

"Do you know how to test it? Do you know what to do with the pure stuff?"

He opened his mouth. Shut it. Opened it again.

"Let's get this done and over with," she said. "You told me that it was quiet during the day. We just killed the two guards outside, and the head of it all. No one knows we're up here right now. Things will never be safer."

Luke's eyes burned—but not from anger. It was from something else, something she wasn't sure she could handle right now. Or maybe at all.

"Rio, it's an unnecessary risk—"

Apex spoke up. "To who? Not to me. Not to fucking Kane. It's not unnecessary at all. And she's right, we don't handle drugs. We're not part of the workers, and never have been. What the hell do we know?"

"Do you want to die here, Rio?" Luke demanded as he ignored the other man. "You want this to be how it ends for you?"

"Oh, absolutely," she snapped. "That's why I let that man murder me about fifteen minutes ago. Instead of shooting him in the heart. Twice."

There was a tense standoff. And then Luke broke away and walked around like there was so much anger flowing through his veins, he had to either move or explode.

When he stopped short, she had no idea what was going to come out of his mouth.

"Fine, but I'm taking her down." He jabbed a finger at Apex. "You're too involved."

"And you've bonded with her," the other man snapped. "So who's the problem here?"

Luke marched right over to the guy. "You don't know what you're talking about."

Bonded? Rio thought.

Before a brawl got started—because, yeah, that was going to be *so* helpful—she double-checked the clip in her gun and walked over to the door out to the hall.

"What's the combination to this keypad?"

Mayhem, who'd been totally quiet, joined her. "I got it."

He put in a pattern and the lock shifted—

"Will you let me get armed first?" Luke bitched.

"We're leaving now," Rio announced as she opened things and stepped out—

Oh . . . *God*.

The man she'd shot had been spear-mounted on the wall, sharp pegs stabbed through the back of his throat as well as in various places down his torso, his body weight suspended off the floor.

"You wanted to do this," Luke said to her in a low voice.

She looked at him. "No, I *have* to do this."

"You don't even know Kane."

"This is about my brother," she blurted. "I was forced to learn a helluva lot of things I didn't want to while trying to deal with his overdose. At least now, I can put some of the knowledge to good use. Let's go."

Rio walked off in a daze, her past tangling with the present—but she had to snap out of all that. Which, as Luke had pointed out, was the survivor thing, wasn't it: Stay focused, stay sharp, stay in the here-and-now. It helped you not get shot.

Besides, when she'd been escorted down here by that guard, she'd had that crushing headache and all those weird thoughts. She couldn't afford to waste this opportunity to mentally record the details of the building.

Forcing herself to plug into her environment, she saw—

Four rooms. There were four processing rooms, going by the layouts down the long hall, and she stopped at the door the guard had walked her out of.

"Here."

Luke stepped up next to her. "We gotta move fast."

"Thanks for the tip." Rio rolled her eyes. "I was going to stroll around and maybe do a little feng shui inside. You know, redecorate some. Maybe design a mural."

Luke shook his head and glanced over his shoulder. "Mayhem, do you have the—"

"Code?" the guy said. "Yup. Aren't you glad when I set this all up, I kept a default?"

"How did they not kill you?" Luke said like he was pondering a law of the universe and wondering why it existed.

"They don't think I'm very smart." The guy stepped up to another keypad and entered a different pattern. "There are advantages to appearing to be an imbecile."

"Well, you're an expert in that," Luke muttered.

When the lock clicked free, Rio opened the way in—and immediately started for the cage of kilos in the corner.

"You stay out here," Luke ordered Mayhem before joining her.

As the door eased shut behind them, she took a deep breath and smelled the unpleasant chemical sting in the air. She hadn't noticed it before, probably because she'd been frantic.

"What happened to your brother?"

Rio nearly lost her stride as she went around one of the worktables. "What?"

"You heard me."

"The testing chemicals are on the desks over there." Clearing her throat, she rerouted her trajectory and went to one of the supervisors' monitoring positions. "This is exactly what I need."

Putting her hand into a wicker basket full of ampoules, she nodded. "Yup, this'll do for testing."

The thing was even trademarked NarcoCheck. She couldn't have done better if she'd ordered the stuff herself.

"Now can you get me in that?" she said as she nodded at the cage.

Luke crowded into her personal space. "Stay behind me."

"Why, what are you going to—"

The shot rang out in the room, sharp and loud, and Rio covered her head and hit the floor. Fortunately, the bullet ricocheted elsewhere—and what do you know, from around the edge of the desk, she saw the chain link uncoil and fall free of the bin.

Rio didn't wait for the all-clear. She rushed over to the cage, opened the front access panel, and reached in to the blocks. Which were marked "H" or "C."

Go *figure what that meant,* she thought as she thanked the Lord for the bene she hadn't expected. And jeez, it meant Apex or Luke could have done this part of things after all.

Grabbing one of the "H" blocks, she went over to the desk. She thought about just taking some of the test solution units with her, but then what if the label on the block meant something else?

There was a pair of scissors by the desk, and she pierced the wrap on the kilo and got some of the powder on the blades. A quick drop from the dropper, and the substance turned yellow. She'd been hoping against hope it would be red for morphine, but what could you do.

"Do you need a cutting agent?" Luke asked.

"No," she said as she paused to inspect the consistency of the heroin. "This is extremely pure. So we're going to use a small amount and dilute it with boiled water."

"How will you be sure of the dose?"

"I'm going to give him it intravenously bit by bit. The effect is fairly instantaneous so we'll know by how he eases."

"Just don't kill him."

Rio focused on his face for the first time since he'd walked through the door into those private quarters. He looked . . . exhausted nearly to the point of sickness, with black circles under his eyes and lids at half-mast. Although she couldn't tell whether the latter was because he still thoroughly disapproved of what she'd insisted she do.

"I won't," she said as she tucked the kilo against her. "Can you take me directly to the clinic?"

"Can't you just tell me what to do? You can stay with Apex and Mayhem in the private quarters—"

"I'll answer that the same way I did to Apex. At least I know what I'm doing."

Luke cursed. Then rubbed his head like it hurt. "Look, we can't stay down there long. This place is going to start waking up soon. Once that happens, we need to get you out fast and it's easiest from where we were. All we do is go right out the other door."

She left that potential argument alone and headed for the exit—except then she doubled back and went around behind the desk. Going through the drawers, she pulled them open one by one—

"Thank God," she muttered as she reached into the big one down by the floor.

"What is it?"

"Narcan pens. In case I get it wrong."

The entire drawer was full of them, loose and out of their boxes, like their use was a fairly normal occurrence. She speared into the collection and took as many as she could fit in her fist. Then she shoved them at Luke, making him hold the load.

"Okay, we're ready."

Luke filled his pockets with the pens. And then stared across the space at her.

"What," she demanded.

"We go down there, you do whatever you have to, and then we're going back to those private quarters."

"All right. Fine."

✦ ✦ ✦

Lucan emerged from the workroom first. Apex and Mayhem were right out in the hall, guns that they'd lifted from the Executioner's stash by their sides. They hadn't changed into the uniforms of the guards, but the weapons spoke for themselves. If any prisoners happened to break curfew and run into them? No questions would be asked.

And up here? Well, the Executioner pegged on that wall like a side of beef was a helluva banner.

"We're going to the clinic," he said. But as if those males didn't know what the plan was?

Lucan stayed by Rio as the four of them proceeded down the corridor. Rio kept looking around like she couldn't believe the scale of the operation.

"Checking out to see if we can take care of your boss's needs?" he heard himself say bitterly. After all, Executioner or not, he shouldn't kid himself. There were still drugs that had to be sold, weren't there.

She glanced over her shoulder. "I'll tell him all about it when I see him."

As she refocused ahead of herself, he pictured her back in Caldwell, living her life. Without him. The stab of pain in his chest made him wonder why he couldn't pull out of this . . . whatever it was . . . with her. Deal or no deal, she was going back down south. He was staying here.

But hey, they'd be able to see each other as they made new deals.

How fucking romantic.

When they came to the stairwell, he opened the door and put his palm up so she didn't immediately follow him. Then he sniffed at the air and listened.

"The nurse is already down there," Apex said. "I told her we needed her."

Lucan nodded and motioned Rio through. As they jogged a descent, the other two brought up the rear.

When they got to the bottom floor underground, he didn't need to tell Rio where to go, which turns to take, how to be as quiet as she could. She went right down to the clinic and immediately inside.

The second they all entered the storage room, the curtain around Kane's bed was pulled back, the nurse's flowing robes like an extension of that which fell from the ceiling.

"You shall not hurt him?" the female said from behind the mesh covering her face.

Rio shook her head gravely. "No, never. I just . . . want to help."

"I never dared to try to secure any of that." The nurse pointed out from under a voluminous sleeve, her gloved hand shaking as if she were emotional. "It's secured and difficult to obtain, and if you are found with it, the consequences are dire."

"I understand. Do you have any distilled water? Or boiled water?"

"Yes, here. Come."

As the females disappeared behind the draping, Lucan crossed his arms so that the gun in his hand pointed out behind his armpit. "I'm not going in there."

"I am."

When Apex started forward, Lucan snagged the male's heavy arm. "You don't hurt her. If this goes bad, and something happens to Kane, it's not her fault."

The other prisoner lowered his chin and glared out of his deep eye sockets. "That depends on what she does. And how he responds."

Lucan bared his fangs. "You can't blame her."

"I can do whatever the fuck I want."

"Not with her you can't."

There was a brief, surging tension. And then Apex pulled away, parting the drapes and disappearing through them. As the lengths of fabric resettled themselves, there were murmurs from the other side.

Pacing seemed like a good idea, so Lucan walked down the lineup of beds. Came back. Went down again. Came back. Meanwhile, Mayhem just stood where he was, staring at the fall of sheets.

Maybe the prisoner was projecting good vibes into whatever the hell was happening at that bedside. Maybe he was having a stroke and hadn't fallen over yet. Maybe he was thinking about absolutely nothing at all.

Total toss-up.

Lucan went to the door that opened out into the corridor. Cracking the panel, he double-checked that there was no one coming. When that didn't seem like enough, he stepped outside and went all the way down to peer into the stairwell.

No sounds. No scents. But that could change at any moment.

All he could think about was how much he didn't want this exposure for Rio or this wasted time. No offense to Kane.

When he reentered the clinic, Mayhem looked over at him.

"You know," the male said, "this place is going to be in chaos when the Executioner's body is discovered. And we need to get rid of the guards in the quarters. For one, it'll keep things tidy, for another, they're going to start to smell. But the real reason is the head of the guards. If they know we killed that kind of personnel? It's going to make everything harder."

The guy did have a point. "We'll figure it out."

"Of course, if you deliberately want to stir up shit, we could just put 'em on the wall. Hang 'em like paintings—oh, we could make a decoration with them. How about high-fiving. Shooting a basket—"

"No."

"You're boring."

"You think this is a Mr. Popular competition?" Then Lucan shook his head. "You're right, though, we should dispose of them. If the head of the guards doesn't know where they are, and we're not obvious about what we did, they won't know who did the coup right away and what went down. They'll have to check all the troops, and because some live off-site, it'll take some time—which we'll use to get Rio out of here. If only there was a way to get them outside. We've got another hour of sunshine left."

"Rio could do it."

Looking over at the guy, Lucan said, "No, she can't—"

"What can't I do?" Rio asked as she emerged from the draping.

"Nothing—"

"Help us take those two guards outside," Mayhem cut in. "That back entrance from the private quarters is—"

"She is not—"

"—going to make it simple and you wouldn't have to take them far."

"—taking them anywhere."

"Sure," Rio said. "I'm strong. I'll move them."

"No," Lucan snapped. "It's too fucking dangerous."

"And you can relax with that." She looked between him and Mayhem. "I heard what you said. I think it makes a lot of sense. The more confusion, the better, especially if you're worried about the head of the guards, whoever he is."

Mayhem shot Lucan a smarty-pants look. "Great, we'll go back to the quarters and—"

The draping around the bed was whipped aside.

Apex locked eyes with Rio, with an intensity that was so great, the male was trembling from it, his huge, lethal body poised to leap on the woman.

"No!" Lucan barked as he threw himself between them. "I told you it's not her fault!"

"What happened?" Rio shoved him out of the way . . . then dug into the pockets of his pants. "I have the Narcan—"

With a surge, Apex jumped forward.

And wrapped his arms around Rio. Letting out a choked sigh, he dropped his head into her neck . . . and held on like she was the only thing keeping him on the planet.

Over the male's heavy shoulder, Rio's eyes squeezed shut and she embraced him back. "Oh, Apex, I'm so sorry, I really tried to help—"

The nurse ducked her hooded head out from behind the drapery. "He's resting comfortably. For the first time since he came to me."

Now Rio's eyes flared back open. There were tears in them. "Thank God he's not in pain."

Lucan exhaled a breath he hadn't been aware of holding.

And wondered what the hell the story with her brother was.

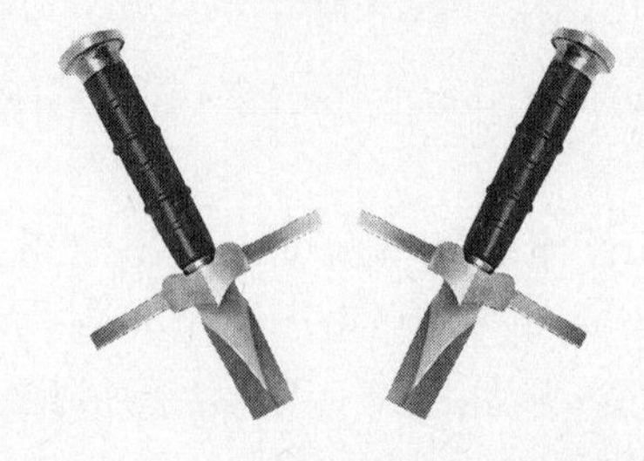

CHAPTER THIRTY-SEVEN

Captain?"

As José came up to the open office door, he knocked on the jamb. "You receiving there, Captain? Willie isn't at her desk."

From out of the private bathroom in the far corner, a muffled voice answered with what could have been anything: *Hello. Not now. Come in.* Fortunately, a second later, Stan emerged from his favorite crapper, as he called it. His frown was deep as a cavern, and at his throat, a tie was in the process of being redone. Or undone. Hard to tell which.

"You taking that off or making sure it stays on?" José asked.

"Wish I didn't have to wear it at all. But the one I put on this morning got mustard on it at lunch. Well, I got French's on my sport coat, too." Stan nodded over to the sofa where a wad of navy blue had been tossed onto the cushions. "Good thing I have second sets of everything in my favorite crapper."

Nailed it, José thought.

"The sacred private head, a joy to behold." He entered and parked it on the hard chair just inside the door. "Where no one but the chief ever goes."

"It's the only throne I have. What can I say."

José nodded. "I'd protect it jealously, too, if I were you. Especially considering how many officers hit the food trucks for lunch."

"That's where I got mustarded, as a matter of fact. And I can't show up at Stephan Fontaine's with part of a ham and cheese on my chest. Right by my name tag."

"Wow, Fontaine's. Fancy."

"Just another rubber chicken dinner."

As they went back and forth, José let his eyes go on a roam. He'd spent so much time updating Stan on cases and problems in the department that he was familiar with every framed picture on the walls, as well as the window that looked out over the back parking lot, and the perpetual clutter on the desk, and the American flag folded military-style in its triangled box on the shelves. Closing his eyes, it was like a video game he'd overplayed when he was a kid, the details projected on the backs of his lids.

Was he going to miss this? he wondered.

No, he didn't think so, he decided.

"I'd be surprised if they serve chicken," he murmured, "much less the rubber kind of poultry, at Fontaine's."

"You're probably right." Stan finished knotting the tie and flipped his collar down. "But at the end of the day, this event is just like any other one. You know the deal. Some rich jackhole's giving money to every nonprofit in town, and we've got that Police Benevolent Fund. Wouldn't mind if some of his benevolence headed in our direction."

"You've always been about the rank and file, Stan."

"Speaking of which, what's going on with our missing officer." The captain sat down in his leather chair. "Any leads on Hernandez-Guerrero's location?"

"No, I'm sorry to report."

Stan cursed and smoothed that new tie. Which looked exactly the same as all of his ties. "Jesus, José. What are we going to tell her family?"

"She doesn't have any."

"Wait, did I know that? I think I knew that. And no boyfriends, husbands, that kind of thing, right?"

"No, she lived alone. There are a couple of cousins out of town, and we're waiting to hear back from them."

Shaking his head, Stan's eyes got a faraway look. "You're lucky you're retiring. I don't know how much more I can take of this shit. What about Officer Roberts? How's his family?"

"Awful. Just awful."

"Goddamn. Least he didn't have a wife and kids, and if that's all you can say about a situation, it's pretty fucking crappy."

As Stan stared off into space, they stayed in silence for a minute, no longer captain and subordinate, just two men who had known each other for over twenty years, in a context that could get really tough sometimes.

"You know," Stan said, "my Ruby used to be great in situations like this. That woman would bend over backwards for any family of a slain officer. She'd cook them meals that froze well—big deal, the whole freezing-well thing. She'd visit and do chores. Pick up kids, if she had to. She was great, an extension of the department."

"Yeah. How's she doing?"

"Good. Her second marriage is going way better than her first. Big surprise, huh." Stan rubbed his face and looked over his messy desk with an expression of hopelessness that had nothing to do with all the paperwork. "She was right to leave me. Too many frozen meal orders, and that wasn't the half of it. You're lucky you're still married."

"I am." José glanced at the window, and wanted to change the subject—like he had some kind of nuptial survivor's guilt. "Light's getting low early now."

"Winter is coming. Anyway, enough about ex-wives and the weather. Tell me what you know so far about Officer Roberts."

"Yeah, so the coroner bumped the autopsy up and performed it this afternoon. I just got the results. We got a bullet."

"Good. Ballistics working on it?"

"Yup. Meanwhile, Treyvon and I went through Roberts's apartment."

"Did you find anything?"

"Nothing we didn't expect. Old takeout in the fridge. Beer cans in the recycling bin. No signs of a struggle or a robbery. We didn't come across any car keys, but they could have fallen out of a pocket when he was in the river. Same with his wallet."

"What about the car?"

"Haven't located that yet. It'll turn up."

"This city is getting too violent." Stan cursed again. "Maybe I just need to go on a vacation, get recharged. Or retire, like you."

"You got a good pension."

"No, I got good debt. I had to second-mortgage everything to pay Ruby off—so she could afford that other wedding dress of hers. And anyway . . . normal life is expensive." He shrugged. "Then again, I could always get another job after this one. Maybe I can open a food truck. Or drive one, as it were."

"Do you cook?"

"Okay, something else then." The captain motioned around his desk. "Come on, I'm too old school for this job now. Look at this shit. Everything's about computers, and has been for a decade. Maybe longer. I'm next to useless."

"The officers love you. You got a lot of loyalty among the rank and file."

"That new mayor, though. She's going to run me out." Stan shrugged. "Maybe I only need a sailboat."

"For, like, recreation?"

"As an escape."

"Have you been on the water before? Do you even swim?"

"Are you just here to poke holes in all my future plans? And I'm just talking about sailing off into the sunset. Hey, so what are you going to do with all your free time?"

José laughed softly. "I'ma start by going an entire week without getting woken up in the middle of the night."

"You have low standards, my friend."

"Fair enough." José got to his feet. "Have fun at Mr. Fontaine's."

"Hey, do you need any other resources to help you with both those cases?"

José shook his head. "Treyvon and I got this. And everyone in the department is helping."

"That's great. That's how it should be." Stan shifted his weight up onto his worn loafers and held his forefinger on high. "Listen, before I forget, can you give me a copy of the most updated report on Roberts? I'm hounded by cameras everywhere I go, and I need to be prepared for the questions with all relevant details. Controlling your expression when you're confronted by shit is harder than you think, and the press seems to know everything."

"Man, I'm glad I don't have your job."

"I just want to be prepared."

"Of course. And I'll get you everything before I leave tonight."

"Hate to ask you to stay late."

"It's my job. At least for another four weeks."

Goodbyes were said, and then José closed the door behind himself and gave a wave to Willie, the captain's executive assistant, who was back at her desk in the waiting room.

Homicide was just down the hall from the chief's suite, and on the approach, he could hear the murmuring voices of the bullpen out in the corridor. Walking into the open area with its cubicles and fast-talking detectives, he felt an old, familiar charge go through him. It wasn't pleasurable, per se, but he didn't dislike it, either.

The idea of never experiencing the adrenaline surge again made him feel like he was in a kind of mourning.

Trying to keep himself from overthinking everything, he headed for

Trey's desk and thought about Stan's chief shit—and was so glad the force didn't have some disconnected bureaucrat sitting in that chair.

If that man was serious about leaving, too, José had another reason to be glad he was retiring.

Things were going to change in the CPD if Stan was no longer in charge.

And not in a good way.

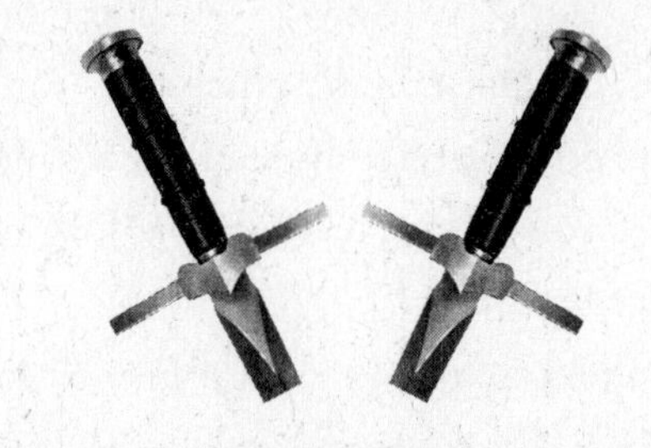

CHAPTER THIRTY-EIGHT

Back at the prison camp, Rio's mind was churning as she returned to those private quarters upstairs. As Mayhem entered the code again and sprang the lock, she walked in and stood over the bodies of the two guards. As an undercover officer, there were rules and regulations about things she could and couldn't do, and she wasn't exactly sure how many she had tripped up in the last twenty-four hours. Then again, everyone back in Caldwell no doubt thought she was dead.

Not that that gave her a pass.

"Just outside, then?" she said. "Where exactly?"

This gruesome task was necessary. She needed to get a sense of the exterior of the facility, and she was running out of time. They were liable to blindfold her on the way out when they left after dark, so if she could see the exterior of the building now, it would make it easier to identify and locate the operation, wherever it was.

"Just right outside." Mayhem went over to the other door on the back wall. "All you have to do is take them down the shallow stairs and leave them right there—"

"This is ridiculous."

As Luke spoke up, they both looked at him. Well, didn't he seem happy. He had crossed his arms, planted his boots, and was the very picture of over-my-dead-body.

Ha-ha, Rio thought grimly as she glanced down at the guards. "Look, I can handle it, okay? You think these are the first corpses I've seen—or handled?"

"It doesn't matter—"

"Yes, it does." She *had* to check out the outside of the building. "And it won't take me any time at all."

When she went to hook her hands under one of the guards' armpits, Luke stepped in. "No. I'll do it. I'll take them—"

"Are you out of your fucking mind?" Mayhem blurted.

"There's a little cover over the door. It'll be okay."

There was a tense pause between the two men, as if they were communicating telepathically. And then Mayhem shrugged as if Luke had won the argument with some really bad logic.

"I guess I'll just make sure she gets out of here alive," the guy muttered. "That's all I got."

"Don't be so fucking dramatic." Luke picked the guard up off the floor, and slung the dead body over his shoulder. "Get the door, will you?"

"You better hope it's cloudy," Mayhem announced.

"Like she said, I won't be long."

In the back of Rio's mind, she tried to find a protest that wouldn't make them suspicious. When she failed, she could only impotently watch Luke—and she couldn't help but note how easy it was for him to lift a heavily muscled man up off the floor. And deadweight was tough because there was little resistance to get a grip on.

She couldn't imagine being that physically strong.

As Mayhem entered a different code on the pad than the one at the other door, she memorized the pattern—and was surprised at the smell of fresh pine as things were opened. Light from an overhead fixture showed off all kinds of new construction, but as with everything she'd seen that had been recently added, nothing was painted or finished beyond the rough-in first stage of the work.

Luke descended four or five steps; then he paused at a second, reinforced door—and looked back at her.

For a moment that felt like an eternity, he stared at Rio like he was memorizing her face.

"You can trust Apex, too," he said roughly. "The bastard's a sociopath, but he feels like he owes you, so you're safe with him."

Dear Lord, he was saying goodbye.

"What the hell is out there?" she asked.

Mayhem drew her away and closed them in the quarters together. Putting his back to the panel, he squeezed his eyes shut.

Then they waited. And waited . . .

. . . and waited.

As time stretched out, Mayhem started to roam around, hands in pockets, hands out of pockets. He looked at a watch on his wrist—that was not actually there—and for the first time, Rio noticed what he was wearing. It was the same kind of loose sweatshirt Luke wore. And his boots were the same. Pants, too.

Like it was a uniform.

"How long's he been gone?" she blurted. Because she was wondering, herself. Worried, herself.

Abruptly, he turned to her, took out a gun that was so big, it surely qualified as a hand cannon—and held the weapon out to her.

"You've got to go and check on him. I can't."

Rio didn't even hesitate. She took the forty. "Open that door right now."

The man went over to the keypad. "Listen, once you're out there, I can't help you. You're on your own. Just please . . . bring him back. He can be an asshole, but I'm kind of fond of him."

"Don't worry. I got him."

✦ ✦ ✦

The sun was low in the horizon, its angle sharp, its rays dulled by the seasonal tilt of the earth on its axis. There was even some cloud cover in the sky, and on top of all that, there were trees around—granted, with not much on their limbs, but the trunks and branches were not invisible.

Yet Lucan didn't make it more than two feet out of the door.

Yes, there was an overhang, but that didn't do shit when that great-ball-of-fire was so close to going down on the horizon: The low position of the sun meant the blinding, strength-sucking golden light hit him like a ton of bricks, the force of it taking his breath away. As he slumped, he lost his hold on the guard's body, but that did not matter.

Instantly, he couldn't see anything.

The world turned into a shapeless, formless bank of white, and he spun around, thinking he was facing the door. Except he wasn't. He put his hands out, but he couldn't find the handle. Couldn't find the building.

He tripped over something. Fell down. Pushed himself up—

Burning now.

Was it his skin? Yes. And the pain was so paralyzing, he landed face-first in dirt.

Holy shit, he thought. This was how he died. He couldn't believe it.

There had been a number of other situational volunteers for the lights-out trophy, from accidents, to fights, to an infection when he'd been a young . . . and then there had been the dreaded transition, because he was a half-breed and that was how vampires matured.

But after surviving all of those assaults on his mortality, he had lived to discover that this, this oven-hot-baking-sheet stretch of asphalt, was how it happened. This sun bath was the answer to the question that every person who was alive, be they vampire, wolven—even human—wondered about in some dark corner of their mind.

And the weirdest thing was . . . he couldn't stop thinking about Rio.

Fear for her life made him try desperately to find the door. Casting his hands out, he dragged himself forward, even though he knew damn well that he could just be pulling himself farther and farther away from safety—

"Luke!"

The voice confused him. What was Rio doing out here? Oh, right. The white landscape around him had to be the Fade—the place where vampires went to spend eternity. And hey, it turned out that the female you wanted to be with was your greeter—

Shit!

"Rio," he mumbled. "Are you dead?"

"Come on, stand up."

In the great abyss of his pain, he still wanted to please her, do what she asked of him. So he attempted to get to his feet.

"Fuck," he groaned as a hold locked around his waist and yanked him forward.

He stumbled into something hard, his face taking the brunt of the impact, and then his balance listed. There was a series of beeps. And then another series—

"Goddamn it, what's the code?" Rio barked.

Lucan weaved on his feet, and the collapse that was coming his way speeded up like it was a boomerang looking for the hand that threw it: One minute he was holding his own against gravity; the next, he was horizontal, his face back in the dirt, his body not responding to all kinds of get-up, get-up, *get-up*'s.

After that, there was a split second of relative silence. Which was followed by a helluva lot of noise.

Bang! Bang! Bang!

"Mayhem! I need the code—he's dying! What's the code—"

Lucan threw his hand out toward Rio's voice, and he got something on her, an ankle, he supposed. "Rio—"

"I need the code! Mayhem—"

"Shh. Rio. Listen to me." When it was clear he wasn't getting anywhere, he used what felt like the last of his strength to yell, "*Rio!*"

There was a pause, and then her voice was very close to his ear. "I'm getting help. I just need to get help—"

"Listen." When she fell silent, he talked fast because he knew he was out of time. "I'm so glad I met you—"

"What are you talking about? I need to—"

Lucan grabbed at thin air—and then happened to snag her hand. Pulling her back down, he said hoarsely, "I wish we'd had more nights and days, you and me. I think we really could have been something."

"Stop talking. Save your strength."

As he went quiet, he wasn't sure whether he was following her directive—or was just about to stop breathing altogether.

He wished he could have told her more because they had had more together. More time, more peaceful surroundings, more kissing.

More . . . love.

But that, his dying heart knew, was not a gift given to the likes of drug dealers and half-breeds.

And more was the pity.

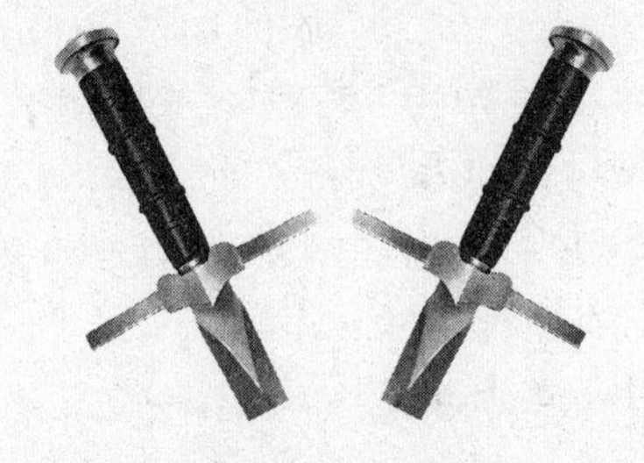

CHAPTER THIRTY-NINE

Through the swirling smoke and terrible grilled-meat smell of burning flesh, Rio restarted with the pounding on the metal panel. She couldn't hear the sound the impacts were making or what she was yelling. All she was aware of was that Luke was facedown on the ground beside an out-and-out bonfire and she needed to get him back inside.

"Mayhem!"

She glanced back at Luke. His big body was in a sprawl, and one of his hands seemed to be smoking—and it was obvious what had happened. Even though there were no gas fumes in the air, he'd clearly used an accelerant on the dead body and tossed a match, and the explosion had blown up in his face and lit him on fire. In a fit of self-preservation, he'd done a stop, drop, and roll, and she worried about what the front of him looked like.

God, she prayed his lungs were okay.

"Help!" she yelled.

Right next to them, the fire was doubling and redoubling, the heat curling off the remains of the guard in ever greater intensity. If the blaze kept growing, she was going to have to drag Luke away—

The door flew open, something breaking through it—a black bag—no, the other guard's body had been used like a battering ram. And as she caught sight of the shallow stairwell, she had a split second image of Mayhem with his arm raised to cover his face, his balance falling away, his body landing back on the pine steps like he'd passed out.

Just before the door clapped shut, she buttressed it with her hip and then she extended her leg and held it in place with her foot.

After that, her superpowers kicked in.

Even though Luke had a hundred pounds on her, she somehow found the strength to hook a hold under his arms and pull him toward the stairs. Naturally, his body caught the damn doorjamb, but then it was on the panel, and keeping things wide as she yanked—yanked—*yanked*—

As his boots finally cleared the threshold, things started to shut and she had a final glimpse of the fire, a final inhale of that horrible stench of burning flesh. Then there was a hard impact slam, followed only by breathing. Ragged breathing. Hers. Mayhem's.

Not Luke's, though.

He was horribly still.

The door at the head of the stairs opened, and Apex's voice barely surmounted the panting. "Jesus."

Things started happening at that point, but she was having trouble tracking it all. Apex picked Luke up and carried him inside, and then Mayhem was next, like they were cordwood being stacked. Marshaling her own coordination—or what was left of it—she stumbled up the steps and tried the door, which had re-closed on itself. It was locked. What was the code?

Apex opened the thing before she could even try it once.

"I got you." He grabbed her as she fell forward. "In you go."

With a practiced move, as if they were dancing, he spun her around and she felt a seat come up to her butt as her legs went loose. It took her a minute to focus, and then she looked across the private quarters. Mayhem was stirring on the floor by the door. Luke was on the bed, sprawled faceup—but at least he was breathing.

Such high standards.

Pushing herself to her feet, she went over on unsteady legs and sat down by him. The burns on his face weren't so bad, just a flushing redness, and his sweatshirt was perfectly intact.

That one hand she was worried about, as it was red and swollen.

And then there were those lungs. He'd clearly breathed in fire, to have that much of a reaction and yet show so little external damage on his body.

"We should get him treatment," she whispered.

Yet even as she said it, she knew there was no way any of them would agree to take him to a real doctor.

After a little while, Mayhem, who had clearly come around, and Apex started talking. She didn't listen. She just sat next to Luke and willed him to be okay.

I wish we'd had more nights and days, you and me.

Her mind was a chaotic storm, too many thoughts swirling around, nothing landing for proper attention.

No, wait, that wasn't true.

She wished they'd had more time, too. And different circumstances.

"Wake up, Luke," she said softly. "Please."

There was no hope at all that he'd hear her—much less respond. But his eyes fluttered—and then opened.

Glowing yellow eyes locked on her face with surprising focus.

"Hi." She cleared her throat as her voice cracked. "You're safe now."

Luke's stare moved around until he seemed to give up on the whole sight thing. And then he said something she was never going to forget.

"Am safe . . . because am with you."

✦ ✦ ✦

Rio stayed at Luke's bedside for . . . well, she wasn't exactly sure how long. It turned out that the quarters had a bathroom behind a partition in one corner, and from time to time, she would get up and refill a glass of water for him, making sure that when he roused, she was there to help him lift his head to take a sip. He had refused to eat the bread and cheese that Mayhem had brought and put on the table with all the handwritten spreadsheets. And Luke didn't seem to be resting when he wasn't conscious—it was more that he passed out and came to in a cycle that could hardly be considered peaceful.

It reminded her of Kane.

Speaking of the other burn patient, Apex, along with Mayhem, was just outside, standing against the locked door by the Executioner's cold body—

Luke made a noise in the back of his throat as if he were coughing, and she bent down closer to him. She had spent a lot of the time staring at his face, tracing the planes and angles of his cheekbones, his jaw, his brow, with her eyes. It seemed incredibly intimate to look at him like that, without him being aware she was doing so, as if they were separated by a crowd and she was off in a darkened corner, admiring him.

Speculating about his life was unavoidable, and she wondered how he had ended up here, in the drug trade, in a place that had its own pseudo police force. Who were his parents? Where had he grown up?

What would he do after this era in his life was done?

Assuming that his end in this business was not a grave.

Then again, the only way out for him was death. People as deep into the trade as he was didn't make it out of this alive. And they were killed in brutal ways.

She thought of the Charger in that alley, the driver shot. And then she remembered the dead guy by the fire escape.

And finally, the hired hitman in that apartment—although who could have seen that big dog coming?

Oh, and then there was the Executioner, who she'd shot.

No, Luke was not going to live long enough to retire: He was just one more cog in the machine that had killed not only Rio's brother, but her whole family.

"I should hate you," she whispered to Luke.

She should hate him for selling the very drugs that had ruined not merely Luis, but her mother and her father. Because that was the thing about illegal narcotics. You didn't have to do them to get lost in them.

Sometimes, it just took a son doing the using, and dying because of it, to take down an entire family.

Unable to stay still, she stood up off the mattress and walked around. Her aimless wander took her over to the folding table, and as she looked at the columns of numbers and dollar signs, it was a relief to focus on something else.

This was invaluable evidence, she thought. The question was how to get it out—

The phone. She had that phone.

Glancing back at Luke, she made sure he was still asleep. Then she took the unit out of her pocket. Of course it was locked, but it was an iPhone, so she swiped up from the bottom.

And accessed the camera.

Turning off the ringer switch, to make sure there were no sounds, she pulled some of the ledgers toward her and faced them right side up. The first picture she took was blurry because her hand was shaking. She tried again. Better.

Sitting herself down, she snapped photographs of each page in each stack, trying to get as much in the shot as possible. After she was finished, she moved on to some of the loose papers, which covered things like staffing the production rooms and schedules for the guards. And then there were order forms for bulk food.

"You have to feed everyone," she murmured. "Of course you do."

Flour. Sugar. Canned goods.

An abrupt image of the kitchen from *The Shining* came to mind, Wendy and Danny Torrance being led by Dick Hallorann through the dry storage room, huge cans of vegetables, boxes of cereal, and jugs of sauces lining shelves.

There had to be a mess hall somewhere, she thought. And support staff, workers whose sole job was to feed the others. The logistics were overwhelming—

The knock on the door by the wall was loud, and as she startled, she dropped the phone. Fortunately, the thing landed in her lap, but as the way in opened, she couldn't put the cell in her pocket without being obvious. She slipped it under her thigh and then made a show of stretching her arms over her head.

"He's still sleeping," she said to Mayhem. "Is all that for us? We didn't finish the first load."

The guy had another big tray in his hands, with more of that bread and the same cheese on it, along with some Coke and Sprite in cans.

"Figured you'd appreciate some backup grub before you leave." He put the meal right on the table, on top of the documents. "It's not much, but it'll fill your belly okay. Underneath is a bag you can put it all in."

"Thank you."

As Mayhem turned to check on his friend, she uncovered the bread with one hand and forced the phone into her pocket with the other.

"I'm not fussy," she said as she tore off a piece and put it in her mouth. "Oh . . . wow. Still warm."

"Fresh from the ovens."

"God, you guys have everything here, don't you."

"Enough to keep going, at any rate." Mayhem smiled at her. "You're an excellent nurse. He's looking better already."

"Is he?"

"Yeah. Aren't you, Lucan."

"Is that his full name?" she asked when there was no response. As the guy just shrugged, she glanced at the back door. "You realize I'm not going to leave until he's better."

Mayhem nodded. "I figured. And he's going to want to say goodbye to you."

"How are things out there? Is everything . . . okay?"

"We'll find out very soon. The sun's down now and things are getting busy. Don't worry, we'll keep everyone out of here. Besides, you know the code on that back door. I saw you watch me put it in. If shit gets bad, let yourself out and run like your life depends on it. Because it will."

She cleared her throat and cracked open one of the Cokes. "And this is cold. Funny what you think of as gourmet, huh."

"Standards change depending on where you are. Well, I'm going to go back out there." The man retraced his steps across the space and then looked over his shoulder at her. "You holler if you need us."

"Actually, I was thinking I'd go check outside to make sure the fire is extinguished. What's the code to get back in again?"

Mayhem's eyes shifted up a little so that he was still staring in her direction, just wasn't meeting her eyes anymore. And then she felt a headache coming on—or maybe it was more like the one she'd had before was returning. Either way, she cursed and rubbed her temples.

"Yeah, you let me worry about that," Mayhem said in a low, serious voice.

"The fire could attract attention, though," she muttered through the discomfort. "I mean, the whole point of not working during the day is to make sure there's no activity, right?"

"You're good. It's not a problem."

"I just thought I'd help—"

"Listen, I really appreciate what you're doing for Lucan. And Kane, too. I mean, seriously, it's amazing—plus, it's clear you've got guts and you've done us a favor with the Exhibitionist. But I'm not giving you the code to entering the building at large. I'm sorry. I can't do that."

"It's totally okay." She put her hands up. "I honestly am just restless and looking for something to pass the time before he wakes up properly. Totally fine."

Mayhem nodded once. "And remember—no matter what happens, the people out in the rest of the building can't get in here—and they can't burn you out, either. The wall is flame-retardant. Same is true in the back. This space was designed to be a kind of fortress."

"Thanks."

There was a moment of quiet. "Rio. That's your name, right?"

"Yes."

"Nice name."

As he disappeared through the door, a shiver went through her. Something was not right about this, she thought. Something was . . .

Shaking herself, she looked over at Luke on the bed. "Paranoia is *not* going to help here."

On that note, she ate some of the cheese. The taste was sharp, but not unpleasantly so, and with the bread? Well, it was pretty much the best thing she had ever put in her mouth—although that was more a commentary on that thing mothers always said rather than the food itself.

Hunger was the best spice. Or whatever the phrase was.

Getting up from the table, she took the makeshift sandwich with her, and the next thing she knew, she was systematically going through the quarters like it was a crime scene—

Well, because it was. Three men had died here, and one of them—the one who was mounted on that wall out there—had been the result of her own actions.

She inspected everything from the bathroom, the changing area, the gun rack—

Rio found the car keys hanging on a nail by the rifles.

Chrysler. A fob with a single black-headed key. Sneaking it into her other pocket, she turned to Luke. Lucan. Whatever his name was. He was breathing easier, now, although that was a relative thing. He still looked like he was in pain, his brows pulled in tight across the bridge of his nose.

Maybe he needed some of what they'd given Kane, even though he certainly wasn't wounded as badly.

Back at the bedside, she lowered herself down onto her knees and looked at the back of his hand, the one that had been burned so badly. Then she frowned. The skin seemed . . . a lot less red and inflamed, as if it was progressing through the healing process, but at a much faster rate than made any sense.

She thought of what the burn had looked like when they'd been locked out in the back parking lot, next to the fire. Not that she had any medical training outside of rudimentary CPR and first aid, but the injury had looked like a third-degree one, what with the uneven blisters that had extended out of his sleeve at the wrist and down his fingers. Now? It was like a bad sunburn, nothing more.

Miraculous.

In the back of her mind, the warning bell that had saved her too many times to count started to ring properly. It had been on the verge of getting serious about its job ever since she and Apex had hurried down that corridor upstairs together—and he had crouched and had to fight through that nothing-wrong hallway like it was an obstacle course of radioactive chemicals.

Rio cursed softly and thought about the strange trance that guard had put her in in the workroom, how her hand with the gun in it had lowered of its own volition.

But surely that hadn't happened, right?

After all, she'd had how many blows to the head over the last how many days? It was more likely that her mind was malfunctioning than there was some sort of mystical anything going on.

And yet she couldn't shake the sense that nothing was as it seemed.

Rio stayed beside the bed on the floor for a little longer, and then she told herself she needed to use this time wisely. Going over to the table once again, she took a piece of paper and a pencil from out of the clutter—and sat down with her back to the door in case she had to cover up what she was doing.

Closing her eyes, she pictured the clinic area. The stairwell. The workroom with its tables and those two desks and the bin of kilos in the corner.

When she reopened her lids, she started to sketch out the plans of everything she could recall about the facility. The effort was not only intel she intended to give her superiors . . . it felt like a test of her cognitive abilities.

If she lost those in this situation?

She was a dead woman.

CHAPTER FORTY

A mere thirty miles away from where Rio was playing amateur architect, V re-formed on a country road out in the middle of nowhere. As he waited for Rhage to hop-along his Cassidy, he took out a hand-rolled, lit up with his Bic—which he'd gotten from the Pit, thank you very much—and looked at the mountains in the distance. The valley between the two ranges was a straight shot of flat and narrow, and he imagined, if he were a nature-loving type, that he'd find a lot of peace and comfort in the landscape. As it was, he was a tetchy, techy sonofabitch with stunted emotional growth, a god complex, and questionable taste in cartoons.

Hey, he liked *Tom & Jerry*. Not that he brought that up around Lassiter.

So no, he wasn't all that impressed by the Mother Earth stuff.

Rhage materialized beside him. "Okay, let's go. And I'll do the talking since you've pulled on your grumpy pants about all this."

"Not my fault the bunch of you have your heads wedged."

"Isn't that your favorite thing?"

They started walking toward a farmhouse that was so picture-perfect, V choked on the quaint. From its porch to the obligatory tree in the side yard, its chimney and the happy-face arrangement of its windows, he would be afraid, if he lived in such a place, that he'd start crapping sunbeams and Care Bears.

He was also aware of wanting Butch to be with them, too—but as a half-breed, the former cop couldn't ghost out and travel in a scatter of molecules. That was the thing with mixed blood. You got some of the characteristics of both sides, but it was a buffet you didn't get to choose from. What your personal rules were got randomly assigned by the fruit salad of your genetic makeup.

So it was ground travel only for Butch, and it would take well over an hour for the brother—

A vibration went through V's body, his marrow going tuning fork on him. And as Rhage stopped short and looked down at himself, it was clear the brother picked up on it, too.

"Is that . . ." Rhage let the words drift as he glanced back up toward the house. "I mean . . ."

At that moment, the front door of the farmhouse burst open and a female in a long dress and a bulky sweater rushed out. She had both palms forward and she was halfway into an epic no-no-no stream.

"—needing. You can't be here!"

Needing? V thought. *Oh, shit.*

The Jackal's *shellan*, Nyx, had gone into her—

"Do you want my mate to help?" he called out. "Jane can come here with the drugs to ease her."

Posie, Nyx's sister, flushed and shook her head. "That's not . . . that's not how it's going to be handled. This was a little bit of a surprise, but females' cycles? They can be unpredictable, especially during stressful times."

She doubled back and shut the door. Then she came down off the porch to them. "I'm leaving as well. For . . . you know, their privacy."

"Are they safe?" Rhage asked. "For the day?"

"They're in the cellar bedroom. I made sure there was food and . . .

Pete already left when the first signs of the fertile time started showing. I only stayed to get the house in order and make sure they'd have what they need."

What a mess, V thought.

Vampire females were only fertile about once a decade—and good fucking thing. The hormones released were incredibly powerful and painful, and his *mahmen*, creator of the species, had set it up such that only constant mating with a male could make the agony bearable. Still, the sex act soothed the cravings only for a short time, so the orgasms had to be constant, for hours and hours. It was either that or drugs. All things considering, the cycle was a brutal system, but considering how high the mortality rate was for females on the birthing bed? It would take something that overwhelming to make them want to run the risks of getting pregnant.

He was really glad his Jane was infertile in her hybrid state—not because he wouldn't have helped during her time, but because the pregnancy stats terrified him.

"Where are you going?" Rhage asked Posie.

"To our grandfather's new place. That's where Pete is. I'll come back right before dawn and double-check they're okay. But Jack has a phone, and . . . things to protect them with."

Things = weapons, given the female's squeamishness.

"Let us know if you or they need anything?" Rhage nodded to the house. "The Jackal's a good male, and I wish my half-brother all the best."

V kept his mouth shut because he thought the pair of them were nuts. If the pregnancy took? The Jackal got to enjoy eighteen months of worrying whether the love of his life, the female he'd bonded with, was going to bleed out trying to bring his fragile progeny into the cold, hard world.

"You know how to reach us," Vishous muttered. Because he didn't want the depths of his douchebagness to be apparent.

Fine, *that* apparent.

"Thank you," the female said.

Relieved to get the hell out of there, V dematerialized off the lawn and traveled north and a little east, knowing Rhage would be right behind him. The needing was not a place for any males to hang around because they couldn't help but be affected and nobody had time for that drama.

The good news? The whole issue of the Jackal tangling up with finding the prison camp was now a moot point, at least for the foreseeable future. If the couple was doing this the old-fashioned way, the male was going to need a waterpark's worth of hydration after it was over, and then he'd have to wait to see if things took. He wasn't going to want to leave his female.

Just as well.

One less cook in the kitchen.

The Audience House was located in Caldwell proper, in a zip code where people had gates across their driveways, access codes to every nook and cranny, and the inflated sense of self-importance that came when you could get whatever you wanted, whenever you wanted it.

As he re-formed around back by the garage, the Federal sprawl was a beaut, even from the rear. Darius, the brother who had built the Brotherhood mansion on the mountain, had constructed this abode as well, and it had been his primary residence—up until he'd been taken out by a car bomb.

After sitting vacant for a little while, the place was now used as a neutral ground for Wrath to meet his civilians to adjudicate disputes, bless matings and young, and generally keep his finger on the pulse of the species.

Opening the back door, V walked into a full-swing kitchen. Uniformed *doggen* were working to prepare a steady stream of fresh-baked goods for the waiting room and the initial wave of appointments. In a couple of hours, the menu would switch to tea sandwiches and cookies.

Lifting his hand to the staff, he turned them down for coffee, tea, soda, water, muffins, Danish, and homemade cake donuts. All in the space of twelve feet. Rhage, on the other hand, was going to get trapped in the calorie net, and come out the far side with a silver tray full of nosh.

At least the chefs would know their wares were appreciated.

Out in the hallway, V kept going and got a clear shot down to the front entrance. The double doors into the dining room were closed, which meant Wrath was in session, and he was not going to interrupt because the news flash he was here to deliver—hopefully without too much noticeable self-satisfaction—was not an emergency—

"Hey, roomie."

V backtracked and leaned into the newly redecorated little sitting room. Butch was parked on the sofa facing the TV, the soft murmur of the newscaster oddly soothing even though it was just a human talking about human shit.

Then again maybe that was why it was soothing. Didn't affect him.

"Check this out." Butch palmed the remote and turned up the volume. "Isn't that your target from downtown?"

Coming over and sitting next to the cop, V looked for an ashtray to put his cig out—

Oh, Fritz, you are a gentlemale and a sailor, he thought as he found one right by his elbow.

And then he wasn't thinking about butlers who anticipated every need before you even knew you had 'em.

To the left of the newscaster's head, there was a black-and-white photograph of a woman who—yup, looked exactly like the one V had been trailing in the alleys in search of more of that iron-cross-stamped poison. From the short dark hair to the intense eyes that seemed haunted, she was—

"Turn it up a little louder," he said, even though he could hear shit just fine.

"—to the CPD undercover officer who had been shot, execution-style, and thrown into the Hudson River, there are rumors that another undercover officer has gone missing. Sources tell us that—"

Butch glanced over. "I mean, that's her, right?"

"Yeah, for real." Well, this was—surprise!—actually a news flash that he cared about. "Goddamn it, we're going to have to start all over again if someone killed her for being a cop."

"The leaks in the department to the press were always for shit. Don't these reporters have *any* common decency?" Butch's Boston accent thickened with all his pissed-off. "If that woman's in the hands of any of the dealers she was going after, they're going to see this and kill her. Assuming she's not frickin' dead anyway."

The newscaster continued to drone on. "One of our reporters caught up with CPD Chief Stanley Carmichael, while he attended a gala event at the home of—"

"Pause it, wouldja?" V asked. "I want her picture."

As Butch hit the remote, V took out his Samsung and snapped a close-up of the screen. The image of the missing officer was shitty, all pixelated, but he could sharpen it up later. Besides, he never forgot a face.

He never forgot anything.

"Okay, got it. Thanks."

Butch hit the button again, and V zoned out as things cut to a female reporter in a red suit shoving a microphone into an older guy's face. As a stream of tuxedos and gowns parted around the confrontation, the police chief lifted his palms and shook his head, all no-comment. And then there was a close-up of the reporter as she summed it up for viewers who had just seen exactly what had happened.

Back to the studio, and now there was another cut. To a news brief where—

Homicide Detective José de la Cruz—according to the scrawl at the bottom—was standing at a microphoned lectern making a statement about the male officer who'd been found in the Hudson River.

A reporter cut through the scrum of questions as he concluded his remarks. "What about the female officer who is missing?"

José looked at the woman. "I'm not prepared to comment on—"

"So you're not denying there is another missing officer—"

"No," the guy said firmly. "I'm not commenting on rumors. Any other questions."

As the news desk reappeared on-screen, the anchor stoked the flames of conspiracy theories and Butch muted it all with a look of disgust.

While V lit up another hand-rolled, his roommate eased back and got pensive. Then he looked over and—

"No," V muttered. "The answer is no."

"How do you know what I'm going to ask?"

Vishous exhaled a stream of smoke. "Because I'm your fucking roommate, that's how."

CHAPTER FORTY-ONE

Lucan woke up in the Executioner's bed. As his eyes struggled to focus, he nonetheless located Rio immediately. She was sitting about ten feet away, her back to him as she bent over the table and scribbled on something.

Before he could say her name, she seemed to sense his stare.

Straightening, she looked over her shoulder. "Hi."

Getting up from a meal that had been brought in by someone, her brows were drawn and her hands fidgety as she came across to him. For a moment, he took her in as if it had been weeks since he'd seen her, noting her pale face, her determined jawline, her strong body in the wrinkled clothes she'd had on for how long now?

She was beautiful to him, in a way that had nothing to do with her physical appearance.

Clearing her throat, she said, "How are you—"

"Hungry."

"Oh, I got this." She seemed excited, like helping his recovery was a test she wanted to pass. "Here."

She moved so fast as she reached for the tray that she spilled some

Coke he assumed she'd been nursing, swiping the can with the back of her hand. With a curse, she mopped things up with a shirt that was draped on the back of a chair—and then she got the tray and brought it over, setting it on the floor by the bed.

Kneeling down, she took a can of Sprite and popped the top.

"How did you know?" Damn, his voice was rough. "That I'm not a Coke fan."

"I had a fifty-fifty chance of getting it right. It's all we got."

He struggled to sit up, and when he did, she gave him the soda and started plumping the flat pillows he'd been resting on—although she didn't get very far with pouffing, and not because the bedding was for shit.

"Are you . . ."

Lucan finished the sentence for her. "I'm okay now."

Her eyes ducked like she didn't want him to know she'd been worried about him. "I guess the gas or whatever it was backfired on you."

"Gas? What are you talking—oh, right." Jesus, he forgot that she didn't know his true nature. "Yeah. Flames."

Fuck. What a mess this all was.

"That was so scary," she murmured. "I thought . . . well, it doesn't matter. It worked out."

Time to change the subject. "Where are Apex and Mayhem?"

"Just outside the door."

Thank God, he thought as he took the Sprite to his lips—with surprisingly sturdy, steady hands, as it turned out. Guess he hadn't lied to her about being better. And when the test sip went down just fine, he gulped the whole thing on a oner.

"Is there another?" he asked with an *ahhhhhh*.

"Absolutely." She went back to the table. "Here, I'll open it for you."

There was a *schhht*, and then he was on to number two. More than food, the sugar and the liquid were exactly what he needed, and his eyes finally came back online fully when he was halfway done with the second.

"You look tired," he said—then caught himself. "Good. I mean. You look good."

Her smile was wry as she sat down next to the tray on the bald floor. Pushing at her hair, which was standing up at odd angles, she looked . . . well, he could only describe it as "adorable," even though that was not a word he associated with her strength, her directness, her sexiness.

Shaking her head, she murmured, "I can only guess what I'm like right now—"

"You're perfect." As she glanced at him sharply, he took another drink. "We're more than even after what you did, Rio. You saved me out there."

"Nah, Mayhem was the one with the code. He opened the door."

"You picked me up off the ground and carried me inside. I don't know how you did it."

"It was more like a drag, and I was motivated, what can I say—"

"Thank you." As emotion came over him, he looked away from her. "Hey, there's a shower. And I don't mind if I do."

Putting down what was left of the Sprite, he got to his feet, and gave his body a chance to collapse. When his balance held, he zeroed in on the tiled corner of the room. There was a partition to stand behind, and after he started the water, he stripped his sweatshirt off—carefully. His skin was still red across his chest, and especially on that one hand.

Good thing it wasn't his dagger—

Rio stepped into view down at the other end of the room. She was by the gun rack, her head lowered, her hand hesitating by the rifles that were lined up, soldiers ready for their shooting orders.

"You can look at me," he said in a deep voice. "I don't mind it."

Not in the slightest.

Her head came up and around. Then she ducked her eyes again. "I'm just worried that you'll slip and fall."

"There's an easy solution. Join me."

What the fuck was he saying here?

As the silence stretched out, he felt like his body had reinflated with strength—and it was not coming from the calories in that soda. Amazing how the mating instinct could kick the crap out of all kinds of minor aches and pains.

And with Mayhem and Apex right outside? And things still momentarily quiet . . .

When she didn't reply, he smiled sadly. "I'll be okay in here. You can just take a load off and relax a little—I won't be long."

"I wish we were different," she said with a defeat he did not associate with her.

We are, he thought. *More than you'll ever know—so you're making the right decision here.*

And yet that didn't stop him from wanting her.

"Just so you know," he said, "I wouldn't change a thing about you. Even in this god-awful light, with everything we've been through . . . you're still the most beautiful female I've ever seen."

Her brows went up high as if she thought he was insane. And then her fingertips traced her own face.

"I feel so old," she whispered.

"That's life, not how many calendar years you've lived."

When she put her palms to her cheeks and tears glossed her eyes, he stepped away from the falling water and went to her.

"I'm not very good when things are okay," she croaked out. "I'm better when they're bad."

Well, they were still in the prison camp. And not on vacation. But why fly the reminder?

Lucan reached out and brushed her hair. "Unfortunately, I can promise you that this quiet is not going to last. This . . . moment . . . is not going to last long at all."

As he stared at her, he wanted to hold her. He wanted to kiss her. He wanted to touch her body so he knew he really was back from the dead and so was she.

"We're like cockroaches," she said as she dropped her hands. "You and me. We just keep going."

Following her lead, he lowered his arm as well. "I'm not sure that's a compliment, but considering you included yourself in it and you have a healthy ego, I'm thinking there has to be a positive spin on the cockroach thing."

"We can't be killed."

He remembered the sunlight on his skin—and did not agree with that. But again, he wasn't going to inject reality into her insect optimism.

When she refocused on him, her eyes were full of shadows.

Lucan waited for—ohhh, maybe a split second. Then he went back into the shower stall and canned the water routine.

As he returned to her, she laughed awkwardly. "How is it that you always smell so good?"

I've bonded with you, he thought.

"Give me your hand," he commanded.

The fact that she didn't fight him made him realize how exhausted she was. And as the contact was locked in by their grips, he drew her over to the bed.

"I'm not tired," she said as she sat down. "I feel like I'm never going to sleep again."

Lucan parked it next to her. "Tell me the story."

Her eyes flared. "What story?"

He had to touch her hair again, he couldn't help it. "The story of your pain."

✦ ✦ ✦

As Rio sat next to Luke on the bed, it seemed absolute bonkers fricking insane that she was having trouble holding it together. Considering everything that had gone down in the last—how long had it been? Five years? Twenty-five? A century? And now, after getting hit by a car, kidnapped, assaulted, and taken in by the drug dealers she was trying to bust, *now* she was losing it?

But something had happened when Luke had woken up and really looked at her properly. And then held his own can of soda. And then asked for another. The humanity of his suffering and recovery had made her forget all about the cop/criminal thing. They were just two people in a shitstorm, trying to survive, and she was so glad he had not—

"I thought you were going to die," she blurted.

When she slapped her palm over her mouth, it was a relief when he laughed. "So did I."

Nodding, she relowered her arm and looked at his . . . rather extraordinary . . . naked chest. And his shoulders. And his . . .

Okay, those abs were sculptured.

"Let me in, Rio," he whispered. Then he shrugged. "And listen, if you're worried about your privacy, where's it going to go, right? I'm just a fucking drug dealer, trapped in this life, going nowhere fast. I have no one, no family, no friends, so I don't talk to anybody about anything. I don't count. I'm a black hole that doesn't matter."

"Don't say that." She wiped eyes that were going blurry again. "How can you say that—"

"It's the truth, and there's nothing wrong with admitting the truth. It'll set you free even when you're in Hell." He held up a forefinger. "Trust me on this."

"What is your truth?" she asked.

"I just told you it."

Rio shook her head. "You're not a black hole. And I can prove it."

He chuckled a little. "If it's a long math equation, you're going to lose me. Numbers are not my bag."

"Me, too. I suck at math."

In the silence that followed, she studied him closely—and knew she was trying to memorize what he looked like. She wanted to keep all the details of him with her for however long she was alive, from the way his blond-and-brown hair curled over his forehead, to how his lips were parted right now and the fact that with his eyes at half-mast, their color seemed more intense.

There were so many reasons to remember that she was a cop and he was part of a criminal enterprise and never the twain shall meet.

Much less make love.

Or, worse, catch feelings.

Still, she extended her hand across the space that separated them—and her fingers trembled ever so slightly as they made contact with the place right over his heart. His skin was warm, but not like it had been when she'd touched him to rouse him as she'd been checking to make sure he was still alive. He'd been running a fever, but now that was gone.

"I can feel you," she whispered. "Therefore you exist—and you are not nothing."

Luke looked down at her palm on his sternum, as if he couldn't understand why it was there—or maybe couldn't believe it. And in the pause that followed, she supposed that there were a lot of things he could do right now: He could kiss her. He could pull away. He could make a joke to try to lower the sudden intensity that was gripping her, and seemed to be gripping him.

Instead, he closed his eyes. And put his hand over hers.

"What are you thinking about," she said, "with your eyes so closed."

"That it's been a long, long time since I didn't hurt in the center of my chest."

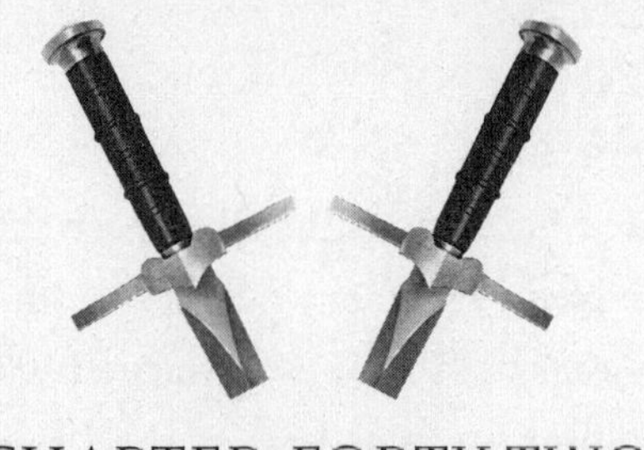

CHAPTER FORTY-TWO

When Lucan eventually reopened his eyes, he found that Rio's whole body was curved in toward him and her face was lifted to his. With their hands linked over his heart and the soft silence between them, he took a deep breath and wondered how he could explain how significant this moment was.

Then again, he wasn't sure he wanted her to know the importance of it all.

But as a wolven who had been abandoned by his clan, he had been an orphan in the world for a very long time. With her now? He felt . . . claimed as family.

"I wish . . ." she whispered.

"What? What do you want."

Rio eased back a little, and unfortunately, took her palm with her. As her eyes shifted away from him, he knew she was somewhere else in her mind—and he missed the contact of her flesh against his.

"I hate the idea of you hurting." She shook her head. "I hate anyone in pain, actually. I'm a wuss."

"You've got a good heart. Like that's a bad thing?"

"It's a little more complicated than that."

"I don't think so."

"Who left you," she blurted. "Who was the person who made you feel like you were so unworthy."

What did he say. What could he say? "It was a whole group of people. My family, actually."

Her head tilted to one side. "What did they do to you?"

"They put me in here." When she looked confused, he wanted to kick his own ass for forgetting all she didn't know, couldn't know. "I mean, I'm in this line of work because of them. It's a long fucking story. Just know . . . I wouldn't choose to be doing what I am if there were any other way for me. I would not be in this life except for everything that went down years ago."

As she opened her mouth, he put his palm up. "And there's no disrespect intended toward you. I don't judge you or anybody else for the way they make their living. I am in *no* position to be critical."

Her smile was tight. "Funny. You wouldn't choose this life, and I . . . wouldn't either in so many ways."

"Tell me."

"It wouldn't make any sense." Rio fell back on the bed and locked her eyes on the ceiling. Then her words came out in a rush. "My brother, Luis, died of an overdose at the age of sixteen. I was the one who found him. I was two years older."

Lucan shook his head. "I am so sorry. Rio. That's terrible—"

"But the destruction didn't stop there. My mother started drinking after he passed. Hard. She collapsed from liver failure two years ago, got on dialysis, and died six months later. Not that we were close or anything. On my father's end, he left town pretty soon after my brother's funeral. Just took off. I have no idea where he is, and after all these years, it's going to stay that way even if I find him, you know what I mean?"

"Wait . . . he just deserted his mate—wife, I mean? And you?"

"There was debt he couldn't cover, he said. Money that was owed to people who were dangerous. Either he left or they were going to come and hurt me and Mom." She glanced over with a hard expression. "But no one ever came looking for him, so maybe it was just a lie—something he told my mother to make himself feel better. I don't know."

After a moment, she covered her face with her hands, and he touched her knee. "So you have no bloodline, either."

"It's true, I'm alone. But it's okay."

"You're not alone anymore."

Lowering her arms, she stared across at him. "You don't want me, Luke. You really don't."

He had to laugh at that. "The hell I don't."

Rio blushed in a way that made him fall for her even harder. "I don't mean like that."

"I'm not your brother, Rio. You don't have to take care of me and you do not have to save me."

"This isn't about him."

"I think it is. I think you're trying to save all kinds of people, in all kinds of ways, because you couldn't do it for him." He shook his head again. "I just don't know why you didn't get out of this life altogether. I don't get the logic. If drugs killed your brother, why are you doing this?"

Her eyes went back to the ceiling. "Like I said, it's complicated."

All Lucan could do was nod. He sensed that there were things she was holding back, but considering the encyclopedia's worth of shit he was keeping to himself? He wasn't going to fault her for not filling him in on everything.

"I don't want to talk anymore," she said as she sat back up.

"I'm not judging you, Rio. Just know that. All the details don't matter to me, and neither do your choices. They're your own to make peace with, and God knows that life can put us in situations where there are nothing but rocks and hard places."

She frowned and seemed to inspect her fingernails, as if she had a manicure even though she didn't.

"You said that your family is making you do this," she murmured.

"Are you involved in the mob? I mean, given this operation's size, I'm figuring it can't be an isolated thing, you know? So many people, so many moving parts."

"Call it whatever you will," he hedged. If it was a truth that made sense to her as a human? She might as well believe it.

God, he hated all the lies he had going on.

But if she ever found out that he wasn't one of her kind? Yeah, no. He wasn't interested in seeing the horror in those eyes of hers.

"Who is it?" she prompted. "Who's your family?"

✦ ✦ ✦

As Rio tossed the question out there, she knew Luke wasn't going to answer it. If he were a made man—and considering how comfortable he was around the dead bodies that had been in this room, and the shooting down in Caldwell, and all the other crap, she had to believe he was—he would never tell her.

She also knew she was in danger of blowing her cover. If she were actually involved in the drug trade at the level she supposedly was, she would never make that kind of inquiry. That was something a cop would do.

Surprise.

"I'm sorry," she said quickly. "That's totally inappropriate. I'm not thinking straight."

"It doesn't matter who I'm affiliated with."

"That's right. All I care about is . . ."

Between one blink and the next, she was back on the floor of that filthy apartment, trussed like a deer, about to be really seriously hurt. And then that dog had come. And then Luke had magically appeared.

"Sure as if I summoned you."

"I'm sorry?" he asked.

"Back at that trap house." She didn't bother to hide the fact that revisiting those memories made her shudder. "It was like I called your name and you came running."

"It was a lucky break for the both of us."

"All because you were there to see Mickie."

As she made some kind of affirming noise in the back of her throat, she hated the fact that she was lying to him, that only she knew they were on opposite sides of things, and not in a way he would ever suspect. They weren't supplier and dealer, staring across the proverbial negotiating table. They were cop and criminal—and the end result was going to be him behind bars, along with everyone else in here who was in charge. He was certainly facing decades for the dealing itself, as well as the money laundering that was inevitably going to be part of an enterprise this size. And then there was the human trafficking that she knew in her gut was going on.

Unless she'd thought all those cubicles, all those workstations, had been for something other than unpaid, coerced labor?

"What are you thinking about now?" he asked.

Nothing good. "Nothing, really."

As she looked over, she stared into his eyes, his incredibly beautiful, yellow eyes. "Can I ask you something?" she said.

"Anything."

"You really wouldn't have chosen this life?"

It was a moment before he answered. And his expression became so grave, and his voice so deep, that she felt as though he were sharing some part of himself that he did not expect to get back.

"I hate it here." His voice became hoarse. "I hate everything about this place. It's cruel. It's inhumane. This is not an existence anybody would ever want. The things I've seen . . . the things I've done . . . I was half dead when I was put in here—and I didn't know how much further I'd sunk until I saw you standing under that fire escape."

"I'm nothing special."

"You are so wrong about that." He laughed a little, and she had the sense he was trying to lighten the mood. "For one thing, I've watched you get hit by a car and walk away from it. That's skills, right there. And now I know you're good with a gun, but we don't have to dwell on that."

Her eyes shifted away to the bloodstain on the floor.

His finger, stroking lightly on her chin, brought her face back to his. "He more than deserved it. And not just for what he'd been about to do to you. He was a piece of evil on the earth, a sick, perverted murderer. Try not to think about it."

"Why did you save my life so many times?"

"I didn't have anything better to do." He winked at her. "All three times."

Rio had to laugh. "Stop it. I'm serious."

"Okay, fine. I needed the exercise. How's that."

Covering her smile with her hand, she batted at his shoulder. "That is not funny—"

"I thought I could maybe fall in love with you, and I didn't want a car, or a bullet, or any fucking thing in the world to get in the way of that. So there."

Rio blinked, her heart stopping. "You don't mean that."

No more joking now; he became dead serious. "They're my words. I picked them because I know what they mean."

"You don't know me."

"And you don't know me."

Shooting him a stare, she pointed out, "Well, I didn't just tell you I'd fallen in love with you."

"I said I might be able to."

Stop, she told herself. *Stop this right now.*

"Well . . . have you?" she breathed. But then she put her hand up. "Don't answer that."

"Why did you ask the question then."

Rio looked away. Looked back. And then couldn't stop herself from falling into a fantasy. "You could leave this life, you know. You don't have to be here. I mean, you could . . . you could just go out that back door and never return. People disappear all the time. My father did it. You could do the same."

"It's not that simple," he said in a hollow voice.

Shit, was she actively encouraging him to become a fugitive from the law?

She gathered his hands in her own. "Listen, you could escape all this, and just—I don't know—you could even go to the police. You could tell them all you know in exchange for immunity and a witness protection program—"

"Why are you trying to get me out when you need me to make a deal with you?"

Rio blinked and realized she might have just given herself away. "Because I'd rather do business with someone I can be objective around. And that's next to impossible with you."

His smile was slow. Sexy. "Are you saying you feel the same way I do?"

"No."

"Yes."

Rio took a deep breath. "I don't know."

"I think you do." When Luke leaned into her, his cologne—that damned cologne, that he maintained was not cologne—got into her nose . . . and went right to her blood. "And I think you want exactly what I do right now."

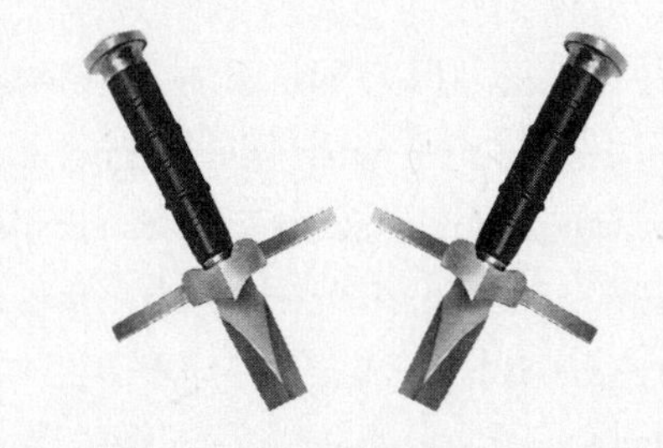

CHAPTER FORTY-THREE

Rio's face was so close to his that all Lucan would have to do to kiss her was tilt in a little farther—and he knew if they got started with that shit, it wasn't going to stop there. Her scent had changed, the arousal she was feeling rising to match his own.

And fucking hell, he wanted her.

"Are we going to do this?" she whispered.

"Yeah, we are."

There was no hesitation on her side when he closed the distance between their mouths, and as he pressed his lips to hers, he had to hold back—or her clothes were going to be ripped beyond repair. As it was, he was already easing her back on the bed, moving over her, pinning her with his weight—

Goddamn, she was gripping his bare back with her hands, digging her fingers into his skin—and he wished she had longer nails so she could scratch him properly, draw blood, make him moan from the combination of pleasure and pain. And there were other good things happening for him. As she shifted so she was under him properly, his arousal made its own way between her thighs.

Screw the nails. He wanted her hot softness more.

As he penetrated her mouth with his tongue, he rolled to the side and swept his hand along her waist, up to her ribs, around the side of her breast. With a restless surge, she twisted her torso—

And put herself right in his palm.

Through her shirt and her bra, he rubbed her nipple with his thumb—and as she moaned in response, she became like water beneath him, fluid and graceful. She was also demanding, though, and very, very hungry.

"I want to be naked," she said urgently.

Well, didn't that make two of them. He wanted to get her naked, too.

Lucan eased back. "Gimme one second."

He kissed her again. Kissed her a third time. Then knew that if he was going to pull out of this, of her, for anything longer than taking his own pants off, he better do it now.

"I'll be right back."

"Don't be gone long," she whispered.

"I won't be. Trust me on that."

With a leap that was worthy of a flying tackle, he launched himself at the door out into the hall. As he entered the code, he punched in the number sequence like he was jabbing the eyes of an enemy. Yanking the way open—

Mayhem stepped into his face. "What's wrong? Has she—"

"I need some privacy."

For a guy who tended to be pretty relaxed, even in a dog fight, Mayhem stayed stressed. "For what?"

"Really."

The other guy blinked like he didn't underst— "Oh."

"Yeah, *oh*." Lucan looked down the hall. "Anything brewing?"

"Apex went down to check on Kane because mess is opening up downstairs—the coast is going to stay clear for a little longer. Like thirty minutes or so? The guards are about to change, though. You may want to hold off on your privacy shit."

Fucking hell. "Just knock if you need to come in. And wait for a second."

"Lucan."

"What."

Mayhem glanced away. "How much do you know about her?"

"Excuse me?" As the other prisoner just continued to stare off into space, Lucan went palms up, are-you-stupid. "I know she volunteered to help Kane. I know she dragged me back indoors when I was dying in the sunshine. What the hell else do I have to know about her."

As the bonded male in him started to prowl around inside his skin, he had to cut that possessive crap quick. His wolf was a hair trigger when it came to defending territory to begin with. Throw in his sexual attraction for Rio?

He might as well have been a bomb waiting to go off.

"Watch yourself with her," Mayhem muttered. "That's all I'm saying."

"And I'll give you a piece of advice. Don't talk about my female to anybody—and that includes me. You're not going to like where it lands you."

Mayhem shook his head and stared down the empty hallway with its closed doors and its dim lighting.

"Fine, you got it," was all he said.

Good decision, Lucan thought as he went back into the quarters. *Good fucking decision.*

✦ ✦ ✦

As Luke stepped out into the hall, Rio covered her face with her palms even though she was alone. Was she really going to do this? Really?

Dropping her arms, she rolled over onto her stomach and wondered what Luke was saying to either Mayhem or Apex. He was propping the door open with his foot, but his voice was low so she couldn't tell the words. Beyond the conversation, though, in terms of the rest of the place getting busy . . . she heard nothing in particular, which she took to mean that any uprising was either contained or yet to come—

Abruptly, Luke pivoted back around, took a step forward, and shut the door. As his eyes met hers, she felt like there was a mask over his facial features, but his eyes. Oh, yes, his eyes. There was no masking what was in them.

And as he stayed put, it was clear he was asking her a question.

So she figured she better give him an answer.

With a slow, sensual pivot on the bed, Rio eased onto her back and let her head fall off the edge of the mattress. Knowing that he was watching, she moved one of her hands to the side of her throat and slowly let it drift downward onto her collarbone. Lower to between her breasts. Even farther so that it was on her stomach.

She stopped just as it came to rest on the center of her pelvis. "I want you. Now."

"Jesus Christ, female," he growled.

As Luke stalked over to her, he stared out from under lowered lids, his gait like that of a predator, his arousal straining against the front of his pants. And with all those muscles fanning out to fill his shoulders, his pecs, his abs . . . he was too spectacular to deny.

Not that "no" was in her vocabulary when it came to him.

He stopped in front of her, and what do you know, her upside-down view was just as spectacular as the face-on ones she'd been enjoying: His torso was magnificent from this angle.

Except then he cursed.

"We can't do this right now," he said gruffly.

"No?" Rio arched—and yup, his eyes went exactly where she wanted them to go: Her breasts. "What's going on out there?"

"There are people coming. And not a lot of time."

"Really?" She brought up her knees and rubbed her thighs together, back and forth, back and forth. "Then we'll just have to be quick about it."

"The guards are changing soon."

"But not now." What the hell was she saying? Was she really— "Not right now, correct?"

Luke started to breathe heavily, his abs rippling as his chest pumped up and down. Behind his fly, his erection jerked.

Rio arched her spine again and reached her arms out. Linking her hands around the backs of his thighs, she put a little pressure into the hard cords of his hamstrings. If he didn't come forward, she would let it be. She wasn't going to beg for sex from anybody, not even him. But if he did—

Luke closed the distance so that the crown of her head rested on the front of his legs. As he stared down at her, his jaw started to grind.

Opening her mouth, she ran her tongue over her lips. Then she bit the lower one.

"Fuck," he breathed.

Extending her tongue again, she flicked it back and forth . . . then she opened her mouth wide.

Luke's eyes squeezed shut and his head fell back. But his hands came forward.

They were such great hands, strong, blunt-tipped, the veins that ran down the backs of them standing out in stark relief.

He undid the button of his fly. "Are you sure this is what you want?"

"I'm not going to beg you." She did some hand work of her own, moving over the front of her shirt. "The timing is bad anyway, right?"

"Really fucking bad." And yet he drew the zipper down. "The worst."

"Couldn't be worse." She drew a circle around her breast, imagining that it was his touch, his fingers. "Ever."

"Ever."

The erection that broke out of his fly was thick and long—and oh, God. Big. And as he wrapped his beautiful hand around it, she bit her lower lip again.

"Rio . . ."

As he hesitated, she shook her head and continued to caress her breast on top of her shirt. "I'm not even going to say please. So don't hold your breath for that. Give me what I want or not. I'll be fine either way—you, on the other, may be uncomfortable for the rest of the night."

With her other hand, she went between her legs, spreading them a little, touching herself through her pants, through her underwear . . . through the insanity that had so clearly taken over her judgment. In this moment, though, all she knew was that she was tired of waging a war against an intangible, disinterested enemy of shoulds, and woulds, and coulds. She hadn't been just a woman in a very, very long time, and staring up at Luke right now? It was impossible to do anything but feel.

And yeah, sure, fine, maybe the concussion(s) had wiped out the risk-assessment portion of her brain.

But she really didn't care.

"I don't get even a please?" Luke murmured.

"No, that's your job. To do the begging."

"Me?" When she nodded, he stroked his shaft with that palm of his. Up and down. "As in . . ."

"'Rio, will you please . . .'"

"Please what?" Another stroke. All the way to the big head. "What comes next?"

"I can't remember. Sorry. You'll have to figure it out on your own."

She brought her fingers to her mouth, pushing them past her lips. Then she let her eyes roll back in her head as she drew them in deep and retracted them. Drew them in deep and brought them back out again.

"Oh, *fuck*, Rio, please suck my cock," he blurted.

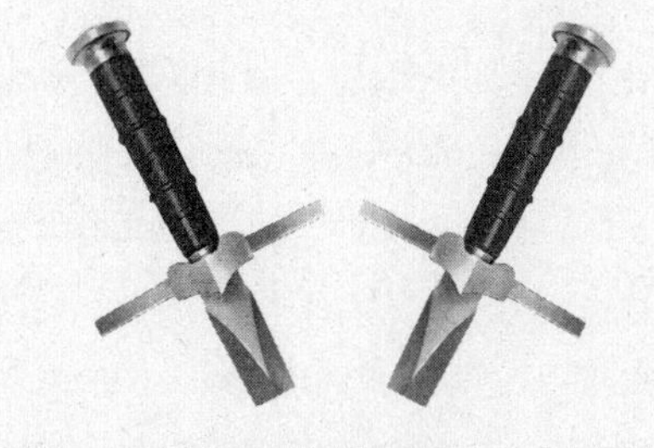

CHAPTER FORTY-FOUR

That mouth.

Those lips.

Those two fingers going in and out of that mouth and those lips, in and out, in and out—and then came the tongue. As Rio licked around the glistening digits, her talented, little pink—

Lucan fell off the cliff and threw out some combination of syllables. He wasn't sure what he'd said, exactly—but "PLEASE" had been in there front and center.

Just like she'd wanted it to be.

And hell, at the rate she was going, he would have said anything she wanted him to—state capitals, names of countries. A goddamn grocery list.

"Well," she murmured, "since you asked so nicely."

Her arms extended out again, and he felt her hands slip around the backs of his thighs once more.

"Gimme," she whispered. "Let me taste you."

With a feeling of unreality, Lucan widened his stance and lowered his thumping erection right into her—

Her tongue came first. She licked at his tip, flicked at it, and teased some more until his legs shook. And then, just as he was about to lose it, just as his whole arm was trembling, when the release was going to happen—

Rio opened wide and took him down.

The shock of exactly what he had expected and had wanted made him go momentarily numb—and that was the only reason he didn't come right away. And then there was the incomprehensible sight of his girth stretching her lips wide, the white slice of her lower teeth flashing, the column of her throat so very exposed—

So tempting to his fangs.

As they tingled and dropped down, a cold blast of warning went through him. No, he couldn't go there. He couldn't let that fantasy, of biting her, of sucking something of hers down deep, get too far.

He was already on the verge of losing control, and he would not, could never, hurt her in any way—or endanger her life by bleeding her out.

"Mmm," she said as she swallowed him down again.

"I gotta touch you," he growled. Or something like that. What the fuck was coming out of his mouth?

Bending over her, he went for her pants, attacking the fly with sloppy, sloppy hands. Meanwhile, where she was working him, she took over where his grip had been, tight, tight palms wrapping around him and starting to pump as she sucked him off.

Yanking down what covered her lower body, she helped him in the effort, kicking off her boots, toeing down the fabric—

Okay, fine, he broke his no-bite rule in spirit when he leaned all the way over and ripped one of his fangs through the hip string of her panties. And to keep it even, 'cuz fair was fair, he tore the other string that went over her opposite hip with his hands.

Lucan went right in with his mouth. Parting her thighs wide, he led with his lips, stroking her sex as she sucked his, the pleasure going nuclear—

As she cried out, he only knew it because her hot breath and cold inhale was what threw him over the edge.

Or no, maybe it was the taste of her. The slick feel of her. The way she cranked over onto her side while she writhed in ecstasy and he had to force her back into position.

Or . . . it could have been the rolling of her hips against his face as she herself came. At the same time he did.

It was the most perfect sex of his life.

And he hadn't even had her yet.

God, why didn't they have more time?

✦ ✦ ✦

Did that count as a quickie, Rio wondered as she turned to the spray in the shower, opened her mouth . . .

. . . and remembered what had been inside of it mere moments before.

Closing her eyes, she felt the throbbing between her legs and relived what it had been like to feel Luke's tongue slick into her, and his lips pull against her, and his—

She popped her lids open and grabbed for the bar of soap. "Not the time, not the place."

But *damn.*

Even though their quick, super-fast, super-sonic session had been, well, *quick,* it was clear that the man had hidden talents, and that he was willing to share them with her. He also had stamina for days, which she took as a compliment. They'd hooked up for all of about ten minutes, tops, but there had been a number of orgasms on both sides—

As arousal thickened her throat and forced her to take a couple of deep breaths, she pivoted around so that the spray dampened her hair. When she leveled her head and opened her eyes again, Luke was leaning against the wall and watching her with his arms crossed and a secret smile on his face. He was fully clothed, dressed in black combats and a black turtleneck that made him look like he was part of a militia.

She smiled back at him.

"You're beautiful, you know that?" he said.

Rio swept both her hands over her head, sluicing water down the back of her skull. As she did, her wet breasts swayed, heavy and gleaming. They were aching for his attention, and she wanted him to know it.

And given where his eyes were, it was a good guess her message had been received.

"You want to join me?" she asked.

"Yeah, I do. Really fucking badly."

Those eyes roamed her up and down—and she decided that he deserved a good look at the back of her so she pivoted on the ball of one foot. When she glanced over her shoulder, he was rubbing his chin as if he had more than accepted all the things she was offering.

And was thinking about where to start.

Except then he abruptly looked away, in the direction of the door. The frown that drew his brows together meant one and only one thing.

"I put your clothes right here," he said as he turned away. "On the chair."

Rio canned the water, the dripping loud into the silver drain. There were no towels—because, hello, this wasn't a Hilton—so as she stepped out from the little tiled section, she sloughed off her arms, her legs, her butt with her hands.

Getting her bra on took some maneuvering because the straps stuck on her wet skin. When it was in place, she pulled the shirt he'd given her on, and then did the same with her pants. The underwear were completely unusable. She wadded them up and shoved them into her back pocket.

The ruined t-shirt and fleece, the ones she had had on before, she left on the floor.

As she came around the partition, she saw Luke over by the bed, tucking a gun into the waistband of the combats he'd put on.

"You can't go out there," he said gruffly. "If you're found, it's going to get bad."

That was when she heard the voices. Outside the door. Loud and insistent.

"Where's your gun?" he demanded.

Rio went over to the table and picked the weapon up. "I've got it."

Luke stared at her. Then came across to her.

She didn't even hesitate. She threw her arms around him and held on tight for a brief moment.

"Please be careful," she said.

God, the idea she might never smell his cologne again . . . and the fact that she wasn't now because he'd sprayed something on himself, something that was like the incense in the clinic.

She pushed back urgently. "Better than that, let's leave together. We'll just go out the back and—"

"Rio, I can't—"

"Yes, you *can*. I'm serious about getting out of the life. You could be free of this—"

"It doesn't work like that, and you know it."

"But I can help you."

"No, you can't, and besides, how would it be for you? If I'm out, and you're still in? Have you thought about that."

"You don't need to worry about me."

"So you think I'm going to come work for your Mozart? Not going to happen." He drew a hand through his hair and looked over at the bloodstain on the floor, which was still bright red. "I don't know, maybe I can get out in a little while, who knows. But it won't be to Caldwell. Your world . . . is not mine."

"It could be."

"No, it couldn't. And you know that." His broad, warm hand stroked her shoulder gently. Then he lifted something up. "By the way, this dropped out of your pocket when I was getting your clothes."

Dangling off his forefinger was the key fob to the Chrysler.

With a locked jaw, he put the the thing in her hand and closed her grip around it. Then he nodded. "I want you to leave now. Go through that back door and drive away—"

A gunshot rang out in the hall and she jumped.

"Goodbye, Rio."

Riding a swell of emotion, she lifted her face for his kiss. But it didn't come.

He brushed her cheek. "Take care of yourself and don't look in the rearview. It's the way of survivors, remember?"

"I don't want to just survive." *Without you,* she added to herself.

"Sometimes it's the best deal a person gets."

As he turned away, she raised her voice. "You said you loved me."

Well, not exactly. But in her desperation, she was willing to play any card she had.

Luke paused. Then he glanced over his shoulder. "You can still love someone, even if you're not with them. And no matter how painful it is, I'm not in any hurry to get over you, Rio."

His smile was heartbreaking, full of pain, and yet no regrets.

Rio teared up as he walked away. He didn't look back when he got to the door. He just punched in the code—and stepped out into chaos.

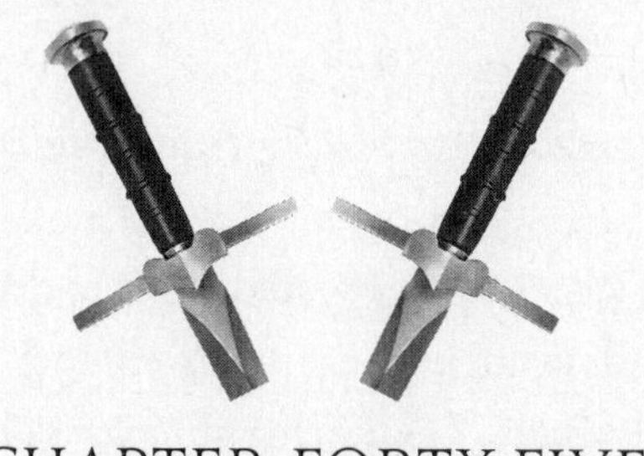

CHAPTER FORTY-FIVE

Lucan made sure the door to the private quarters closed behind him—and then he assessed the seven guards who had lined up in front of Apex and Mayhem.

"Okay, who shot who," he said to the group as he palmed his gun. "I'm not seeing anybody on the floor."

"Misfire," Apex drawled. "The one on the end was cleaning his gun. He didn't mean to try to put a bullet in me."

Lucan looked down the line to the guard in question and bared his fangs. "You gotta be careful. Accidents can be deadly."

The guard took a step forward. "You want to explain *that*?"

It was pretty obvious what the "that" was. The Executioner was where he'd been left, no change there, and it was clear the decomposition process was starting, the blood pooling in the feet and ankles, which were now purple; the face utterly white; the blood no longer flowing out of the piercings of the pegs, but congealing beneath him on the floor.

"Explain what," Lucan murmured amicably. 'Cuz sometimes it was good to make people say things out loud.

"*That*." The male pointed. "Right there."

Lucan glanced over. "Why, that's a door. You use it to go in and out of when you—"

"You're in deep shit, Lucan. I wouldn't get cocky."

Down at the end of the hall, the stairwell door opened, and prisoners started to file through. The lineup of lowered heads, and wrinkled, dirty clothing, and desolated shuffling was a reminder of where they all were. No freedom. Just servitude.

The fact that none of the workers looked up at the congregation in front of the Executioner's dead body was a commentary on how tired and ill they were.

Lucan thought of what Rio had said. About getting out.

He retrained his stare on the guard.

"Well, if I were you"—he walked right up to the guy—"I'd remember who did *that*. And enjoyed it while it happened. You know what my kind is like. We relish the kill and it doesn't matter the context—sometimes it's to defend our territory. Sometimes it's to settle a score. And sometimes it's for fun."

"*Wolf*."

The female voice cut through everything, including the footfalls of all the prisoners filing into the workrooms.

"Great," Lucan muttered, "another party checks in."

The head of the guards was tall as a male and just as well muscled, her dark hair pulled back in a severe twist, her affect one of total dominance. And yet even with all that, her eyes were actually the most dangerous part about her. Lucan had learned the hard way that her peripheral vision was incredibly sharp. The only thing better? Her aim. Gossip had it that she'd made her money as an assassin in the human world.

Lucan didn't question that backstory. Then again, he really didn't give a fuck.

"You rang," he said as he looked at her.

"I see you've done some redecorating." She walked forward, her body shifting lithely under the armored plates she wore on the front and back of her torso, as well as down her legs. "Proud of yourself?"

He had to give her credit for all that gear under her weapons. A lot of males who were all about the engagement and the militia shit were too proud, too overconfident, to protect themselves. What they saw as an admission of weakness, she saw as preservation.

She was smart like that.

Which was how she'd managed to quietly gather power, first under the Command, then under the Executioner. And now, it didn't take a genius to figure out she was going to make her big move.

But he couldn't let her do that, although not because he wanted to play king himself.

"It was about time to change things around here," Lucan announced. "A new set of rules. So I'm taking over—"

"Are you." The smile on the female's face was about as warm as a winter squall. "You're underpowered for a coup on the wall, just the three of you."

He nodded over his shoulder at the body on the wall. "We're doing okay so far."

"Just because you killed him, you think you're in charge."

Raising his voice, he said, "It's time to end this whole fucking thing. Centuries of people falsely imprisoned, working in deplorable conditions, suffering so a series of despots can pocket the money—"

"Okay, we're done with your sermon, wolf. Step aside now and I'll thank you for your service to me—and there will be no repercussion. Argue even one word and I have fourteen other guards in the wings—and another twenty-five I can call in. You're not going to win this fight, wolf. You're going to wake up dead."

"Isn't that an oxymoron?"

"No, I'm originally from Boston. It only makes sense to people from the six-one-seven. But I digress." She smiled again, her eyes slicing into him, through him. "You three have few weapons, little ammo, and no cover. As I said, if you have a death wish, I'll indulge it now, and then hang you and your accomplices up next to the Executioner. Or you can stand down, let me into the private quarters, and do your fucking job on the Caldwell streets."

Lucan shook his head—and prayed Rio had done what she needed to do to save herself. "Not the way it's going to happen."

The head of the guards looked at the door. And smiled again, in that carnivore kind of way.

Under different circumstances, he would've gotten along with her better.

"Is there someone in there?" The female stepped in more closely. "Someone you're protecting. Somebody that you have to hide because she's not supposed to be here?"

"You've got it all wrong. But it's a nice thought."

"So you just love reeking of incense, then?" The female slashed a hand through the air. "It doesn't matter. What does, is the fact that this isn't a game, wolf. I'm not going to let you take over this whole operation with a human just because you're greedy."

"I don't give a shit about money—"

"I know the dealer you've been negotiating with is here. I've scented her in the stairwells, and she's under that stench you've doused yourself in. I think you're looking to cut everyone out, and make a fortune for yourself—and it's not that I can't respect the goal, but I'm not going to allow you to take control."

"You should write fiction, you've got a knack for it."

"I'm done talking. Let me into those quarters. Or I'm going to pave the way in over a bleeding corpse."

✦ ✦ ✦

Rio stayed frozen where she was for—oh, maybe a second and a half. Then she frantically patted her pockets. The phone. Where was that phone.

Had he taken it, too?

Glancing around the floor, she didn't see the thing anywhere, so she dove for the messy blankets of the bed, shoving the covers out of the way, splaying her hands wide, searching for that glossy little screen—

"Thank God," she muttered as she found it trapped at the foot of the mattress, in the one corner of the sheets that was still tucked in.

Her hands were shaking so badly she nearly dropped the cell, and she looked to the door. Tightening her hands around the key fob, she closed her eyes and told herself she had to go.

Take care of yourself . . .

She was a fucking cop, for godsakes, and she was on the job. Everything that happened here at this site was about two things: lining up evidence to arrest and prosecute everybody in charge for illegal drug trade and staying alive to deliver that evidence into the hands of the prosecutor.

So the innocent could be cleared and returned to their families and loved ones, and the wrongdoers could go to jail for their crimes.

That was it.

And now was the perfect time to get out.

With one last look at the door Luke had disappeared through . . . she wheeled away and stumbled for the back exit. As she passed by the gun rack, she threw out a hand, grabbed one of the rifles, and slung its strap over her shoulder. Snagging a box of ammo off a shelf, she went to the numbers pad.

She punched in Mayhem's pattern from memory and the lock unlatched.

In the end, she had to glance back one last time. No more gunshots out there, and the voices had dimmed down. But who the hell knew what was happening.

The pull to change direction was so powerful.

. . . and don't look in the rearview.

"Shit."

On that note, she broke out into the stairwell and rushed down the fresh pine stairs, entering the code a second time and shoving the lower panel wide. Outside, the night smelled of fresh earth and coming snow.

And soot from the fire.

There was no ambient light anywhere. All she could see were shapes within the darkness: a lineup of vehicles, the soaring flank of the building, the stick-tree forest like a sketch that had yet to be colored in. As she attempted to get her bearings, her thundering heart in her chest was loud in her ears, and her lungs didn't seem to be working—

What the hell was that clicking sound?

Oh. Her tongue in her own mouth.

Putting out the key fob, she pressed one of the buttons. Somewhere over to the left, there was a beep and a flash of orange, so she hit it again. Tracking the strobing, she found the SUV parked grille-in between a truck and a box van with no side windows.

When she tried the door handle, she realized she'd just managed to lock the thing really tight. She pushed the other buttons, raising the back end, and then—

The alarm was loud as a scream, the flashing headlights and taillights like a bad concert come to life. Shoving the fob out in front of herself, like it was a gun she could shoot the SUV with, she scrambled to—

Silence.

Looking around, she held her breath. When there were no sounds of people rushing up to her—or shooting at her—she scrambled down to the rear hatch and shut it with the fob. As the panel lowered itself automatically, she got a quick view into the back thanks to the glow of the interior lighting. The seats had all been put down, as if there had been cargo of some sort loaded in there, and the white powder residue told her everything she needed to know about what exactly had been transported.

Rio raced around and yanked open the driver's side door. Getting behind the wheel, she locked everything up and started the engine. As the headlights exploded to life, that was when she got a proper look at the building. It was brick with cream mortar that was streaked with the grime of the ages. Rows and rows of windows stretched five stories up. And wings that seemed the size of airplane hangars flanked either side.

What the hell was this place, she thought as she put the engine in reverse.

Backing out of the spot, she hit the brakes and stared through the windshield.

Fumbling to find the right button, she lowered the window next to her and then she got out the phone and swiped up to bypass the code requirement. She took pictures of everything, including the back door she'd come out of and the burn marks on the pavement.

Then she hit the gas and kept snapping the pictures as she followed the lane down the rear of the building. Emerging from the lee of the wing on the right, she came around the front and stopped again.

"Where have I seen you," she whispered as she took more pictures with the phone. "I know you from somewhere . . ."

The open-air porches were the thing that jogged her memory: There were open-air porches across all the levels of the wings, the center core of the building the only part that was solid.

"Go," she told herself. "You have to *go*."

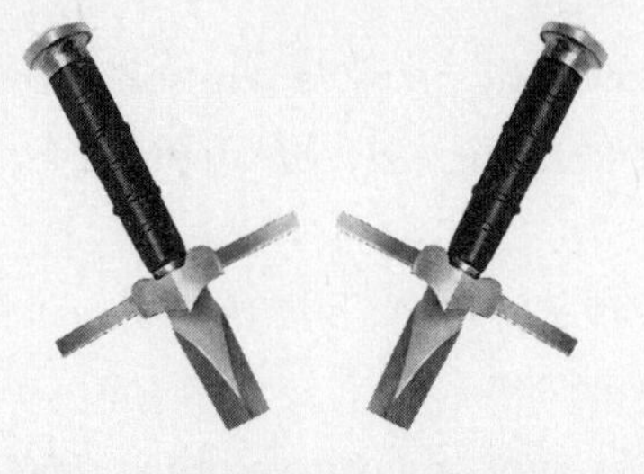

CHAPTER FORTY-SIX

As Lucan stood in front of the private quarters, he shook his head at the leader of the guard squad. "Fine, you're going to have to shoot me if you want to get in there."

The female seemed surprised he wasn't following orders, even with the threat of death. But come on, like he hadn't had countless I'm-going-to-kill-you's in his life? She was going to have to do better than that if she wanted to impress him.

"I have nothing against keeping human pets," she said as she got nose to nose with him. "But you don't shit where you eat, at least not on my watch. She is not welcome here. So you're going to let me in there to deal with her, and then you're going to go the *fuck* down to Caldwell and finish what you started with Mozart."

Lucan glanced at Apex and Mayhem, trying to gauge their readiness to fight. Both of the males were rock steady, prepared to use their guns.

"You know," he said, prepared to work his leverage, "if you want to get the deal done, you need me. I'm the only one who knows who the contacts are down in Caldwell. Sure, you can re-create it all, but it'll cost you time and money. And as for her? I don't know what the hell you're talking about, but you better do the math on her role, too. She's Mozart's right-hand woman. You bury her? We lose the deal, and Mozart is going to come after you with everything he's got. You'll end up defending yourself instead of making money."

"You honestly believe humans can get in here? They're weak, and disorganized on their best night. Against my males, they don't stand a chance."

"You keep telling yourself that."

"I gave you an opportunity to be reasonable." The head of the guards nodded off to the side. "But it is what it is."

There was a shuffling. A moan of pain. And a scent of fresh blood—

The flank of guards that had gathered parted, and before Lucan's eyes could properly focus on what was coming forward, Apex let out a curse and lunged forward.

Toward Kane, who was being dragged forward by two heavily armed males.

Lucan caught the other prisoner's arm and yanked him back. "Don't give her more than she already has," he hissed quietly.

Kane's head lolled on his shoulder, fresh blood running from his raw wounds, his breathing a rattle in lungs that had been burned on their insides.

"Oh," the head of the guards murmured, "did you think it was your corpse I was going to step over? You're right. I need you, but I don't need him."

"You *bitch*," Apex spat. "Let him go. He's no threat to you!"

"The Executioner and I had few secrets." The female talked over the prisoner's protests as Lucan stepped in front of Apex to hold him back. "And what ones we did have were on my side only. So he told me about your little attachment, your—loyalty, let's call it—to this aristocrat. I had questioned how deep this abiding regard went, but then I realized, it is in your species' nature. You are a pack wolf without a clan, and the reflex to create that which is intrinsic to your DNA forges ties wherever they are found. You pick up people like trash at the side of the road, and it fills the wheel wells of your car. But you can't help it, and I am not going to resist using your defect to my benefit."

Lucan narrowed his eyes. "Be careful there, female. You know what else they say about wolves?"

"What."

He looked at her exposed throat. "We bite."

"Oh, that's original." She smiled coldly. "I didn't see that coming. Now get the fuck out of my way."

When he didn't move, she took her gun out.

"Shoot me," he said. "I don't give a fuck."

And he meant it. There was no future for him and the female he'd bonded with. No real future, anyway. So what did he care?

"Will you stop trying to be my target? It makes you look desperate." She swung the muzzle around and pointed it at Kane's chest. "*He* is who I'm going to shoot—"

"Kill him and you have no leverage over me."

"No, I'll just find your girlfriend. I followed her weeks before you did. Even if she leaves here, I know where she lives, what car she drives, where she goes at night. I will give her to you in pieces. Now get the *fuck* out of my way."

Apex growled and tried to lunge for the female, but Lucan wheeled around and locked the other prisoner in a bar hold. As their eyes met, there was a struggle, but the other male stilled.

Not now, Lucan mouthed.

"Thank you," the head of the guards patronized. "And yes, I'll bet she's left after all these delay tactics of yours. Like I don't know what you're doing with this posturing?"

There were a series of beeps and Lucan glanced over his shoulder. The female was entering the code, and as the lock released, she smiled back at him.

And stepped inside.

Lucan nodded for Mayhem to come over and keep holding Apex in place—because goddamn it, Lucan was going into those quarters and checking to make sure Rio was gone. Except as the guy stepped up to assume the corralling job, there was a mistake in the transfer of duties.

A slip of the hands was enough for Apex to break free and go raging bull toward the guards who were holding Kane up off the floor.

As a fight broke out, Lucan had to let his two comrades handle themselves. He lunged forward and caught the door just before it shut, slipping into the private quarters.

The head of the guards was over by the rifles, her long, blunt-tipped fingers traveling down one of them as if she were caressing the blooms of a vase full of red roses.

"I have coveted these guns." She glanced over at him, seemingly unsurprised he'd followed her. "They can take out a dangling cherry from its stem at two hundred yards."

Lucan looked around without trying to be obvious. "Do me a favor."

She arched a dark brow. "Excuse me?"

"Let Apex have Kane. Things are getting ugly out there, and if you're all about taking control—which appears to be true—you're going to want those guards without a lot of broken bones, right?"

The female came over. Stared at him. "I thought you wanted to be king of the mountain."

"No, I want to end this place."

"So you and I are at odds, even though you're willing to give me power."

"Did I say I would give you anything?"

"You don't have a choice."

With that, she walked back to the door. Entering the code, she opened the thing—and recoiled.

The fresh scent of blood and the gurgling sounds of death said it all.

"Hey!" she called out. "Enough. *Stop it.*"

The female palmed her gun and discharged a series of bullets into the air—with all the calmness of someone putting in a lunch order at a drive-through.

In the aftermath, there was nothing but silence and the smell of gun smoke.

She looked back at Lucan. "You're going to Caldwell now and completing your job. And you know, if your girlfriend plays by my rules, I might let her live, if it's beneficial for me."

"Fuck you."

"Her life is in your hands, wolf."

Bide your time, he told himself. The female was right, he and Mayhem and Apex were not enough to hold control. Not right now. But with the right plan?

He needed time to think.

Grinding his molars, he muttered, "Yeah. Fine."

"Bring Kane in here," the female ordered out into the hall. "There's a bed—okay, fine, let him do it, for fuck's sake. He wants to play gurney, I don't give a shit."

There was a pause. Then she opened the door wider and held it in place with her strong body.

Apex didn't look at her as he passed by with Kane in his arms. Good thing. The light in his eyes was capable of blowing a mortal right out of their boots.

And hey, at least Rio was nowhere to be found.

As Apex laid Kane out gently and sat on the bed beside him, two guards with shiners like they'd been hit with a set of two-by-fours took up res against the far walls.

Lucan shook his head as he tried to see whether Kane was still alive. "You better hope you didn't kill him."

The female shrugged as if she didn't have a care in the world. "Whether he lives or dies doesn't matter to me. 'Adapt and overcome,' that's my motto."

"So you're a parasite."

"No, I'm a predator." She paused by the command table. "Well, well, well . . . look at this."

The female picked up some papers and went through them. Then she drew them to her nose and sniffed.

"These were your female's." She smiled in that cold way of hers. "I can scent her on them. Such a little artist she is, but she wasn't drawing you. Disappointed?"

As the pages were turned around, Lucan came forward and didn't bother hiding his intensity.

The head of the guards' satisfaction was like the bloodstains on the floor, something that penetrated the space around her: "Seems like she wanted to remember exactly what the layout of our facility is."

Taking the papers from her, he frowned. They were, in fact, line drawings, floor by floor, of the sanatorium. Every room, staircase, hallway, and connector that Rio had been through. Down to the scale. And the head of the guards was right. The paper had Rio's scent on it.

She had done these.

"But she's not here anymore, is she," the other female said. "Because you told her she better save herself—too bad humans can't dematerialize, isn't it."

When he remained stonily silent—because that was what you did when you discovered someone was using you—the female filled the void with conversation.

"Why did you bring her here to the prison camp. And do not lie."

"She needed to see the production." He shrugged like he didn't care. "It's a big order. She said she wanted to make sure we could handle it."

"Why be so secretive?"

"She's a goddamn human."

"The Executioner wasn't going to jeopardize the funds flow. She was safe. Why hide her."

"I don't trust anyone inside these walls."

"Not even your Kane?"

Lucan glanced over to the bed. Apex was curved over the other male, as if he were trying to breathe for the aristocrat by will alone. The fact that his own face was bruised and there was blood on his mouth didn't seem to be something he even noticed.

"Kane is not mine," Lucan corrected.

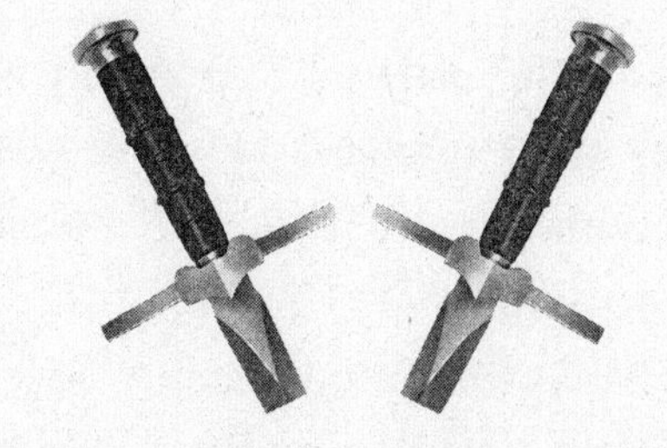

CHAPTER FORTY-SEVEN

In retrospect, José had cursed himself.

That was what he decided as he finally left the homicide division's bullpen and hung a louie to head down the empty corridor to the chief's suite. When he got to the outer door, he wasn't surprised to see that the window to the waiting area was dark, but he had permission to go in so he tried the door handle.

Fortunately, things had been left unlocked and the motion-activated lights came on as soon as he put a foot inside. No doubt Stan had told Willie to leave things open because he'd been expecting the updated report on Leon Roberts sometime after she left for the day.

José certainly hadn't thought it'd be this late before he'd finished his typing—he glanced at his watch and cursed. Nine frickin' p.m. He'd had to call home twice. Once at six, when a tip on a cold case had come in, and then again at 7:30, to let his wife know he needed to stay and do write-ups.

There had been a great deal to add to the report, and not just in terms of the autopsy or ballistics. Lot of people were calling with leads on Roberts's death. José had fielded them all afternoon long. He didn't think anything was going to materialize from any of it, but you never knew. So he and Trey had returned thirty-three calls, all of which he'd logged manually into the system from notes he and the kid had scribbled.

Not that Trey was a kid.

And now he was here, giving Willie's empty desk a wave in the darkness and going over to the glass door to Stan's crib, feeling like he was a hundred years old.

The wave thing was pure habit, really. Every time he came in here, he walked by Willie's desk, waved at her, and went to open Stan's door. She never stopped him, no matter what Stan was doing—even if there was a meeting going on or the chief was on the phone.

Willie always said he was the only one allowed to interrupt like that.

So there was no hesitation as he passed by. Like the trained seal he was, he followed his greeting routine and went directly to Stan's inner door. It wasn't until he started to turn the knob that his tired brain woke up and pointed out that this entry was absolutely going to be inaccessible after hours—

Things opened no problem.

"Of course you don't lock your door," José murmured as he entered and overhead lights came on automatically.

Stan was such a product of the eighties, when battening down the hatches the second the sun went behind the horizon for the night had not been a thing. Then again, this was the police station, so everyone was getting checked in as they came into the building itself. And there were cameras everywhere.

Well, out in the hall there were cameras. Not in here.

"Whatever."

José walked across the red-and-blue carpet and then stood over the piles of paperwork on the desk. Man, compliance would have a fit if they knew all this . . . departmental shit, whatever it was . . . was unsecured. But that was the way Stan was. Too trusting. Then again, who could find anything in this—

The sound was so quiet that, had José not been standing still as he contemplated where he should put the report in the midst of the mess, he never would have heard it.

And if it had not repeated, he wouldn't have bothered to do anything about it.

But the soft noise was a phone. A cell phone on vibrate.

Setting the report down on the corner of the desk, not that there was any rhyme or reason to that particular location, he followed the *brrrrrr'*ing, *brrrrrrr'*ing to the door to Stan's private crapper.

"You forgot your phone, Stan," he said as he pushed the door wider.

The sound was still muffled even as he leaned into the sacred space—and then, before he could zero in on the where, things went silent. He glanced around the counter. Nothing there, out in the open. And on the back of the toilet—only golf magazines. And he wasn't going into the guy's drawers—

The sound started up again.

José bent down. Bent farther. The phone was vibrating in the lowest of the cabinet's drawers.

He pulled the handle slowly, sliding things open. But for godsakes, he'd known the guy his entire professional life. What was he going to find other than toilet rolls—

There was a button-down shirt wadded up in the drawer. Blue-and-white-checked. No doubt another mustard casualty.

Reaching in, he pulled the cotton folds out.

Underneath them was a black nylon wallet . . . and a cell phone. And as the caller hung up again, or things went to voice mail, the vibration stopped.

With a sense of total disbelief, José took a pair of nitrile gloves out of his pocket. Yet after so many years in his job, he'd learned to trust his gut.

And his gut was telling him that what he was about to find was going to break his fucking heart.

Leaving the phone alone, he picked up the wallet, tore open the Velcro, and—

Officer Leon Roberts's face stared up at him from a driver's license that had been slotted into the see-through half of the two flaps. And across on the other side . . .

. . . was the Caldwell Police badge the man had earned and done proud.

✦ ✦ ✦

"You know, you're quiet. Even for you, you're really frickin' quiet."

As V stopped under the fire escape and looked up, he wondered, if he stayed silent, whether Rhage would move on to another topic. Like, food. Or . . . food.

Or maybe . . . food?

You know, just to mix it up.

"Hello?" Hollywood prompted.

"I'm focused on what we're doing here."

Rhage stepped in front, and given his size, it was like the earth had coughed up a big, blond, beautiful mountain. With a piehole that, with no pie around, was flapping in the wind.

"And we've walked aimlessly for how many blocks now?" the brother said. "What's wrong."

"Fine, you want to chat? Answer me this. How does getting in our three hundred and fifty thousand steps tonight correspond to conversation—"

"V, what's up your ass." Rhage crossed his arms over the black daggers that were holstered, handles down, to his massive chest. Then he winced. "Actually, how 'bout you just tell me what's on your mind. I think I better leave your ass and what may, or may not, be inside of it out of this. No offense."

V leaned back against the club. As the music was really bumping, the vibrations coming through the cement walls were like a massage chair.

"What did you dream about, Vishous," came the question he dreaded.

He shook his head. "You don't know me."

"The hell I don't. What did you see." When there was no reply, the brother said, "Who died."

"Who said anybody died?"

"You don't get visions about happy shit, V. Like never once have you told me you've had a dream about a bag of Lay's Sour Cream and Onion. Or Doritos. Hell, some Snyder's of Hanover pretzel nubs would do nicely."

"Nubs?"

"Yeah, with peanut butter in them. They're awesome." Rhage shrugged. "I mean, I'm assuming you'd mention it if you've seen any of these snack foods in my future. Like, have you?"

"Let me get this straight. You're putting nubs in your mouth, but you're worried what's doing with my ass?"

"Don't hate the pretzel. And let's get back to the issue at hand."

"Right. We're trying to find the missing female officer posing as a dealer, and this is where we saw her last."

"What the hell did you see over day."

Okay, this was the problem with Rhage. The brother was a tenacious motherfucker—and he actually had spot-on instincts.

Oh, and then there was the ass-slapping fact that V kinda wanted to talk about it. Hey, Rhage's *shellan* was a therapist, right? That was halfway to goal.

Not that he was looking to get his head shrunk.

The words came out of his mouth fast: "I dreamt that José de la Cruz's head got blown off his shoulders."

The brother rubbed his eyes like they stung. "Butch's former partner."

"No, another human with that name in Caldwell—" V put his hand out. "Sorry. I'm being bitchy."

"It's okay. You must be freaking out. I mean, what do you do with information like that?"

"And no timeline. None. It could be ten years from now. Or tomorrow night."

"Or tonight—"

"Holy shit," V cut in. "It's that guy."

Rhage wheeled around and squinted through the darkness. "You're right. From that thing."

V stepped around Hollywood and shitkickered his way across the street, falling into the wake of a human male who was six feet tall, but only about a hundred twenty pounds. The addict was in the same clothes as he'd been in the other night, when that undercover cop had walked him to the Holy Mother of Salvatory Stuff a couple streets over.

"My guy," V called out. "Hey."

The man glanced over his shoulder, got one look at the two pieces of trained killer on his tail—and took off at a surprisingly fast bolt. Then again, maybe he'd had training in these kinds of sprints.

V just loped along in his trail, knowing damn well that that body didn't have a marathon in it. Sure enough, three blocks down toward the river, there was a sudden drop in forward motion. And as the classic respiration triangle manifested—the guy bracing his arms on his knees and making plenty of torso space for his labored breathing—Vishous and Rhage pulled up alongside.

Flash Gordon looked up from his panting. "I dint—I—dint—do—it—"

"Take your time," V muttered. "We'll wait."

Palming his tin of hand-rolleds, he popped the top and put the offering in the human's face—and like the cigs were the hookup to a ventilator, or at the very least an oxygen mask, the guy reached for the nicotine with quaking fingers.

"Here, I'll get you one." V did the job with his gloved hand. "Only tobacco. But it's Turkish. The best."

"Th-th-thanks, man."

The cigarette went in between thin lips, and then the man kicked his head forward for the Bic that was offered. As he puffed up, the habit kicked in and calmed the hyperventilating.

Three inhales later, and the guy said, "I dint do it. Really."

"I'm not accusing you of anything." V thumbed over his shoulder. "Neither is my brother."

Eyes that would have been considered rheumatic in an eighty-year-old went back and forth.

"We're not related by blood," V explained.

"Oh."

"Listen, I know you've got to be somewhere." V motioned around in a circle, indicating all of downtown. "So I'm not going to waste your time."

"Okay."

"I want to know about a woman you were with the other night. She's about this high." V put his hand out flat at about five feet, nine inches tall. "Short dark hair. Had a leather jacket on. She helped you over to that dry-out tank—"

"Resource facility," Rhage cut in with a glare. "And hey, pound me for getting some help. That takes courage. Good luck with your recovery."

As Hollywood put out his toaster-oven-sized fist, the human put his open palm over the knuckles in confusion. And then when Rhage clapped the man on the shoulder, V had to catch Flash Gordon before he eggshelled onto the sidewalk.

"You know the woman I'm talking about?" V prompted. "You need her description again?"

"I, ah . . . yeah, I know her."

"Great. Do you know where we can find her? You got a cell phone number or an address for her?"

The man fell quiet, and paid a whole lot of attention to the end of the hand-rolled. Then he smoked some more. Meanwhile, the city kept going. A couple of cars—a sedan and a truck—went by, and then some twenty-ish men in tight jeans and narrow-shouldered jackets slicked across the intersection.

"Hello?" Rhage said.

V reached into his back pocket. "Here. This hundy'll help. I get how times are tough."

The human's eyes flared as he focused on the folded bill.

"Just answer any of my questions and it's yours." V held the Benji between his fore- and middle fingers. "Telephone number. Address. Regular place of business. Anything you know would be a big help."

The human cleared his throat. Then he dropped the hand-rolled and stamped it out with a Converse All Star that had seen better days. And nights.

Flash Gordon shook his head. "Nah. I ain't telling you nothing. Rio, she's good to me. She cares about me. She makes me take care of myself better even when I don't feel like it. I can't tell you nothing. Sorry."

The human straightened from his sagging posture, and even though he was still shaking, like he expected to have a gun put to his head at any second, his lips were shut and staying that way.

"Okay." V nodded. "I can respect that."

To a point.

By passing the human's nobility and free will, he entered the man's mind, and took a brief stroll around. The guy was currently sober, but that was not going to last—and he was feeling bad about being determined to score, like he was letting that undercover buddy of his down. In the end, though, the man didn't know anything specific about the woman, other than her street name, Rio, and the fact that she was supposedly high up in an organization run by a guy named Mozart.

Pulling out, V didn't bother patching anything up. It was better not to mess with the man much, because God knew that brain was damaged enough from the drug use.

In response, the addict winced like he had a headache, and those eyes went back and forth again between V and Rhage, all other-shoe-drop, bracing for some kind of retribution.

Vishous tucked the hundy in the man's pocket. "Keep the money. Go get a hot meal, it's going to be a long night."

Flash Gordon stammered some thanks, and then he shambled away, looking over his shoulder a couple of times before he disappeared around a corner into an alley.

"You've got a good heart under those daggers, Vishous."

"Whatever," V muttered as he started walking again. "Let's keep looking. At least we have a street first name now. But if she's undercover and she's missing? She's going to wake up dead."

Rhage caught up with him easily enough. "Hey, that's what Butch says all the time. It's a funny saying."

"Yeah, I know."

"It doesn't make a lot of sense."

"Yeah, I know."

Christ on a crutch, V thought to himself. Finding that prison camp was a real pain in his ass on so many levels, true?

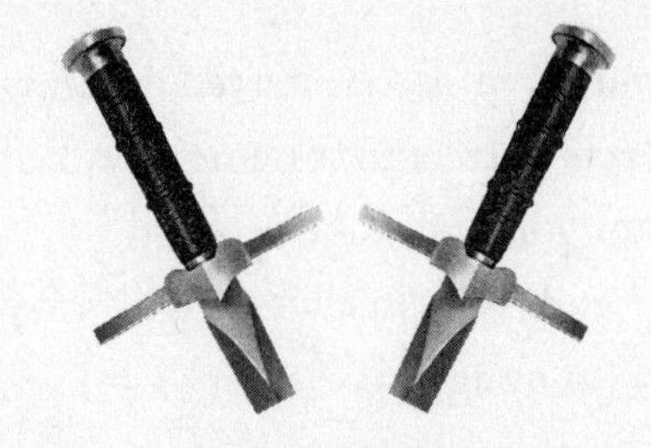

CHAPTER FORTY-EIGHT

Hello?"

When Rio's third call to her direct report, Leon Roberts, was finally answered, she had a split second of relief. Except then the man who'd picked up repeated the greeting—and she knew it wasn't Leon.

"Hello . . . ?"

Without conscious thought, she stomped on the brakes. The SUV's knobby tires immediately grabbed on to the pavement and brought her to a screeching halt in the middle of the narrow strip of country asphalt. As a surge of fear gripped her, her peripheral vision sharpened, the pine trees on either shoulder coming into almost painful clarity in the glow of the headlights.

Roberts was never without his cell phone. And she'd called him so many times over the last three years, she'd know his number and his voice anywhere.

"I can hear you breathing," the man on the other end said. "I know you haven't hung up."

No, she hadn't. But where was Roberts?

"And I think . . . I think I know who this is. Even though this number is not in Leon's contacts."

Rio covered her mouth with her free hand. Oh, God, she knew this voice. She knew who this was.

Tears speared into her eyes and she blinked quick.

"If I'm right about who you are," the man continued, "you need to listen carefully. Do not . . . don't come home. Wherever you are, if it's safe, stay put. It's not good here . . . at home. Do you understand what I'm telling you? I think I know who you are, and that means you know what I'm telling you and why I'm telling it to you like this."

Drawing the cell phone away from her ear, Rio stared at the time count as the seconds moved quickly.

Then she snapped the thing back in place. Lowering her voice to disguise it, she said, "Detective José de la Cruz."

There was a brief pause. "Yes. And I think you can guess why I'm answering this phone."

All at once, she was back downtown, racing to meet Luke for the first time, accepting a call on her own cell phone. Clear as a bell, she heard Roberts's voice in her ear, telling her her identity had been compromised. And there had been something else when she'd been busy talking over him. He'd told her he'd sent her something. Hadn't he?

What had he sent her?

Suddenly, there was no air in the SUV so she put down the window a little, the cold night coming in.

"Home," she said in that falsely low tone. "Go home."

Then she quickly ended the call.

Maybe he'd figured out what she was trying to tell him. Maybe he wouldn't.

But either way, Detective José de la Cruz of homicide had just saved her life.

Someone on the inside was after her. And had killed her colleague and friend because of it.

Holding the cell phone to her chest, she tried to breathe, tried to think. And sometime thereafter, she realized she had come to a stop next to a green-and-white highway sign.

Walters 10

Upstate. She was seriously upstate.

The idea that she couldn't go back to her apartment made her feel as if she were in a foreign country and did not speak the language. Then again, she had no idea where she could go, who she could talk to. What was safe. What she should do—

Another set of headlights rounded a curve in the road, coming toward her.

Snapping to attention, she threw the phone out of the window and into the opposite lane; then she punched the gas and continued on. She was in a stolen SUV, owned by drug suppliers, with a phone she'd lifted off a guy she'd shot and killed, stuck in an information vacuum where the wrong move could end her up where Roberts had.

Wherever that grave was.

Rio kept driving until she came into a little hamlet with a diner/grocery store combo, and a bank, and a gas station. She wasn't hungry—but then she had no money.

At least the tank was full.

That gasoline, and this vehicle she didn't own, were pretty much the extent of her assets.

God, what was she going to do? She'd assumed that as long as she could stay out of Mozart's way until she could get to the station, she'd be fine. But now that was not an option.

She had to find a safe place to collect her thoughts and figure out what she needed to do. But like she knew this area at all?

✦ ✦ ✦

As Lucan walked out of Willow Hills's front entrance, the sense that things were closing in, smothering him, suffocating him, was like a tangible stalker, tight on his heels. He knew what he was supposed to do, knew where to do it, knew what he had to accomplish to be successful.

But in the very short distance between the Executioner's private quarters and this very large, awfully decrepit exit, he'd made up his mind: Rio wasn't going to be involved in what happened next. He was going to deal with Mozart directly. That way, he could make sure Kane stayed alive while not endangering her, and then he could . . .

Lose his fucking mind quietly and calmly.

Great plan.

But come on. She'd known she was in danger. He'd rescued her, for fuck's sake. The conversation should have been about her getting out of the drug-dealing life, not him, but he'd been too distracted by emotion to be as smart and logical as he should have been. And wasn't that always the way.

Closing his eyes with a curse, he slowed his breathing and got ready to dematerialize. Just get ghost and go. Leave in a scatter of molecules—

When nothing even remotely heading-out happened, he reopened his lids and looked back at the sanatorium.

All those lives stuck underground, suffering in lesser degrees until they dropped dead and were slung out of the building's body chute to roast into ash by the sun. No one to mourn them, nobody missing them. Forgotten.

For fuck's sake, most of the people in there couldn't remember why or how they'd ended up in custody.

But they were going to have to wait for another savior to come along. He was not it. He was no hero, and never had been one.

Once again, with the closing of the eyes. Then the breathing. Deep breathing . . . slow. Easy—

When he still filled out his clothes and stayed stuck to the ground, when his body remained heavy and full in his skin, and the landscape continued to be unchanged, he lost his temper and started hoofing it. Another couple of hundred yards, he tried to dematerialize again. And then one more time, a further hundred yards along.

His head was just too fucked for him to concentrate enough to ghost away.

Long fucking walk to Caldwell from where the hell he was.

Man, this night just kept getting better.

Zipping his leather jacket up, he entered the scruffy tree line, pushing bare limbs out of his face, making his way to the chain-link fence. He was forced to claw his way up the thing and swing himself over the top. As he landed with a curse, he kept going.

Guess he was just going to have to "borrow" a human's car off the county road.

Yeah, 'cuz there were so many people wearing out the pavement up here this time of night. He'd have a better chance of getting hit by a bus—

Monte Carlo.

Monte-fucking-Carlo, he thought as he fell into a jog.

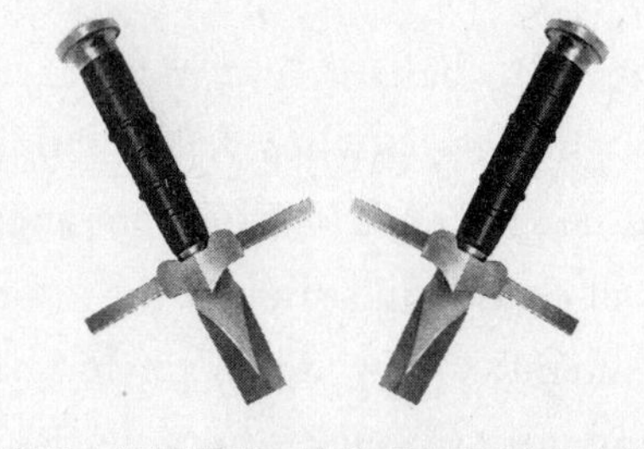

CHAPTER FORTY-NINE

José pulled his unmarked over to the curb in front of Officer Hernandez-Guerrero's apartment building. When he got out, he made sure his jacket was open so he could get at his gun.

It was that kind of night.

The neighborhood was quiet even though there were no private houses, but congregations of tenants, corralled under communal roofs. Then again, this was a working-folks zip code where nine o'clock was wind-down time, even on the weekends, all kinds of TV-blue light strobing in the sliding glass doors that opened to shallow, one-unit porches.

Hitting the sidewalk, he went up to the front door of the building in question and entered, passing by the mailboxes. At the second door, he took out the keys Stan had given him from before and unlocked things. It didn't take him long to get to the missing officer's apartment, and he snapped on gloves before breaking the seal he had put on the doorjamb.

As he hit the inside lights, he knew the layout like the back of his hand, not that it was complicated—and he went through each room, one after the other, turning on any lamp or overhead fixture that he came to.

He looked under the sofa, the bed, and in all the cupboards, all over again. He went through drawers wherever he found them, in the bedroom, in the bath, in the kitchen. The closet got another deep dive as he checked the pockets in coats, and searched the floor under the hanging clothes with his flashlight. Going down on his hands and knees, he opened shoeboxes, and went through empty duffles.

Nothing.

Maybe he'd gotten her message wrong—

The knock out by the living area was soft. So was the "Hello?"

José got back up to his feet with old-man effort, his high school football injury squawking at the weight he put on that bad knee.

"Yup," he called out as he came around into the living area.

A woman who was about six months pregnant was leaning through the main door. When she saw him, she smiled tentatively.

"Um, hi, I'm Elsie Orchard, I live across the hall."

"Hi." He got out his badge and flashed it. "Detective José de la Cruz."

That smile disappeared, all kinds of worry replacing it. "Is everything okay?"

"We're doing our best. Can I help you?"

"Yeah, so . . ." She brought forward something from behind her back. "I was getting my mail today, and the post office guy couldn't fit this in Rio's box? He said there wasn't enough room because it hadn't been emptied in days. I don't know what it is. I promised him I would give it to her, but she's not . . . here."

As the woman held out an eight-and-a-half-by-eleven envelope, her hands were shaking. "Is she all right? She's really nice. She always helped me if I were bringing groceries in—and when the lights went out from that storm back in August, she knocked on my door and made sure I had a flashlight. My husband was gone. It meant a lot."

José wanted to make the sign of the cross as he accepted the piece of mail, but nothing good would come out of further alarming any of the neighbors, especially if they were pregnant. "Thank you so much."

"Is there anything I can do to help? Where is she?"

The eyes that clung to his were scared rather than hopeful, and the woman ran her hand around the gentle swell of her belly, as if she were trying to soothe herself.

"Have you seen anything unusual in the building?" he asked, just to give her something to respond to. "Or at this apartment?"

"No, I haven't. I wish I had. Our place faces the street that way and . . ."

José let her keep going, let her tell him everything she could think of. Sometimes, you just had to invite people into the investigation because it was the right thing to do. Caring neighbors and family members who were suffering deserved air space.

Plus, you never knew when a helpful tip would be dropped.

"Anyway," she concluded sadly, staring down at his gloved hands.

"Here's my card." He held one out to her. "Call me if you think of anything else?"

The woman nodded and then went back across the hall. He held the door open and watched her until she gave him a wave and locked herself in. He hoped her husband was home tonight. She was going to need some support.

Closing Officer Hernandez-Guerrero's front door, he took the envelope into the kitchen. Everything was neat and clean, so there was nothing to push out of the way to get a flat, clear space on the counter.

Unlike on Stan's desk.

As a feeling of dread swamped him, he turned the piece of mail over. The name and address were written in fine-point black ink, and the penmanship was bad, everything scrawled and tilted to the left, like someone who wasn't right-handed was trying to write like they were.

No return address in the upper left. Postcode over the stamps was Caldwell.

Heavy and stiff.

Photographs.

Ordinarily, he wouldn't open potential evidence on his own, but this was not ordinary, considering what the hell he'd found in the sink cabinet in Stan's crapper.

Taking out his Swiss Army knife, he slid the blade into the flap and cut carefully down the seam. The back had been taped in a sloppy fashion, the wide, shiny swaths pressed into a mess.

José put the knife down and slid out . . .

Black-and-white glossies.

At first, his eyes refused to focus properly on the two figures who were facing each other. When things finally became clearer, he found that the images had been taken at a distance, but from a telephoto lens, so they were laser accurate—

Stan was on the left.

And on the right, a tall, elegant man in a tuxedo.

Stephan Fontaine.

There were easily fifteen pictures, and the succession of them told a story. There was an argument going on, both men leaning in, gesturing with hands, throwing up arms in frustration. And then . . . there was one where a photograph changed hands. The first image of it didn't register. But the second caught the old-school picture at just the right angle.

It was Rio. It was Officer Hernandez-Guerrero.

Why in the hell would Stan be providing the picture of an undercover officer, whose identity was known only to Stan and one or two others on the entire force, to a civilian?

Under any circumstance, it was a breach in protocol and confidentiality. Under the fact pattern that one undercover officer was dead—and had likely been the person taking the pictures—and Rio was missing?

The photographs looked like a negotiation, where Stephan was giving Stan something, and Stan . . . was providing the identity of Rio in return.

Now, José freely made the sign of the cross over his heart.

Then he turned the envelope back over and stared at the handwriting. He was willing to bet his almost-mortgage-free house that analysis would show the writing was Leon Roberts's. If it didn't, it was because he'd tried to disguise his cursive by using his opposite hand.

The man had been going to Rio directly because he didn't trust internal channels, not even internal affairs.

And he'd known her life was in danger.

The question, almost as important as what Stan had gotten for the intel . . . was why Stephan Fontaine would need or want to know who Rio was.

CHAPTER FIFTY

Lucan would have let his wolven out to run if he hadn't needed to keep a set of clothes on himself. As it was, he got through the woods as fast as his two-legged form could take him, even though under his skin, his other side chomped at the proverbial bit to get free and four-paw the ground.

Now was not the time for that.

And that abandoned farmhouse was only a mile or two away.

He was about two hundred yards from the property, scaling a fallen tree in a hurdle, when the scent first reached his nose. Slowing, he had to make sure he was catching it right.

Gasoline. In the middle of the woods?

And it was fresh—accompanied by oil and exhaust. The bouquet of it all was faint, but unmistakable.

Tracking the smell, he changed direction, moving laterally over the acreage to make sure he didn't catch anyone's attention—

There it was. Tucked into a thicket of brambles that was so dense, the silver SUV might as well have been covered by a tarp of evergreen vegetation.

Was it possible, he thought as his heart quickened.

"Rio?" he whispered as he closed in on the vehicle.

Circling the tinted windows, he couldn't see much inside, but it was locked.

Lucan turned and looked through the interlacing branches of the tangle. That farmhouse was just in the distance—but he felt like it was across the country. Surging forward, he all but shot himself out of a cannon as he raced to the back door. But just as he grabbed the knob, he stopped and made sure his instincts weren't sensing anything.

"Rio," he said out loud. "It's me. Don't shoot."

Lucan knocked. A couple of times. Called out her name again.

The door squeaked as he opened it, and he spoke up louder as he leaned into the kitchen. "Rio. Don't shoot."

His voice echoed around the abandoned rooms.

"Rio?" He stepped in. Closed the door. "It's me."

What if she were injured, he thought—

Across the way, the cellar entry opened a crack, and he put his hands in the air. "Just me. No one else—"

He didn't get a chance to finish the sentence. Rio raced out and threw herself at him. As his arms wrapped around her, he held her so tight, he had to force himself to loosen his grip for fear of crushing her.

"I thought you were going to Caldwell," he said.

She pulled back. "I can't."

"Why not?"

When she just shook her head, he felt his fangs tingle. "What's going on?"

Rio broke away and walked around the fallen plaster pieces, the discarded trash, the broken kitchen chair that was just organized kindling as opposed to anything you could actually sit on.

"It's not safe for me right now. I came here because I needed a place to think for a minute."

There was a temptation to get into her mind, to take all of her secrets and consume them because he was impatient and frustrated. But that would be a violation of her, sure as if he touched her when she didn't want to be or spied on her when she was naked and didn't know he was there.

It was wholly inappropriate.

"Mozart came after you, didn't he." As she looked over at him sharply, he knew he was right. "You don't have to say anything you don't want to. But you can't pretend I didn't save your life back in that shitty apartment building. It had to be him."

"He's a powerful man."

"What went wrong? I thought you were his second in command."

"Look, the less you know, the better." She put her hands up. "And I may not be who you should deal with anymore."

"But Mickie is dead. So who do I go to?"

"Mozart himself," she said with a harsh laugh. Then she shook her head. "No, that was a joke. Do *not* go try to find him—"

"What do you know about the man."

She didn't even hesitate. "Nothing. He's impossible to find, a ghost."

"No one is that good at cover. No one."

Rio came back at him, her eyes pleading. "He'll kill you. That man is a soulless monster."

He thought of those drawings she'd done of the building and knew the head of the guards was right. They were not mementos of her stay; they were blueprints for an infiltration.

She was using him. And yet . . . her body couldn't fake arousal.

And was he any better than she was, with all he wasn't telling her?

"I'm not worried about Mozart, I have some tricks up my sleeve." Lucan brushed the side of her face. Then he paused as things took on a different intensity. "You know something, I love when you look at me like this."

"Like how."

"Like you want me to touch you."

The next thing he knew, her hands were on his shoulders. And he was leaning into her.

"Rio . . ." There was no time for them. There was no future to be had. All they had was the present. "*Rio.*"

"Kiss me," she moaned, like she'd read his mind.

Lucan dropped his head and found her lips like she was the air he needed, the food he craved, the sunlight he could no longer be in. And against his own, her mouth was as hungry as his was, the contact desperate and needy.

Without any rational thought in his head, and every sexual instinct in his body roaring, he maneuvered them over to the door she'd emerged out of.

"Come on," he said, taking her hand.

As they started down the cellar stairs, he turned back and threw the dead bolt. It wasn't copper, so it wasn't going to do shit to keep out any vampires, but at least humans would be denied access.

For as long as it took for an intruder to break down the damn door.

Then again, it wasn't like he and Rio weren't armed.

On the lower level, he couldn't not kiss her again. She'd lit a candle in a stout, corroded holder, and the fragile light was like a distant star in the night over by the bolts of fabric he'd first settled her on when he'd had nowhere else to bring her.

He helped her stretch out, holding her hand to steady her as she got down on her knees and lay on her back. Joining her, she arched her body and he kissed her some more, his hands finding their way under the shirt he'd given her.

The layers that covered her came off, melting away as he undid buttons, unzipped zippers, stripped off the shirt, her pants, and her bra.

No panties. He'd ruined them.

"You're so beautiful."

"You always say that." She smiled up at him. "I'm thinking you're biased for some reason."

It's because I love you, he thought to himself.

Lucan kissed her in a lingering way. Then he sat back and just watched the candlelight play over her pink-tipped breasts, and her stomach, and the graceful curve of her hips. As his eyes traveled down her naked body, she moved her legs together, her thighs shifting restlessly, like she was wet and hungry.

Taking his time, his hands followed the path of his stare, stroking down her throat, lingering over her collarbones. Her breasts lifted as she arched, but he teased her, letting his fingertips cross over her ribs and curve up to her sternum.

He made a circle around one of her nipples, and as she gasped, he pinched her gently. Then he full-on caressed her, relishing the softness, the tautness, the silk—until he couldn't help himself. He lowered his mouth to her and tasted her, one tight tip and then the other.

When his hand went lower, she opened her legs.

She was so undone for him, so vulnerable and powerful at the same time. She was ancient and she was new, a mystery and an answer, a secret and a truth. The contradictions made him desperate and that made him aggressive—but he relished calling on his self-control. He enjoyed the torture of keeping himself in check.

Slipping his hand between her thighs, he found her slick heat, and as he stroked her, penetrated her, he watched her writhe in the candlelight. With an erotic moan, she brought her hands to her face, bit down on a couple of her fingers, and then she put her arms over her head, twisting, turning.

She slapped her legs together at where he was pleasuring her as she came, holding him in place, locking her knees tight.

The rhythmic releases compressed his fingers, and he imagined his cock was inside of her.

Like she read his mind, she popped open her eyes. "I want you in me. Now."

✦ ✦ ✦

Rio was feeling like liquid heat underneath Luke's hot stare and very talented hands. But it wasn't enough. Fortunately, as he retracted his touch and immediately started stripping, it appeared that the foreplay hadn't been sufficient for him, either.

In the candlelight, he was magnificent fully naked, his very male body hard and thick with muscle, hard and thick . . . where it counted the most.

When he came back down to the bolts of fabric, she held out her arms and opened her legs wide. She was done with the anticipation part of things. She needed him—

"I can't wait," he growled.

"Good."

As he settled into the cradle of her sex, his tremendous weight made her feel pinned—and she wanted that. She wanted to be under him and pressed into the softness below her. She wanted him buried deep—

Rio cried out as his blunt head probed at her. Then she got what she wanted. With a decisive thrust, he entered her and stretched her wide, the sex better than the best she had ever had—and they hadn't even started moving yet.

That little slow-up was promptly addressed.

Luke retracted his hips. Thrust again. Retracted. Thrust. The rhythm got faster and faster, and rougher, too—until he was pounding into her. Against the onslaught of him, it was all she could do to just hold on to his massive shoulders, her teeth clapping together, her core both numb and hypersensitive—no, wait, that was her whole body.

Her nails dug into his skin, and at one point, she nearly bit him in the biceps.

The orgasm tore through her, the pleasure so great it registered as pain, too—and then he was locking against her body. Then locking again. And again.

It didn't stop.

Maybe later she would marvel at the stamina. At the moment, she was too blissed out and off the planet to do anything but absorb everything he pumped into her . . .

. . . until he finally went still.

As he collapsed on top of her, breathing hard, she stroked his back with slow hands. Even though the full weight of him was on her, she felt as though she were floating.

"I better let you breathe," he said in a hoarse voice.

When he went to roll aside, she pulled at him. "No. Not yet."

"I'm too heavy."

How could she explain that she needed him to hold her down? She felt as though her pinnings were gone, her tethers cut, her balloon off and floating over the landscape of her life. She had no family, it was true, but her job, her mission, her . . . obsession . . . had been a grounding sure as all those Thanksgivings and Christmases, birthdays and weddings, that other people enjoyed. Okay, fine, her sense of home involved crime and danger and dead bodies, and required a constant, nagging self-preservation instinct, but it was still what was familiar to her.

What got her out of bed in the morning.

What gave her purpose.

Now, she didn't know who to trust—and not in a "the streets" kind of way. As in inside the Caldwell Police Department itself.

When Luke shifted off eventually, he took her with him, the pair of them entwined together with him still inside of her. Reaching behind himself, he pulled some of the bolts of fabric over them.

"Please don't go after Mozart," she said as she stroked his face.

His eyes held hers in the candlelight—and she felt as though he could see through her. "Why, because you are?"

Yes, she thought, that was what she had decided to do. It was the only way to guarantee her safety inside the department. Someone in there had compromised her to the man, and if she could apprehend him herself, and turn him in? Then she'd be okay.

It was the only way to survive.

And besides, Mozart didn't know for sure whether she was dead or alive, so that gave her an advantage.

"Rio? Where'd you go in your head?"

Refocusing, she shrugged.

"There are other dealers in town." She tried to keep the sadness out of her voice. And failed. "I really wish you were not . . . I wish I could help you get away, that's all."

"You need to get out of this life, Rio. It's killing you from the inside, like a disease. You already lost your brother and your parents to drugs, don't lose yourself."

"It's too late for that," she said grimly.

Riding a sudden surge of emotion, she wanted to grab on to him, and start talking a bunch of crazy shit about not just him going underground but her as well—except she knew better than that. Fairy tales didn't exist in the real world, and certainly not between cops and drug dealers.

They were silent for what felt like a lifetime. Then he spoke up.

"You need to leave here first," he said. "So I can make sure no one is following you."

"This can't be the end," she whispered to herself. Although technically this was their second goodbye, wasn't it.

"It has to be. And you know it. We are not good for each other."

The man was right, of course. "I'm so tired, Luke. I've been running for so long."

"I feel the same way." He brushed her lower lip with his thumb. "And I'm sorry if I was rough with you when I mounted you."

"You're perfect." She stroked his chest, over his heart. "Besides . . . it has to last a lifetime, doesn't it."

For a moment, as he looked into her eyes, she felt like his resolve was wavering. But then he nodded curtly and pulled the bolts of mismatched fabric off of himself. The way he was careful to tuck her in made her tear up.

She hated being taken care of. Looked after.

Except for by him.

His pants had been tossed all willy-nilly aside, and as he bent over to pick them up off the concrete floor, she got a helluv'an ass shot. And then he was stepping into them and pulling them up his thick thighs—

Something fell out of the combats' back pocket—a bundle of papers, the square they had been forced into unfolding now they were out of the confines they had been in.

Inside the folds . . . she saw something she recognized.

Rio reached out and pulled the wad toward her. As she flattened the pages, she gave the sketches of the facility she'd drawn a quick once-over.

Not like she needed to review them in depth.

"I know you're a cop, Rio." When she looked up sharply, he put his palm out. "It's okay. I won't tell anybody—even if they torture me, your secret is safe. But just do us both a solid and don't try to lie to me now. You engineered staying longer than you had to under the pretext of helping Kane, you clearly took notes on the layout, and you're all but begging me to get out of the business. If you were a drug dealer, you'd be talking about the deal—and you never have. Not even once."

Looking down as he did up his fly, his hair fell forward and hid his expression. And then he pulled on his sweatshirt and a jacket that hadn't registered. To get his boots on, he sat on the floor next to the makeshift bed, and she watched as if from a vast distance as his strong hands did the laces up.

Then he was still.

When he stared over at her, his expression was full of sorrow. "I know you used me. I'm never going to really be sure how much of what you did with me was real, and how much was about seducing me for your own purposes. And the truth is . . . I don't want the truth. I'd rather just leave things right here and be able to pretend that you cared about me. Even if it was just a little."

Rio threw out her hand, but he shifted away from her touch.

"I'm just going to choose to believe in my fantasy," he said. "They're never real, right? But they feel great, don't they, especially when there's nothing to compete with them when it comes to hope and validation.

And hey, for me, I have one further than most people. Mine is not just a conjecture, conjured by the mind, but an actual memory. A tangible experience."

She squeezed her eyes shut. "Luke, it wasn't like that for me—"

"It was. But you always were too good for me, and I've known this all along. And not just because I'm a drug dealer and you're—"

Sitting up to cut him off, she held a stripe of blue velvet to her chest. "I *never* lied to you."

"Except for about who you really are." He looked down at his hands. "But like I said, it's okay. You have very, very good reasons for keeping that shit to yourself. I don't blame you, and I'm just lucky I got to be with you, no matter the reason or the pretext."

"Please let me explain."

"There's no way you can without more lies, and I've made peace with the ones that are already between us." Luke turned to the stairs. "I'll give you some privacy to let you get dressed. See you up there."

He walked away, moving in that beautiful way he did, and as he disappeared up the rickety stairs, tears started to fall from her eyes.

But if she was honest with herself . . . how else had she thought things would end?

"Oh . . . God," she said into the candlelight. "It's really over."

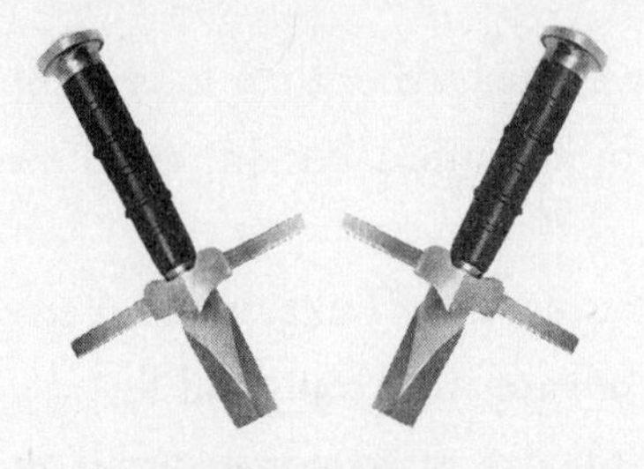

CHAPTER FIFTY-ONE

When Rio emerged into the kitchen, she opened the door slowly. Luke was over at the chipped counters and the ruined sink, leaning back with his arms crossed over his chest and his eyes on his boots.

He looked up and smiled a little. "You ready to trade?"

"I'm sorry?"

"Keys." He held out a collection of silver slips on a metal ring. "To the vehicles? It's better for you not to be in something that came from my place."

He tacked on the extra explanation because clearly her brain wasn't processing anything and he knew it.

"Oh, right." She walked over to him, fishing around in her pockets. "Here."

Their hands barely touched as they exchanged what they had, and she looked out over his shoulder at the old car in the dull moonlight.

"I can't believe this is happening," she said, unsure what part she was referring to.

"I'm going to ask you to do something for me."

"Anything." *Within reason.*

"Close your eyes, and forgive me."

"For what—"

All of a sudden, there was a piercing headache in the front of her brain, and her thoughts got muddled. At first, she had no idea what was happening—but then she remembered the way she had felt as the guard had somehow commanded her body in that workroom.

I only took as much as I absolutely had to, she heard Luke say in her mind.

A wonky feeling of disassociation took its time receding, and then she rubbed the eye that stung. "I've got a headache."

"Goodbye, Rio."

She wanted to hug him, but she could feel her emotions already starting to choke her. And then there were the fuzzy thoughts in her head, nothing organizing into anything that made sense.

"Goodbye, Luke," she mumbled.

"Ladies first."

With her heart in her throat, she turned away. Opened the squeaky door. Stepped out into the not-really-much-colder night because the house was unheated.

She looked back as she closed things up. Luke was still leaning against the counter, staring at his boots, a lone figure in an abandoned, ruined kitchen, with the weight of the world on his very strong shoulders.

Her fingertips lingered on the dusty glass. And then she turned away to the car.

As she got inside the Monte Carlo, she was aware of the mental spaciness persisting, but at least the pain in her head was easing, and she knew what to do with the car key, and where the pedals were, and how to put the engine in gear.

She remained absolutely clear, however, on the fact that her heart was breaking.

Turning the POS around, she headed off down the lane, moving the car around potholes in the dirt and a fallen trunk.

Images from being with Luke flashed in front of her eyes: Coming awake in the clinic and finding him beside her. Kissing him. That shower in the private quarters. She remembered the other two men, his friends, and the patient as well. Plus her executing that . . . well, Executioner.

There was also her squeezing into the dumbwaiter. And hiding under the locked-up blocks of drugs in that room.

And yet . . . something was wrong. She couldn't seem to recall where she had been. It was like a dreamscape, where nothing exactly fit together, even though all the pieces were intact. Also, the harder she concentrated, the more indistinct everything became, and the more her head hurt.

Where was she going, she wondered—

The animal ran out in front of the car so fast that she couldn't swerve to avoid it, and the thing was so big that when she hit the poor thing, the whole car bucked and got thrown to one side.

"Dammit!" She punched the brakes and squeezed the steering wheel hard.

Shoving the gearshift into park, she opened the door and leaned out, but she couldn't see anything. With a shaking hand, she released the seat belt and put one foot on the ground, and as she stood up, she decided that everything that could go wrong was going to—

It was a dog.

A big dog. Maybe a wolf . . . at least going by the size of the rear paw that was extending out from the front wheel.

No growling. No moving. No wheezing.

She'd obviously killed it.

Sagging in her own skin, she wanted to break down. It felt like everything was working against her, and though she knew her own life was in danger, and she'd just lost the man she loved—the idea she'd hurt an innocent animal was utterly unbearable.

And then there was the reality that she had to move it out from under the car if she was going to continue driving.

"You got to do this," she muttered.

And wasn't that the theme song of her largely dark and depressing reality at large.

Pulling herself together, she palmed up her gun, and stepped around the door—

Rio froze.

Then she slowly brought her free hand to her mouth and just barely caught the scream from breaking out of her throat.

There was a human foot on the ground in front of the wheel. Not a paw.

So she was either losing her mind . . . or her eyesight.

Stumbling around to the front of the car, she saw something that her eyes simply refused to process. There was . . . some kind of change happening to the dog . . . the wolf . . . it was *changing*.

The wolf was changing.

Right before her.

Its white-and-gray fur seemed to be retracting back into the skin underneath, and a series of cracking noises, like bones or joints were breaking, sounded out as limbs reshaped and pushed the feet and the hands forward. And then there was the face. The muzzle sucked back to become a chin, mouth and nose, while the head expanded, a rounded skull taking the place of the canine square top.

Rio took a step back. And another.

She knew she should care that she was spotlit in the headlights, but her brain was taken up by—

She hit something solid.

And as she gasped, she smelled that cologne Luke always wore.

Jumping off of him, she wheeled around—and played a horrific game of connect the dots as her eyes fluttered: *Blink*. She saw the dog that burst through the door into that apartment and attacked the man who was going to kill her. *Blink*. Luke was there in ill-fitting clothes, freeing her from the stakes in the floor. *Blink*. She remembered Apex being brought to his knees in the weak sunlight of that hallway. *Blink*.

She was back dragging Luke to the back door's stairwell, pulling him out of the sunshine as his skin burned. *Blink.* Nocturnal. *Blink.* "Mates," not "married." *Blink.* The fuzzy thoughts she'd suddenly had after Luke had stared deeply into her eyes before she'd left the farmhouse. *Blink . . .*

I only took as much as I absolutely had to.

Rio pointed the gun at Luke, horror and disbelief overcoming her.

"What the hell are you," she demanded. "*What the hell are you!*"

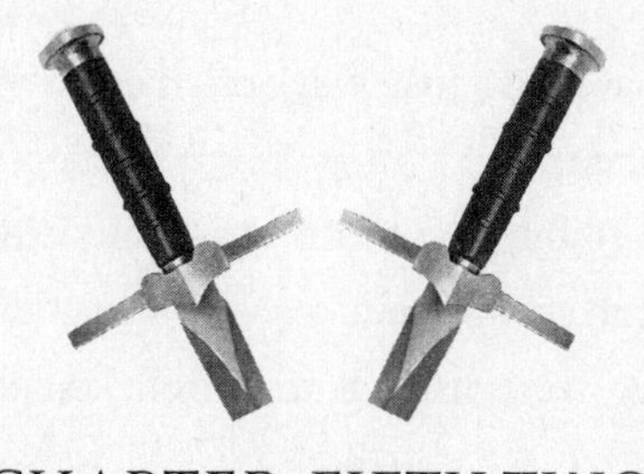

CHAPTER FIFTY-TWO

One great thing about unmarked cars, particularly the older ones, was that you could kill all the lights. No head- or tail- or running. Nothin'.

In the modern era, where everybody and his uncle was playing nanny to the child you hadn't been for years, it was nice to have the option to just say, *Hey, I don't need to attract any goddamn attention right now so I'm going dark. Thanks.*

As José sat behind the wheel and stared across at the parking lot behind the station house, he was watching Stan's office up on the third floor. He knew he had the right set of windows because homicide's lineup was always lit, and the ten glowing glass panes in a row grounded him. Plus, hey, the building wasn't that big anyway.

Stan was moving around in his digs. And he went into the bathroom—José knew this because the little slot of a window that didn't match any of the others in the facade went bright.

José glanced across to his passenger seat. The envelope that the nice pregnant neighbor had brought over to Rio's apartment was sitting on top of Leon Roberts's wallet and cell phone.

The rest of the case that José was constructing was in his head.

And his broken heart.

"Helluva way to go out," he muttered—and didn't know whether he was talking about Stan or himself.

Then again, they were in this together. Just like they had started together—

As his phone went off, he jumped and shoved his hand into the inside pocket of his sport coat. Extracting the thing, he had to brace himself—

Only to deflate. "Hey, honey," he murmured.

His wife's voice was worried. "Where are you?"

"I'm . . . working a case."

"Oh, I thought you were coming home."

"So did I," he said roughly. "How's your day?"

"Long." He heard a rustling and a thump and could picture her putting that huge bag of books and her laptop onto the kitchen table. "I've got an exam next week, so I'm just going to sit myself down and start studying while I wait up for you. How late are you going to be?"

"I don't know. Could be . . . hours."

"Okay."

The easy way she said the two syllables was why they were still married. The woman was patient, and smart, and everything that was good in his life.

"I'm going to take you on a vacation." His voice cracked. "Your semester is ending at the same time I get out. You and I are going on a . . . a married-moon. A week away, anywhere you want to go. You pick."

Her laugh was surprised. "José, you hate to travel. You know this."

"Not this time, I won't. You and me, anywhere you like, it's my gift to you."

There was a hiccup on the other end of the line. "Really? You're serious."

"I'll even get a passport for the first time in—well, actually, it might just be the first time."

"Oh, José . . . I love you."

"I love you, too—"

"Be careful out there tonight. It's cold, and—I don't know. I got a bad feeling for some reason."

So do I, honey, he thought.

"It'll be fine," he said as Stan's private bathroom light turned off.

José didn't really track what was said as they ended the call, but as he hung up, he very clearly decided that this week away was a gift for them both. Maybe it could be a yearly thing, a tradition as she worked her way through her PhD.

Up on the third floor, all of the chief's lights went out, including the ones in the waiting room.

Before José put the phone away, he made sure that the ringer was on silent. Then he extended his seat belt out and resettled it across his sternum.

If Butch were here, that cop from Southie would have driven him nuts as they waited, rambling on with sports scores and twitchy, impatient shifts in the seat. The bastard had been the worst at stakeouts. He was an action man.

Had been.

And soon José would be in the past tense, too. Well, in terms of being on the force.

God, he wished his old partner were here. Butch would know how to handle this—actually, no. Butch would just walk up to the chief, shove the guy up against the wall, and start counting down to a beating.

Fuck protocol and all that—

The rear door to the station house opened, and a lone silhouette stepped out. The chief had a reserved space right next to the exit, and Stan looked around before he got into the sedan. The guy always parked ass in, so as he started the engine, his headlights came on, flaring across the mostly empty lot.

José ducked down even though he was all the way across the street in a pocket of shadow.

Stan's car cut across the empty lines, and at the kiosk, which was also unmanned at this hour of night, he stopped and swiped his card. For a brief instant, security lights pierced the windshield and illuminated his face.

He looked death-knell grim.

Hanging a louie, he started down Muhammad Ali Blvd. And after a lead of maybe five car lengths . . .

José left his spot and oiled along after the chief of police, keeping his own lights off.

How had he known the man had to go back to the office tonight? Because someone who was disorganized and forgetful enough to leave all the doors unlocked in his suite after hours . . . was still going to have enough self-protective instincts to remember the mistake he'd made.

And return to get the evidence that connected him to not one, but two, homicides.

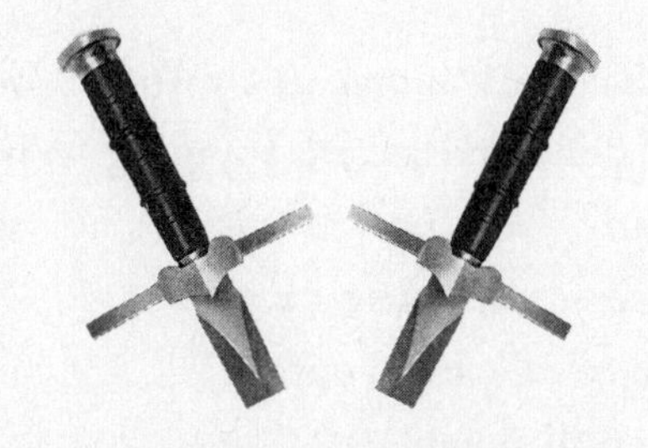

CHAPTER FIFTY-THREE

In the glare of the Monte Carlo's headlights, Lucan put his hands up, in a move that was like the universal sign for choking when someone couldn't breathe: When you had a gun in your face, you got those palms high and away from your body. Especially if you were armed yourself and didn't want to get popped for a sudden movement.

Meanwhile, the woman who was staring down the muzzle of her gun . . . had just put two and two together—and come up with what in her tradition would be called *werewolf*.

Not exactly news that made somebody feel calm and relaxed.

And to that point, Rio was shaking so badly, he had a thought that she was liable to pull the trigger by mistake—and deadly was deadly, whether you meant to or not.

"Rio."

He meant to go on from there. But what could he say?

"What are you," she repeated. This time with a cold levelness to her tone.

"I am . . . what I am."

"That's no fucking answer."

"I don't know what you want me to say. You know what's going on—"

"No, I do not! I don't understand anything. What the hell is that—what the hell are you?"

"I'm not any different than I ever was—"

"You're not human!" she cried out.

"And haven't been all along."

She seemed to lose her voice. Or maybe she was worried it was her mind.

"I didn't know it." She emphasized the point with the muzzle of her gun. "It was a helluva detail to leave out."

"And what would you have done. Seriously, think about it. I walk up to you on the streets of Caldwell and tell you, 'Hey, I'm a half-breed wolven, pleased to meet you, how 'bout we do fifty million dollars in drug trade over the next two months together. Great. Sign here.'" He leaned forward. "That would have gone just great, right? Smooth as fucking glass."

As his temper started to get away from him, he turned from her and walked up and back on the dirt lane. If she wanted to shoot him? Fucking fine. Good luck getting his bastard, no-good, double-crossing cousin out from under the Monte Carlo—

"This is your cousin?"

While her words cut through his internal—or supposedly internal—monologue, he snapped into focus and realized he'd said all that out loud.

Fine. Whatever.

He wheeled around and marched right up to her. "Okay, you want to know everything." He jabbed a finger over her shoulder. "That was a fucking prison you were in back there. And there isn't a goddamn human in it. The drug trade is so we can survive and have the bare minimum for food, water, and health care." Now he poked his finger at the dead man-like form wedged under the car. "And that male, along with a couple of others, were who put me in this hell back in the eighties. So there. You know all my story."

As her eyes went back and forth between him and the dead body, he snapped, "If you shoot me now, you're going to have to move both of us out of your way before you can hit the gas. I'd recommend you have me get him off to the side first before you do me like you did the Executioner."

There was a tense moment. And then she slowly lowered the weapon.

"I don't understand any of this," she mumbled.

"Your understanding is not required. Reality really doesn't give a shit about rational and reasonable. Trust me, if I've learned nothing else during the last—"

"What's the other half," she interrupted. "What's your . . . other part."

Lucan looked up at the sky.

Then he leveled his head. And curled his upper lip.

For the first time around her, he let his fangs elongate—and had to ignore a tingling hunger as he considered all the soft places on her he could sink them into.

"I'm sure you've heard the myth," he said in a low voice. "But you humans have it all wrong. As usual."

"*Vampire,*" she whispered in terror.

✦ ✦ ✦

Annnnnnnd it was time for a little breakie-poo.

Rio's legs made the executive decision without any consultation from her mind or the pesky free will thing that usually controlled negotiations between the body and the brain: One second, she was standing. The next she was in a sit, right on the shoulder of the lane.

The good news—maybe it was training—was that she had the forethought to make sure she didn't pull the trigger on the way down or on impact. And now that she was on her ass, literally and figuratively, she put the nine millimeter on its side on the dirt.

Then she crossed her hands in her lap like she was in church.

After a moment, there were noises: Shuffling, pulling, a grunt or two. She couldn't tell what Luke was doing exactly, but she could guess the general gist of things.

Then his face was in front of hers. He even waved his hand before her eyes.

"I don't understand," she heard herself say. Which was what was going through her mind over and over again.

Luke knelt down. "I can make it go away."

"What?"

"I can make you forget everything. You won't remember any part of this. It will be as if it never occurred."

That explains it, she thought.

"The guard. And then what you did in the . . . back at the . . ." She winced as her head hurt. "You do that to people, don't you. Manipulate their memories."

"It'll be easier on you."

"No," she said weakly. "I don't want that. My . . . mind . . . is not yours to take."

When he didn't respond, she started to relive everything—just to check and see what might have been taken: "My cover was blown and Mozart sent someone to kidnap me from my apartment. I woke up in his actual house. He didn't show me his face—he drugged me—" She paused and looked at the front of the Monte Carlo. "What's that growling? I thought he was dead—"

"Sorry." Luke slapped a palm over his mouth. "I get a little . . . aggressive sometimes."

Rio turned herself to him and looked at him properly for the first time. "You attacked that guy with the knife. That was you. It wasn't a stray dog."

"Well, technically, it was the wolven in me. But yeah, I sent him forward to save you."

"You sent . . ."

"It's like having two people in one skin. I'm mostly in control. But in certain circumstances, he comes out, and he does what he does. He's very dangerous."

"Why didn't he hurt me?" Was she really talking like this? "Because you told him not to?"

"No, he knows you. He knows . . . you. That's the only way I can explain it."

"You look so . . . normal."

"No, I just resemble a human on the outside." He frowned. "Tell me about Mozart. He was the one who hurt you?"

"I'd never actually met him in person until he kidnapped me. The communications with him are all done through screens and VPNs. I was getting close, so fucking close. But he found me out because . . ." She took a deep breath. "I think someone in my own department tipped him off about me. Another officer, who was undercover like me, was killed—and right before he was, he tried to warn me. That was the night I met you."

"Jesus."

"Which was why I can't go back to Caldwell. I don't know who to trust—but I can't let Mozart win. I just can't." She closed her eyes. "Even if it's the last thing I do, I just want—"

"To kill him?"

Rio shook her head. "I want to jail that bastard. He's everything I've ever worked against. He's murdered so many people, and I just . . . I've spent eighteen months closing in on him. I want him to go to prison for the rest of his natural life." She lifted her palms. "After that, I can retire. I'm finished in this racket anyway. My cover blown, my life a mess."

They stayed there long enough for a shooting star to pierce the blue velvet of the night sky . . . and travel all the way across the visible plane of the universe.

"You know, you're still as easy to talk to as ever." She smiled a little. "I mean, this is remarkably unweird for being totally bizarre."

"That's because it has always been, and still is . . . me."

Rio looked down at her hands and remembered running them over his body. And the way it had been to make love with him. And the connection she felt—and still did.

"You know," he said, "I could help you."

She lifted her head up. "How?"

"I can help you get to Mozart."

"But . . . how?"

Luke tapped the side of his head. "We have tricks, remember. If you want to find Mozart, I can help you."

"But why . . . why would you do that? If the drug deal supports the . . . the prison . . . if that money is needed to feed and clothe and—"

"You don't have to worry about all that. You just have to ask yourself if you want to get Mozart bad enough . . . to work with a wolven-vampire cross to get the job done."

Rio shifted her eyes to him—and focused on his face. All of the features were achingly familiar, exactly the same as they had always been.

"We're survivors, remember," he said in a low voice. "We stay in the present because it's all we have. But survivors also settle scores. In the right way."

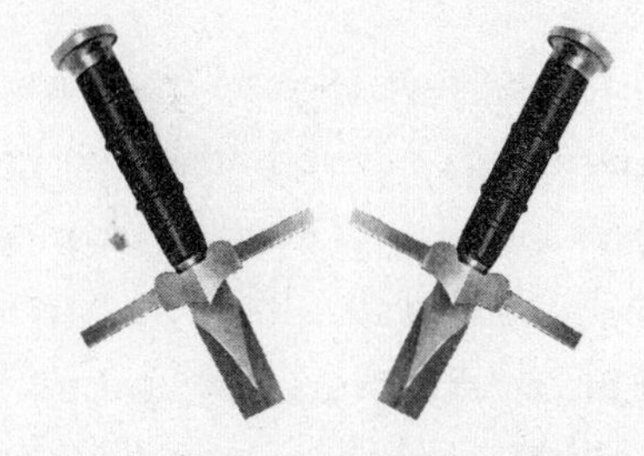

CHAPTER FIFTY-FOUR

Captain Stanley Carmichael's home was a Cape Cod, set way back on a lot that could have handled a much bigger structure. As José eased to a halt on the back left-hand corner of the property behind the house, he put his unmarked in park.

Stan had pulled up to his garage, turned off his car, and gotten out. He was now walking down the long asphalt driveway to the mailbox—like he'd been so distracted as he'd driven in that he'd forgotten to grab the day's allotment of bills, flyers, and bullshit.

José glanced around to make sure there was nobody nosy checking out where he was. That was a nope. The other houses were separated by equally large parcels of land, the neighborhood being more farm country than suburban, regardless of its proximity to the Northway.

As Stan started the return trek up the drive, José thought back to when the guy had moved all the way out to the edge of the city limits. It had seemed like an impulse move after the divorce, and not a bright choice for a guy who had never been a cook or a cleaner, and was no doubt going to settle down with someone else right afterward.

Or at least try to.

Stan had cleared up the mystery about a year later. The place was apparently the spitting image of the house he'd grown up in. So that was the drill. Emotions and real estate were frequently linked together.

As José watched the man walk along, he had a realization that he was waiting for his mind to change its conclusions: Surely there was another explanation to all this, one that reconciled the man he knew with the kind of monster who could murder an innocent civil servant for the purpose of one of two things.

It was either extortion because Stan knew that Stephan Fontaine was a fucking drug dealer crook . . . or because Stan was on the take and delivering on a deal he'd brokered.

Either way, Stan had been the one to compromise Rio's cover.

And perhaps she'd had something to do with that murder scene under that dealer Mickie's apartment. Fortunately, it appeared she was still alive, so she could give her own testimony about that.

As soon as it was safe for her to do so.

Stan stopped next to his car and looked at the sky. Like he was searching for some grace or something.

Or for possibilities of where the wallet and the cell phone might have gone.

"Time to go to work," José muttered to himself as he turned the lights of the unmarked on and put the car back in gear.

Hitting the gas, he went around Stan's acreage, and then he pulled into the driveway. As his lights swung around, they picked his old friend out of the darkness, spotlighting him. The guy looked old, with his graying hair, and exhausted, with his wrinkled suit, as he lifted his arm to shield his eyes from the glare.

José put the unmarked in park and opened his door. As he got out from behind the wheel, he said, "Hey, Stan."

There was a pause. And then the chief of the Caldwell Police Department slowly lowered that arm of his.

"José. What are you doing here?"

"I think you know, Stan. I think you know exactly why I'm here."

✦ ✦ ✦

Downtown Caldie was hopping, people all over the streets, going in and out of bars and clubs, eating and drinking indoors because it was too cold to be in the open air. As Rio stared out of the Monte Carlo's smudged-up window, she still wasn't sure this wasn't all a dream. And yet it seemed so real.

Down to Luke's cologne. Or . . . scent.

"Where are we going?"

As Luke put the question out there, she directed him over another three or four blocks. She wasn't sure exactly where—

"There." She sat up. "There he is. That's the guy."

Luke didn't vary their speed and didn't look over at the tall, well-built man who stood in the inset doorway of an office building that was shut down for the night. He just kept them right on going, smoothing his way around the block.

"His street name's Chins." She glanced across the interior of the crappy car. "The rumor is he's Mozart's eyes on the street. Mickie was jealous of him. I tried to get close to him, but he's a totally separate operator. He just watches, and does deals to make it look like he is one of the rank-and-file others. He's our best bet at a connection who might actually know Mozart."

With a nod, Luke went around the block a second time—and then rolled up in front of the guy.

"Wait!" Rio said. "He's going to see me. Drop me off—"

"It's not going to matter. Trust me."

As she ducked anyway, Luke cranked his window down. "Hey, you got something for sale?"

Rio turned her face away, as if she were inspecting the car door.

"What you looking for," was the gruff response.

"Actually, I changed my mind. I think I'll just take what I need."

When there was only silence, Rio glanced over. And then stared. There was no contact between the two, no weapons out on Luke's part . . . and yet Chins was standing there as docilely as a trained seal.

"Thanks," Luke muttered. "And you're not selling to anyone under eighteen anymore. You're going to start carding 'em, motherfucker."

Chins stepped back from the car as Luke hit the gas, and Rio twisted all the way around to look out the rear windshield. The dealer remained standing at the curb, his hands up to his head like it hurt, confusion on his face as he glanced around like he couldn't figure out what had happened.

"I don't know Caldwell," Luke said. "But he's been to a house. A big-ass house with white columns in front. There's a gate and a stone wall. Trees in the lawn. I don't have an address, though, or a number or anything. I also don't have a real name. And there's no phone number. He never calls, is only called."

"You're sure it's in Caldwell?"

"Yeah, it's somewhere in Caldwell." Luke looked over. "He wasn't going there to report on business. They're fucking. He's in love with this guy, Mozart, and it seems like the man feels the same."

"So, wait . . . what is the house like again?"

"All I can tell you is that it's got columns across the front. Six fluted columns with curlicue tops. And a pair of carved dogs."

Well, Rio thought, at least that narrowed the neighborhoods down. There was only one in Caldwell that would have a house like that.

"Take a left up here," she ordered. "I have an idea of where to go."

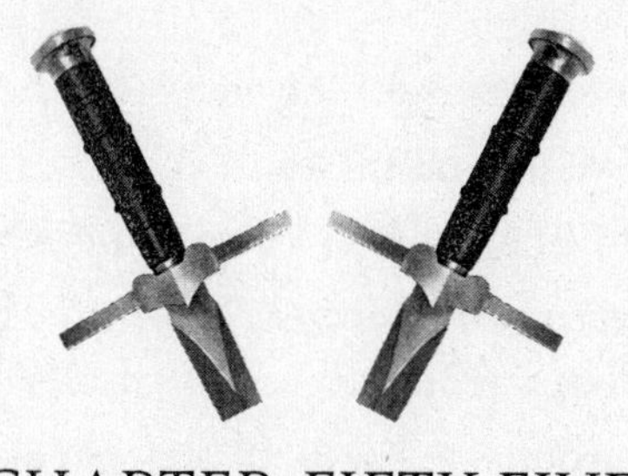

CHAPTER FIFTY-FIVE

"Come on, José, you think I'm a mind reader? I can barely remember what I had for breakfast. Getting in your brain is way over my pay grade, even as chief. Hey, can you kill the lights. Christ."

"I know you're aware of what I've found."

"Religion?" Stan put his mail on the trunk of his car and started for the inner pockets of his jacket. "Oh, wait, you already were a churchgoer—"

"Keep your hands where I can see 'em." José upped the volume on his voice. "Stan, don't make me—"

It happened so fast, and in any other suspect confrontation, José would have handled things differently. But the past and present had milkshaked on him, the presence of a suspect looking like his old friend, sounding like the guy, too, making him sloppy and slow: Just as José drew his service weapon, Stan unholstered his and pointed it at José's heart.

"What the fuck is wrong with you," the chief said. "What the *fuck* is going on with you."

They were squared off, nothing between them but thin air, two muzzles pointed at two mortal torsos.

"Why did you do it, Stan. You killed Leon Roberts, and you sacrificed Hernandez-Guerrero to Mozart. Was it for the money? Was that the end game?"

There barely was a pause, as if Stan had been holding on to his truth for too long.

"Oh, easy for you to say. You got a wife and a family. You got holidays and weekends, and people waiting for you to come home. You got hot meals made for you, the ones you like, the way you like, and a warm body sleeping next to you. Fuck off with the judgment, okay? I come home every night to an empty fucking house—"

"Stan, you gotta put that gun down—"

"—and you know what I think about?" The man jutted forward on his hips, his tie hanging loose. "You know that pension I got? Half of it went to Ruby. The money I spent twenty-five years earning by showing up to work and kissing ass until I got promoted high enough to get kicked in the ass by the mayor's office is now paying the mortgage of the house she lives in with her new fucking husband."

"Stan, listen to me. I know you're not going to shoot me, and I don't want to shoot you. Let's just talk."

"We are talking, José," the guy snapped. "You know what the best thing about under-the-table money is? It's mine. I don't have to report it to the fucking government and I don't have to give it to my ex-wife. Thank fuck she couldn't have children or I'd be up to my ass in college bills right now, just like you are—"

"I can help you." José raised his voice. "Listen to me, with what you know about Mozart, you can get a deal. He's the big fish, not you."

"You think I don't know that? Have you seen his house? I keep telling him that only the president has a bigger, fancier facade." The guy spat out a curse. "And besides, I don't need much. I just want enough to get me out, my golden parachute that I'm *owed*."

"I know you didn't mean to hurt Roberts—"

"Fuck Roberts. He's just another goddamn weight around my neck. You all are. Arguing about money, equipment, days off, time off, pensions—it's never enough. Nothing I ever fucking did was enough for any of you, and you know what, I don't have to give a shit anymore. I've taken care of myself, and I'm not sorry, and now I'm going to take care of you—"

There was just an instant, a split second, of dropped attention, that gun listing off to the side as Stan continued to rant.

Slow motion. It always happened in slow motion, didn't it.

Knowing that he was seconds from his own death, José pulled his trigger, and the bullet discharged—and given that he was just a few feet away from point-blank range, there was no question of that slug not hitting home in the center of Stan's chest.

The impact blew the man back off his feet, the headlights' harsh illumination making him look like he was in a Marvel comic strip, a super-villain in a cheap suit and a bad tie taking justice right through the heart.

With a sickening thud, he bounced off the trunk of his own car and slumped to the pavement, his body ending the roll on its back, facing the heavens above.

José stayed where he was, the smoke from the barrel of his gun rising up, the smell of the powder in his nose. Then he got his phone out of the pocket that he'd have put a handkerchief in if he'd been that kind of a man.

Before he called for help and backup, he turned off the microphone recording he'd triggered on the unit just as he'd entered the driveway. After that, he stared at Stan for a moment and then slowly lowered his weapon. The man's mouth was working, so José went over and knelt down.

Last words, and all that. Guess he was hoping for an oops-I-take-it-all-back.

It was just autonomic function, however, muscles in the neck and face spasming randomly. The hit had been right in the center of the chest. José couldn't have done a better job if he'd been a surgeon with a scalpel.

Looking down at his phone, he had to put a numeric password in because he hated the new kind with facial recognition. When it became clear that his hand was shaking too badly to hit the keys in the right sequence, he decided to just make an emergency call to the police station.

'Cuz this sure as shit was an emergency.

Except his fingers were still trembling—and he had a thought: If he couldn't put in four digits for a password, why did he think he could do seven? Or maybe even ten if the local 518 area code was needed?

He was concentrating on the phone screen so intently . . .

. . . that he didn't see Stan marshal his last strength . . .

. . . to lift his gun right up at José's head.

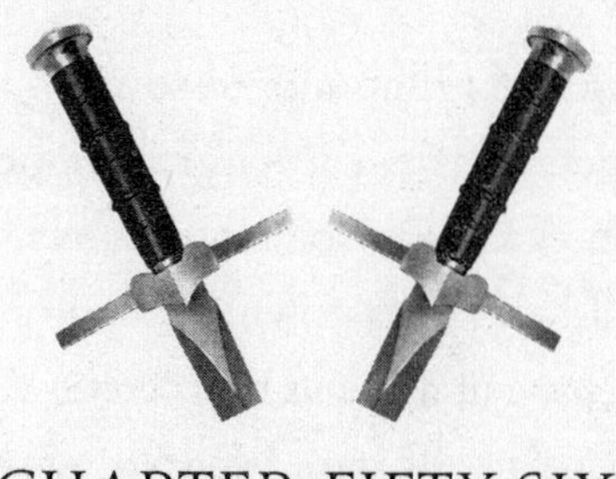

CHAPTER FIFTY-SIX

Stephan Fontaine."

As Rio spoke up, Lucan looked away from the lineup of cutesy pie shops and well-tended restaurants he was driving them by.

"Who are you talking about?"

"Stephan Fontaine. The columns." She pointed up a hill. "Head there. I think I know the house."

"Roger that."

He had no idea where they were, but Rio was in charge, telling him in no uncertain terms which turns to take, where to go. And he knew, without seeing any big houses yet, that she'd taken him to the right neighborhood. From the streetlights with their graceful arches, to the trees that had been planted alongside the sidewalks, to the complete and utter lack of litter, it went without saying that they were in rich people territory.

As he piloted the piece-of-shit Monte Carlo up the rise, the estates started—and they were in the same exact vein as the white birthday cake he'd gotten from the memory banks of that dealer.

"Who's Stephan Fontaine?" he asked.

"He's this philanthropist who moved to town a couple of years ago. He's always in the papers and on TV for giving away money? He's got his name on a wing at St. Francis hospital, and he endowed a chair in economics at SUNY Caldwell. He's done a bunch of other stuff, too." She glanced over. "But he lives in a house with columns. Six of them. There was an article in the *Caldwell Courier Journal* about the renovations he did on this mansion he bought. And the house is up here."

So Lucan kept going. And as they went along, in the back of his mind, he was missing her already.

It seemed ridiculous to be mourning Rio's loss while she was right next to him. For fuck's sake, he could reach right out and touch her—not that he would. He'd terrified her enough.

He was *such* a prize.

"Here! Stop!"

He hit the brakes and looked across the car's beat-to-shit interior.

"That's it. That's the house."

The mansion was set far back on a rolling lawn, behind a set of sturdy gates and a stone wall that was federal-penitentiary-worthy. The columns were indeed six, right across the front, tall as evergreens and more than capable of holding up the pediment and slate roof above them.

It was exactly as the memories of that dealer out on the street had detailed.

"Service entrance," Lucan said. "Let's go around back. That's how the guy would get on the property when he came to visit."

It took them some time to find an alley cut-through in the street, and then he trolled by the back of several estates, staring into the trees and wondering how many hidden cameras were tracking this old junker as it violated the pristine neighborhood's roadway.

"Is this it?" Rio asked as she leaned into the windshield. "This entrance here."

"Yeah."

Lucan pulled into a service port on the far side of the rear gate. There was a carriage house locked in by the stone wall, and through the iron bars of the fence, he could see a pool area, and then the back of the mansion.

"How do we get in?" she murmured.

"It's not going to be a problem."

"But how are—" She stopped herself, as if she were remembering the way the drug dealer downtown had been handled. "Okay, let's do this."

After he turned off the engine, they got out and met at the front grille—and he pressed the keys into her palm.

"You take these. If anything goes wrong, I want you to get in and drive away. Don't worry about me."

Her eyes bored into his own, and he had a feeling she had questions, so many questions. But now was not the time. Never was the time.

"All right," she said after a moment. "I will."

Lucan made a move like he was going to kiss her—and stopped himself in time. Stepping back, he nodded.

And dematerialized away. Right in front of her.

When he re-formed on the far side of the locked gates, she was covering her mouth with both hands. He hated the fact that he'd freaked her out again, but they needed to get inside and it was the work of a moment for him to—

Two German shepherds came barreling around the side of the pool house, the dogs trained to not bark when attacking. Their scents gave them away because he was downwind, however, and then there were their pounding paws over the short grass.

Lucan wheeled on them and crouched down. The growl that came out of his throat was not from him. It was his other side talking.

And that pair of perfectly trained killers pulled up like they were about to go off the edge of a cliff.

Moving forward, he backed them away, his snarl submitting them, his eye contact promising them what would happen if they misbehaved: He would school them like they were pups. Instead of eighty-to-ninety-pound fully grown males.

After he'd driven the dogs behind the pool house, he turned around and jogged to the gate—and that was when a guard came out of the side door of the cottage. The guy was pissed off and out of uniform. Or maybe he was just a paid caretaker.

The man noticed the Monte Carlo and Rio right away.

Meanwhile, Lucan stalked up behind the human male. And just as the man said, "Can I help you—"

Subduing him was the work of a moment. Lucan just threw an arm around that throat and hauled the torso back against his own.

Which was when he discovered that the "caretaker" was, in fact, armed.

Lucan caught the gun that came up, took control of the weapon, and calmly put the muzzle to the man's temple. "You're going to let her in now."

There was a little too much going on in his own brain for him to get into the guard's noggin and grab access codes or some such. So the Smith & Wesson worked just fine. Or should have.

When there was some argument, Lucan bared his fangs—

"No!" Rio said. "Don't kill him! Everyone on-site is taken alive. They could all be in on the enterprise. *Everybody* lives."

Bummer. And inconvenient.

But like all bonded males, he did what his female said—and put his sharp-and-shinies back in his upper jaw.

Shit, he could really have used a nice bloody fight to take his edge off.

✦ ✦ ✦

As the gate started to open, Rio slipped in as soon as there was a space big enough to fit through. On the far side, she looked into the wide eyes of the guard and knew this was madness. But she wasn't turning back.

"Let's go," she said.

As Luke brought the guard along, he handled the other man like he didn't weigh a goddamn thing, and when they passed by the pool house, she glanced around, wondering where the dogs were. God, she remembered the attack on that hit man back at Mickie's apartment building, the ferocity of it all had been so shocking, from the flashing teeth to the grinding jaws, the muzzle running red with blood, the victim's midsection ripped open, his throat a raw wound.

Abruptly, she recalled coming to, just as it was all over. The wolf had wheeled around on her.

Tears had run from her eyes, both for what she had seen . . . and for what was going to be done to her.

The wolf had approached her, its massive body moving in a coordinated prowl. But instead of attacking her, it had whimpered. Nuzzled at her legs as if it wanted to get her loose if it could. And then it had lain down beside her, like it was protecting her, its regal head up, its eyes shifting to the door, its nose sniffing like it was testing the air for the scents of enemies.

She clearly had passed out again at that point. Because the next thing she remembered was Luke releasing her from all the ties.

"You took the clothes of the attacker," she said. "Back when you saved me . . . you needed something to wear, and that's why everything was too small on you."

Luke looked over. And so did the guard—who, she realized abruptly, was in flannel pajama bottoms and a SUNY Caldwell t-shirt.

"Yeah," Luke said with a nod. "And I didn't want you to know what I was."

On that note, they arrived at the mansion's rear flank. There was a terrace that ran all the way down the back of the house, but there was no outdoor furniture on it. Obviously, things had been put away for the winter.

And inside, everything had been shut down for the night: All the rooms were dark, no lights on in the lower level. Up on the second floor, however, there was a bank of fixtures still glowing.

"Where are we going?" Luke said to the guard. "How are we getting in."

"I can't tell you."

"Yeah, you can."

The guard threw out his proverbial anchor. "You're going to have to kill me now. Because if I let you into his house? He's going to do so much worse to me. Just . . . fucking shoot me."

Well, Rio thought, at least they knew they were in the right place.

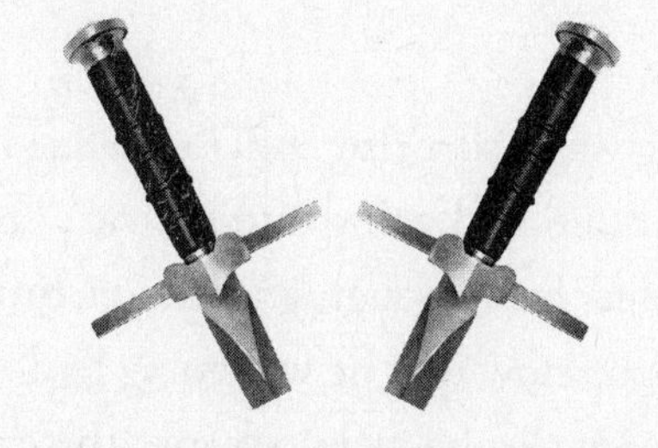

CHAPTER FIFTY-SEVEN

In a split second that lasted an eternity, José saw the gun of his old friend coming up in his peripheral vision, but it was too late to catch the weapon. And yes, it turned out that the old wives' stories were true: Your life did flash before your eyes right before you died. In a quick series of heart-wrenching images, he saw himself and his wife on their wedding day, and at the births of their children. He visualized holidays and weekends, and Christmases and Fourths of July.

It was everything that Stan didn't have and had decided he'd been cheated of, as if some robber had come into his life and taken at gunpoint all of the stuff he'd been due solely by reason of him being alive, character and responsibility and commitment having nothing to do with any of that end result.

God, José didn't want it all to be over. And not like this.

Knowing he was fucked, José winced and got ready for pain. Or maybe it would happen so quick, he would feel nothing.

He'd been so close to getting out of the CPD alive—

The discharge was so loud because it was right by his ear, and he felt heat, a flash of heat, right by his cheek—

Ping!

The metallic ring was a surprise until he realized it was the lead slug passing through his brain and going into the car's steel panel. And now came the collapse. He'd seen enough gunshot victims in the immediate aftermath of impact to know that he was going to do what Stan had just done: Slump to the side. Probably knock into the car, too. Then maybe he'd land on Stan's legs.

After that, lack of consciousness. Followed by death.

And finally, the pearly gates, hopefully—thanks to all those novenas and Hail Marys—

José's eyes flipped wide—and he fell backward onto his ass, but not because he was dead: A tremendous man dressed in black leather, with black hair, icy white eyes, and a goatee, was standing next to Stan . . . and holding Stan's gun.

Somehow, the harsh-looking savior had come out of nowhere and taken control of Stan's gun just in the nick of time, diverting the discharge into the car.

Instead of into José's head.

José lifted his hands and felt around himself for injury. Opened his jacket wide. Pushed at his neck, his cheeks. Ran fingers through his hair, down to his scalp.

Then he focused on the strange man, a cold wash of awareness going through him.

"I know you," José breathed.

"Yeah, you do, but only in your dreams."

Stan made a clicking sound and a groan—and the man with the goatee transferred his attention to the guy who was actually dying. There was a split second of pause . . . and then that menace in black leather crouched down, bared his enormous teeth—Jesus, were those fangs?—and hissed at Stan.

Who promptly seized up in terror and started grabbing for his chest, like he was having a heart attack. A mortal struggle went on for a moment or two, and then . . . Stan Carmichael breathed his last breath.

The man in leather chuckled a little and relaxed his mouth, his upper lip lowering to cover those tremendous teeth.

"You know," he said conversationally, "I've been accused of scaring people to death before. Now I've actually done it. I'm so adding this to my résumé."

Those icy eyes swung back around, and José noticed that there were tattoos at one of his temples. Also noted that there were weapons around his waist, and undoubtedly inside the jacket given all the bulges.

Yet José felt no fear, and not just because he was in shock.

"In my dreams," he said as a headache flared under his skull. "I've seen you in my dreams."

"Butch says hi."

"He does?" God, he felt so confused. And yet also totally clear. "Really? He's still okay?"

"Yeah." The man glanced at Stan. "He would have been here in person, but he couldn't keep up with your car on foot. So I'm his stand-in."

"You saved my life."

"I did, true."

"Thank you."

The man stared at him for a long time. Then tilted his head. "You know, you're welcome. And there was no way I was going to let you die. It'd break my roommate's heart and I can't let that happen."

"Butch is your roommate?" When the man nodded, José smiled a little. "So you'd really know if he was okay. Good."

"Yeah. Well, I gotta go. You got any message for Butch?"

"Tell him to go to church."

"He does. Midnight mass, Wednesdays and Saturdays, without fail. We moved the work schedule around to make sure he could go."

"Church is important." José rubbed over his eyebrow. "You're going to take my memories now, aren't you."

"It's for the best—"

"How did you know this was going to happen?"

There was a pause. "It's my curse. To know the how, but rarely the where, and never when. So in most cases, I just have to follow my gut."

"I'm sorry."

"Thanks, my guy—"

"Wait." José put his palm up. "Keep taking care of Butch, will you? I tried to. I failed. But I think . . . I think you're doing a much better job than I ever did, aren't you."

The man got really serious for a second. But then he smiled a little and nodded.

"You're a good man, José de la Cruz. And let's just keep this between ourselves, shall we? I've heard that true Good Samaritans don't need their deeds to be known, and although I've never been much for that whole savior shit before—and probably never will be—I got a soft spot for the Boston cop we both respect so much. Besides, he'd get all emotional when he thanked me and really, who needs that."

The stranger who was not really a stranger stood up, and José found himself bracing for a familiar sting—

"One week?" the man in leather said. "No, you take that pretty wife of yours away for two weeks. You guys go and enjoy yourselves. Happy retirement—"

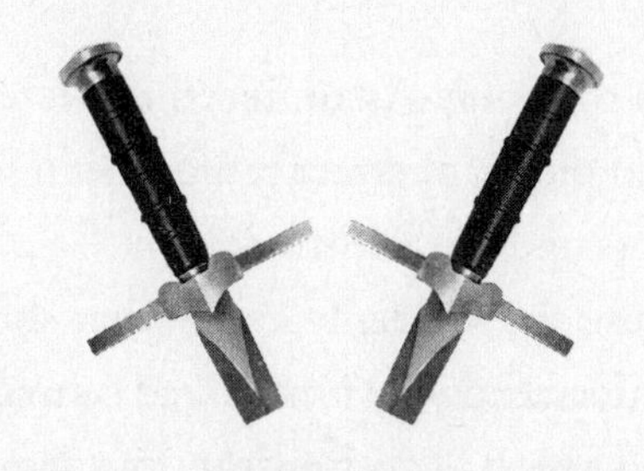

CHAPTER FIFTY-EIGHT

We have to make some noise. Sorry—"

Before Rio could ask what Luke was talking about, a gunshot rang out and then the guard dropped to the terrace and didn't move.

"I thought I told you not to shoot him!"

"I didn't," he hissed.

Meanwhile, an alarm started to go off inside, shrill and very loud, and the countdown to police arrival got rolling.

"I just knocked him out," Luke said. "Before I shot the lock."

Okay, that explained why one of the French doors was lolling open.

"You ready to do this?" he asked.

Without another word, Rio entered first, but it wasn't like she knew the layout any better than Luke did. Still, it didn't take a genius to know that whoever was upstairs was going to do one of two things: They were either going to come down with a weapon, or they were going to call for reinforcements.

Which might, or might not, be Caldwell Police.

Probably not on that one. Assuming they were in the right place, Stephan Fontaine had plenty of street resources, in spite of all his legitimate business contacts and philanthropy.

Taking off at a run, she suddenly knew what she was looking for—and yet she didn't understand why it mattered so much, given the alarm, given everything. But she had to find the fountain. It would confirm that which was still only speculation at the moment.

If she could find where she had been held, though, she could make the final connection, plug the background in with the foreground.

She raced through a blur of rooms, dining, sitting, a library, a study—

And there it was. The fountain was around the last turn, in that room she remembered, with the chair she'd been tied to. As she skidded to a halt on the black-and-white marble floor, it was all as it had been: The falling water, the golden clock on the mantel, the drapes.

Turning around to Luke, who had been following her, she saw past his shoulder a man coming down the formal staircase in a silken robe.

And for a moment, she froze solid. Especially as Stephan Fontaine looked right at them.

They were in the shadows, though, because he had failed to reopen the heavy curtains from when he'd brought her here.

Why, she thought. Why had he taken the risk?

And as soon as she wondered that, she knew the answer: Because he believed he could. Because he had been safe in this house, and hidden from his Mozart games for so long, that he believed he was invincible. With all his money, legally or illegally gotten, the world was his for the taking—and people like her, people like her brother and her parents, didn't matter. He had his fortune, and his power, and his fake status, and all the lives that he ruined along the way didn't matter.

Rio started running before she knew she was going to go at him, flashes of the past spurring her on, images of Leon Roberts's face, of the white hair and skin of that hired killer at the apartment, of Mickie dead on that sofa . . . of Spaz shambling around the alleys of downtown, caught in a trap that he would never get out of . . . giving her the strength of a linebacker.

Just as Stephan turned to her as he heard her footfalls, she launched herself into the air.

She took him down hard, the gun in his hand flying free, the breath exploding out of him. And she didn't stop there. Rage blinded her until she saw nothing but her vengeance as she pounded at him with her fists, hitting him, kicking him, scratching him. At some point, she grabbed him around the throat and started strangling him.

All around, the alarm continued to sound, but it wasn't nearly as loud as the roar in her heart, in her soul.

"Luis!" She yelled her brother's name. "*Luis* . . ."

And then it was over. As fast as it had begun, it was over. She was pulled off her prey, just ripped away, and she fought whoever it was—

"Rio! Rio!"

Her name. Spoken in that voice, that deep voice that made it through her fury when nothing and no one else could have.

Luke shoved his face into hers. "Do you want to kill him or not?"

"What?"

"Do you want to kill him?" When she didn't respond, Luke put a gun in her hand. "You can shoot him if you need to, it's your choice. But you told me you wanted him to go to jail, not a grave. I just have to make sure you know what you're doing—and we're also out of time. I hear the sirens."

"How will they know what he did?" she mumbled. "How will he—"

Luke glanced up and cursed. Then refocused on her. "What do you want to do? You don't have a lot of time unless you want to be here when your colleagues arrive. You said you didn't know who to trust. This place is about to be filled with cops."

Rio broke out of his hold and leaned over Stephan Fontaine. His face was bloody to the point of being unrecognizable, but he was breathing, though otherwise motionless. The silk robe he was wearing was ruined, all stained and torn.

Luke had been right to peel her off. Even a minute more, and she would have killed him.

And justice had to be served.

"There's only one person I trust," she said gruffly. "Let's go."

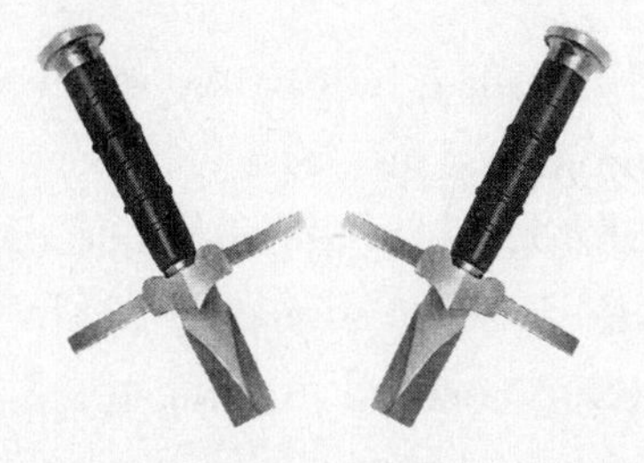

CHAPTER FIFTY-NINE

Hello? Hello? CPD dispatch, can you identify yourself?"

José blinked and looked at his phone like it could have been a toaster oven—and why would that be the case here outside of Stan's house?

Next to Stan's dead body.

It was a moment before everything came back to him.

"—hello?" the woman said over the connection.

"Ah, this is Detective José de la Cruz." He had to clear his throat. "My badge number is oh-fiver-nine-four. I need immediate assistance at seven-niner-two Eastwood Lane. We have . . ."

José focused on the face of his old friend. Who he no longer felt he knew. Who he no longer saw as the chief of the force.

"We have a gunshot death." The dispatcher asked some questions that ran together so he cut through things. "I shot him. In self-defense."

There were many questions then, and he answered them as well as he could—

There was a gun in Stan's hand. Wait . . . that wasn't right, he thought. Or was it?

As a headache threatened, he gave up on everything. And a little later he was off the phone and just leaning back against Stan's car.

All of a sudden, the details of the night became very clear, from the cold temperature, to the smell of someone's fire in their fireplace, to the whiff of gas like the vehicle needed a tuning up.

It was so quiet out here.

But Stan had missed the very peace he had sought. On all levels.

José looked down at the phone in his hand. Then he made a call.

His wife picked up on the second ring. "Hey you, are you on your way—"

"I'm okay." His voice got so rough it all but dried up. "I'm okay. It's all okay."

"José? What happened. Oh, God—"

"I'm all right." He closed his eyes and covered his face, even though there was no one around to see him get emotional. "I love you."

"Where are you—"

"I'm at Stan's house."

"Oh, good, you'll be safe there."

José took a deep breath. "Listen, we're going for two weeks. Our vacation is gonna be two weeks, okay?"

"Yes," she said gently. Like she knew he was cracked wide open and would find out the details later. "Hey, have you called Treyvon?"

"No. Not yet. Why?"

"I'm just gonna call Treyvon. I'm going to put you on hold—"

"Backup's coming. I just . . . needed to hear your voice. 'Cuz you're my wife . . . and when the world makes no sense to me, you're the one I want to call."

"I love you so much." She sniffled, and he pictured her snapping a tissue out of a box. "You come home when you can."

"I will."

They hung up and he let his hand fall into his lap. Then he just breathed. In and out. In and out. In and out—

The phone rang again and he answered without looking. "I swear,

I'm okay." When his wife's voice didn't come back to him, he frowned. "Hello?"

There was a pause. And then a woman said, "Detective de la Cruz?"

He straightened. "Yes?"

"I think you know who this is."

"Rio?" He shouldn't use her name, but her threat . . . was gone now. Or at least half of it was. "Where are you—the shit's hitting the fan—"

"I'm safe. I just need you to know that Mozart is Stephan Fontaine."

José closed his eyes. "I know, I know—I have proof. You were right to tell me to go to your house. Leon Roberts sent you pictures of Stephan Fontaine meeting with a source inside the department. That source gave up your name to him and made you a target. Leon had been following leads as part of an internal affairs investigation that was top secret, and he was killed . . . for his courage."

"Thank God you believe me." The woman exhaled long and slow. "But there's another piece. There was just a break-in at Fontaine's house. His caretaker was overpowered and Stephan was gravely injured in an attack pursuant to the home invasion. He is alive, however. I just want to make sure that he's taken into custody and that all my reports are used to charge him. He needs to be behind bars for the rest of his life."

José lowered his voice. "Are you injured?"

"No."

"Be honest."

"Nothing a bandage around my knuckles won't handle."

He chuckled. "Good for you."

"I'm not coming back."

"To the CPD? Or at all."

There was a long pause. "I need a fresh start. It's been . . . too long. Too much."

José closed his eyes again. "Yes, it has been."

"Thank you for warning me."

"Thank you for your service. And I just want to say . . ." Off in the distance, he heard the familiar sound of sirens closing in—and wondered how long it was going to take before he didn't feel like they were something he had to get involved in. "Take care of yourself, Officer, and happy retirement."

"Listen, don't tell anyone you spoke to me. I think it's best that I just . . . remain an unsolved case."

"Okay. I can do that."

"Thanks. Bye."

"Goodbye."

He ended the call just as the first of the squad cars came screaming down the country-ish road, heading for him.

And for Stan, who had retired in a fashion as well.

CHAPTER SIXTY

Rio ended the call and looked over the lip of the quarry. It was a helluva spot, this set of cliffs and the huge pool below, especially with the twinkling of downtown off on the horizon. After a moment, she hauled back and slung the phone into the water that was so far down the drop.

Then she turned and faced . . . the man/male/wolf/vampire who had gotten her off that mansion's property and safely out here, away from prying eyes.

Luke was leaning back against the Monte Carlo, his arms crossed, his eyes on her. He was so still, and magnificent, and . . .

As she started to walk over to him, he straightened. But he didn't smile.

"You reach him okay?" Luke asked.

"Detective de la Cruz has everything they need. It's all going to come out, everything that Mozart was and did is going to land on his head. A man lost his life to get that information to me, and to try to save my life. The department will honor him by prosecuting that asshole."

"That's good."

"Yeah, it's everything I wanted. So I can say goodbye. You know, say goodbye and be at peace with it all."

Luke nodded and rubbed his hands together. "All right, then. I guess this is it. I, ah, I'd say see you later, but—"

"I meant goodbye to Caldwell and my life there."

"Oh. So you're going to disappear, go underground. Do you have enough money? I mean, not that you need my help—"

"Well, see, I thought you might need mine."

He blinked. "I'm sorry?"

Rio walked around in a little circle. "I thought a lot about things while we were driving down from Walters. And also, as we came out here just now."

"I figured you were silent because you were scared of me."

"Scared of you?" She stopped in front of him. "How could I be scared of you? You've saved my life three times. And you're . . ."

"A monster, right?"

Rio reached up and put her hand to his face. "A mystery. Never a monster."

Luke closed his eyes as if her touch was both the most painful thing he'd ever felt and the most soothing. "Rio . . ."

"Yes, I thought maybe, since you helped me, I could help you."

"With what?" His lids opened slowly.

"Liberating the prison." As his brows shot up, she nodded. "That's what you're thinking, right. You were going to kill Mozart because you don't want the deal to go through. So you can undermine the power structure, free the falsely imprisoned, save Kane, and make sure Apex and Mayhem are okay. Right?" When he didn't respond, she prompted, "Right?"

"Well, yes. How'd you know?"

"I know you better than the few hours we've been together suggest I should. I truly feel like . . . I know you down to your core." She laughed a little. "Well, except for the whole werewolf thing."

"Wolven," he corrected.

"Wolven, then. And then the vampire is just . . ."

"Vampire."

"Ah. Good. I've got that down then already."

Luke shook his head. "What are you talking about here, Rio?"

"I'm talking about helping you free those people, no matter what their species." She stepped off from him. "I'm dead, technically. I have no existence in Caldwell."

"A ghost?"

"That's right, I'm a ghost." She smiled and pointed to him. "You're a wolven and a vampire. And I'm a ghost. It's true love."

He recoiled like she'd shocked the hell out of him.

"Yes," she whispered. "I'm still in love with you."

"So you were in—"

"Yes, I was. And I am." She shrugged. "The thing is, survivors also need to believe in the future. And I'd like you to be my future. I know so much of this seems impossible, but let's do it together. Let's figure out the plan—I have training, I'm a great shot—"

"I know that already. And after what you did to that Fontaine guy in his front foyer, you're also really good in a bar fight. You've got fists of steel."

"You say the sweetest things." She moved back in against him, tilting into his body, and putting her arms around his neck. "Let's face it, you need me."

"No shit." He lowered his mouth to hers. "I totally need you, Rio, and I love you—I don't understand how you feel this way, too. And honestly, you don't know what you're getting into."

"When do we ever?" She stroked his hair back. "Life is a series of unexpected surprises, some good, some bad . . . some life-changing, whether we know it at the time or not. And that night I met you under the fire escape? My life was destined to change—and now, if you're not in it, it's empty. Give me a future, Luke, it's what this survivor needs."

"Well, how can I argue with that?"

They kissed deeply, tenderly. And when they finally pulled apart, she knew, without a doubt, that she had found the man of her dreams.

Wolf.

Wolven. And vampire. Whatever, like those details mattered.

"Are you sure about this?" he asked.

"Yes."

"Then let's go back to Walters and fuck some shit up."

Rio laughed out loud as he led her over to the Monte Carlo, where, like a gentleman, he held her door open for her, and helped her into her seat. When he came around and got behind the wheel, they linked their hands and held on.

"Back to Walters," she ordered.

With that command, they were off into the night, on a quest of justice and liberation.

And true love.

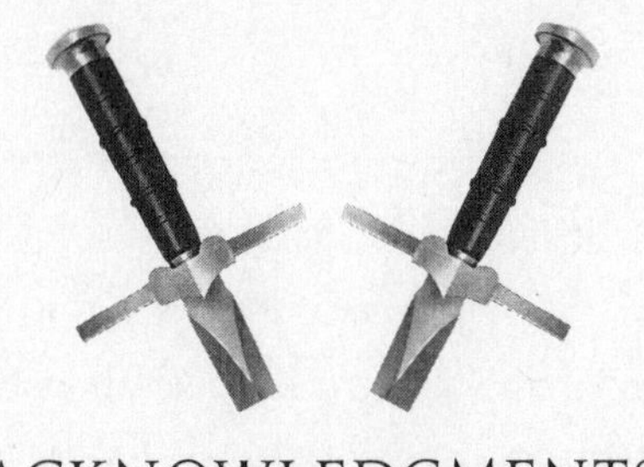

ACKNOWLEDGMENTS

With so many thanks to the readers of the Black Dagger Brotherhood books! This has been, and continues to be, a long, marvelous, exciting journey, and I can't wait to see what happens next in this world we all love. I'd also like to thank Meg Ruley, Rebecca Scherer and everyone at JRA, and Hannah Braaten, Andrew Nguyen, Jennifer Bergstrom, Jennifer Long, and the entire family at Gallery Books and Simon & Schuster.

To Team Waud, I love you all. Truly. And as always, everything I do is with love to, and adoration for, both my family of origin and of adoption.

Oh, and with all my gratitude to Naamah, my Writer Dog II, who works as hard as I do on my books, and to the Archiball!